LAURA HAYDEN

AMERICA
the BEAUTIFUL

TYNDALE HOUSE PUBLISHERS, INC., CAROL STREAM, ILLINOIS

Library of Congress Cataloging-in-Publication Data

Hayden, Laura.
    America the beautiful / Laura Hayden.
        p. cm.
    ISBN-13: 978-1-4143-1939-1 (pbk.)
    ISBN-10: 1-4143-1939-8 (pbk.)
1. Women presidential candidates—Fiction. 2. Political fiction. I. Title.
    PS3558.A8288A8 2008
    813'.54—dc22   2007051777

Printed in the United States of America

14 13 12 11 10 09 08
 7   6   5   4   3   2   1

To my family,
who understand and respect
my dedication to my work.
Most of the time. <g>

ACKNOWLEDGMENTS

Someone we all know once said it took a village . . . Ha! It takes far more than that. First, I'd like to thank my critique group—Pam, Karen, Angel, Jodi, and Paula—for their unwavering support. In addition, many thanks to Becky Nesbitt, Jan Stob, Kathy Olson, Ethan Ellenberg, and Lee Hough. All of them contributed to this book with their keen insights and excellent editorial comments. I'm also very grateful to Dr. Dale Hayden for his insight into politics from a historical standpoint.

Most importantly I want to thank Denise Little. It's not a requirement that your editor be your friend, but I'm so very thankful that she is both.

One last note—I'd also like to thank the dedicated folks behind TheGreenPapers.com Web site. It became my single most important source for up-to-date information about a constantly changing political calendar. Thanks, guys!

"IF I CAN FIND the ammunition—and it's looking good that I will—what I want to know is just how far we're prepared to go in using it." Kate Rosen looked around at the people gathered in the penthouse suite of a Dallas hotel. "I know we want to win, but—" she turned to face the most important person in the room—"this could get ugly."

Emily Benton, with a term as governor of Virginia under her belt and nearly a lifetime in politics before that, stared in obvious disbelief at her best friend and political manager, the person who had helped engineer her many previous successes.

"Of course it's going to get ugly, K." Emily pushed her honey blonde hair over her shoulder in a characteristic gesture. The shade, as well as the style, had been carefully calculated for maximum public appeal. Feminine but not fussy. "This is politics. Not just any politics either. This one's for the White House."

"Exactly," Kate said. "When this thing is finally over, the last candidate left standing is going to run this country. I intend for that person to be you. But I also want you to have the moral authority to do the job well. As my father always said, 'You can't take the high road if you insist on playing in the gutter.' If the campaign gets too dirty, it'll undercut everything we're trying to achieve once you're in office."

"Maybe you have a point, but as *my* father always said, 'If you don't play to win, you won't win,'" Emily said. "I intend to be the first woman president of these United States, to go down in the record books as the woman who broke the gender barrier to the highest office in the land. And I'll do whatever it takes to succeed."

That's nothing new, Kate thought. Emily always played to win. It was her signature strength, something she'd learned as a baby on her father's knee, sitting not in the family living room but in the smoky power centers where old-time politics had lived—in boardrooms, in back rooms, and in hotel rooms far less well-appointed than this one.

Kate knew such old-fashioned images lingered in the minds of the American public. They believed politicians still forged their deals in smoke-filled back rooms over good single malts and a couple of Cubans. But knee-deep in the twenty-first century, the big decisions were far more likely to be made over Chinese takeout in a smoke-free room of a business-friendly hotel.

Today's politicians realized the importance of mobility and access. Not like the good ol' days, when news releases had to be timed to take advantage of printing press schedules and personal appearances were positioned to make the six o'clock news, when all of America stopped what they were doing to watch. In today's world, the latest information and gossip circumnavigated the globe in nanoseconds, news channels ran around the clock, and virtual newspapers didn't need to wait for print runs.

Today, Dallas. Tomorrow, Denver. The next day, Des Moines.

One hotel room looked pretty much like another to this crowd of political experts, advisers, and operatives, but all of their lodgings had to have the minimum of creature comforts—ergonomic desk chairs, excellent cell phone reception, in-room faxes, high-speed wireless Internet, twenty-four-hour room service, and a gym with unlimited access. And, of course, room enough to accommodate a candidate's inner circle of advisers, who could be called up at any time for a powwow just like this one. In fact, two key members of Emily's kitchen cabinet, Dozier Marsh and Chip McWilliamson, were there representing the broadest spectrum of politics: Dozier, from the old school, brought a sense of history and experience as a political adviser, and Chip, a Silicon Valley whiz kid, engineered their campaign in virtual arenas—MySpace, Facebook, Flickr, YouTube, Second Life, and of course, EmilyBenton.com.

But both of them remained silent as Kate and Emily hashed out the current battle of political philosophies—restraint versus going for the jugular. Undoubtedly neither wanted to get caught in the cross fire. Since Kate and Emily had been having discussions just like this one since they were teenagers, Kate actually enjoyed the debate. She knew Emily was the best person for the job—and had known it for nearly twenty years. But she and Emily still had fundamental differences in their approaches for achieving that goal.

Everyone watched Emily as she rose gracefully from the desk chair and walked over to the window to stare at the city beyond. Reunion Tower was putting on a light show in the night sky, looking like some giant electronic dandelion. Kate reached over, snagged a four-dollar bottle of water, and opened it. She might as well kick back and get comfortable as she watched Emily perform. She cracked the seal on the bottle and thought about how much time it had taken her to suppress her inner cheapskate, who insisted that tap water was good enough for slaking her thirst.

After six months of preprimary positioning, hotels like this one had become her natural habitat, and part of that nature included not thinking twice about guzzling four-dollar bottles of water. Kate had been away from her home so long and so often that even her dog, Buster, had trouble recognizing her when she finally got back for a change of underwear and to pay bills. The campaign was taking its toll on Kate. Yet Emily thrived on the pressure. Kate supposed it was because she was born to it.

While Emily paced back and forth, talking about her vision for the campaign and how much she wanted—and America needed—her to be the next president, Kate thought about how well suited Emily was for the job because of her background, because of her vision, and because of her aptitude for governing.

But only a person who'd lived under a thick layer of rock would fail to recognize the Benton name and associate it immediately with politics. Emily's family had been big in government for three generations, with Emily representing the fourth. Over the years, the Bentons had spawned three large-city mayors, five state representatives, two governors—including Emily, three senators, four members of the House, and one president. The Bentons shared not only a successful political platform but a proclivity to identify and expose their opponents' biggest weaknesses, thanks to surgical strikes of spin and political intelligence that would have made the air force proud.

And Emily was no different.

Kate sipped from her water bottle, then cleared her throat. Time to get Emily focused back on the issue at hand. "We're going to make this happen, Emily. As per your instructions, I've had our people out digging on Talbot for months. They've got leads on a couple of good stories that are panning out well. If you're prepared to use what we find, repercussions and all, I'm pretty sure it will bring him down. But Talbot's got people doing the same thing to you. Remember, playing cutthroat politics can rebound on us, in the polls and in salvos from the other candidates. The competition's worried about you. No, not worried. Running. Running scared. They're slowly realizing you just might win this election, so they're arming themselves with every sling and arrow they can find. If we start lobbing cannonballs at them, there's no telling what they'll fire back."

"Let them. It's not like my life isn't an open book. I grew up in the public eye. There's nothing the world doesn't know about me."

Ha! Kate thought, then paused to draw in a deep breath. She and Emily had a long, strong, and deep friendship. Emily wasn't often the type to shoot the messenger, but she'd taken her share of shots at Kate. The fact that Emily trusted Kate totally meant that she also felt free to behave her worst around her best friend. It was like two sides of a coin. Just as Emily's best could be breathtaking, her worst could knock Kate flat. In a way, Kate knew those knockout punches were a tribute to their friendship. Emily had faith that Kate would stay by her side, no matter what. That faith was mutual.

Kate figured that's what friends were for. If your best friend wouldn't tell you the truth, who would?

Kate braced herself, then let the words go. "Don't be sure. Here's the bad part. My source in the Talbot camp tells me that his people are putting out feelers to Nick. And I have to admit that it's a smart tactic. What better way to derail our campaign than by bringing your ex-husband on board theirs?"

Emily didn't move. That was bad. She was very controlled in public, another lesson learned from her very public childhood. But Kate knew Emily well enough to see the anger in the way her friend stood, the muscles in her shoulders and back unusually rigid.

But then Emily's voice betrayed her, revealing something else mixed with the anger.

Regret?

"Oh, well. I knew they'd make a play for him sooner or later. I just didn't think it would be this soon."

"Emily, honey, it's been a long time," Dozier "Bulldozer" Marsh said softly. He'd been leaning against a wall, having waved away a seat when they started their powwow. He pushed away from the wall now and straightened, commanding the collective attention of everyone in the room except Emily, whose back was to everyone.

He might be past eighty these days, but Dozier still moved like a man twenty years his junior. The old hands on Emily's team swore he kept young by living on the blood of the lesser beings who had dared to stand in his way. He'd survived more nasty political campaigns than any four dozen politicians alive. Part of his success was due to the fact he'd aligned himself with Big Henry Benton, Emily's dad, becoming a key member of her father's legendary inner circle. After a couple of beers, Emily could often be persuaded to tell Kate hair-raising stories about her Uncle 'Dozer. So Kate knew the legends were true—and, if anything, understated.

Usually a thundering voice in any discussion, Dozier spoke now in uncommonly tempered tones. "I know the divorce was messy. What divorce isn't? But that piece of buffalo chip matters less than a stinging ant in a wasp nest." He stepped across the room and joined Emily at the window, throwing a fatherly arm across her shoulders. "Nick's been out of your life . . . what? Twelve years?"

Chip McWilliamson spoke from across the room, his comment almost too quiet to hear. "Longer than you were married . . ."

"Exactly." Dozier turned briefly to acknowledge the younger man's contribution, then faced Emily. "He's been out of your life so long that Talbot won't get a blessed thing of any use from him. He's hiring the boy solely to throw you off your game. You're not going to let him get to you, are you?"

Emily took a deep breath and evidently shook off whatever emotions had threatened to swamp her. She also stepped away from the protective arm of Dozier Marsh.

Emily Benton stood in the shadow of no man.

"Get to me with Nick? Sorry. No way. Talbot's made a big mistake, tipping his hand like this. If he's prepared to hire Nick, willing to tolerate being in the same room with him, then my opponent's demonstrated just how low he'll really go." She sounded almost as if she believed her own words. "Better than that, Talbot's camp is proving just how desperate they are."

Emily turned her back to the Dallas skyline and faced her inner circle, the occupants of this room. "So I guess that answers your question, K. We're going to need a wide variety of weapons and all the ammunition we can get. From handguns to howitzers. And we'll use them. We'll use them all. Nobody messes with me and comes out unbloodied. In fact, nobody messes with me and comes out alive—not in politics!"

She smiled. Kate and most likely everyone else in the room noted the glint of steel in her gray eyes, one Kate knew meant an unstoppable amount of dogged determination. But there was more in that expression. Looking past the classic beauty of Emily's face, Kate knew her friend's curling lips formed something less than a smile and more like a stylized snarl.

It was Emily's war face.

Kate had first seen that particular expression during their days together as law school roommates at Georgetown University. That look always meant trouble—not for Emily but for anyone who dared to oppose her, from the cafeteria worker up to the dean of the law school. Kate had survived as Emily's friend by knowing when to feed the beast and when to keep her fingers away from the gaping maw.

And now it appeared that Emily Benton had just declared war to the knife.

Talbot, Kate figured, was history. And Nick, being

caught in the cross fire, would be an acceptable casualty along the way.

Emily caught Kate's eye and held her gaze for a moment. It was a clear signal: time to strategize, and that meant a tête-à-tête between just the two of them. Kate turned to her companions, about to make a suggestion that it was time for Emily to get some rest, but Emily beat her to the punch with her usual blunt honesty.

"K and I need to be alone to talk." Her smile grew less predatory as she addressed Dozier and Chip. "You two need to get some sleep, anyway."

Dismissed, Dozier stepped over, bussed Emily on the cheek, and paused to lean down and touch foreheads with Kate, a gesture she didn't particularly like but tolerated for Emily's sake. "Don't let her stew too long," he said in a loud stage whisper.

Kate responded with a small wink.

Chip seemed reluctant to leave. Lately he'd been jockeying things around to put himself closer to Emily, and Kate was pretty sure it was part of his thinly veiled bid to become the First Gentleman of the United States. But Kate knew his efforts were futile and had told him so on several occasions. In his favor, he was smart, handsome, and ambitious, but he was also too young, too inexperienced, and much too naive in the world of politics.

Emily needed somebody who would challenge her. Chip couldn't even influence her.

Yet he persisted, and Kate and Emily weren't above using his dogged determination for their own purposes. If nothing else, he was an attractive bit of beefcake to drape on Emily's arm at Washington social events.

He served his purpose, and his governor, well.

Chip tried and failed to hide his besotted smile as he stepped closer to Emily. His face betrayed an obvious desire for a good-night kiss, but then his common sense prevailed. "Sweet dreams, Governor Benton."

She shrugged off the formal title that sat so oddly on Chip's lips and sent him away with a brush of her hand. Her smile had now lightened to something bordering on sociable. But the moment the door closed behind the men, her more pleasant expression disappeared.

Now that it was the two of them, Kate and Emily, the real dialogue began. Kate knew that Emily trusted no one else but her when it came to the big issues.

"Nick can hurt us. Hurt me."

"I know. So what are you going to do about him?"

"Short of killing him, I don't know. Yet."

"Seduction?"

Emily flopped onto the bed with a sigh. "He *was* good in the sack. I'll admit I still miss that aspect of our marriage. But . . . no. If I seduced him, it'd simply prove that we consider him a threat. He'd love it. Then he'd hold it over me like a WMD for decades."

"Assassination?" Kate widened her eyes at the obvious exaggeration.

Emily released a deep-throated laugh. "Don't tempt me. Some nights, I actually have dreams about pulling the trigger. Luckily dreams aren't actionable."

"Discredita-shun?" Kate said in her best Cajun accent, a fair imitation of Nick's slight Louisiana twang.

"Please. Don't remind me," Emily complained, squeezing her eyes shut in mock pain.

They'd all met in New Orleans a long time ago when they were four law students on a last fling before taking the bar—Emily and Kate from Georgetown and Nick Beaudry and his roommate, Wendell Conway, from Tulane. Wendell and Kate had been a minor flash in the pan, and they'd gone their separate ways only a few months after they'd hooked up. However, Nick and Emily had been flint and steel, and the sparks from their constant clashes ignited a roaring fire of a romance, culminating in the social wedding of the season—held in the White House, no less.

The honorable William R. Benton, president of the United States, had escorted his niece, Emily, down the aisle in the East Room, taking the place of her father, the late Henry Benton, his brother.

As the maid of honor, Kate had the perfect vantage point to see the look of longing on her best friend's face, but she knew the expression had less to do with the wedding night and more to do with Emily's realization that she was one step closer to living in the White House. Emily's political dreams of achieving the presidency had been finalized in grade school.

Nick and Emily had been the picture-perfect political power couple, a photo favorite of newspapers and tabloids alike. A trace of Native American blood slightly darkened Nick's Black Irish good looks, which made him a perfect contrast to Emily's blonde, all-American beauty. Hollywood couldn't have cast the roles better. In public, they were a dream team.

But in private Kate saw firsthand how flint and steel could create wildfires of a different sort. Nick and Emily brought out the worst in each other, probably because they were so much alike—always looking out for themselves, never thinking about the team.

Five rocky years later, Nick chose Emily's very public thirty-first birthday party bash to rise unsteadily to his feet in front of everyone and declare it was either politics or him and that Emily needed to choose. Now. Before answering him, she calmly blew out the candles on her cake, cut a slice, and held it out to him. Shocked by her silent reaction, he automatically reached for the plate. That's when she smashed the cake into the pleated front of his expensive hand-tailored tuxedo and motioned for security to remove him from the room.

Kate managed to smooth over the disruption with the usual dodge of "too much wine and strong antihistamines" as the justification for Nick's bizarre behavior. No one bought it, but it dulled the gossip to whispers. The next morning, Nick helped shred the remainder of his reputation by being picked up doing ninety on the George Washington Memorial Parkway in a drunken haze and in the company of not one but two known prostitutes.

From that point on, it was easy to paint Emily as the good woman ridding herself of an unfaithful and feckless husband.

However, it hadn't been as easy to remove Nick from Emily's heart—or from her politics, for that matter. He stayed in Virginia for a while, but Emily's influence meant he met nothing but roadblocks in his pathway. He eventually returned to Louisiana, where he was shunned for the requisite three years before being allowed back into parish politics. Eventually, he achieved a comfortable status as a gentleman state senator. In public, he and Emily remained civil, albeit cool, to each other, but there were always sharp, coded looks between the two of them that even Kate couldn't decipher.

And now, after having tried to slice away at Emily's political ambitions once before, it appeared he was getting ready to pick up the knife again. And twist.

"We fight fire with fire," Emily said. "Right?"

Kate remained silent, trying to figure out exactly how to drop the last bombshell.

"Right?" Emily repeated. She took one hard look at Kate. "All right, Rosen. Spill it."

Kate drew a deep breath. "Talbot isn't hiring Nick as a consultant. There's talk that Nick will become his deputy campaign manager." That meant Nick wouldn't merely be trotted out every now and then for maximum embarrassment value. Instead, he'd be part of Talbot's inner circle, available for round-the-clock information and influence. During his five years in the Benton family's good graces, Nick had learned which family closets held which family skeletons. He knew enough about the past transgressions of the Bentons to cause some major problems for Emily and for the rest of her relatives in politics. Kate figured that he was in this for payback, and he was going to make the campaign as ugly as he could for Emily.

That, Kate figured, would be ugly indeed.

Emily obviously reached the same conclusions as Kate; she let loose a string of expletives that, no doubt, she'd learned at her father's knee. Times like this, it was best just to let her burn off the excess anger. Kate had learned long ago to let her friend yell, scream, throw things, whatever it took to bleed off the worst of the temper. To Emily's credit, she had the self-control to never do it in public. But Emily never felt the need to rein in her impulses around Kate—for better or for worse.

So in private, all bets were off.

It took nearly five minutes for Emily to run out of steam and invectives. After circling the room, growling like a caged tiger, she finally flopped onto the bed again, spent.

Long experienced in dealing with Emily's intense emotions, Kate stood over her friend, her arms crossed. "You finished?"

Emily sighed. "Yes."

"Good. Now, can we discuss what to do next?"

"Simple." Emily rolled over to her side and propped up on her elbow. "We fight back. You dig. Dig deep. Look in places even he doesn't know about. Get me every bit of dirt on Nick Beaudry you possibly can. I was married to the guy. He was no saint. And I've heard he got worse, not better, after I kicked him out. You can find the ammunition we need if you look hard enough."

"But . . ." Kate thought about how much she hated this aspect of politics. Yes, everyone who got into politics knew it would happen to them. Yes, it was part of the game. But Kate always felt that digging for the ammunition of a good mudslinging match left her soiled. Only her loyalty to Emily could make her do it. "But you know how I feel about that stuff."

"But nothing. I know you don't like it. I also know I can count on you to do it right. I don't want unsubstantiated rumors. I don't want innuendo. Those things can come back to haunt a campaign. I want facts. You have never given me anything that I couldn't take to the bank. So I'm counting on you, K." Emily yawned and stretched. "Is there anything else of earth-shattering importance we need to talk about?"

Kate consulted her planner. "You've been asked to speak at the Dexter Avenue Baptist Church in Montgomery."

Emily groaned. "I thought you weren't going to push your religious initiative policy thing at me until I got into office."

"I'm not pushing. Though you know how much that religious policy 'thing,' as you call it, means to me. This is a request they made on their own through the local campaign office. I didn't set it up."

"When do they want me?"

"Sunday, the twenty-third."

Emily groaned. "By speak, you mean preach, right?"

"Not really. More like speak. It's a celebration of the end of the Montgomery bus boycott."

"I'm fine with the civil rights aspect, but there's no way that I'm getting up on a pulpit and doing some fire-and-brimstone song-and-dance routine."

"I don't think they'd expect it of you."

"No, but they'd expect me to sit there and look interested. Rapt, even. And sing hymns." She made a face. "They always want me to sing."

"Look, if it bothers you that much, you don't have to do it. I can tell them you have family obligations and regret that you are unable to come."

"It might even be true—I've got an obligation to keep my family free from the problems Nick can cause."

"True." Kate paused. "One question, though."

"What?"

She took a moment to formulate her question. Since Emily had promised to create an Office of Religious Initiatives once she got into the White House, and since she planned to put Kate in charge of it on top of her obligations as chief of staff, then maybe Kate needed to ask a very basic question of her friend now. They'd discussed the issue before, but it was one Emily was adept at sidestepping. "I've never understood why you hate doing appearances at churches so much. It doesn't make sense. You go to church when you're home."

Emily picked up the empty bottle of water and tossed it toward the trash can. "Because it's good politics to be seen there. No one complains at home when I sit in the back pew and use my BlackBerry during the service. No one expects me to be a mover and shaker in the congregation. I don't have to join the choir, teach Sunday school, or run the outreach program. I just have to show up. Every once in a great while, I let them trot me out front and center. But they know I won't do it often or for long. I like that. It's the religious version of 'don't ask, don't tell.'"

Kate grinned, then realized that Emily wasn't kidding. "C'mon," she said. "Churches aren't just collections of people who get together to show off their nice suits on Sunday morning or show off what notable person is in their congregation. Churches stand for something. And those congregations would appreciate hearing what you stand for."

"It's not that simple, K. You know I believe in God and all that, but it's hard to explain."

"Then try. Explain it to me, at least," Kate said.

Emily remained on the bed, staring at the ceiling. "Let's just say that I know where I stand politically. Where I stand before God is a totally different question that I'm not ready to investigate. Until I am, I'm steering clear of standing in front of any congregation. Out of sight, out of mind."

"Emily!" Kate exclaimed, torn between horror and fascination with her friend's reasoning. "You can't avoid God by ignoring him."

"Maybe not, but maybe he'll ignore me if I stay in the back of churches, not in the front. And that's my plan until further notice."

"Avoiding the subject doesn't make it go away," Kate said. "I don't want to sound like I'm repeating myself, M, but sooner or later, you need to come to terms with your faith." Kate frowned. "I don't think anyone can survive long-term in politics with their spirit intact without a true and sustaining belief in God." She glanced toward the bedside drawer, which she knew contained a Gideon Bible. "These days, my faith is all that keeps me sane sometimes."

"If you can't survive in politics without religion, then how do you explain what happens on Capitol Hill every day?" Emily asked. "You sure see lots of lip service to God but not much actual faith. And talk about all that bad behavior and sinning. Hooboy! As far as I've seen, Washington's fruit of the spirit is mostly rotten tomatoes." Emily crossed her arms. "I may not be preaching from every handy pulpit, but I've always stood by my words. So if I get into a pulpit to preach, I need to mean it. Until I can mean it, I'm staying out. Period." Her face and her posture softened slightly. "It's not like I'm ignoring God completely. Once I'm in office, I can make things happen. I did it as governor. So you know I can do it as president. I can lead by example. Appoint good people to the bench. I've even agreed to your religious office plans, haven't I? I know it's been tried before, but I think you can really make it work, especially since I've got your back." She made eye contact with Kate, then turned away.

Kate studied her friend, knowing the gesture signified an end to the conversation. She sighed. "So what do I do about Dexter Avenue Baptist Church?"

"Send flowers or something. Anything else?"

"Nothing pressing."

"Good." Emily unclenched her arms and rolled over onto her back. "As you go out, will you send Chip in here?"

Although dismissed, Kate didn't move. "Do you think that's wise?"

"Wise?" Emily released a short bark of laughter. "Not particularly. But I need a distraction right now. And Chip's good for that. And for keeping his mouth shut."

Emily's change in subject meant she was finished talking about Nick for the time being, and Kate was supposed to simply play along.

So she did. "Chip may be asleep already," she said.

Emily's expression—it was hard to call it a smile—bordered on predatory. "Or he may be waiting impatiently by the door. Either way, I want him."

As she walked out, Kate allowed herself a sigh of exasperation. Pausing outside the door, she tried one last time to make her friend consider the consequences of her actions. "He could be a weak link."

"You worry too much."

"That's my job," Kate said to the door that closed behind her. "It's what you pay me for." But Emily wasn't listening. And she would be waiting for Chip.

When Kate knocked on the young man's door, a few

rooms down the hallway, he responded much too quickly. Emily was right. He *was* waiting for her. He failed to hide his momentary disappointment in realizing it was Kate at his door, not Emily.

"Expecting someone else?" Kate asked.

He blushed and Kate suddenly felt decades older than he was. She continued with the charade. "Emily needs to speak with you for a moment."

"Aahh." He swallowed his smile and nodded.

"Briefly," she added.

He nodded again and scampered off to their boss's room.

Kate didn't want think about what they did in there. If the two of them were strategizing without her, great. If it was an affair, she didn't want to know what was going on. Maybe, like Emily, Kate was avoiding a subject she just didn't want to think about. And as she'd told Emily, ignoring the truth wouldn't change it. But, she thought with relief, at least Emily wasn't bragging about it.

Maybe the relationship with Chip was just another instance of "Don't ask, don't tell" that was a part of Emily's life right now.

It was times like this that Kate pushed aside their friendship and looked at Emily strictly as her employer. That sort of compartmentalization of emotion had saved their friendship more than once. Although Kate had her friend's ear, sometimes it was much more important to be her adviser, her nursemaid, or her conscience.

Or her mind reader.

But right now Kate didn't dare try to read her old friend's mind.

Kate slid into the desk chair in her room and flipped open her laptop. She'd already anticipated Emily's command to look into the darker corners of Nick Beaudry's life in order to short-circuit his effectiveness.

Fourteen new e-mails waited in her in-box and she hoped that at least one of them would help her start the new scorched-earth phase of the campaign.

Before she could settle in and start reading the messages, her cell phone rang.

It was Dozier Marsh. "Kate, got a minute?"

Kate tried to give herself permission to lie, but something deep inside her refused to take the liberty. As she'd told Emily, her faith was all that was keeping her sane these days. And that meant telling Dozier Marsh the truth. No matter how much she didn't want to.

"Sure. What's up?"

"We need to talk. Now."

"NOW'S AS GOOD A TIME AS ANY."

"Not on the phone. I'm an old man who doesn't trust modern technology. I use these cell contraptions only under duress. No, I want to talk face-to-face."

"Would you like for me to come to your room?"

Dozier rumbled in laughter. "What? And give the gossips some tasty new fodder?" His accent deepened suddenly. "It might put a little shine on my reputation, but it probably wouldn't do much for yours. I can just hear people asking 'What kind of campaign y'all runnin' here?'" His laughter faded. "What say we meet downstairs at the bar?"

"I'll be right there."

Kate really didn't want to go, but Dozier was the sort of colleague she felt compelled to please as much as possible. After all, he was a living legend in the field. But even though he'd pulled his weight in the political arena for decades, she didn't kowtow to him because of his gender or his age. She was the first to admit he wasn't the easiest man to work with. But she never hesitated to contradict him when he was wrong or to disagree with him when their philosophies differed. Their worldviews failed to converge more often than not, but she picked her battles with Dozier carefully. He belonged to the age where men were men and women smiled and nodded in agreement.

Kate didn't.

She still hadn't figured out why he'd joined their camp. Yet Dozier, the total old-school politician, had seemingly thrown his considerable weight behind Emily without a second thought about her gender. It wasn't that Kate doubted his sincerity, but she was puzzled over his unexpected enlightenment on the issue of how important it was to have a woman candidate for president of the United States. Agreement on that basic issue was, at best, rare for a man of his age, his position, and his experience. Key words: *man* and *age*.

But Dozier defied the stereotypes, at least when it came to the thought of Emily as president. He was all for it. As for the rest of his life, he was a poster boy for the bad old days.

Kate supposed Dozier's support of Emily was a testament to the power that Big Henry had held over all of them, the sense of unending and unerring loyalty he had inspired in the people around him. Even more surprising to Kate than how much loyalty the old guard felt to Big Henry's memory was that the legacy of such loyalty had been handed down smoothly from father to daughter in a business that was more often a matter of father passing the mantle of power to a son.

But these days, politics was much more a business than it

had been in the good ol' boy network days of yore. Whereas iconic power had once been enough to put a man in the White House, now it would take an entirely different set of strategies, strengths, image control, and finances to put anyone, much less a woman, in the Oval Office.

Unlike many of her opponents, Emily had found a comfortable balance between the old and the new as she assembled her campaign—taking full and unabashed advantage of being a Benton, with all the privileges therein, but conducting a campaign for the twenty-first century. Of course, one of the Benton family traditions was to do whatever it took to get what they wanted.

Sometimes, Kate thought, *by hook or by crook.*

By that measure, Emily was a Benton down to the core.

When Kate reached the small table in the corner of the hotel bar, Dozier was on his feet. He raised one finger and the cocktail waitress trotted over. "Yes, sir, Mr. Marsh?"

Dozier beamed in pride, a wide grin that almost shouted, *"They still remember me."*

Kate hid her smile. More likely the young lady simply remembered the name of a heavy tipper.

He tapped his empty glass. "I'll have another bourbon and branch and the lady will have . . . ?" He turned in deference to Kate.

"Diet Coke."

Dozier made a face but refrained from voicing his usual disdain for her choice of a lightweight tipple. He waited for the waitress to leave before leaning forward and speaking in a low voice.

"Nick's going to be a complication, isn't he? A big complication."

"No names, please." Kate had learned long ago that private discussions shouldn't be held in public places. Proper names needed to stay right out of all but the most private discussions. At least the bar was mostly empty and Dozier was making a concerted effort to tame his usually booming voice. And the man had a point about the problems of men and women meeting in private. She just wished Emily was as mindful of carefully practicing that campaign strategy.

She leaned forward, matching his pose. "*He* very well could be a problem."

"Then what are you going to do about *him*?"

"Me?"

"Yes. You. Semantics." He made the censuring grandfather face. "Or *our friend*, by way of you. What is our friend going to have you do about *him*?"

"We don't have any plans other than to do some basic investigation."

"Then find something on him. And fast. I don't really care whether you use it or not. Our friend simply needs to know that she has leverage she can use to derail, discredit, or expose him. If she thinks she's in a superior position, she won't feel the need to make hasty and perhaps desperate decisions. I know the girl. I've known her since I dandled her on my knee at her daddy's political rallies. It's a matter of knowing she has the power rather than a matter of using it." He shifted back in his seat and looked up, an obvious sign that they were in danger of being overheard.

The waitress placed the two drinks on the small table. "Will there be anything else, Mr. Marsh?"

"Just the tab. Thanks, honey."

She deposited the check and slipped off.

Kate took a fortifying sip of her soda. She *so* didn't want to have this discussion right now. She'd rather have had time to sort through all the pros and cons. But Dozier liked to be listened to, acknowledged. It was the price they paid to have access to his library of living history—a vast and very personal knowledge of presidential campaign strategies from the last thirty years.

She decided to speak her mind. "Do you honestly believe she will just sit back and wait for him to make the first move if she has the power at her disposal to stop him before he even begins?"

"No," Dozier answered quickly, as if he'd anticipated Kate's rebuttal. "She's very much like her father that way. She's used to being on the offense. Hank always made sure the first cut wasn't just the deepest, but that it was fatal."

Since they were playing dueling platitudes, Kate offered her own. "Knowledge is power. And she's not going to *not* use the power if it's just sitting there, an obvious and easy solution."

"Then that's quite a dilemma, isn't it? Put a loaded gun in her hand and she's apt to shoot first. Trouble is, she might be shooting herself in her own foot. There's a chance that any first strike on her part could be interpreted as desperation. And that becomes a candidate's image nightmare. Worse, in her case. She'll have to combat 'the woman scorned' mantle. That sort of thing."

His machinations weren't lost on Kate. "You like playing the devil's advocate, don't you?"

His dentist apparently believed in art for art's sake; Dozier's wide smile exposed a set of too-perfect teeth. "There's more to me than just my good looks." He reached over, covered her hand with his, and lowered his voice till she could barely hear him. "You're in a tenuous position, my dear, and I don't envy you one whit. When it comes to Emily and Talbot himself, all bets are off. Anything you two find and use against him is fair game. As far as that goes, Emily will be far more circumspect and careful about constructing an anti-Talbot campaign. But I don't trust her judgment when it comes to . . . our new complication."

Kate stared into her glass, holding back the words *I don't either.*

Dozier continued in a normal tone. "The only solution I see is for you to arm yourself but not necessarily her. She may have the power to order the nukes . . ." He squeezed Kate's hand. "But you're the one who will need to decide if you turn the keys to the launch system or not."

"Gee, thanks," she said. "I just love playing nuclear strategist in this little scenario. I think you sat in on one too many defense budget discussions."

"Maybe so. I'm just concerned that this so-called 'religious initiative' concept you're pushing is going to make you less . . . effective when it comes to what needs to be done."

Kate felt herself stiffen in her seat. "How so?"

"Turning the other cheek doesn't really work in politics. You should know that. You end up with handprints—no, footprints—on both cheeks."

"My faith makes me who I am," Kate said. "I try every day to live what I believe. I think that makes me a better politician and a better person. Our friend does, too. She has no problem with who I am."

"I won't either, as long as you continue to do what has to be done. There's a reason that I support the separation of church and state. Politics is a messy business and not one for somebody who likes to keep their hands clean."

"I do my job and I do it well." Kate fought to keep her words quiet and her tone level.

"I know it. And you're good for our friend. But the first time I see you backing away from the fray because of your faith, I'll make sure she knows about it."

"You do that," Kate said.

"I will. Keep your eye on the prize. Isn't that what they used to say in those old church rallies? Keep your eye on the prize—and don't let anything stop you from grabbing it."

Dozier polished off his drink and signaled for the cocktail waitress, who approached with a ready smile.

"You need another round, Mr. Marsh?"

"Thanks, darlin', but no." He patted his protruding stomach. "Got to keep my girlish figure." He shot the waitress a wink, and for a brief moment, Kate feared she might have to launch herself across the table to intercept a less than appropriate gesture. Dozier and bourbon often made for a bad combination, resulting in feminist rebellion by his intended target, where he'd aim to swat a fanny, deliver an inappropriate comment, or worse. But tonight, despite his slam of Kate's personal convictions, he seemed to be on his better behavior—that, or the hotel was watering down their drinks. The only thing he did with his hands was wave away Kate's attempt to pay for her soda and then sign the bar tab to his room with a grand flourish. To end the evening on a high note, he tucked a twenty in the waitress's hand, basking in her grateful smile.

"Any time I can retire to my bed warmed by the smiles of two beautiful women, I call that a great day." He rose to his feet and held out his arm. "May I escort you to your room, Kate, dear?"

She remained seated and, instead of accepting his hand, thumbed away a bead of condensation from her glass. "I think I'll sit here and finish my drink. But thank you, Dozier."

He turned and graced the waitress with a smile that still held a great deal of charm. "Alone, again. Both of us. Pitiful, isn't it?"

He waited for her to contradict him. Everything was fine until the woman reached over and patted his arm, which appeared to shatter his illusion that he was still the sort of man young women yearned to be with. Instead, he was the sort of man that reminded young women of their fathers.

Or grandfathers . . .

His smile dimmed slightly and he lost some of the spring in his step as he headed to the bank of elevators.

The waitress lingered at the table. "You need anything else, ma'am?"

"No, thanks."

After a moment of awkward silence, the woman spoke in a low voice. "Uh, excuse me, but is he . . . like, famous or something?"

Kate toyed with the straw in her drink. "He used to be."

"A movie star?"

"A politician. Former Speaker of the House."

"Oh." Disappointment filled her face. "I thought he was somebody important."

As the woman walked away, Kate contemplated those words. Along with everything else Dozier had said to her, they hung in the air around her like a bad smell.

Emily always complained—mostly in private—that one of the main problems with the American public was their woeful ignorance of the American machinery of government. Then again, Emily had been born into that machinery and had been groomed to become a royal cog in the American political apparatus since birth.

Kate, on the other hand, had had a normal childhood, with her occasional exposure to donkeys and elephants occurring solely at the zoo. While eight-year-old Emily had dined on foie gras with dignitaries, Kate had wolfed down Happy Meals with her Brownie troop. Their lives, their worlds, couldn't have been more different right up until the moment that they intersected. And yet, once that happened, they'd been best friends for years.

Why, she was never sure. They were very different, but opposites did tend to attract. Outside of a church, Emily never met a crowd she didn't like. Kate couldn't conceive of a life without a strong church home. Emily always knew what she wanted. Kate asked God for guidance at every stage of her life. Emily sought the presidency for the platform it would give her to change the world. Kate sought to give Emily her dream because she'd seen what an effective leader Emily could be. But she'd never want the job for herself—the thought of being in the public eye that way made her shudder. The two women liked different movies, read different books. But in the end, she trusted Emily to be a great leader, and Emily trusted Kate to be a great supporter. What they lacked in common ground, they made up for with a common trust in each other's abilities. Their skills complemented each other. They knew they were different, and that was the basis of their well-forged friendship.

Between the two of them, their interests weren't simply all across the board; they filled the board. They were smart women who, between them, possessed an insanely complex understanding on a wide variety of topics, concepts, and areas of expertise. Emily appreciated and valued Kate for knowing what she didn't and Kate did the same for Emily.

Emily wanted to rule the nation. Kate wanted to make that possible.

Together, they were Batman and Robin.

Kate leaned back in the chair.

And if Kate had any say in the matter, come feast or famine, her best friend was going to become the first woman president of the United States.

Kate sighed, polished off her soda, and left. She rode the elevator with a too-young couple who couldn't keep their hands off each other. It'd been like that with Emily and Nick, she remembered. It wasn't that they were too young but that they'd been absolutely consumed with each other. Kate had assumed that their white-hot flare of attraction would eventually either cool down to something manageable or fade away completely and Emily would move on to the next guy, suitable or not.

But the flames continued to burn. As the old Southern phrase went, they "got married in a fever." But five short years later, the flames of passion had turned into a destructive inferno, obliterating everything and everyone in its path.

That inferno was still burning entirely too hot. On both sides.

Kate glanced at the couple, who were ignoring her and going at it like a couple of minks. At least they were still fully clothed. Kate counted her blessings. Still she couldn't help but wonder if the strength of their passion would turn on them someday too. . . .

She left the elevator before they got any more serious about their pairing, found her room, and ten minutes later tucked herself into the bed, fumbling to turn out the lights.

She'd planned to check her e-mail.

Hang it all, she thought.

E-mail could wait.

The next morning, Kate awoke to an earlier alarm than usual. Last night, making plans to get up early to catch up with e-mail had seemed a wise decision, but now all she wanted to do was roll over and go back to sleep. Her personal scheduler in her Palm Treo showed that the limo wouldn't pick them up until nine thirty for a ten thirty flight. Emily's cousin Richard had placed one of his company's corporate jets and its pilot at their complete disposal. If the campaign's transportation scheduler couldn't get a donor jet for any of their planned excursions, they always had Richard's plane as a backup, which they'd needed for this particular trip. Election laws forced them to set the value of their corporate jet travel at the same price as a first-class ticket on a commercial carrier for both Emily and Kate. All other staffers rated the economy ticket rate. But the $3,000 or so price tag for a cross-country trip from Dallas back to D.C. was chump change when compared to the real price tag for a charter jet undertaking the same trip.

And it was funny how the money paid to Richard always

seemed to turn up again in similar amounts as personal campaign donations from employees of his various companies. . . .

Despite what campaign laws said.

Before Kate could climb out of bed and turn on her laptop, her cell phone rang.

"Hotel gym is on the fourth floor. Meet in ten minutes." It was a statement, not a question.

Kate yawned. "As long as we can stop for an Egg McMuffin on the way to the airport."

"Fast food is going to kill you someday."

"Yeah? Maybe I'll get some rest then. Meanwhile it's my reward for meeting you in the gym at this hideous hour."

Fifteen minutes later, Kate nodded her greeting to Perkins and McNally, the two Secret Service agents who stood guard outside the hotel gym. As an active candidate, Emily had full-time Secret Service protection. She hadn't, so far, needed it for more than the expected number of idle threats from the far-off lunatic fringe, something for which Kate was very thankful.

Kate headed into the fitness room. Emily was already on the treadmill, running full speed.

Kate said nothing as she stepped up on the next machine and started her exercise for the day. She and Emily had had an unwritten pact on gym trips since they were in college together. If the spirit was willing, no business in the gym until well after the flesh was weak.

They'd been running for twenty minutes before Emily finally spoke.

"You . . . going . . . home . . . for . . . Christmas?" Emily said the words on each beat-slap of her feet against the treadmill belt. She wasn't winded, but the rhythm of her words revealed her level of concentration.

"If you can spare me. I know it's brutal with the early primary schedule. I was hoping to see Mom and Dad. And Brian and Jill are expecting again." Her brother and his wife were currently stationed at Langley Air Force Base, which theoretically had the whole family living in the same state for the first time in years. That made holiday attendance at their parents' house almost mandatory. Besides, Kate loved the holidays. Sure they were commercial, Christmas trivialized by pop culture with more Santa and Rudolph than Christ in the mix. But there was something about hitting the midnight Christmas Eve service with her family that made the holiday season complete for Kate and ended her year on a high note. It gave her a chance to evaluate her life and her relationship with her Savior, and she always resolved to try harder to live her life in his image as the next year dawned. Lately, she'd been thinking long and hard about that image.

"Kate . . . you're going. And the fact that . . . I'm . . . letting you . . . no . . . making . . . you go . . . is a sign . . . of how very much . . . I love ya, babe. . . . How many . . . kids does that make for Brian now?" Emily asked. "Nineteen?"

Kate chuckled. "Three. And from what Jill says, this is their last."

Emily's arms pumped hard. "She always says that. It's about time."

"They seem happy. And the kids are great."

"If you say so. Oh, don't leave town without getting the presents I have for your folks. I found that crystal critter your mom's been talking about. The one with the dragon sitting on the egg?"

"She's been looking for that one for years."

This was the Emily that Kate enjoyed the most. The one who never missed a birthday or holiday, who looked out for the people around her. The one who, in the middle of a hectic run for a national office, not only remembered her mother's collection of crystal figurines but, more importantly, knew which ones she wanted and didn't have.

Kate grinned. "At this rate, you're going to beat me out for favored daughter status. All I found was a scarf with a drawing of a baby dragon."

Emily had said more than once how envious she was of Kate's ordinary life and her ordinary parents. Kate had invited Emily along on her trips home several times, and as a result, Emily had forged some pretty strong connections with Kate's mom and dad, who had all but adopted Emily as their third child. Emily practically glowed in the warmth of that love. Kate had spent time with Emily's family, too, long enough to know just how lucky she was in her own relations. Although the Benton clan embraced Kate as an official Friend of the Family, Emily's mother remained distant, not only from Kate but seemingly from her own daughter, too. It gave Kate a window into the reason for Emily's reserve with just about everybody but Kate and the reason for her friend's unstoppable drive to succeed. It was as if Emily had to prove to her family every day that she was worthy.

When the Bentons got together to celebrate holidays as a family unit, Claire Rousseau Benton didn't even attend. But Emily did, and she happily joined in every contest with her supercompetitive cousins.

Competition—whether for office, for money, or for a flag

football touchdown—was highly valued in that family, and Emily definitely embraced her family's values.

Emily punched the speed control on her treadmill and the machine picked up the pace. "Found your dad . . . that new sand wedge . . . he's been . . . talking about."

Good thing I didn't get it, Kate thought. Anticipating Emily's largesse, Kate had gotten her father a monogrammed golf bag and, thanks to the celebrity aspect of running a presidential campaign, had it autographed by Tiger Woods.

She smiled. Sometimes rank really did have its privileges.

"What?" Emily challenged.

"Nothing."

"C'mon. . . . You're grinning. . . . Why?"

Kate caved. "Because I figured you were going to get Dad the sand wedge, so I got him a golf bag."

Emily grinned back. "We make . . . a formidable team, sister-friend." She held out her hand and Kate slapped it.

"We do, indeed."

A warm sense of connection with Emily ran through Kate.

"BFF . . . best friends forever . . . right?" Emily gasped.

"You bet."

They ran for another couple of minutes with Kate nudging her treadmill's speed higher until their feet pounded in a simultaneous rhythm.

Belatedly Kate realized what sort of strategic mistake this was. She'd learned long ago not to give Emily any sort of open challenge such as matching treadmill speeds. To Emily, it became an invitation to prove how much faster, better, and smarter she was than her competition, even when that competition was her best friend.

Therefore, Kate knew what was coming next.

"About . . . ready . . . to . . . stop?" Emily asked.

Kate wasn't ready, but "Who can last longer?" was yet another area of contest between them. Emily would never voluntarily stop if Kate was still there, plodding along. Emily couldn't let anybody, not even Kate, beat her. She'd run until she dropped. Literally.

Bentons never gave up. Not first. Not ever. It made for interesting family football games.

"Okay, I've had enough," Kate lied.

Once they landed back in Virginia, she'd go home and the first thing she'd do would be apologize to Buster the Wonder Dog. Then after he was sufficiently loved on, she'd strap on her iPod, jump on her own treadmill, crank it up to whatever speed she liked, and run until her bones ached, her joints screamed, and her heart pleaded for rescue. A real workout.

It wasn't until Kate reduced her speed to a sedate cooldown crawl that Emily reached over, sped her own machine up, and took her last "I'm so much faster than you" show-off sprint.

Emily needed to demonstrate her superiority; Kate understood that. In fact, she deliberately fed into Emily's overwhelming need to win by always making sure there were small successes for her friend to savor as often as possible. A string of small, even inconsequential, wins allowed Emily to better cope with the tougher issues, the harder battles, and heaven forbid, the occasional loss along the way.

That insistence on winning was one of the things that made Emily such a good politician. She never gave up. During Emily's years as governor, she accomplished things all the pundits said were impossible because she just kept pressing until everybody came to the table—Republicans and Democrats, elected officials and bureaucrats—and gave Emily what she needed. Virginia was a much better place these days because Emily never gave up. It had better roads, better schools, lower taxes, and a better safety net with a significant participation of charities and churches in that safety net—that was Kate's baby. Emily had been really good for Virginia. Kate couldn't wait to see what would happen when she got her hands on the whole country. The people who said Emily could never win the presidency . . . well, Kate figured they'd never dealt with Emily. She would go the distance, just as she was doing now on the treadmill, if it killed her.

The run for the presidency was the big picture. Down on the ground at M Central, Emily's drive to succeed meant that Kate shut down her treadmill a little earlier than she liked every day. Kate figured it was worth it to keep Emily happy. 'Cause if Emily wasn't happy, nobody was happy. And all of Kate's plans to change the world for the better depended on Emily being happy.

Letting Emily win was a lesson taught to Kate by a very wise woman who had forgotten more about the art and craft of politics than Kate would ever know.

Marjorie Redding, image consultant to four presidents, including Emily's uncle Bill, had been the person to formally identify Emily's driving need to succeed in all things at whatever cost. Marjorie might have been older than dirt, but she knew her business well, catering in confidence to clients who were seeking very public careers in either politics or the media. Marjorie had wisely pointed out Emily's consistent knee-jerk reactions to competition in a private conversation with Kate as the campaign manager and Dozier as Emily's chief political adviser.

"How can we . . . fix this?" Kate had asked. She couldn't quite shake the mental image of Emily filleting a psychiatrist long before he dug into the gooey inconsistencies beneath her shiny candy shell.

"The key to image consultancy is to change or tone down those aspects of a candidate's personality that appear to be weaknesses and to exploit and build on those aspects that appear to be strengths," Marjorie explained. "You do the opposite against an opponent, of course. You wear down the strengths and accentuate the weaknesses. In fact, a good consultant can even use an opponent's strengths against him. Think of how Karl Rove used Kerry's military service to take him down in the 2004 election against George Bush."

She sat back, obviously pleased to have an audience.

"Rove was worried that Bush's National Guard service didn't stack up well against Kerry's time in Vietnam. So the Bush campaign worked up a strategy. And shortly thereafter, a few Vietnam vets who'd served with Kerry and many more who hadn't but who wanted to denounce him joined forces with a well-heeled group of Bush supporters from Texas to form an organization called Swift Boat Veterans for Truth. The organization paid to make four commercials in which those people told their stories. Then they paid to have those commercials played all over the airwaves to anybody who would listen. By the time the election was over, Kerry's supposed advantage of military service had been turned into a terrible liability.

"President Bush and Karl Rove claimed to have nothing to do with those ads. But a number of Rove associates and

Bush advisers had connections to the Swift Boat campaign. They resigned from the campaign as soon as those connections became known during the buildup to the election. And no one was ever able to track a firm connection back to Bush or Rove. But I like to think Rove planned it and pulled it off. As a political ploy, it was masterful."

She pointed a gnarled finger at an eight-by-ten glossy photo—Emily's official portrait. "I'd like to think I can do the same for Emily one day."

"Think of Emily as a piece of banged-up furniture." Dozier added his folksy translation. "We take reality, polish up what we can, sand off any burrs we can, and spackle the remaining holes. By the time we're done, she'll be a showpiece."

The woman released a rare smile. She was evidently used to Dozier's homilies. "Emily is no banged-up specimen. It's not often you bring me such good material to start with." She gave Emily's photo a slow once-over. "She's pretty in an understated, classic sort of way. Excellent features—she has the Benton eyes and the Rousseau chin. Thank heavens," she muttered under her breath.

Emily's mother, Claire, had brought European bone china–delicate features into the hearty Benton stock. Dominant genes meant that all the Benton men bore a strong resemblance to each other—be they father, son, uncle, brother, or cousin. And as for the sisters, it was a general consensus that the Benton features looked far better on the men in the family.

However, no geneticist in the world could have dipped into the Benton-Rousseau joint gene pool and recombined the DNA better than the genetic permutation that had spawned Emily. The Rousseau line softened the harshness of the Benton features, and the Benton strength removed the air of delicacy from the Rousseau lineage.

As a result, Emily might not have been as beautiful as her mother or the other Rousseau women, but she was the most beautiful Benton woman ever born. She totally lacked the faintly masculine-horsey looks of her female cousins.

One particularly astute columnist had described Emily as looking as perfect as a china doll—but with the durability and unbreakable nature of a rag doll.

Along with beauty and stamina, Emily possessed a quick wit, a steel-trap mind that embraced all things academic, a strong, clear voice, a drive to serve her country, and an unmistakable lifelong love of politics. Essentially, she *was* the dream candidate.

And yet Marjorie still had her work cut out for her back then. After they finally met, she'd circled that younger Emily like a tiger sizing up its prey.

"Today's female politicians are a new breed," Marjorie had preached. "It's not a matter of trying to look and act more like a man but to find a way to champion your feminine qualities and present them as assets, not liabilities."

She walked one more circle around Emily, then paused to her side. "Any children in your future?"

Emily glanced at Kate. "No. I can't have them."

Marjorie shifted until she stood in front of Emily, skinny arms folded, her soul-piercing gaze and body language screaming in doubt.

"Can't or won't?"

No one stared down Emily Benton. "Does it matter?"

"What matters is how you present the idea. So let me ask it again. Can't or won't have children?"

Emily closed her eyes, drew in a deep breath. "It's a personal question, but I don't mind sharing." She opened her eyes, now glistening with slight moisture. "One of the greatest joys in a woman's life—or so I've been told—is to give birth. What I *do* know is that one of the greatest responsibilities in life for any person is to nurture a child, to help him or her grow up healthy and wise and to find the right path in life. I've always regretted that I've been unable to share in the joy and the responsibility of being a mother, and I can't help but appreciate and maybe even envy a little those women who do have a chance to have children."

The delivery was perfect, the sentiment possessing just the right balance of wistfulness and acceptance of untenable fact. If Kate hadn't known better, even she would have gotten a little choked up. But Kate did know better. Kate had been there several years ago when Emily first mentioned how she couldn't afford—wouldn't afford—to take the necessary time out of her life to have a child. Much less raise it.

It . . . Not *her*. Not *him*. *It*.

Marjorie appeared completely unmoved. "That's a start, but the wording could be better. Instead of saying that giving birth is one of the greatest joys in life, say that one of the greatest joys in life is 'to become a mother.' This way you don't risk alienating adoptive parents." She continued without a pause. "So when did you have your tubes tied?"

Emily blinked.

Marjorie pointed at her face. "If you have a reaction like that, everyone will know the truth. The American public will *not* be thrilled to realize you had elective surgery. When was it done?"

Emily paused for a moment; then her lips thinned. "I

had an emergency appendectomy while on vacation in Aca-pulco. My father bribed the doctor into tying my tubes at the same time and leaving no paper trail."

The woman raised one eyebrow. "Without your con-sent?"

Emily looked shocked. "Of course not. I begged him to do it. K can tell you that. She was there."

Kate bit her lip. What she could tell them was that she knew all along that the ruptured appendix claim had been a lie from the beginning. Emily had planned the trip for the express purpose of having the tubal ligation procedure done outside of the prying eyes of the media. Emily had thought she'd tricked Kate with the faked pains and even more faked insistence that her father be called. Emily had exploited both of them—using Kate to lend credence to the trip as a carefree vacation and Big Henry for his ability to use his good sense to buy her a suitable surgeon as well as the man's medical silence. Whether it had been an arrangement between father and daughter, Kate honestly didn't know.

Marjorie seemed to infer all of this without explanation. "You planned ahead. Good. Most people I work with don't think that far in advance when it comes to their political ca-reers. If anyone asks about your trip, stick with your original story—vacation in a foreign land, unfortunate health prob-lem, Daddy comes to the rescue, and you have surgery there. If anyone ever looks hard and starts to draw a connection between your infertility and your trip, then your camp hints that the surgeon was less skilled than advertised and that the infertility was due to complications from what should have been a simple operation. If they look into the surgeon's background and he comes out clean, your fallback position is that the procedure was done to you without your knowledge by your manipulative father. That it was *never* a matter of your choice. And, Miss Rosen, you know nothing about this, correct?"

Kate fully expected Emily to step forward and defend the memory of her late father. Big Henry may have been a scheming cutthroat in the boardroom and the scourge of every marble-lined corridor in the District, but everything Kate knew about him substantiated that he truly, unconditionally loved his only child, Emily.

So if Emily could swallow the idea of using her father as a posthumous scapegoat–slash–contingency plan, who was Kate to argue? She gave Marjorie her most innocent stare. "Me? Sorry, I wasn't listening. You were talking about . . . what? Taking a vacation?" It was an evasive nonanswer that seemed to satisfy both Emily and Marjorie. The truth was, she wasn't sure who was to blame—Emily or her father. And not knowing freed her from lying and violating her personal code of conduct.

Kate believed in the Ten Commandments—all of them. That included the ninth commandment, the one that made politics such a tricky business for Christians: you must not lie. Practical politics was all about shading the truth. Sometimes being a Christian and being a political consultant was a tough mix. Kate did her very best to live up to her faith. She tried always to stay on the right side of that bright line of the truth. But occasionally it was a real struggle.

She prayed she'd never hit the point where her beliefs made it impossible for her to go on in politics. In fact, Kate firmly believed God had placed her in politics to do whatever she could to change the world for the better. And that potential ability was what made her look forward to getting up and going to the office every day.

And on that day, at least, her conscience had stayed clear. Mostly, anyway.

Emily locked eyes with Dozier, the last real member of her father's inner circle, the man who represented Big Henry's generation of politics. "If it comes to that, are you okay with blaming this on Dad?"

He shrugged. "I can believe he might have done something like that. As far as that goes, I always had my suspicions that he might have engineered it." A paternal smile spread across his face as he gazed at Emily. "I had no idea you had the gumption to do something like that at such a tender age."

"It's not like I was sixteen." Emily didn't blush easily or often, but she did this time as if she were indeed some schoolgirl. "I was twenty-two at the time."

He beamed. "And a visionary."

Marjorie tapped her watch. "I don't have all day to validate your past actions. We need to work on your present to assure your future."

From that moment on, Emily didn't question a single suggestion made by Marjorie Redding. Kate agreed that the woman had no political ax to grind, so it didn't become a matter of Marjorie trying to change what Emily believed or why but one of simply coaching them all on how to best present Emily's appearance, philosophies, and plans. Some of the changes Marjorie suggested were alterations in Emily's appearance, softening her usual dark suits, using more subtle touches of color. Marjorie simplified Emily's makeup as well, which actually took a couple of years off her looks, even though she had been a well-documented forty-two at the time and was forty-four now.

There was no lying about Emily Benton's age; the media loved repeating the story of how her father, a young politician under JFK's tutelage, was supposed to be in Dallas that fateful day in November when the president was assassinated. However, Big Henry Benton had stayed back in Virginia to tend to his wife during her difficulties in childbirth and had thus missed being an eyewitness to the death of Camelot.

John Connally had been sitting in what would have been Henry's customary place near JFK, and he was wounded in the chest and the thigh. Big Henry, who was taller and broader than the Texas governor, might have being more seriously injured or even killed. Hank had said publicly that he wished he'd been there to take that bullet for the president.

What he said privately was that, unlike Kennedy, LBJ got things done. That was something Big Henry admired in a man.

What Hank didn't know then was that he'd eventually get his wish. Years later, an assassin would take Hank's life while trying to kill the president.

Emily's legacy was a complicated one.

Emily and Kate worked with Marjorie Redding for three and a half weeks, taking copious notes, learning about hair and makeup and posture, going shopping, and cultivating a better speaking voice, etiquette with the masses, and of course etiquette with the media. . . .

Including the members of the media who now stood outside the doors of the hotel gym in hopes of catching a disheveled Emily in her sweaty gym clothes.

They were mildly disappointed when Emily emerged, having showered and changed into an identical set of workout clothes that lacked unsightly pit stains and *aroma du athlete*. Emily had taken to heart Marjorie's commandment number twenty-seven: "Never let them see you sweat." Marjorie had also suggested that Emily show off her athletic figure on occasion as an obvious way to remind America that Emily Benton had a strong, healthy body to go along with her strong, healthy mind.

Not to mention a great pair of legs.

Lights strobed and the media surged closer to her and Kate. The two Secret Service agents and three hotel security personnel closed around Emily to form a flying wedge to get her to the nearest elevator. Kate had to plow her way through the crowd in the slipstream behind the candidate and the Secret Service. Practice let her push through the crowd with only moderate jostling.

One voice rose above the rest. "How'd the workout go?"

"Not bad," Emily answered, "although I'd rather have run outside. But I don't think most of you could have kept up." She gave them an encompassing look and an infectious grin. "Make that *any* of you."

"How long did you exercise?" This time, Kate could identify the speaker—a reporter holding an NBC-logoed microphone. His cameraman had obviously been chosen for his height, towering over all the other media types.

"I try to get in six miles a day, but it's hard when I'm on the campaign trail. So I hit the treadmill instead. But if any of you are runners, you know it's not the same."

Another disembodied voice said, "If you're elected, are you going to run every day at the White House?"

A small contingency of reporters called out the correction, "*When* you're elected . . ." and then all laughed. It had become a joke among the press corps. For the first two months of her campaign efforts, whenever anyone said, "If you're elected," Kate had corrected them with "You mean, *when* she's elected. . . ."

Now, no matter what city they visited, a Greek chorus formed within the media ranks to provide the correction automatically. It not only established a more easygoing rapport with the media, but it became a not-too-subtle reminder that key members of the press stood behind Emily's bid for the Oval Office.

"If elected, I will run. If not elected, I will . . . run." The media crowd erupted in laughter.

Emily paused rather than posed for a couple of shots, gave them a congenial sound bite or two, then begged off, citing the late time and their flight arrangements as the culprit.

The Secret Service split the crowd to allow her clear passage to the elevator that hotel security had commandeered for their exclusive use. They proceeded nonstop to the thirtieth floor to let Kate off, and then Emily and the security contingency continued on to her suite on the thirty-third floor.

It wasn't until Kate got into her room and pulled off the towel she'd slung across her neck that she saw the piece of paper. Judging by the way it fluttered to the floor, it had been tucked in the folds of the material.

It landed writing side up and she could read the note without even bending over or touching it.

YOU WILL *DIE.*

KATE WAS FAR MORE CONCERNED about how she received the message than what it actually said. At least that's what she told herself. After all, Emily received threatening messages all the time—in e-mail, through the regular mail, and on the phone. They came with the territory, and she shrugged them off without a second thought.

This time, though, the threat had come from inside Emily's circle of safety. Somebody had been so close that Emily or Kate probably could have touched them. They had certainly touched Kate or come dangerously close.

Contemplating that, Kate couldn't help but have second, third, or even fourth thoughts about the note and their safety.

The fact that Emily's dad had been assassinated added real bite to Kate's fear.

Kate tried to tell herself that death threats tended to be annoying but weren't necessarily a sign of certain doom—

just a sign of someone's certain stupidity. None of the people who'd threatened Emily in the past had ever tried to put their threats into action.

But this threat writer had been close. Too close. Kate's hands shook because she knew that the only opportunity anyone had to place the note in the towel was after their workout. The towel had come from Kate's room, not the gym. She'd opened it up and slung it around her neck before heading down to meet Emily. No hidden note in there then. Nobody'd had access to it while they worked out; the Secret Service had prevented anyone from entering the gym while they were there.

Rank had not only its privileges but its privacies, too.

Therefore, a reporter—or at least someone posing as the media and running with the pack—had tucked the note in one of the folds of the towel as Kate had shouldered her way through the crowd with Emily and her Secret Service detail.

Someone who wished Emily harm had been close enough to touch them. . . .

Been within arm's reach.

Kate felt a chill spread across the back of her neck and cascade down her shoulders until her hands shook so badly she had to clench them into fists to stop the shivering.

Maybe the note had been meant for her. Not Emily.

Then again, probably not.

For once, she wished she were more like Emily, who took these sorts of things in stride. After all, her friend had practically grown up as a public figure. But Kate hadn't. She hadn't grown up on a huge horse farm in Virginia. Hadn't gone to private school. Hadn't hung out with the rich and the famous. Hadn't spent the better part of her life having her every whim catered to. . . .

Hadn't seen her dad's blood coat her hands as she'd administered CPR while he was dying from a gunshot wound. . . .

But Emily had. Her school might have been private, but almost every other aspect of her life had been spent in the unblinking eyes of the public. Yet she'd survived her exposure, determined to succeed. Fear wasn't allowed to be part of her world.

Never in Kate's life, not even when she actively worked as a lawyer, had she ever incited the wrath of someone to the point where she received a death threat. Sure, she'd received some angry phone calls and a handful of letters threatening legal action, but no anonymous notes and certainly no death threats.

So it stood to reason that this threat was aimed at Emily. That is, if anonymous note writers followed the laws of reason and logic.

Somehow, that thought didn't help at all.

Her stomach slid sideways as she hit the speed dial on her phone. So far during this campaign, she'd called the security alert number exactly twice and always on Emily's behalf, never her own. Neither time had turned out to be a real emergency, though she hadn't known it when she'd called.

She hardly knew what to say.

But Agent McNally seemed to understand her rambling explanation and reached her door in less than a minute. Once there, he listened to her tale and appeared to come to the same general conclusion she had. Somebody was after Emily and had gotten within touching distance of the candidate. He repeated Kate's story verbatim to a higher authority by radio, then listened intently to the response. While doing this, he pulled the room curtains closed, choking out the morning sun. Then he examined Kate's bathroom for bogeymen. He also slipped the note into a plastic evidence Baggie.

"Change in plans." He pointed to his watch. "We're leaving for the airport in fifteen minutes." He glanced at her clothes, which she'd laid out on a chair before heading to the gym, and then at her almost-packed suitcase sitting on the edge of the bed. "I've been ordered to stay here while you change and pack. Another detail is with Ms. Benton. You okay with me staying in here while you get dressed? Or would you rather have me wait outside in the hallway?"

Kate had no problems admitting to herself that, under the circumstances, she appreciated having an armed Secret Service agent standing guard only one door away from her rather than two. She pulled out the desk chair. "Sit. I'd feel more secure if I knew you were nearby while I change in the bathroom." She glanced in the mirror, noted how pale she was. She needed to toughen up. "I'm sorry I'm such a wuss. Your job is to protect Emily, not me. Maybe you should go back to her."

"No, ma'am. She's got full protection and she'd be the first to say your safety is important too. In fact, Ms. Benton said any threat toward you is a threat toward her."

Now thoroughly embarrassed, Kate backed up a few steps and pointed her thumb over her shoulder at the bathroom door. "I . . . I'm just going to take a quick shower, but I promise I'll be ready in ten minutes."

He looked doubtful at her estimate but gave her a grim nod. "Ten minutes," he repeated.

Kate grabbed the clothes she'd laid out and took the world's quickest shower. Afterward, she dressed at the speed of light in the bathroom, towel dried her hair, slapped on some makeup, and emerged to watch a wry smile flit briefly across Agent McNally's usually stoic face.

"You weren't kidding, were you? Six minutes, fifteen seconds."

"I never kid about the important stuff." Kate shoved her wet gym clothes in a waterproof bag, then tossed everything into her suitcase. After giving the room a brief check to look for any last-minute forgotten items, she closed and locked her suitcase and rolled it to the door. She knew that McNally wouldn't offer to take her bag, not because he wasn't a gentleman, but because he was required to have his hands free in case he needed his gun.

That thought both soothed and frightened her.

He joined her at the door and kept his voice low, as if relating details to her on the sly. "So far, all press IDs have checked out, but one guy is missing—a new face in the crowd that nobody from the local field office or any of the media reps recognized. The suspect left shortly after you did, using a different elevator. We reviewed the security footage and the elevator records and we tracked him to the lobby floor, where he exited and got into a car waiting at the curb."

"So, there's no . . . imminent threat?"

"No, ma'am, and we're not convinced the note was actually serious. If its writer wanted to kill you or Emily, why send a threat first? Why not just strike? However, we still think it would be better to push up your departure from this city. Dallas has a bad rep when it comes to political assassinations."

Kate tried to smile at what she hoped was the agent's little joke, but her mouth wouldn't cooperate.

McNally took pity on her. "In all honesty, Ms. Rosen, I really do think the note was meant for Ms. Benton. The guy probably knew he couldn't get to her, so he slipped it to you instead. Or perhaps you two simply got your towels mixed up. It's probably just some nut job trying to shake you both up. We've got the hotel's surveillance tape plus all of the press footage. We'll get this guy before he can eat lunch. He's got to know it."

"It feels weird to say I hope you're right, but . . . I *do* hope you're right," Kate said. She grasped the handle of her roller suitcase, wishing she could grab hold of some courage just as easily. "Ready when you are, Agent McNally."

This time, the Secret Service didn't have her ride with Emily as was their usual custom. Normally, Emily and Kate rode together to the airport, and they'd spend their time reviewing the day, deconstructing the success or lack thereof of their campaigning efforts. Once on the plane, they looked forward rather than backward, planning the next whistle-stop, speech, or appearance.

As she watched out the limo window, she realized that the Secret Service must not have completely discounted the idea that she might be the target of the threat. By putting her in a different car, the agents were keeping her out of Emily's orbit until both women were safe on the jet.

Minimizing collateral damage . . .

Now, not only had Kate's sense of security been disrupted by the threat but it had messed up her time with Emily. Kate's stomach growled. And this complication also had made her miss the breakfast sandwich Emily had promised her. . . .

And somehow, she didn't think the Secret Service wanted to stop at a McDonald's on the way to the airport. Especially after the threat she'd just found.

Once they reached the private hangar, McNally opened the car door for Kate, retrieved her suitcase from the trunk, and handed the bag off to the copilot, who carried it up the stairs to stow inside the jet. After thanking McNally, Kate climbed the stairs as well.

Time to face the music, she thought. *I hope Emily isn't taking this as hard as I am.*

She wasn't.

"Aha, here's our troublemaker. Late as usual." Emily leaned out of the galley in the rear of the plane and waved.

"I'm tired of taking messages for you," Kate quipped as she stowed her briefcase.

"Who's to say it was for me?"

"Me. You're a bigger target than I am. Ask anyone."

Emily grinned. "You're so right. Better sit down and buckle up. They're raring to go up front. Schedules to keep, you know."

Kate settled herself in one of the buttery-leather seats and fished out the seat belt.

Chip, playing flight attendant, trotted over with a cup of coffee for Kate. "Two sugars, one cream, just the way you like it." He was being unusually solicitous. Either he'd had a fabulous night's sleep or he was playing the sympathy card to curry Emily's favor.

Or both.

Or perhaps it was something else.

Kate refused to think about it.

At least he and Emily were both in glowing good moods.

"Thanks, Chip." Kate accepted the coffee and debated rifling through the small galley to see if there was anything to eat other than snack foods. She pivoted in the chair, about to ask Emily if there was anything to scavenge on the plane when a heavenly aroma hit her.

"Even if I'm a bigger target than you are, I bet you're hungrier." Emily placed a familiar-looking bag in Kate's lap, and before Kate even opened it, she knew what was inside.

"You remembered!" She fished out a paper-wrapped object and opened it, revealing a still-warm Egg McMuffin.

"It was that or listen to your stomach howl all the way home." Emily dropped the flippant attitude as she settled into the chair next to Kate. "You okay, K?" she said in an uncharacteristically soft voice, adding a quick hug.

Kate knew Emily had spent her childhood without ever being hugged except when the cameras were rolling. It said volumes to Kate about how much her friend cared when Emily reached over to reassure her.

Kate inhaled deeply, finding comfort in the aroma of the food and her friend's obvious sense of concern. "Yeah. The whole threatening-note thing just took me by surprise. That's all. I'm actually fine. Thanks."

"You sure?"

"Sure as I can eat this before the pilot finishes his preflight." She demonstrated by taking a bite. "See?"

"Don't talk with your mouth full," Emily chided. She paused, then gave Kate a look of penetrating concern. "Just remember that a message like this isn't an actual threat. It's somebody's lame attempt to throw us off our game. And no one manipulates us like that. Right?"

Kate nodded.

"If we allow this note to distract, discourage, or derail us, then that reprobate has won; he'll have achieved maximum damage simply because of three lousy words." She glanced at Kate, then at Dozier and Chip. "No way we're letting him do that, right? Right?"

Kate found an odd sense of solace in Emily's fierce determination to let the matter drop. Her stirring words reminded Kate of one of the things she loved about Emily: her undying dedication to those she held nearest and dearest. Once, when Buster had gotten into a bag of chocolate candy and had to be rushed to the vet, Emily was the one who left a highly charged political dinner to sit in the waiting room with Kate, distracting her with idle gossip, doing anything she could to keep Kate from worrying about her pup. And another time, Kate's mother got lost in downtown Richmond and couldn't get Kate on the phone. Instead, her mother called Emily, who was in the midst of an important meeting with two other governors and who stopped to give Kate's mom directions so that she could get to a sale at a local department store.

Family came first and Kate's family was Emily's family. That's why Emily had earned not only her support and her friendship but her vote as well. And her tireless determination to bring as many other voters as she could to support her candidate and her friend. Kate took another bite of the sandwich that Emily had gone out of her way to get and silently vowed to do everything she could to get things back to normal.

After a brief moment, Kate realized the best way to regain confidence, reestablish control, and reclaim a sense of peace was to get back to business as usual. She reached for her briefcase. "Since we didn't do the eval in the limo, let's do it now."

Emily rewarded her with a broad smile and an "attagirl" wink. "Give me the breakdown."

An appearance evaluation consisted of an after-action report measuring the effectiveness and efficiency of delivering their campaign message and gauging the reaction of the target audience to that message. They also looked hard at how well they reached and utilized the media outlets at each location and how effective their print, television, Web, and radio ads had been.

In the last twenty-four hours, Emily had been the guest of honor at a charity fund-raiser luncheon for the Junior League of Dallas and had done four major network news interviews, including one with Fox News on the infamous grassy knoll where the tale of the birth and death of political regimes was trotted out yet again. More importantly, she delivered a keynote address at a dinner sponsored by the largest Hispanic news organization in the U.S. There, Emily had made perfect use of her fluent Spanish to mention her immigration reform proposal. She'd outlined a worker visa program that would provide a fast track to citizenship for the more than twelve million Hispanics living illegally in the United States. The audience interrupted her more than a half-dozen times with standing ovations. As a result, she received the endorsement from the Hispanic Mayors Council, virtually ensuring that she would carry Texas in November. It could also put New Mexico, Arizona, and California in her pocket.

That was also a feat her opponent, Charles Talbot, could never achieve—not only due to his ironclad stance on closed borders but because, even with coaching, he couldn't speak Spanish, not even phonetically.

Talbot actually prided himself on writing his own speeches and made pointed and often insulting references to Emily's many speechwriters. What he failed to realize was that Emily's speeches might be written by some of the sharpest word slingers in the business—including a Pulitzer prize winner—but it was Emily's pitch-perfect delivery of them that elevated those cleverly crafted words into oratorical splendor. And Emily made sure her policies and her politics were central in every speech she gave, no matter who wrote it. She was in charge of her presidential run, not the consultants and image burnishers who surrounded any serious candidate, and it showed in every word she spoke.

In fact, no other candidate—Republican, Democrat, or Independent; national or regional—could speak as eloquently or as effectively as Emily Benton. After all, it was in her blood. Emily came from a long line of silver-tongued politicos, living and dead.

They all had reason to be proud of her after this run through Dallas.

Kate consulted her laptop for the dozen or so evaluation reports, fed to her by junior staffers. "We got good reviews and good press from the Junior League appearance. They raised $125,000 for their community assistance fund and we had over two hundred new supporter sign-ups from the event, which sounds tame only until you consider that they represent some of the most influential women in the city." She turned to Chip, whose milieu was the virtual campaign trail. "What sort of impact did you see online?"

He had his laptop open as well. "Besides the usual network

and cable coverage, the in-depth releases were picked up in fourteen major online-only markets. We've seen almost two hundred new off-site blog references over the last eighteen hours and another 350 supporter sign-ups from the Dallas/ Fort Worth area on the English site with almost a hundred new on-site blogs started. But that's not all." He paused for maximum effect. "We got 697 sign-ups on the Spanish site overnight. Of those sign-ups, almost two hundred requested and paid for campaign kits from the online store."

Emily punched the armrest of her seat. "Now that, ladies and gentlemen, is the way to run a campaign. Remember, Kate, back in college, when we used to dream about making a White House run together, to bring the voice of women to the top spot in politics?"

"You bet," Kate said, thinking of how young and naive they'd been. "We were going to save America, just the two of us."

"Well, the day's at hand. Now, let's make sure every appearance I make has this sort of payback." She turned to Kate. "You just earned that week off with good behavior, just in time for Christmas."

Despite the sense of triumph, achievement, and momentum they attained from the postevent assessment, the three-word note she'd intercepted still continued to haunt Kate as they flew back to Reagan and then drove to the campaign headquarters. She decided that the distraction was understandable. As long as she didn't allow it to derail her, she'd mitigated most of the damage.

She made herself take a calming breath. But it wasn't until she stepped into her office and saw Buster the Wonder Dog waiting for her there that the ugly words faded from her memory. Kaleesa King, the staffer who always babysat Buster while Kate was on the road, had given him a bath and decked him out with a new bandanna embellished with the Benton campaign logo.

Kate sat on the floor of her office and allowed Buster to slobber all over her until he fell into her lap, an exhausted heap with the exception of the tip of his tail, which wiggled back and forth almost too fast to see.

She nuzzled his head. "You don't know how much I missed you, Buster."

His tail started a new oscillation.

She turned to his babysitter. "Was he really good?"

Kaleesa knelt beside them and patted Buster's fuzzy snout. "He's always good. But he always misses his momma something fierce. Don't you, Buster-Boy? Gimme four." She held out her hand and he lazily lifted his paw and dropped it into her palm.

Kate couldn't help but grin. "Cool! A new trick. Gimme four, Buster."

He stared at her, bedevilment in his eyes, staunchly refusing to move a muscle other than his perpetual tail motion.

"C'mon, Buster. Give me four."

He continued to wag but otherwise stayed still.

"Please?"

Kaleesa leaned down and made eye contact with the dog. "Buster. Give her four."

He eyed Kate, then Kaleesa; then with grave reluctance, he placed his paw in Kate's outstretched hand.

"Good boy!" Kate reached over to her desk, pulled open the side drawer and fished around blindly until she found the jar of dog cookies. Buster jumped up in anticipation of the treat and proceeded to run himself through the various commands he knew—sit, sit up, lie down . . . hoping that one of them would result in the reward.

Kate held the treat up. "Give me four." The dog clawed at her leg until she put her hand down low enough to accept his paw. "Good boy," she said, feeding him and then stroking his clean fur. "Good Buster."

Kate held out a twenty to the young woman, their usual fee for overnight dog-sitting services with pickup and drop. "Thanks so much for keeping him, Kaleesa. I always feel so bad when I have to leave without him, but knowing he's with you helps me feel a little less guilty."

As usual, the young woman hesitated but then took the money with a ready smile. "We really love having him around. He's great with the kids." She stooped to ruffle his ears. "And so well mannered. Right, Buster?" She fished a small calendar from her pocket. "Next week on Wednesday, right?"

Kate nodded. "Just the one night. Then, after that trip, he and I are headed to my parents' house for Christmas. Mom and Dad have two cats that he loves to terrorize. It's just not Christmas for me unless it's accompanied by the sound of hissing cats and a crazy, howling dog."

After saying their good-byes, Kaleesa left and Buster stood at the door, perplexed. After a moment, he let out a howl of what sounded like abandonment.

"Buster? What's wrong? C'mere."

The dog stood at the door, obviously pining for Kaleesa.

He wants her. Not me. The revelation slammed into Kate, leaving her with a queasy feeling in her stomach, worse than hitting an air pocket at twenty thousand feet. Was Buster forgetting her and throwing his affections to the person who spent more time actually caring for him?

Kate remained on the floor in her office, trying to combat the sudden sense of doubt and fear that ran through her. Her brain insisted that, of course, the threat had been meant for Emily, the very public candidate, not her behind-the-scenes campaign manager whom few people recognized. And Buster was just an animal with a temporary sense of loyalty to the person who fed him last.

But it was her secret heart that worried the threat was real and Buster now preferred someone else over her.

Forever.

She felt a twinge of pain, low in her gut, and even as the first tear threatened to slide down her cheek, she smiled. *Aha,* she thought. She wasn't losing it. Her tears were perfectly normal. *PMS,* she told herself. *It's nothing more than PMS.* She scrambled to her feet, found her Palm Treo, and pulled up her calendar.

The dates coincided.

Hormones, not insanity.

A sense of relief washed over her. She opened the bottom desk drawer, pulled out her candy jar, and placed it next to the telephone. It was a visible warning to all who entered that the next few days might be a little rockier than usual, but that she was self-administering the best medicine she could find to counteract the symptoms of PMS. It was one of those situations where sharing her medication benefited everyone around her.

Chocolate for everybody!

She reached in and unwrapped a Hershey's Kiss, and as she ate it, she felt some of the day's tensions slide away. And then her cell phone chirped that she'd received an incoming text message.

L. McCormick: NEWS!

Kate stared at the word on the screen. LuAnn McCormick only sent text messages when she couldn't bring herself to speak face-to-face or ear to ear. A text message from her was never a good sign.

She dialed LuAnn's cell and the young woman answered on the third ring.

And she had a ready complaint.

"Don't call when I text you," she whined. "You're supposed to text me back."

"I don't like getting bad news via text. I want to hear either the sympathy or the sorrow in your voice," Kate said.

"How do you know what I've got isn't good?"

"You only text when it's bad. So stop stalling. What's going on?"

"Okay, okay." The young woman drew in a deep breath. "My friend called."

Kate sighed. Everybody was LuAnn's friend. The young woman had an uncanny knack for charming every man she ever met, which in the District wasn't an easy task. However, for whatever unfathomable reason, men would meet her, fall madly in love with her, and—for years following the meeting that had initially converted them to her minions—do anything she wanted. And yet she didn't flirt, didn't make untoward promises, and certainly didn't deliver in a way that you'd think necessary to keep a platoon of men on the hook.

"Which friend, Lu?"

"Ricardo from data research."

The sounds in the room swelled as Kate's senses grew acute—the murmuring fountain on her credenza, the squeaky wheels of her desk chair. That's what always happened when she prepared for bad news. Her eyesight sharpened. Hearing sharpened. And bad news? It had a bitter tang.

And bad news leaked from CNN by one of their prime data crunchers in the Washington bureau had the worst taste of all.

"The latest poll?"

"Yes," LuAnn whispered as if worried about being overheard. When the girl swallowed hard, it was like the rumble of thunder in Kate's ears. "You've dropped twelve points."

Kate closed her eyes and drew in a sharp breath. They'd anticipated a small loss as the holidays drew near but not twelve percentage points. She glanced out the door at Emily, holding court among the staffers with her usual engaging smile, probably regaling them with tales of the current fashions in the Junior League set.

Emily wasn't going to like this one bit, which meant that that cozy little domestic scene outside Kate's office door was about to fall apart.

And the world as they knew it was going to collapse in on itself.

AS EXPECTED, their world imploded; their sense of accomplishment shattered into a million little pieces.

It was Kate's job to reassemble those pieces into a viable and effective campaign plan. This time, despite Kate's best efforts, the staffers hadn't been quite so insulated from the fallout. Sure, they knew their candidate had feet of clay—all candidates did—but they'd never seen Emily in a full tirade, and Kate was bound and determined to limit their exposure.

After Emily's initial outburst, Kate calmed her long enough to hustle her into her own office, where they could continue the explosion in private, behind heavily sound-proofed walls. Kate had anticipated the eventual outing of her friend's temper and had spent extra money to increase the insulation in Emily's office, which muted her loud rants to a mild murmur.

Lesson one: Don't get the candidate angry.

Lesson two: If she does blow a cork, soundproof rooms

are important, as are shiny objects to distract her. But it was critical to make sure those shiny objects didn't have any sharp edges or points.

To Emily's credit, once she calmed down, she took the blame herself—for the drop in the polls and for her unseemly reaction.

"Sorry, Kate. I didn't mean to let fly in front of the troops."

"It's understandable. I know to take what you scream with a grain of salt the size of a salt lick. But they haven't learned that."

"You *did* warn me it was too early to switch our attention to the other party, but I thought you were wrong." Emily shook her head. "I should have listened to you."

As much as Kate wanted to say it, *I told you so* was not and would *never* be the right response. Instead, Kate offered a better interpretation of the situation. "Look at it this way. No effort we made was wasted. Maybe a bit premature but not wasted."

"True, but it also means we have to work twice as hard, twice as fast, to recover lost ground. Henderson can't hold the party together against Talbot—he's not strong enough. He'll crumble like the sand castle he lives in. We have to regain that ground as soon as possible."

Mark Henderson had many of the same qualities Emily did—he came from a political family with a long, successful history, had a circle of strong advisers guiding him, and possessed good looks and even better health. Their basic political views even paralleled each other.

Closely.

The biggest difference between the two of them was their

gender. And that small genetic disparity had provided an easy detour around the electorate's speed-bump reaction to the concept of a woman in the White House.

Have two candidates with similar politics?

Vote for the man!

Emily paced the room. "Forget Talbot for right now. We concentrate on Henderson." She stopped suddenly. Then she stared at Kate. "Whatever ammunition you have on Talbot, I want twice that much on Henderson. Look in every shadow; track his every footstep. He can't be as clean as he pretends— nobody is. Go back to his college days. We all slipped up in college, once or twice."

Kate held her tongue. On a normal day, that would be her cue to remind Emily that they both screwed up far more than once or twice in college, but she knew this wasn't the right time or place for such humor.

Emily continued, unaware of Kate's restraint. "In any case, there's got to be something out there that can expose his weaknesses and disrupt his campaign. Find it and bring it to me."

She stalked toward the door and stopped, turning around. "Mark my words, Kate. If anyone is going to break the glass ceiling in the Oval Office, it's going to be me. And after I make the history books for being the first female president, the next chapter will be about all the great things I did in office. And no one—not Henderson, not any other man—is going to stop me."

She took a deep breath, opened the door, and made one of her miraculous emotional changes, joking with the aides and volunteers.

It wasn't a mask; it was just how Emily worked through

things—getting everything off her chest in a private pow-wow with Kate, where Emily could rant and rave but do no harm. Once the worst of the upset and shock bled away, she was back to normal, ready to cope and, better yet, succeed.

Dismissed, Kate returned to her office and stared at her computer screen. She could hear Emily giving the staffers assurances that she was fine, she'd just suffered a momentary upset.

Kate knew that Emily's congenial side was firmly back in control. She'd apologize to the campaign workers, then either have pizza or pastries brought in as part of the apology or go to the kitchen herself and whip up a batch of cookies.

Yes, alert the media. The candidate could cook, thanks to her mother, who had tried to expose her only child to a world outside of politics, including a six-month stint at a Parisian gourmet cooking school as a teen. Emily's mom had lost a husband to politics long before he'd been assassinated, and she'd had every intention of making sure her daughter wasn't sucked into the family business.

Emily had returned from France with some basic cooking skills but also with even more determination to follow in her father's political footsteps.

As far as Emily's mother was concerned, the whole French excursion was a total bust. Even if Emily did learn to cook.

One of those lingering skills Emily had learned in that long ago summer was a particularly good cookie recipe that she'd worked to perfect. Sure, a pan full of chocolate chip cookies might not heal the world, but it would pacify a group of staffers and make them forget any concerns about the emotional status of their candidate.

It seemed trite and an obvious ploy, but Kate had seen it in action often enough to know it generally worked.

And it would work again.

Except on Kate.

Emily hadn't actually apologized to Kate.

And Kate was the one who had to go digging for dirt on their opponent. She hated that part of her job. Given the guy's squeaky clean surface reputation, it was going to take serious digging to rattle the skeletons in the closet. She always felt a bit dirty when she started the process. She knew that by judging others she was putting herself in a position to be judged. Never mind the Golden Rule. . . . Politics generally played by its own golden rule: do unto others as they would do unto you—but do it first.

She took no delight in finding anything awful on the other candidates. But typically, the depth and breadth of what she had found and would find always made it easier for her to place even more faith in Emily. Kate knew all of Emily's deepest, darkest secrets. Compared to the other candidates of either party, Emily clearly stood above the rest.

"The cream of the scum," her friend often joked.

But the more Kate learned about the others, the more strongly she was convinced that the country needed Emily.

The only trouble was . . . learning about others was scary. It made her feel unclean. She justified doing it by telling herself she was following Jesus' admonishment to "render unto Caesar that which was Caesar's." Kate believed that if a person aspired to become a temporal power, then that person should live by temporal laws. Any failure to do so called into question that person's suitability as a leader. And leadership was important. The country she loved needed not just *good* leadership but *excellent* leadership—the kind Emily had demonstrated in the past. If Emily's opponents couldn't live up to Emily's potential as a leader, Kate felt that it was both the right thing and the Christian thing to make sure the public had at its disposal all the facts to make a good decision.

On the more personal scale, digging into other people's backgrounds was time-consuming, so much so that Kate worried that her much-anticipated family Christmastime might be melting away right before her eyes. It took time, patience, and ingenuity to burrow deep into the landscape of a person's life in order to dig up . . . something. Anything. To find fault or guilt or evidence wherever it was—hidden, dormant, or forgotten.

She told herself that discovering the truth was no sin, but still she wondered if she was merely trying to justify her actions. Even though Kate's goal was to ferret out the truth and not to make up any falsehoods, this kind of work always left a bad taste in her mouth and dirt under her nails. She told herself every time her conscience screamed at her that, unlike some other well-known political advisers, she stuck strictly to the truth. She made sure that her evidence was ironclad before she shared it, much less used it. And she never, ever used anything she found against an innocent—unlike those political activists who slammed innocent kids for using government benefits they were entitled to, back in the battles over funding the State Children's Health Insurance Program.

But the truth could be a weapon against their opponents. By signing on to the political game, Kate figured they also signed on to have their backgrounds checked, their lives exposed, their pasts examined minute by minute. And if they didn't know that, they were fools.

Emily was sinking in the polls. She needed a weapon. It was Kate's job to find it.

In fact, Emily needed more than a weapon. She needed a thermonuclear device to use against her opponent rather than a mere slingshot.

And if Kate wanted to have any semblance of a Christmas holiday, exactly where was she going to find an armed and ticking warhead in less than a week?

✶ ✶ ✶ ✶ ✶

Contrary to popular belief, Kate didn't know where all the bodies were buried. Neither did Emily Benton or any other candidate. No single political pundit or media maven knew all the answers. But thanks to one source she'd carefully cultivated, Kate did have a fair idea of what questions to ask.

And of whom.

She punched in the number on her cell phone from memory, having never trusted it to a silicon chip or a piece of paper. There were some things you never wrote down.

A voice answered, "And you want?"

"Caller ID has certainly had an impact on basic telephone etiquette. I'd hoped we could start our conversation with something like 'Good afternoon' or 'How are you today?' or simply, 'Hello.'"

Carmen del Rio's laughter wasn't particularly harsh, but neither was it warm and inviting. "I forget you have some semblance of manners. Please forgive me. Good afternoon, Miss Rosen. How may I be of assistance?"

"I need some direction," Kate said. "On a delicate matter."

Carmen had the phlegmy, raspy cough of a lifelong smoker. "Don't you always? Who, this time?"

"Mark Henderson."

The woman sounded tired and not the least bit surprised at Kate's request. "Let me check my files. I'll call you back in an hour or so."

As the various candidates of both parties had begun to declare their intentions to run for president, Kate had started building a dossier on each person who expressed any serious interest in the race. She examined every aspect of their lives that she could with her available resources. As she often told Emily, Google was a girl's best friend.

Kate didn't stop with just the candidates. In addition, she delved deeply into the lives of each candidate's inner circle of campaign advisers.

"Know thy enemy." It was a necessary mandate in the world of American politics.

She knew there was no shame in digging up old records, looking for details concerning the candidates' pasts, because she knew that the opposition returned the favor in full, with interest, delving into her background too.

Of course, Emily's life had been an open book thanks to her larger-than-life family, and Kate's life was beyond boring in comparison to practically anyone in politics.

Thanks to the unconditional love of her parents, who made sure she'd had a strong moral grounding—not to mention Kate's personal commitment to Christ from a young age—Kate had barely gotten detention, much less ever made any police blotters. The worst thing she'd done as a rebellious teen was sneak out to meet a girlfriend at the midnight movies. She'd faced the usual temptations of youth but hadn't got caught up in the claws of drugs or alcohol. Her mundane temptations weren't the kind that made front page headlines or dossiers put together by other candidates.

Most political types, she knew, hadn't been so lucky.

Kate knew which campaign workers for the opposition had expunged juvenile records. She knew what sort of crimes they'd committed and which ones had been whitewashed away. She knew which adviser had bought himself out of a college cheating scandal, which campaign manager's underage sister had been prominently featured in a Girls Gone Wild video. She knew which three candidates liked to watch porn in their hotel rooms. She knew who had DUIs, who'd done rehab, who had lapsed, and who'd stayed sober. She knew who had edited their Wikipedia entries and why.

It was a telling comment on her generation and its amusements, she supposed, that the file containing her distilled knowledge about her opponents' frailties was so thick.

And it'd taken a lot more than a batch of gourmet cookies to get that kind of information.

Kate had gone at her various targets in a roundabout way. She'd done her share of straight research. She had even occasionally hired help.

But instead of breaking her back and the bank trying to send out a dozen different investigators to claw through the lives of a dozen different presidential contenders, she'd put a great deal of time, effort, and substantial cost into finding the goods on one person: the biggest power and information broker in D.C.

Carmen Maria Angelina Conchita del Rio knew everything

about everybody and kept most of it to herself. The first time Kate met her, the woman had reminded her of one of those Hollywood stars of yesteryear. It was as if Carmen had thrown the names and appearances of Carmen Miranda and Dolores del Rio in a margarita blender and donned the result. To look at her dark beauty—fading now but still apparent in the purity of her bone structure—no one would ever guess that Carmen held and protected the secrets of hundreds of politics' biggest names from all parties. She looked more like she should star in *Sunset Boulevard* than like the repository for cataloging all the worst acts of America's political underbelly for two generations.

But that's what she was.

What was known for certain about Carmen del Rio was that she'd worked as a research assistant for the *Washington Post*. She had been very good at her job and never forgot a single fact, figure, or detail. Later, she became a secretary in the FBI office that handled all of the District's black bag jobs. Beltway rumor had it that she'd helped make the worst of J. Edgar's secret files disappear by stuffing the most dangerous ones in her underwear and taking them home. That was pure speculation.

When asked about it, Carmen always derailed the questions by swearing she'd never worn underwear when she was a young woman.

A statement like that usually got conversations moved into a whole different direction fast.

There were rumors that before she'd joined the *Post*, she'd been a CIA operative, a call girl, the mistress to two presidents, a nude model, a madam, a gospel singer, and a dozen other improbable occupations.

What wasn't speculation in the District was that Carmen had, for many years, been *the* person to go to when somebody needed insider information on anyone in Washington's political, social, or business scene.

These days Carmen was no longer dependent for her support on her information business. She'd married one of the wealthiest and most influential businessmen in the area and lived in an ivory castle west of the Potomac. Although she reigned over a staff of servants who waited on her hand and foot, she still paid close attention to whispers on the east side of the river.

What Kate knew as fact was that Carmen's vast knowledge of who was who, and what they'd done to get there, extended as far north as Boston and as far south as Atlanta. No gossip, rumor, innuendo, or whisper escaped her attention or her assessment. But Carmen had long since retired from her information-brokering business, to the relief and dismay of politicos everywhere.

So Kate had tried a different tactic on Carmen. Even if Kate could bring herself to attempt blackmail, it would have been useless. No matter how awful the deed attributed to Carmen was, she wore the legend of her past like a badge of honor. Perhaps it was because she could buy anybody and everybody off. Or perhaps it was because her life was so colorful that any new chapter of debauchery merely added to the aura.

Whitemail—now that was another issue entirely. The day Kate learned that the "open book" of Carmen's life was nothing more than a carefully crafted work of fiction was the date Carmen del Rio became permanently in her debt.

Kate's incredible good luck occurred the day her own

mother casually mentioned that a picture she'd seen of socialite matron Carmen Maria Angelina Conchita del Rio looked incredibly like CarrieAnne Rivers, who had been her best friend in sixth grade, when her father had been assigned to Fort Sam Houston while in the army.

It had been an innocent comment that gave Kate a unique starting point for her journey of research. As a result, she unraveled the long and involved tapestry that CarrieAnne/Carmen had woven for herself out of whole cloth once she left San Antonio to seek her fortune. Of the laundry list of career paths she'd supposedly taken, she'd definitely been a secretary. And a gospel choir singer.

The rest? Kate never found a single trace of evidence to support those wilder claims.

Armed with the facts, Kate had struck a deal with Carmen; in exchange for Kate's silence about Carmen's completely innocuous past, the woman would help guide her in any reasonable investigative request.

However, there was a definite protocol to follow. Kate's requests had to be made with the same deference that she would show a respected elder in her own family. In return, Carmen would never quite hand her the smoking gun but would only point to where that smoking gun might possibly be found, often still in the hands of the person who pulled the trigger.

Through the years, Kate had found it to be an effective working relationship. Carmen's uncheckered past remained a closely guarded secret.

Kate's cell phone rang fifteen minutes after making the initial call.

Carmen never identified herself, but then again, her rasp

was unmistakable. "Henderson just made a radical flip-flop on a federal wetlands bill today. Money changed hands three days ago at the Grand Ambassador Hotel on Twelfth. Find the security camera feed from the elevator. The guard is young, greedy, and impressionable. Get the goods from him before he gets a better deal from someone else."

"Thank you."

Carmen hesitated, then answered, "You're welcome," as if she hadn't had much practice saying the phrase often or to many.

This time, Kate did have the number she needed in her speed dial. District Discreet had a double-D logo, which made most people assume the company might be an escort service. But instead, District Discreet was one of the most efficient and effective private investigation agencies in the Metro D.C. area, with reciprocal licensing in the District, Virginia, and Maryland. The fact that its owners, Lee Devlin and Sierra Dudicroft, were both statuesque blondes with impressive double-D attributes had been a happy coincidence.

Or so they said.

"Lee? Kate Rosen here."

"What can we do for you and Madam President?"

Kate smiled at the optimism. "From your mouth to God's ear. What we need is a little footwork to uncover a piece of security footage from the Grand Ambassador, three days ago. The interchange took place in one of their elevators between Mark Henderson and persons unknown. Money exchanged hands."

"Usual terms?"

"Agreed. I've heard that the informant is on the hotel's security staff and is both young and greedy."

"I'll call back when I have something."

"Thanks, Lee."

Four hours later, Kate was home, trying to chip a frozen dinner out of her freezer when Lee called back.

"Can you meet me at the office? Actually, in the garage of the building?"

"Now?"

"It'll be worth the effort."

Kate abandoned her dinner plans with some relief in favor of fast food on the way. She polished off the last of her meal as she turned in to the parking garage and took a moment to wipe away a smidge of ketchup from her chin. While looking in the rearview mirror, she saw movement behind her in the well-lit garage.

Her doors were locked, a lifetime habit reinforced by D.C.'s unusually high crime rate. Reaching over to her purse on the passenger's seat, she kept her eyes on her surroundings as she found the canister of pepper spray she kept there. The spray would be more of a detriment than a defense if she tried to use it within a small, closed space like the car. But she wanted it at hand.

She angled the mirror, trying to find the source of the movement, and was surprised and relieved when she saw Lee Devlin headed her way. Kate unlocked the car and had barely moved her purse out of the way before Lee opened the passenger door and sat down.

"Head there," she ordered, holding out a shop directory for the Fashion Centre at Pentagon City.

Kate complied without asking questions. Visuals without verbal explanation usually meant Lee was concerned about being overheard. It took fifteen minutes to finally get across the Fourteenth Street Bridge, into Arlington, and into the parking deck for the shopping center. During that time, Lee fiddled with Kate's car stereo and didn't say a word.

Kate doubted seriously that her car had been bugged but figured Lee's sense of caution was a good idea. If Lee was wrong, no harm done. If the woman was right, it might mean preventing a world of hurt.

Once parked, Lee motioned for Kate to follow. They ended up in the bottom floor food court of the mall. Lee found an empty table in a corner and they sat down. Reaching into her briefcase, she pulled out a personal DVD player and a set of earbuds. She plugged them in and offered Kate one bud.

"Cloak-and-dagger usually isn't your style," Kate said as she accepted the earpiece. "You were really that concerned that my car was bugged?"

"Why take chances? Besides, this stuff is *that* hot." Lee started the player.

The color footage was crystal clear, not the grainier security camera version Kate had expected. It was probably a testament to the level of precaution and protection employed by the Grand Ambassador, which was known for its discretion when catering to and protecting highbrow clientele. Conversely, such stiff security measures meant that its patrons might be surprised at how few truly private corners the hotel possessed.

A man stood in the elevator car, his craggy face in profile. The door slid open and Mark Henderson entered. His aide-de-camp tried to enter as well, but Mark shook his head. "Not enough room. Take the next car." It was clear that there were only the two men in the elevator and ample space, but the aide nodded and stepped back out of view.

The door closed and the car rose a few feet. Profile Man—he looked familiar enough that his identity lurked on the outskirts of Kate's memories—reached over and hit a series of buttons that stopped the car with a slight jolt, but surprisingly the action didn't fire off any alarms. That was suspicious from the get-go.

"Here." The man held out an envelope, which Henderson accepted, then opened, revealing a thick wad of bills. "Twenty grand. Just like you said."

Kate stared at the scene as if it were something out of a bad movie. Cash? In this day and age? Any smart candidate realized there were easier ways to move funds, legally or illegally, than handing over a wad of cash. Henderson couldn't be that stupid, could he? Would he, like one member of Congress, try to hide it in his freezer in packages of frozen food? She thought the man had more class than that, not to mention brains.

Kate smelled a setup. She turned to Lee, who was also watching the screen closely but wearing a smile as she did it.

"You don't expect me to believe this, do you?" Silently, she added, *Carmen didn't think I'd fall for this, did she?*

Lee shook her head. "Don't worry—just keep watching."

They continued to look at Henderson and Profile Man as they held a cryptic conversation straight out of a grade-Z movie, complete with stilted dialogue, monotone delivery on Henderson's part, and gross overacting on the part of Profile Man. It was as if he had to compensate for the lack of talent of his wooden costar. It was like a really bad grade school production of *Law & Order*.

The proverbial bell rang in the back of Kate's head.

She hit Pause on the machine and the action froze.

She knew exactly where she'd seen Profile Man before. It was on an episode of that very show, *Law & Order*. A couple of years ago, the young son of one of her legal secretaries had been a bit player in an episode. Everyone in the office had attended a party on the night the episode aired. The proud parents kept playing back their child's key scenes in the courtroom. Profile Man had played the evil villain against whom the young witness had testified.

"That guy." Kate touched the frozen figure of the Profile Guy on the screen. "I've seen him before. He's an actor."

Lee nodded. "Yeah. His real name is Mickey Meyer, but his SAG card is under the name 'Mitchell Mays.' He lives in Baltimore, and he gets a good amount of work in shows that shoot on the East Coast, especially in New York City." She patted the machine with affection. "I think this tape may be some of his best work. He definitely needs to add it to his demo reel."

"So we have actors, dialogue, and intrigue. All this lacks is an underlying score in a minor key. So why in the world would Henderson set up this sort of elaborate charade?"

"Just wait. Something is coming up in a second here and it'll prove just how far your opposition will go to have a little fun at your expense." Lee hit the Play button and the action continued. As Henderson and the man walked out, Henderson slapped the man on the back, secretly depositing a bumper sticker that read, *Vote for Benton*.

Kate groaned. "That man has entirely too much time on his hands. What? Is he in negotiations to host *Saturday Night Live* and this is audition footage?"

"Look at it this way: he knows you're looking for some dirt, so he whispers something in the right ear and he leads you to this . . . this parody sketch. 'Ha ha, fooled you. Don't you know you're wasting your time?'"

"He expects me to believe he's got time—this close to the primaries—to play a stupid practical joke like this?"

"Who knows? In my opinion, this is simply flashy misdirection. Smoke and mirrors. I think he created fake footage to keep you from looking harder. My bet is he was counting on you finding this and not digging any deeper."

"Then he made a mistake."

"I'll say." Lee stopped the machine, opened it, and exchanged the disc with a second one. Moments later, the machine stirred to life again. "But we weren't fooled. So we dug."

This time the picture was a bit grainier. It looked like a different elevator car with the same basic interior as the other one, but the camera angle was different. The footage was black-and-white and had the mild distortion of a wide-angle lens, typical for a security camera. A 6 was superimposed on the lower left corner. When the elevator moved, the number changed to 5 and obviously represented the current floor.

Kate studied the screen. "This is a real feed, right?"

Lee nodded. "We checked. The camera's in the right location. Even the reflections from the door line up correctly. We can validate that this footage came from the real camera in the real elevator. It has the right date, camera code, and floor readout. If you noticed, the other one didn't have any indicators other than the date."

As they watched the tape, a group of kids entered the elevator—loud, obnoxious and profane—then exited en masse three floors higher. That's when Mark Henderson entered the car. One floor later, two burly men stepped in, and one shifted slightly so that a somewhat chunky brunette could enter as well. One man held a soft briefcase and he leaned down slightly to place the bag on the floor next to him. They all rode in silence until the car stopped and the two burly guys departed. Kate noticed that the man never stooped to retrieve his briefcase but simply left without it. The doors closed and the elevator continued moving down.

At the next floor, Henderson stooped for a moment, going nearly out of frame, then straightened and walked out. The doors closed and the woman's posture changed from rigid to relaxed. The mirrored wall of the elevator reflected a small smile that flitted across her face.

The screen went black.

"I WANT TO SEE THAT AGAIN."

Lee complied and they watched the jerky silent-movie reverse action until they reached the beginning of the sequence and the footage went forward again at normal speed. They watched in silence until the man started to place his briefcase on the floor of the elevator.

Kate hit the Pause button. "There," she said, pointing at the frozen screen. "That's when he drops it." Although it was blurred by the motion, the bag appeared to be made of dark fabric and had some sort of insignia or initials on the side facing the camera.

She advanced, then froze on Henderson as he dipped out of camera view. Advancing frame by frame, she watched him rise back into view, hiking a dark strap over his shoulder. She stopped it again as he stood in complete view, the bag with its unreadable insignia tucked under his arm.

"It's a handoff," Kate declared softly. "It could be

documents. Or private records. But it's not necessarily something illegal."

"But it could be. It could be money or drugs, just as easily."

"C'mon, Lee. The first version was a total farce. But it doesn't make this second one any less far-fetched because it's less staged. Today's crooked politician doesn't play 'switch the briefcase' in public elevators. It's too . . ."

"Trite?"

"I was going to say *risky*. But *trite* works too."

"So if you were to take a bribe, how would you do it?" Lee raised her hand to cut off Kate's sputtering denials. "Don't answer that. I don't want to know."

Kate ignored the gibe. "Putting aside the theatrics, do we know who those two guys are?"

"Funny you should ask. Yes, we do. They're on the security staff for Maynard, Seaforth, and Black, a firm lobbying against the new wetlands bill on behalf of their client Fair Energy Source."

Kate squinted at the screen. "There's no telling what the logo is—I can guarantee you it's not MS&B's. It doesn't matter, anyway. The question is, is this footage real or simply a more realistic fake?"

Lee tucked a strand of blonde hair behind her ear. "I think it's real. Here's the scenario Sierra and I pieced together. Henderson didn't realize until after the fact that the hotel's security camera caught his money exchange. Maybe one of the hotel's rent-a-cops decided to try a little blackmail. 'Pay me or I'll turn the video over to . . . somebody.'"

"It's happened before. Of course, the blackmailer'd have to figure out what to do with the footage. Who to go to.

How much to ask for. I've seen these cases prosecuted. It's trickier than TV makes it look," Kate said.

"Exactly. So apparently Security Junior asked for help from an older and wiser security guy on how to best approach possible buyers. It turns out that he confided in the wrong man—Security Senior was already on the lobby group's payroll. But Senior couldn't simply make the footage disappear without raising the suspicions of Junior. To make things worse, Junior had already contacted a 'news'—" Lee used finger quotes to signify her distaste—"show and they'd already agreed to buy the footage." She sighed. "Evidently, the concept of a bidding war was beyond his comprehension."

"A *news* show? Don't tell me; let me guess. *Bramble and Friends*."

Lee nodded.

Bramble and Friends was a tabloid show that delighted in airing every bit of real or imagined scandal they could purchase. Unlike *The Daily Show*, Bramble took the "fake news" scenario in a dangerous and often litigious direction, not looking for intelligent laughs but for titillation and ratings. So far, Kate had kept the show's prospective anti-Emily stories off the air by feeding Bill Bramble with real leads, albeit small and harmless ones, on the other candidates.

As her grandmother always said, a well-fed dog is less likely to bite. . . .

Lee continued. "So Security Senior goes to Henderson directly and they come up with the idea of creating a really bad fake and substituting it for the real footage. After all, the show will air it, no matter what. The show doesn't care what's real and what's not. Junior will get paid and that's all that matters to him. When the fake footage hits the air tomorrow minus the bumper sticker punch line . . ."

Kate supplied the obvious answer. "Henderson's camp will be ready to discredit the footage by showing the whole tape, making clear that it's a joke, and then place blame at the most likely culprit for the leak, the person who has a history of leaking stuff to the show—me. I'll look naive at best, greedy at worst, for falling for the faked footage."

Lee nodded. "Emily will come across as totally desperate for having okayed your actions. Combined, it'll do some harm to both of your reputations. Maybe even completely derail her campaign."

"Plus it distracts everyone from the idea that Mark Henderson actually did accept some information or money or whatever from someone representing the lobbying firm. They may even forget that, immediately thereafter, he made a 180-degree turn on his position on the wetlands bill."

Kate's mind began to churn, examining and discarding a hundred possible tactics to counteract Henderson's plans. The only way she could stop the show would be to give them something of more value. But she had nothing to trade other than the ammunition she'd been gathering on Charles Talbot. And it was neither the right time nor the right place to use any of that material.

Her stomach began to churn as hard as her mind.

"But wait." Lee opened the player and replaced the second disc with a third. "There's much, much more. And this is the best part. Trust me. Watch."

Kate swallowed the worst of her rising revulsion and watched.

It appeared to be the same elevator, several hours later

by the time stamp. The same woman, obviously pregnant rather than just chubby, stood in the elevator, alone. The car beeped; then the doors slid open. Mark Henderson entered and turned around to placidly face the closing doors. But once they did close, he turned and shot the woman a look of undisguised lust. She threw her arms around him.

"Oh, baby, I've missed you," she moaned as he began to kiss her neck.

"I know. It's—" several muffled words—"to be apart." He pulled away from her but shifted his hand from her shoulder to her stomach, bypassing any territory in between, which Kate found awfully curious. To her surprise, Henderson cupped the woman's stomach, of all things, then leaned down and said something the microphone didn't quite pick up.

"He's doing fine," she responded. "Kicking like a mule. The doctor says—" more muffled words—"a sign he's healthy."

"Like his old man," Henderson said, paternal pride etched across his face. "Right, Junior?" He turned to the woman. "I've been—" several indistinguishable words—"to name him after my father."

"I was hoping we could name him after—"

The elevator dinged in warning and the two of them stepped apart as if they'd not been in midembrace and mid-word only moments before. Two older women stepped in, filling the newly created gap between the man and woman. One of the ladies immediately zeroed in on the pregnancy like a moth to the maternal flame.

The lady spoke loudly as if she was compensating for a hearing loss. "Oh, I remember those days, but it was an awfully long time ago. My youngest is thirty-nine," she said with a grin. "How far along are you?"

The young woman responded congenially, as if asked this question much too often by total strangers. "Seven months."

"It won't be too much longer, then. Those last two months literally fly by. Your first?"

The young woman nodded.

The elevator beeped as it reached the next floor. Henderson exited without any comment to the woman he'd been kissing, much less to the other two ladies.

The conversation continued after the doors slid closed. The second woman chimed in. "Picked out names yet?"

The pregnant woman nodded. "We're thinking about naming him after his grandfather."

"Then you know it's a boy."

The elevator beeped again and the young woman stepped forward, shooting them an apologetic look as if leaving in midconversation was a sign of bad manners. "Have a nice day," she said as she exited. The doors closed behind her and the first woman remarked, "Pretty girl . . ."

Then the video clip ended.

Kate stared at the blank screen, not quite sure what she'd witnessed. Finally she turned to Lee. "Is that real?"

"Seems to be. We have the entire footage for a six-hour period with this piece smack in the middle—no signs of tampering, insertion, or editing whatsoever. We can't say that about the other clips. In fact, someone slipped up, because we have two sets of footage with the same date and time code for the same elevator. They forgot to erase the real footage from the hard drive."

Kate tapped the DVD player. "I want to see it again."

Lee complied and Kate watched both sequences again,

looking for similar lapses in logic, continuity, anything to help prove this piece of footage was as flawed as the earlier ones.

"What's your assessment? Real or not?" Kate asked.

Lee patted the DVD player. "It passed every sniff test we could come up with. Trust me, we looked hard. The pregnant woman's name is Kellie Scarborough, she's not an actress, and she's really pregnant. She's a secretary in an auto insurance branch office in Tysons Corner."

Lee pulled some notes from her purse and read aloud. "Remarkable coincidence number one: Mark Henderson's campaign headquarters is in the same building. Remarkable coincidence number two: Shortly after learning she was pregnant, Scarborough stopped using the obstetric clinic that's on her insurance plan. Instead, now she goes to a very ritzy and exclusive ob-gyn in Falls Church who isn't on her insurance plan, so someone is paying big bucks for her prenatal care. As it happens, Henderson's brother, Malcolm, is a pharmaceutical rep who visits the clinic often."

Kate waited. It was clear Lee wasn't done.

Lee fast-forwarded to the part where the ladies engaged the pregnant woman in idle chatter and froze the screen. "These ladies are Margaret Naismith on the left and Sheila Rand on the right. They're sisters from Portland and Seattle, respectively, attending the U.S. Scrapbooking Guild conference."

"I didn't know there was a U.S. Scrapbooking Guild."

"Me, either. But we checked. It's legit and the sisters are charter members of the organization as well as registered for the conference. They're rooming together at the Grand Ambassador in room 607. And for the record, they entered the elevator on the sixth floor."

"So you think this woman really is pregnant with Mark Henderson's child?"

"She certainly appears to think she is. More importantly, he appears to believe it as well." Lee removed the disc and placed it and the other two in slim jewel cases.

"Oh, and one more thing. Kellie Scarborough is a scrapbooker too. That's why she was at the hotel; she was also registered for the conference. But here's the curious part. Although she makes only $45,000 a year as a secretary, which isn't a lot in the D.C. area, she somehow managed to cough up $350 a night for three nights in the Grand Ambassador so she could rest between workshops even though she lives less than two miles away in a very nice—emphasis on nice—Crystal City apartment. Just four Metro stops away on the blue line. She could have gotten home in less than twenty minutes. Plus, she's been eating a lot of expensive room service steaks, skipping the usual rubber chicken conference food at mealtimes." Lee closed the lid to the DVD player. "She certainly takes her hobby very seriously, doesn't she? To cough up enough money to cover all that? On her salary?"

Kate closed her eyes. Henderson hadn't been the biggest thorn in their side until recently, with his unprecedented poll gains. Emily's plan had been to not openly antagonize the man so that when he eventually tossed in the towel, he'd throw his support to her as he got out of the race.

It made sense. The two campaigns had a lot in common. More than once, Henderson had been sympathetic to their common political agendas and background. In particular, he'd talked with Kate about the fact that both Emily and his wife were lamentably infertile and how much he wanted kids.

Kate shot up in her seat, the word flashing in her mind like a neon sign. *Infertile. Infertile. Infertile.* Was Henderson so desperate for an heir that he had done an end run around his wife's problem and gotten another woman pregnant? That could be explosive. Her better nature tried to offer an explanation. Maybe he and his wife were having a child by proxy. But given the look in Henderson's eyes, Kate didn't think that was the case. Her better nature lost out. No, she was pretty sure Henderson fathered that baby the old-fashioned way. And in an adulterous relationship.

Even if it was true love, Henderson wouldn't be able to explain it away and keep his political ambitions intact. Any way it panned out, letting this info into the public debate would ruin Henderson, plus devastate his wife. Kate was almost certain his wife didn't know diddly about this girl and her child-to-be. And who knew what letting this cat out of the bag would do to a young woman who was seven months pregnant by a married man? what it would do to her baby?

Kate drew in a sharp breath. The important question she should be asking was whether this was on the other side of that bright line Kate always called her "What would Jesus do?" acid test.

Could she, in good conscience, use any of this, knowing it would affect not just one unfaithful man but the two women who loved him? and the innocent child who had yet to be born?

"What am I supposed to do with this?" Kate asked.

Lee sighed. "If you paid me more, I probably would have made the same leap in logic you just evidently did. But my job is to simply find this stuff. It's up to you how and when to use it."

"It's not up to me," Kate said, tucking the jewel cases

into her purse. "It's up to Emily. And I'm not sure I want to hear what she has to say about this. But I know what I'm going to recommend she do with it."

★ ★ ★ ★ ★

Emily was fascinated.

"Let me get this straight. He films himself taking a fake bribe in order to cover up the fact that he took a real bribe? Explain to me in what universe that makes sense."

Kate hadn't shown Emily the other footage with the pregnant woman. She wasn't sure why she'd hesitated. Maybe it had something to do with Dozier's comments about nuclear strategies. Or maybe it was because no child, born or unborn, should be tangled up in the sharpened cogs of political machinery.

She offered her best explanation. "It makes sense if you're desperate. You can't stop shows like *Bramble and Friends* when they've gotten their hooks into a story. They bought that footage and you know they're going to show it. The only thing Henderson can possibly do to mitigate things is substitute his patently fake reel for the real one. He gets a good laugh on the show, and if he's lucky, he blames the fake on someone else. Like us, for example."

"Of course he's going to blame us. Everyone knows I'm the only candidate who hasn't been openly skewered on the show. Everyone already thinks you're sleeping with the producer."

Kate stared at her friend in shock. "Emily!"

Her friend shrugged. "Well, it's what they think. It doesn't matter if it's true or not. I don't care either way."

"Emily!" Kate said, making no effort to hide her exasperation.

"I know; I know. You don't sleep around. You're still waiting for the right man to come along." She grinned. "I'm looking, too, but what's the harm in doing some sampling along the way?"

"Emily!" Her friend knew just where to needle her—long practice and native talent had rendered Emily's barbs an art form.

"Don't get your panty hose in a wad, Kate. I was kidding."

"Can we get back to talking about the show?" Kate demanded. "Not my sex life—or the lack thereof?"

"Fine. Whatever people think about you and your producer boyfriend—" Kate rolled her eyes—"I bet they now say you two have had a falling out and the show won't go out of its way to protect me any longer." Emily began to pace the room, kicking at random furniture legs during her circuit around the space. "It'd be so much easier if you'd just slept with the man when he asked."

Kate straightened in indignation, which was hard to do when she was slumped on the end of a modernist, low-slung leather couch. Emily's designer taste ran more to high style than high comfort. "Doug didn't ask." She felt her face begin to flush. "And I wouldn't have even if he had."

"C'mon, K. Loosen the chastity belt, will ya? You're cutting off your circulation. I was there, remember? Doug Lamb did everything short of undress you in public at that last press dinner. He was making a move for you and you ignored him."

The heat of blazing embarrassment scorched Kate's cheeks.

"I can't believe you're saying these things to me, Emily. They're uncalled for. They're—"

"They're *mean*, Kate." Emily stopped pacing in the middle of the room. "They're mean *and* vindictive." She glared at Kate, then threw her hands up in exasperation. "Get with the program, sister. I'm doing this on purpose. I'm trying to rile you up. You work better when you're mad. So get mad, Kate. Blow a cork." Her voice rose. "Use that remarkable brain of yours to figure out how in the world we extricate ourselves from this and salvage everything we've been trying to do for the last two years. Do your job."

Kate had been slow to recognize the drill. She hated it and she knew it was far less effective than Emily realized. Kate would always go to the wall when Emily appealed to her better half. But Kate pretended once again that the kick Emily had tried was just what she needed to spur her to action.

In reality, Kate figured she was manipulating Emily instead, trying to goad her into coming up with a suitable plan that wouldn't involve the revelation of Henderson's infidelity.

Her mind raced ahead. She couldn't let this turn into a media circus with that poor pregnant girl at its center. The only really appropriate way to spin this—the only way her conscience would allow her to play it—was to keep the footage under the table. Tell Emily she'd handle it. Get a private meeting with Henderson and Ted Fontini, his campaign manager, and show them the clips they had with no overt threats. Let them draw their own conclusions concerning how much shucking and jiving it would take to knock the images and the words Henderson had said to a pregnant woman not his wife out of the memories of a scandal-hungry American public. That would be Mission: Impossible 2008.

Henderson and his advisers would soon realize that they couldn't possibly recover from a revelation like that—not when it came complete with indisputable visual aids. They'd soon realize that their best means to secure Henderson's political future and his current marriage—or possible pending divorce—and achieve a good life for his as yet unborn child would be for him to initiate a quiet side step out of the race for president. But if he played ball with Kate, dropped out of the race, it wouldn't be a scorched-earth situation. He could run again. Getting out of Emily's way today wouldn't end his current career in the Senate or affect his chances of running for office again. Kate would bury the evidence. Emily would get what she wanted. And Henderson could do the right thing—whatever that was—by the women in his life. She figured that there was nothing like incriminating footage in a competitor's hands to spur him on to make that little kid's world right.

Best of all, Kate thought, the decision would be his, not theirs. Now *that* was a satisfactory outcome, she decided. Not only did it do no lasting harm to her conscience or her soul, it gave Henderson a chance to repair his fractured world rather than try to pick up the shards of a shattered life. Henderson clearly needed to change his course. Now he had the opportunity and the motivation to straighten out and fly right.

Emily stopped pacing again and stared at her. "A smile? Is that a real smile on your face?" She dropped to the miserably designed couch, falling into a boneless sprawl next to Kate. "See? My insidious plan worked and now you have a newer, more insidious plan, right? So? What is it? What do we do? Who do we do it to?"

Kate hesitated. The only flaw in her plan was that she might have to let Emily see the third clip. From that point on, it'd be an uphill battle to keep her friend from trying to blast it from media mountaintop to media mountaintop. How could she stop that from happening? Could she keep Emily from going for the throat?

"I have something that may work."

"For heaven's sake, what, K?"

It took less than two minutes to outline the basic plan. She had to tell Emily what she had, though she didn't intend to show her friend the clip. It took Kate well over an hour to dissuade Emily from using the evidence right away to blast the gentleman senator from Michigan out of political waters for the rest of his life. But no matter what Kate said, assured, or explained, Emily insisted on at least seeing the footage before she would agree to Kate's plan. After another hour of argument, Kate finally relented.

It was the first time Kate had seen the footage on a big screen. Witnessing Henderson's betrayal against his wife in an almost life-size plasma version made it all the more real, and that, in turn, made her job even harder. Kellie Scarborough, the Other Woman, was no frowsy blonde bimbo out to snag herself some political bigwig sugar daddy. She looked normal. Nice, even. Despite the poor quality of the footage, she had a visible glow about her. Plus, Kate couldn't help but notice the way she held her belly with obvious maternal instincts. Kate even liked the way she'd made polite responses to two somewhat intrusive women in a hotel elevator.

Kellie might have been having an affair with a married

man, but she clearly loved him and their unborn child. She was nothing more than an average young woman who'd made the mistake of loving the wrong man. Everybody made mistakes, Kate knew. Christ had called her to love others the way he loved them and to treat them as she wished to be treated herself. She couldn't live with the thought of being the person who destroyed all that hope for the future in the young woman's eyes. Worse, she couldn't stand being the person who made sure Henderson's wife knew he'd betrayed her on such a fundamental level.

Henderson deserved the chance to tell his wife himself and ask for her forgiveness.

Watching the video, it was clear to Kate that Henderson had something in his eyes that transcended lust and desire—it was . . . love? Maybe it was not as much for the woman as for the unborn child. *His* unborn child. But it was love, nonetheless. Henderson simply couldn't fake something like that.

Kate felt pity and sorrow as she viewed the footage—nobody in that fractured family was going to come out of this unscarred.

Emily watched the video with the anticipation and enthusiasm of someone watching the season finale of a favorite television show, oohing and aahing over the action, wanting to replay "the good bits." In Kate's opinion, there really were no good bits, not in light of what was likely to happen next.

"I can't wait to see that smug so-and-so's face when he gets a load of this. Just think of all those loyal campaign workers in tears when they realize he's just a lying, cheating—"

"No," Kate said softly.

"What?"

"We don't release it to the public. Nothing good will come of that."

Emily stared at Kate as if she'd completely lost her mind. "Are you crazy? Of course something good will come from it. He'll drop out of the race. In disgrace."

"We need him." Before Emily could contradict her, Kate continued. "We need him to back out quietly and give you his endorsement. If you threaten him openly, he won't do it. His pride won't let him. But . . ." She stood, now getting the advantage of superior positioning to drive home her point. "But if we present him with the footage under the table, give him a chance to save face in public, we can convince him to give you the endorsement."

"Blackmail, you mean."

"No. Not at all. Honorable behavior on both sides."

"Same outcome, perhaps. But it's not nearly as satisfying as watching him squirm under public scrutiny, listening to his feeble attempts to explain how he forgot all about his 'promise to moral America' while he cheerfully slept with his current mistress who now carries his illegitimate child. You know what they say: 'Pride goeth before the fall.' And I do so want to see him fall a very long way down. Why, he—"

"Emily, stop." Kate sent a small prayer heavenward that Emily might see the whole picture. For Kate's sake, for Henderson's sake, for that innocent child's sake, Emily had to listen! "We *have* to play it my way. Taking the low road means exposing you as the source of the leak. That could be just as bad for you as for him. You'll look too ruthless, too unfeeling. Sure, he'll go down. But so will you. Voters don't like an angry candidate. Do you want to risk that?"

Emily opened her mouth, prepared to argue the point. Kate kept talking before her friend could get a word out.

"Seriously, it could cost you points. You don't want that. What goes around, comes around. But if we do this my way, Henderson steps out of the race and stays in power, and he owes us favors. Forget the possible blowback if we leak this stuff. Do you want to give up that leverage? If we go public, the backlash could be a career killer for you just as much as it will be for Henderson. Listen to me. You don't have to destroy him to clear the path for yourself to the nomination. Yes, he made a bad moral decision, but it's not for us to judge."

"The Bible says to smite your enemies," Emily said.

"I'm not sure you can apply that to this context, M. Maybe a more applicable reference would be Jesus' instruction to 'Love your neighbor as yourself.' If we use Henderson's mistake like a club and pound the guy into roadkill, it's not just bad politics. It's a sin. And I don't want that sin on my conscience. Give the man a chance to save face and bow out on his own terms. Look, if you can't do it just because it's the right thing to do, think of it this way: You'll inherit his support. You'll have markers to call in. And he'll still be out of the way. It'll be better for you, not just better for him. Remember, whatever you think of Henderson, there are innocents involved here. His wife. The child."

"You didn't mention his girlfriend."

"Her too. She fell for a married man. She shouldn't be branded with a scarlet letter because of it. Let Henderson and those poor women find a way to work this out on a personal level, not as the center ring in a public media circus. Remember what it was like for you when your marriage to Nick fell apart? You can spare Henderson's wife that kind of trouble. Wouldn't you like to do that?"

Kate said the next words softly, but firmly. "You only need to stop him on a political level. You're too good to stoop to destroying him personally."

Emily contemplated Kate's warning for a while, then finally nodded. "I see your point." A wistful look filled her face. "But it would have been so much more fun my way."

✶ ✶ ✶ ✶

The meeting began as Kate hoped. Emily managed to hide her unholy glee under a facade of concern and disappointment that her esteemed opponent had made such a tragic error in judgment. The word *blackmail* never entered the picture as Kate played the footage. Henderson, eaten up with guilt, and Fontini, numb with shock, both agreed that it'd be better if the footage wasn't released. They also agreed that perhaps Henderson should step out of the picture for this election cycle and work through his personal problems before running again.

Kate offered her condolences and her hopes that Henderson could resolve things in his private life. She meant every word of that. The look in that young woman's eyes was haunting her.

Henderson appeared to be too catatonic to react, though Fontini thanked her for handling this so discreetly.

Kate didn't bring up the discussion of a possible endorsement at that point. She'd already discussed it with Emily.

Henderson and Fontini both needed to come to grips with the end of this stage of their political plans before she or Emily could broach the subject. Asking for Henderson's support could wait for a follow-up call a day or two later when both men realized how close they'd come to public humiliation and career meltdown.

But Emily was refusing to follow the script they'd agreed upon.

She refused to temper her triumph with mercy. She just came right out and said what she wanted—and this time it was clear that what she was up to *was* blackmail. When she mentioned the word *endorsement* to Henderson, it was like a hot breeze fanning the smoldering embers of the man's presidential plans. Instead of dousing the last hope of any flame, it transformed that last spark into an inferno.

Kate could see the outrage rise in Henderson's eyes.

"I'm not ready to make these sorts of decisions right now, not without discussing it with my advisers," Henderson said with a sudden sense of purpose. He stood. "We'll get back to you on that."

If Kate had been a violent person, she would have strangled Emily. As it was, she had to pray for patience. She waited until the two men departed before she released a sigh that she wished could be a scream.

"You blew it."

"No." Emily shook her head. "I didn't."

"Yes, you did. You needed to let Henderson come to the conclusion he should support you himself. Instead, you assumed he'd already accepted the inevitable. You pushed him too early for the endorsement and now you're not going to get it. He's going to blame you, not himself, for the fix he's in. He'll probably become a bitter enemy, not the ally you could have made him."

"Ridiculous. Why? Our platforms aren't that much different."

"It doesn't matter. He's furious. He's going to shoot the messenger. You."

"No," Emily said with her usual air of certainty. "Wait until his press conference. You'll see. He'll hold off until ten o'clock tonight for the announcement, hoping he'll get a network news break-in on prime time in three time zones and the lead story on the West Coast local news. He wants to go out with a bang, but he'll be lucky to get a crawl on the bottom of the screen, instead."

Kate could see the gears turning in Emily's head. "Too bad the networks aren't going to want to interrupt their Christmas specials for the likes of him."

Emily's glare of righteous conviction wavered slightly. "Yeah, too bad. . . ."

That evening, Kate tried to distance herself from the television, the Internet, and her land and cell phones. But all of them conspired to continually interrupt what she had hoped would be a peaceful evening. By 10:02 p.m. Eastern, there had been no news crawl, no breaking news, no hint of Henderson's self-removal from the race for the party's nomination. It appeared that the last hour of prime time would be saved from "A Special News Report."

Somewhere in the back of her head, Kate wondered if that meant Emily's untimely push to control Henderson had resulted in the man's decision to dig in and attempt to spin the press his way. He wouldn't be the first senator to play that game. Senator Larry Craig had survived an embarrassing arrest in Minneapolis. David Vitter had showed up on the D.C. Madam's phone logs with barely a ripple on his immediate career after he apologized to his wife and the voters. Ted Kennedy got through Chappaquiddick, and that was much more scandalous than what Henderson did. In the bad old days, Bob Packwood had tried to brazen out so much bad behavior with women that it had forced the moribund Senate Ethics Committee into action. Maybe Henderson was gearing up a classic, weepy "flawed man" scenario in the hopes of appealing to legions of equally flawed constituents.

As long as he withdrew from the race, Kate hoped Emily would leave well enough alone. But if Henderson didn't act soon, Kate was terrified that Emily would take things into her own hands.

And at one minute past eleven, Kate watched in horror and dread as she saw the grainy footage of Mark Henderson kissing his pregnant mistress in the elevator air as the lead hourly story on CNN. Moments later, the story broke on all four major networks as they cut in on the local news, a rarity. The timing was classic—it hit the late night news on the East Coast and in the Central time zone and broke into the prime time feed for Mountain and Pacific.

The news release couldn't have been better calculated for maximum saturation and exposure.

Oh no. Those poor women. Kate said a small prayer for the innocents caught up in this nightmare.

With her breath caught in her throat, Kate logged on to her e-mail account and watched as the mail started pouring in from friends and foes alike, all with subject lines like "!!??!?!!!!," "Is This YOU!!!!?," and "Why didn't you tell me???" She turned off her instant messenger after the fifth acquaintance popped up to chat.

She hit speed dial and managed to retain some semblance of control when she reached Emily. "I hope you're proud of yourself."

"What?" Emily sounded nonplussed. "I did what I had to do." It was said in a matter-of-fact delivery. Just like her.

"Are you so sure about that?"

"Henderson had it coming. He refused to play ball. I don't need his endorsement now, K. His supporters will come to me on their own. And wouldn't we rather have independent-minded people come to us—folks who can think on their own rather than be told what to believe? To be told who is worthy to follow?"

"What if someone traces the video back to us?"

"They can't. It didn't come from us. You saw me give Henderson the only copy we had of the footage."

"Then how . . . ?"

"Never underestimate the abilities of a woman scorned."

"His wife?"

Emily laughed. "None other. She's been pumping herself up with fertility drugs, undergoing all sorts of hideous and, as I understand it, really painful testing. She's been doing anything and everything she can to get pregnant. But it only takes one whisper concerning the possibility of her dear hubby having put a bun in his mistress's oven and boom! She goes for the jugular. Once a little birdie told her where to look for the goods, she got them and used them. And boy, did she use them—slam, right in the kisser, baby. Too bad she wasn't his campaign manager. I gotta applaud her efficiency—maximum damage with maximum exposure. The girl's got talent."

"Let me repeat the part of your little story that concerns me most: *someone* had to tell her *where* to look."

Silence.

Kate was shaking, but she forced her voice to stay level. "Emily, all it takes is for one slipup for this to all get back to us."

"She doesn't even know it came from us. C'mon, K, I'm not stupid. There's no way to connect her to us. It came to her from a friend of a friend of a friend. And at that, I made sure it was an anonymous drop." There was a long moment. "Kate, all I did was expose Henderson for what he really is—a liar, a cheat, and a real dog to do this to someone he supposedly loves. If anything, I'm protecting her and showing her she can't trust a louse like him. When my marriage went on the rocks, I came out stronger for it."

The words were hauntingly familiar; Emily had said the same things about her own ex-husband. *"Kate, he's a liar, a cheat, and a real dog to do this to me. I'm supposed to be the person he loves most. . . ."* Kate had said to Emily then, "If you trust God, you'll come out of this adversity a better person." She doubted that Emily had heard the "God" part of that statement.

Kate drew a deep breath, then expelled it along with another quick prayer for strength. She seldom took on Emily head-to-head, but this was going to be one of those times. Emily needed to hear a few home truths.

"Listen to me carefully. You've taken a big risk, one we didn't necessarily have to take. Don't you *ever* take a chance like this again. You need to be a role model. You need to keep your head above the fray. You can't get elected if your hands aren't clean."

There was a moment of eerie silence between them. Then Emily said quietly, "You're right."

The admission startled Kate. "Say that again?"

"You're right," Emily repeated. "I wasn't looking at the big picture." Then Emily Benton said two more words that Kate had seldom heard her utter together.

"I'm sorry."

It nearly poleaxed Kate. That—Emily's ability to see what mattered and change her course—was one of the things Kate loved about Emily.

However, Emily was also capable of ducking when times got hot. Kate noticed that Emily didn't say, "I'll never do it again . . ." because they both knew that was a promise she couldn't keep.

✷ ✷ ✷ ✷ ✷

The next morning, Kate woke early to an uneasy feeling in the pit of her stomach and a general sense of malaise. The feeling made her want to stay in bed for a year or so. If she'd had anything alcoholic to drink the night before, she would have figured she was hungover. But having imbibed nothing stiffer than a mug of Sleepytime tea, she decided it was an emotional hangover from the events of last night.

Despite the pseudo-heartfelt apology, Emily had still screwed up things further by adding a unique "coat the fan with excrement" complication. Left on its own, Kate's original plan would have resulted in the desired bottom line—Henderson stepping out of the campaign and throwing his support to the Benton camp.

But, no. Kate had negotiated while Emily had decided

to go all scorched earth on her opponent. Emily had not only engineered the ruin of Henderson's personal and professional life, she'd thrown three more souls into the media woodchipper with him—the wife, the girlfriend, and the unborn baby.

Now Kate would need to spend an inordinate amount of time making sure everyone knew that Emily didn't have a woodchipper, had no idea how to use a woodchipper, and even if she did, would never have shoved three of the four people involved into said woodchipper.

All the while knowing that Emily just loved that nasty old woodchipper.

And if people didn't believe Kate's song and dance . . .

Kate didn't want to contemplate that Herculean task. In fact she didn't even want to be awake. She wanted to go back to yesterday and do it all over again—only this time without Emily in the room to mess things up. She wanted to seek forgiveness from God for not doing more to stop Emily from going all medieval on her opponents.

She wanted to call in sick and lie in bed until some other horrible political mess took precedence in the news cycle.

She wanted to go home with her dog and get a job where her heart wasn't reamed out and chewed up on a regular basis.

But if she didn't get up and go to work, she couldn't help make it right.

Maybe there was something she could do to help smooth it over, for Emily and for Henderson.

When she reached M Central, it was abuzz with the news of Mark Henderson's humiliation at the hands of his angry wife. Staffers were joyous about the possible repercussions.

Kate knew she couldn't correct them. But she could ask them to have a little compassion.

She did.

They didn't.

They were too excited about what this might mean for their adored candidate, Emily Benton.

Kate buried herself in her office and hung a Do Not Disturb sign on the doorknob. The only person who ignored it was Emily, who showed up with Kate's favorite breakfast in the world, an Egg McMuffin and a grande Cinnamon Dolce Frappuccino.

Kate's stomach betrayed her by growling at the aroma.

Emily held out the bag. "C'mon, you know you want this."

After a moment's hesitation, Kate accepted the bribe. "I'm such a fast food junkie," she moaned as she unwrapped the sandwich and then took her first bite. No matter where they were, home or away, she could always rely on the consistency of her beloved Starbucks McMeal.

"Your appetite for swill is one of your more interesting qualities." Emily sat down in the side chair. "Did you see the *Post* this morning?"

Kate shook her head. "I'm avoiding all media. I figure that's the only way I can keep my spirits up and my breakfast down."

"Don't be silly. Despite your concerns, the whole story is playing out perfectly. Infertile wife intercepts a call from hotel security about returning an article of clothing left behind in her husband's hotel room. Trouble is, not only is it an article of women's clothing, but it's from a very trendy maternity shop. Then with just a little snooping, she realizes that her feckless husband is not only canoodling another woman but has gotten said woman pregnant. Oh, the inhumanity," she deadpanned, then laughed.

"It's no laughing matter," Kate said. "That baby hasn't done anything to deserve the mess you made of its life."

"Maybe. But Henderson? He was an honest-to-goodness two-timing scumbag and he got caught. Womankind should link arms and lift their voices in solidarity, rejoicing in the spectacle."

"Don't rejoice in someone else's failure, Emily. It's not becoming. Worse, it's not right. You've got skeletons in your closet. One day they may come out to haunt you. Don't you want to have your friends and opponents treat you with mercy if that comes to pass?"

"It wouldn't happen. They'd be on me like wild dogs."

"All the more reason," Kate said, "to try to set a good example. They can learn from you. Some of the victims you're gloating over are innocents. What about Henderson's wife? Remember what you felt like when you found out Nick was cheating on you? I bet she feels even worse. Sure, Henderson was in the wrong, but he, like every person, lives at the center of a web of relationships. Going after him shakes that web. Those tremors we started hit everybody who knows Henderson, guilty and innocent alike." Her stomach lurched on cue. "I feel sick about my part in this. Just sick about it."

"Don't look now," Emily said, "but you're channeling your mother. I guarantee that Henderson's wife is better off knowing she couldn't trust him. And don't get me started on the girlfriend. She blithely ignored the fact that he was married. She needs to learn not to play around with guys with wives. Don't you think the country is better off now that they know what kind of man he is?"

Kate sighed. "On that point, maybe I can agree. But not on the rest of it."

Emily released a self-satisfied sigh. "Well, we made that happen. I call that a win-win situation. Feminism at its finest."

"It's a win for you," Kate said, "and a win for your campaign. But not for me. I keep thinking about his wife. What did she do to deserve this?" Kate stared at her beloved breakfast, her appetite vanishing. "I feel so bad for her. And what about that unborn baby?"

"Trust me. Everybody will get over it. You'll see. When I'm president, I'll address some of the laws that make this all such a tragedy. That baby should have an equal chance with any other baby, legally and morally, whatever his mother did. It's something that a female president can make happen."

"Emily, I know you'll be a great president. I've seen you in action. You don't have to convince me. But that's in the future. You need to be a great person, too. And that's for right now. Try for a little mercy."

Emily took a deep breath, obviously ready to argue with that conclusion, but she was interrupted.

"We have a big problem." Chip McWilliamson stood in the doorway, his face pale and pinched. "I have a friend who works for the Maryland State Police. He told me they got a 911 call from Mark Henderson's housekeeper. She just found Mrs. Henderson dead. Of an apparent suicide."

"Oh no," Emily said.

Kate put her head in her hands. She tried not to cry, but the tears came anyway.

SHOCK BLANKETED THE ROOM, muffling all sounds except for the fountain on Kate's credenza. Instead of being soothing, its sound was intrusive, like an annoying buzz in the back of her head.

After a few moments, Kate dried her tears and looked at Emily, whose face was white with shock. Kate figured hers probably looked worse and was grateful she couldn't see it. She wasn't looking forward to facing her mirrored image.

Rather than say the words that scalded her brain and burned the back of her throat, Kate controlled herself and simply said, "Leave."

Emily nodded, adding in a low voice, "I understand. We'll talk later." She paused at the door before exiting. "Just so you know, K, I didn't see this coming. Not at all."

As the door closed, Kate leaned back in her chair and closed her eyes to prevent tears from welling up again. She told herself that if she cried, it would be because of the potential damage Emily had caused to their campaign. Not because her whole moral justification for her actions in digging up dirt on Henderson had crashed down on her head like a house of playing cards. Not because she had, indirectly, gotten the blood of an innocent woman on her hands.

Sure, she'd never meant to hurt that woman. But she'd been the person who kicked the rock that started the avalanche down the hill.

How was she going to live with herself?

Kate didn't really know Henderson's wife beyond an occasional moment or two at various political get-togethers where the ebb and flow of crowds caused their paths to cross. They'd probably shared not more than a dozen words, all of them polite.

But whether she knew the woman or not, Kate knew this: because she'd dug around in the shadows of a political opponent's life, the man's wife had chosen to take her own life. Had Kate seen that coming? Of course not. Then why did she feel so bad, so guilty, over this?

Had she known that it would hurt Henderson if what she found got out?

Yes.

Had she known his wife would feel anything like the kind of overwhelming despair that would drive a person to suicide?

No. Absolutely not.

So why did she feel like a murderer?

"Consequences." She heard her favorite law professor's voice in her ear. George Madison Canton had been in his mideighties when he taught Advanced Ethics. When he spoke, his voice always rang with the authority of a long and rich lifetime of experience. She could hear him just as

clearly now as she had then, his stentorian voice echoing through the lecture hall.

"There are always legal, moral, and ethical consequences to every action you take," he'd said. The trick, he had said then, was to anticipate the probable outcomes but not to get bogged down with the infinite possibilities of any course of action.

Should she have anticipated this particular consequence? Could she have foreseen this outcome when she tapped the fountain of information named Carmen del Rio? Should she have predicted that because of her investigation, Lee would find not only a spent shell casing of corruption but the entire smoking gun?

More important, could Kate have anticipated Emily's decision to go public without consulting her?

Maybe, she told herself.

Then her self-defense mechanism clicked on. Had Emily spent any time considering the possible repercussions of releasing that video?

When it came to the big picture, Emily was like a chess player, plotting strategies, calculating her moves six, seven, even a dozen steps beyond the current picture. It's what made her a good lawyer and an even better politician. It was going to make her a great president.

Obviously even Emily hadn't anticipated this.

Emily had figured that the wife would react just as she had and kick the bum out, preferably in public.

But as Professor Canton had always said, "The ethical person accepts responsibility for the unfortunate as well as the fortunate consequences of his actions."

Kate was the one who triggered the investigation, who

hired the people to dig the dirt, who took the results of her research to Emily, who allowed someone else to control the knowledge. In essence, the whole chain of events began with Kate.

She'd acted, and someone had died.

She finally put her head down on her desk and cried, letting the tears pour out. And she prayed.

Lord, please forgive me. I don't know how to forgive myself.

Time passed. Her tears slowed, then stopped.

And Henderson's wife was still dead.

The peace that confessing her sins usually gave her refused to come on this day. Christ could forgive anything. But Kate couldn't. Not her own sins. And she could never, ever forget.

Kate sat at her desk, rehashing her every action, every reaction, going back and recognizing the possible outcomes she'd obviously missed earlier. After almost an hour of tearing her own actions apart for a review of her motives and methods—interrupted on occasion by frantic sounds beyond her closed door—Kate knew what the bottom line was.

She'd blown it.

She'd stepped out of bounds, over that bright line where she asked herself, "What would Jesus do today?"

Maybe she couldn't change the past.

But she *could* change the future.

"No."

"Yes."

Emily stood up and slammed her palms down on her desk as she leaned forward. "Then let me put it another way. No way in heaven or earth will I accept your resignation."

"It's the only way to save your campaign," Kate protested. "You'll need to redirect the fallout. The most effective way to do that is to blame me."

"No. Let someone else be the sacrificial goat."

"It won't work. You have to cut hard, cut deep, and cut high so that everyone knows you've removed the gangrene from your staff. Firing a couple of low-level staffers won't work. Firing me is the only way to assure your supporters that you personally had nothing to do with the leak and that you take something like that very seriously. If you can't fire me when the situation warrants it, the press will have a field day, blaming your inability on your gender."

Emily moved from behind the desk and circled the room like a caged tiger circling its dinner. "They'd be wrong. But no matter. If you walk, then we fold our tents and slink away. I'm not going to try to run a campaign, much less the country, without you." Emily slammed into the seat by the window. "You're my chief of staff—now and later, in the White House. You *know* that." She turned away so that Kate could see only her profile. Emily's expression was unreadable from that angle. "I can't imagine trying to be president without you at my side. How did that *Newsweek* reporter put it? 'Every head of state needs someone to help them also be the heart of the nation.' You're the heart in this campaign. Everyone knows that. But what they don't know is that you're far more than the heart—you're the brains, the brawn, the soul, the conscience. You keep me honest. You keep me sane. I cannot and will not continue this campaign without you."

She remained facing away, but Kate thought she saw a single tear trickling down her friend's face. The last time she saw Emily cry was . . . when?

The day Emily's father was murdered. Twenty or so years ago. But then again, everyone in America had seen Emily Benton in tears that day.

The footage had made heavy rotation on every media outlet.

"Don't make any decisions now," Emily said in a broken voice. "Take the day off. Go play tourist. Go sleep." She sniffed and swiped at her face. "Make it Buster's Day Out. But whatever you do, don't make any rash decisions. Not right now, okay?"

Kate sighed. Nothing good ever came out of hasty decisions. She swallowed hard. "Okay. I'll sleep on it. But I *am* serious."

"I know you are."

★ ★ ★ ★ ★

As tempting as it was to go home, curl up with Buster, and collapse like a deflated balloon, Kate couldn't do it. But she did want to shed her remaining tears somewhere private, so she decided that a day away from the office would be wise.

Gathering her purse and coat, she glanced at the various pictures and plaques hanging on what she called the "I love me" wall. Above her framed law school diploma hung a picture of Emily and her, with caps, gowns, colors, smiles, and assurances of rosy futures. They were young and full of themselves as well as full of detailed plans, outlining their rise to political prominence, Emily in the forefront and Kate in the background.

Such grand plans . . .

Beside that photograph hung a smaller one of the two of them, taken years later. Maturity had tempered their enthusiasm and added some new lines to their faces, but their grand goals remained the same. Kate stared at the third person, off to the side of the photograph.

Wes . . .

An insistent voice in her mind said, *Call Wes.* . . .

She reached for her cell phone.

John Weston Kingsbury had been a literal godsend one fateful day in August during Emily's first year in office as governor of Virginia.

Emily's pet project, the highway expansion bill, had passed six months prior and the new construction had already begun. The plan had been to expand one of the state highways to a six-lane toll road to alleviate traffic on the I-95 corridor. Working hand in hand with Maryland, they'd forged a consolidated program to create an alternative parallel road as a bypass, pulling traffic to the east of Washington, D.C., and its legendary Beltway congestion. To meet up with its Maryland counterpart, the last ten miles of the toll road had to be angled away from the original state highway.

Everything had progressed nicely until the state started acquiring the necessary property by eminent domain. The projected location of the toll road ran smack through the middle of a privately held "training" compound owned by a group that called themselves the New World Militia. As with antigovernment groups like that, they were none too happy about the prospects of the state taking their property under the "guise" of a highway program. Their leader firmly believed it was a conspiracy to disrupt and disband the group and its militia.

Emily wouldn't back down.

She pushed through the land seizure. When the road crews showed up, they were met with enough guns and sufficient ammunition to overrun a small South American country.

The Feds and the military were ready to step in and claim federal jurisdiction due to the compound's close proximity to Fort A.P. Hill, a major military training facility. But Emily managed to keep some control of the situation. She got it set up as a joint operation between state and federal officials. It was that or worry about the threat turning into a live-fire demonstration for the military trainees.

But it was Wes Kingsbury who saved the day.

Emily and Kate had met Wes at Georgetown years earlier, but time and distance had weakened the bonds of friendship and the women had both lost contact with Wes. It wasn't until Daniel Gilroy, the leader of the New World Militia, made his armed stand in his "compound"—a four-room cabin in the woods—that Wes reappeared in their lives.

Gilroy fancied himself the group's spiritual head as well as its military leader. No one was quite sure what religion he followed, but it seemed to consist mostly of misquoted and mangled passages from the book of Revelation. In Kate's opinion, when somebody carrying a large and loaded gun quoted badly from any religious text, much less Revelation, that was probably a sign of looming trouble.

As soon as Wes had heard about the standoff with the NWM, he contacted Kate's office, knowing that was a quicker route than trying to reach Emily directly at the governor's office. When he volunteered his expertise to help with the situation, Kate learned that since they'd last met, he'd earned a doctorate in divinity in addition to his law degree and had become an expert on religious and nonreligious cults.

Wes explained to Kate that he'd spent the last four years researching the NWM and interviewing as many of the members as would talk to him. He promised that Gilroy was familiar enough with him to know he wasn't what the militia members called a "police stooge" or a "federal sock puppet."

Thanks to Wes's expert guidance and the unpleasant echoes of Waco stationed in the forefront of everyone's minds, Emily coerced the Feds into standing down. Then she proceeded to throw out most of the rules in the standard FBI negotiator's handbook. Since no blood had been shed on either side and Gilroy seemed rather entranced with Emily's famous family, she agreed to negotiate on behalf of the United States and to do it on the front porch of Gilroy's cabin headquarters in full view of FBI snipers.

Not to mention CNN, Fox, and MSNBC.

News cameras cranked to maximum zoom to record the sight of the governor of Virginia and the Reverend Wes Kingsbury as they sat in rocking chairs on the cabin's porch, sipping iced tea and calmly cutting a deal with a heavily armed cult leader. Said deal included the state's agreement to shift the highway project a mile to the west, which meant it only clipped rather than bisected the NWM property, and instead of purchasing the land, they would trade it for a larger piece of adjacent property that was actually better suited to the group's needs.

As part of the deal, Gilroy agreed to surrender to the local authorities if no one else at the compound was held responsible for following his orders. He also promised to provide restitution for the two local and three state police vehicles that his supporters had hit with stray gunfire. The only fluid shed in this particular debacle had come from the radiators of two of the cruisers. It was a blood-free end to the crisis.

But the scene that caught the attention and earned the admiration of the American public was of Virginia governor Emily Benton, sans makeup and dressed in jeans and a University of Virginia T-shirt, accepting Gilroy's sidearm as a measure of his faith in her. Like an expert, she pulled the clip and ejected the round in the chamber, then put the gun in her waistband and escorted Gilroy off the property, his hands behind his head.

It was a dream photo op, and a good chunk of the world tuned in to watch live.

Emily Benton as Wyatt Earp, bringing order to the wild frontier.

In Kate's estimation, that was the day the Oval Office truly became an attainable goal for Emily. It was also one of the reasons that she knew Emily would be a great president. Any person who could pull that off was ready to negotiate on a worldwide stage.

Even when Emily's detractors complained that she'd caved to an armed terrorist by agreeing to his demands, she managed to keep her cool. She won the debate by pointing out that while the negotiations had progressed and Gilroy was distracted, most of his so-called supporters had flown the coop, scattering to the winds. Without a leader, they were nothing more than widely dispersed, aimless malcontents. The tense situation had practically evaporated without a shadow of trouble.

More importantly, the militia members remained unorganized, undirected, and unimportant, an assortment of outsiders scattered across a large landscape instead of concentrated in one place and causing trouble. The Feds' methods in similar standoffs in both Waco and Ruby Ridge had made martyrs and revitalized movements that had lasting reverberations—including a blasted federal building in Oklahoma City.

But Emily's methods had brought peace and prosperity in only a few hours.

The press had a second heyday a week or so after the standoff when, with Kate's encouragement, Emily and Wes went out on their first date. After the Nick fiasco, Emily had retreated from the idea of any relationship. But it was obvious to Kate that Wes was everything Nick hadn't been—responsible where Nick had been negligent, mature where Nick had been juvenile.

Loyal where Nick had been unfaithful.

But after Nick, Emily wanted no strings, and Wes Kingsbury firmly believed in family ties. They drifted from the beginnings of an intimate relationship to a friendship that was better for both of them in the long run. Wes had since married and had a child. And now he was the unofficial religious adviser for the campaign. He was just the shoulder Kate needed to lean on.

He sounded chipper as always when he answered the phone. "Kingsbury, at your service." There was road noise in the background.

"Wes, it's Kate Rosen. Got a minute?"

"Always for you. I'd ask how things are, but judging by what I've seen of the news, I suspect I know. How are you holding up?"

"Well enough." She couldn't help but hesitate; asking for help didn't come easy. "Uh . . . you have any time to talk? Like soon?" *Like now?*

"Hang on." The background noise changed from loud to soft.

Guilt flooded her again, though this time of a less terrifying variety than the kind she'd been burdened with all morning. "I didn't get you in the car, did I?"

"Nope, not at all. I just finished doing a breakfast seminar for some folks in the State Department. How's Emily?"

"How do you think?"

"I'd bet she's holding it together nicely, as usual," Wes said.

"I guess you could say that. I'm afraid I'm the one who needs some counsel."

"Legal or religious?"

"Probably both. Can we meet somewhere? Maybe today? If you're not busy, that is . . ."

"Not at all. You have perfect timing. I'm standing here at the Foggy Bottom Metro station and I don't have another appointment until two. I can get to M Central in about fifteen minutes."

"I was thinking of meeting someplace else." Kate's voice threatened to break. "Anyplace else but here."

"Oh, man. Is it that bad?"

"Yeah," she managed to say without sniffing.

"Okay, how about halfway in between? There's a Starbucks at the Crystal City Metro station. What say I meet you there?"

"Great."

"If I get there before you do, you want your regular? That cinnamon thingy?"

"Sure, thanks. And if I get there before you, grande black, right?"

"Yep."

It was a brisk four-block walk in the cold and wet to the King Street Metro station and a nine-minute ride on the blue line to the Crystal City. As she entered Starbucks, she heard Wes call her name. He'd commandeered a table in the corner and already had her favorite caffeine ready for her arrival.

Wes stood as she approached, helped her with her coat, and held her chair as she sat. He allowed her to get settled and take a few sips of her coffee before he spoke. "So tell me what happened."

Kate launched into her tale, keeping her voice low. She told him everything she could, sparing nothing except the names of the people involved. Rule one of public meetings: Don't be overheard. Rule two: Don't use full names in case you fail to obey rule one. Rule three: Don't bawl like a baby in public. That one was tough for Kate to follow today.

The only thing she left out of the story she told Wes was that Carmen del Rio had been her source. Not even Emily knew that.

Wes listened intently, nodding or inserting the appropriate sympathetic sounds in all the right places. After she finished, he sat back in his chair and took a sip of his coffee. "So let me get this straight. You feel guilty because your *friend* went against your advice, and instead of waiting for the situation to rectify itself, she jumped the gun and set up a chain of events that resulted in this morning's headlines."

"Not just guilty. In the wrong. Soiled and torn. And devastated by it."

"So," he said, "you blame yourself for the results of an action that you counseled against in the first place."

"The situation does sound a bit different when you put it in those terms," Kate admitted. That was one of the reasons she'd sought his guidance; Wes had a way of cutting through all the unnecessary details and getting to the real meat of a situation or problem.

He shot her his famous lazy West Texas smile. "Of course it does." He leaned forward. "There's been a tragedy here, but I don't think you had any way of knowing what was to come. Life's like that, which is why I think there's more going on here. What's your real problem, Kate?"

She stared across the room, her eyes focused on nothing in particular. *In for a penny* . . . "You know our friend. When things go bad, she always trots out her infamous 'No one got hurt, no blood, no broken bones' motto. But this time, someone did get hurt. An innocent bystander. I know what our friend is capable of. She can do just about anything she sets her mind to. When she's pulling miracles out of a tough political standoff with the legislature over funding for Medicaid, that's a good thing. When she unleashes the nuclear option and a woman dies, it's a bad thing. I knew what she could do. I never should have put the weapon in her hands. God forgive me, I made what happened possible."

Wes studied her face, and she fought the urge to turn away from his interest.

"A woman died?"

"Yeah. His wife. Suicide."

"I'm not aware of anything beyond the death of the man's political career. I take it this news item hasn't been released to the general public yet?"

"Not yet, but it won't be long. By the evening news, if not earlier." She lowered her voice to a whisper. "That suicide? We drove the woman to it. If we'd left well enough alone, given him some time and his dignity, he would have stepped out of the picture. With or without his endorsement, we would still be ahead of the game and his wife would still be alive."

Wes reached over and put his hand on top of Kate's. "I'm so sorry."

She fought to keep control. "Thanks."

"But you keep saying 'we.' Were you part of any decision to leak the info to anyone else besides the man himself?"

"No, but—"

He raised his hand to cut her off. "'No' is sufficient. So tell me, why is any of this *your* fault? Tell me exactly what *you* did wrong."

Kate started and stopped several explanations but couldn't quite bring herself to say anything aloud. How could it not have been her fault? She thought about it; then she knew.

"I broke the Golden Rule. I did unto another what I wouldn't want done unto me. I dug up dirt on an enemy. And my actions had severe consequences. It makes me question everything about my life—right down to the way I earn my living."

He leaned forward and covered her hands with his. "I'll tell you what I think. You're in a business that practically eats its young. And you've just found out that there are prices you're not willing to pay in order to stay in it. Is that right?"

"Pretty much."

Wes sighed. "There are two sides to your issue. As part of your job, you went looking for proof of political corruption. You found it. Then by accident, you found proof of moral corruption as well. You know how I feel about politics. I'm not sure I could live with spending my days digging up dirt on political rivals, even though I know it's part of what politicians like to call 'business as usual.' But here's the important part to remember when you're trying to analyze your conscience: You didn't set the guy up. You didn't prey on any of his weaknesses. You didn't do anything to tempt or lead him astray. All you did was find the dirt he'd created on his own."

He squeezed her hand with obvious affection. "Your instincts were right, Kate, to present him with the evidence and let him determine what to do on his own. You gave our friend excellent advice, but she didn't choose to follow it. So tell me, exactly why is any of this your fault? And as far as that goes, wouldn't things be a lot worse if you weren't around to give our friend advice on a regular basis?"

"Yeah."

"So isn't that your answer?" Wes asked. "You stay because our friend needs you. Is it enough?"

"I don't know." Kate rubbed at the pain in her forehead, but it didn't go away.

It was the lifelong story of her relationship with Emily.

Emily wanted things done, and Kate stayed behind the scenes and tried to make sure they were done right. Emily worked the public arena and bulldozed her way to success. Kate made sure that success did not bring with it unfortunate consequences. But sometimes Emily wasn't content to point and order and instead took it upon herself to act, ignoring the counsel of those around her.

This time, the situation had played out Emily's way, not Kate's.

And Wes understood the root of the problem without a word from her, perhaps because he'd been in that same place himself more than once—trying to give Emily what she wanted and avoiding any unfortunate fallout.

His hand tightened on Kate's. "Don't kick yourself when others make a bad decision despite your good advice. If you're telling yourself that you should have known better than to hand her something like that, then stop. It was reasonable to expect that she would respect and follow your recommendations. She usually does listen to you. No one could have anticipated she would go off half-cocked like this. Not you, not me, and certainly not anybody else. Not even our friend."

Kate toyed with her coffee. It was totally unappetizing at the moment. "The fact that she didn't listen to me is moot. The problem now is that someone will eventually trace the information back to me, and that will lead to her, of course. When that happens, the excrement will hit the fan."

"*If* that happens, then remember that you're not helping her by protecting her. She's a big girl. She made this decision against your advice, so she should take the heat herself."

"It's not that cut-and-dried."

Wes stared at her, long and hard, as if looking straight into her soul. To his credit, he wouldn't judge her, but somehow she knew he could see all the small black stains, all the places where she had taken the wrong road, made the wrong decisions. "No, it's never that cut-and-dried. And it never will be, not as long as politics are involved." He paused and gave her a questioning look. "You've made a decision about this situation, haven't you?" he asked softly.

She leaned back in the chair and closed her eyes for a moment. She told herself it was because she didn't want to see his expression. But she knew it was the only way to keep her tears to herself. "What else can I do? I've put in my resignation as her campaign manager."

"Oh, Kate." He sighed. "If you were doing this because you wanted to change your life, I'd be the first to applaud you. But you're not. You're doing this to protect her, aren't you?"

She nodded.

"No one who knows you will honestly believe that by leaving you're trying to duck out of the publicity backlash and the resulting firing squad." His gaze narrowed as he stared at Kate as if trying to read her motive in her eyes. "You really think this is going to draw the fire away from our friend, right?"

She nodded again.

He pulled back and glanced around the room at other customers, who appeared to be paying them no attention. When he leaned forward again, he had a look of conspiracy in his eyes. "Look, it's okay—admirable even—to stand beside a friend who is in trouble, but in this case, you shouldn't stand in front of her and take a bullet meant for her. I understand sacrifice as well as, if not better than, the next man, but you'll only be saving her from that one bullet. You won't be saving her from herself." He released her hand and sat back, crossing his arms. "It's going to take a power higher than you and me to do that."

"I'm not sure God is the answer here."

"Of course he is. You and I were both raised to put our faith in God. Our friend was raised to put her faith in only one person—herself."

"What's wrong with believing in yourself?"

"Nothing, but if you do that *instead* of believing in God, then you're in danger of letting your love for self color or even override all other decisions. When a person is raised to believe she's the center of the universe, she expects everything and everybody to revolve around her. If she doesn't like the direction things are going, *she* doesn't shift positions—she expects everyone else to shift to accommodate her." His lips quirked slightly. "Sound like someone we know?"

"What are you trying to say?"

"Two things. First, don't get all caught up in revolving around her. God should be at the center of your universe, not . . . our friend. You should take your troubles to him and ask for forgiveness and his guidance."

"I have."

"Good. Then continue what you've been doing—living your beliefs every day in everything you do. Even in politics."

"But it's not always so straightforward. Politics is all about winning. In this case, it's about our friend winning. Assuring that happens is my job. Still there are lines I'm not willing to cross to perform my duties."

"I understand that. In fact, I applaud it. Our friend counts on you too much sometimes. It's fine for her to be important in your life, but I'm just reminding you that she's not the center of everything. Only God is the center of everything. So do your job every day, keeping that in context. And keep God at the center of your life, no matter how much our friend would like to take his place there."

Kate looked up, surprised.

Wes patted Kate on the back. "Go ahead," he said. "Smile. That last bit was supposed to be a little joke."

Kate managed a weak grin.

"You know our friend," Wes said. "She does tend to believe that the ends justify the means, no matter the situation; but you aren't so easily misled."

"I'm a regular GPS."

Laughter danced in his eyes now and his famous grin threatened to break out again. "There's hope for you yet, Kathryn Marie Rosen."

A weight began to lift from her shoulders and her heart. "So what do you think I should do?"

"Don't resign. She needs you. She needs you to remind her that she's not the center of the universe. Even more importantly, she needs your conscience to help lead her when she leads the nation. She needs to know when she's disappointed or disillusioned you because you represent . . ." He hesitated as if having a hard time finding the right words. "You reflect the hearts of the real people. She may not readily accept God as the center of her universe, but she might accept the good of the people as the true center, and that's a start. And she looks to you to provide that center."

"Wes—"

"No, think about it. When our friend gets into the Oval Office, she's going to be bombarded by decisions every day, none of them small. When she becomes president, every decision she makes—perhaps even which Boy Scout troop to let into the Oval Office for a meet and greet—has a huge number of consequences. It'll be easy for her to see only one aspect of that picture—how the outcome will affect her. You need to be there to remind her to look at the moral and ethical costs of each decision she makes. To help her keep the nation and its people at the center. She's capable of greatness. But she'll only achieve it if you're behind her, providing her with the moral compass she needs. I think our country needs that greatness. The question is, can you work with her after this to provide it?"

"She's not without a heart and a soul. She's always got her eye on the big picture. She's not going to overlook something that critical."

"No, but she might not value the cost to others for her actions as much without your input."

"You overestimate my influence. She didn't listen to me this time."

"And look what a royal mess she's made because she took matters into her own hands. If any good comes out of this tragedy whatsoever, it's the object lesson that she's learned about the frailties of human nature. In particular, she should have learned to listen to you next time. And maybe she's learned a little humility, too."

His tone grew earnest. "Look, this is a big thing, staying with her after this. I think you need to pray about it. But I also think that you have a role to play on the world stage. Our friend can give you a platform for that role. What about that religious initiative we've been talking about? Don't you want to be there to help give religion a more official role in her administration? I can't think of a more qualified person to make Christian compassion a muscular arm of the federal government. Not just to bring hearts and minds into the fold but to bring peace and a helping hand to those in need." Wes had been the one to first come up with the concept of a new faith-based initiative. He took it to Kate because he knew she was the only one who could get Emily to agree to it. Kate took it to Emily. Emily had been more than enthusiastic—she'd made it part of the platform she was running on. "She's not trying to get out of that, is she?"

"No. She's behind it all the way. If anything, she's higher on the idea than ever. Maybe this debacle has proven to her that she needs to consider running her ideas, thoughts, and policies through a religious filter as well as a political one."

"We can hope. But you do realize that if you quit, the religious initiative disappears too?"

"No, it won't. Maybe I'm cynical, but she likes the way it plays on the campaign trail."

"But is it just a gimmick to her?" Wes asked.

"Maybe. She always tells me it'll be my baby. But you could pick up where I left off."

"Nope. Not going to do it." He crossed his arms with mock sternness. "I'm going to play the guilt card here. Our friend needs you. The religious initiative needs you. Both will flounder aimlessly without you."

"Oh. Great." She pulled the lid from her coffee and stared into the cooling liquid. "Kate Rosen. Moral Compass."

"Exactly. And I think that you'll be an excellent one when you get into the White House. For all Emily's flaws, her strengths are in picking her advisers." Wes's face lit up. "She does that well, if I do say so myself. Speaking of moral compasses . . ." He reached into his pocket, pulled out a small polished stone, and slid it across the table. The cross engraved on it also had the points of the compass—N, E, S, and W.

"Just consider this a little gift to help my favorite moral compass get her bearings and decide which direction to take."

Kate managed her first real smile of the day.

He grinned back. "That's much better. Pray about all this. Follow your heart and your conscience. But remember that there's more than just your life bound up in all of this. What will the world look like with our friend as president? That, I'm almost sure, will happen. And I think it could be a good thing. But you have to ask yourself, what will it look like if you're not standing behind her?"

Kate traced the engraved lines on the compass with the tip of her forefinger. "So . . . you really think I shouldn't quit?"

He nodded. "You can do more for her, and more importantly, you can do more in God's name if you stay with her. If Christians don't venture out into the world and work to lift it above its troubles, what good are we? Promise me you'll think about staying on. Seriously."

"I will." And she meant it.

"Why don't we pray about it? Here. Now. Why don't you ask God for his guidance?"

They bowed their heads together. Kate closed her eyes and took a deep breath. Wes was right, as usual. "Dear Lord, thank you for Wes's good advice. Help me to remember that you are directing my steps. Help me understand what happened today, and give me the strength to follow your calling for me, whatever it should be. And give me the wisdom to know what you want me to do, whatever path I should follow. My life is in your hands."

Their soft *amen*s sounded together over the buzz of conversation in the busy coffeehouse.

"Keep your heart open. You'll know what to do." He slid a quick glance at his watch.

"Got an appointment?"

"Yes." His expression changed to a mixture of sheepishness and paternal pride. "I'd forgotten Dani has a well-baby check this morning." He reached inside his jacket. "She's growing like a weed. Have I shown you the latest pictures?"

Kate spent the next few minutes oohing and aahing over the latest "first moments" of his baby's world, immortalized on her doting father's cell phone camera. After extracting sufficient attention and praise for his daughter, Wes stood, gave Kate a hug, and asked her to give him a weekly update on the campaign. Then he left.

Once again, Kate was left alone with her conscience, but now her worries didn't feel quite as suffocating as before, thanks to Wes and her prayer. When she gave her cares to God, the burden on her heart always lifted.

Kate sipped her coffee and contemplated her past, her future, and the decision she would soon have to make about her present.

Life would have been so much easier for her had Emily and Wes been able to take their budding romance into something more definitive and permanent. As much as Kate liked Wes's wife, Anna, she couldn't help but believe Wes would have been the perfect husband and soul mate for Emily. With

Wes's strong morality and Emily's political strength, they would have been an amazing power couple in the White House.

Not only could he have helped her be wiser and more thoughtful, Wes would have easily been embraced by the American public as the First Gentleman.

Water under the bridge, she told herself. *Deal with what is, not what I wish could be.*

She took a last deep draw from her coffee, then capped it and stood.

I guess I better go back and let Emily know my decision.

KATE STAYED.

Actually, Kate left the next day for her parents' house, but only after assuring Emily that yes, she would remain on as campaign manager. As long as Emily listened to her when it came to issues of morality and conscience. And as long as Emily agreed that the religious initiative she'd promised to support remained a viable program in the planning.

Emily hated being told what to do. But she knew that Kate had never steered her wrong in the past. And the recent debacle was still fresh in both of their memories.

Emily'd had to agree to several points before Kate promised to remain in her position. Those important points included an agreement that there would be no unapproved deviations from the plan of attack they had carefully constructed when the campaign started and that Emily would make no surprise end runs around Kate's strategies.

Kate stood in front of Emily's desk. "If you disagree with

me or the course of action we're taking at any time, then tell me. To my face. Don't go behind my back. This point is a deal breaker. I'll never forget how I felt when I saw that video on the news feed. You follow the plan, or you tell me why in advance. You don't run off the rails and leave me to deal with the consequences."

"I promise I won't." Emily squeezed her eyes shut for a moment. Kate knew the action wasn't for any reason as sentimental as stopping a stray tear or two. Emily didn't operate like that.

If anything, she was holding back something she'd really rather say—not that Emily specialized in taking a more circumspect tack to a situation.

But this time, Emily surprised her.

"I'm sorry," Emily said with more honesty than Kate expected. "I guess I lost the vision for a moment there. I promise you. I won't lose my way again."

"Good." Kate waited a moment, fully expecting the earth to stop rotating on its axis. As rare as it was for Bentons to apologize once, twice was . . . unheard of. Bentons explained, they deconstructed, and they sometimes regretted outcomes, but they seldom out-and-out apologized. However, Emily had learned how to do so, begrudgingly, over the years. It had taken quite some time before she realized that, contrary to popular belief, the ground would not swallow her whole for having uttered an apology or acknowledged a weakness. No matter what Big Henry had taught her. . . .

Now that Kate knew she'd driven home the importance of the agreement, she decided it was time to let Emily pull herself off the sharpened stick of guilt. Kate swallowed hard and let the subject at hand go. "Now that the air is clear, you said you had presents you wanted me to take to Mom and Dad. As you recall, you promised me a whole week off at Christmas."

The look of tension on Emily's face faded into a guarded but pleasant expression. "Indeed I did. And I'd really appreciate it if you'd take them with you. Oh, I also picked up a couple of things for Brian, Jill, and the kids, too."

And as easy as that, their world was mended.

Christmas in Washington, D.C., was the same hustle and bustle as any other time of the year but with bright lights and red and green decorations. And more people trying to cram a lot more packages onto the Metro.

Christmas away from the hustle of Washington, D.C., still possessed a sense of bustle but a kind that Kate could actually enjoy. As soon as she got to her parents' house, her mother put her to work immediately. At least her mother called it work; Kate called it family holiday tradition and she'd been jonesing for it for at least a month.

Over the course of the next six days, they ate too much, gave each other far too many presents, spoiled the kids and animals just a shade shy of rotten, and had a thoroughly Norman Rockwellian holiday, complete with snow and a picture-perfect, heart-lifting Christmas Eve service.

The weather even delayed her trip back to D.C. by one day, but the campaign staff forgave her when she arrived lugging several heavy boxes of assorted goodies that she and her mother had baked during their snowy incarceration.

No pecan had been left behind, unused.

When Kate finally reached her desk, having deposited the goodies in the break room, she had a forest of pink "While You Were Out" notes waiting for her and an insistent light on her voice mail.

Six of the notes were marked simply, "Call DD ASAP."

Kate fortified herself with a cup of coffee and a piece of divinity before she returned the call.

"Where are you?" Lee sounded both excited and guarded.

"In my office."

"On your cell or your private line?"

"Private." Emily had insisted that both she and Kate have private landlines that didn't go through the switchboard.

"Close and lock the door and sit down. You won't believe what we found. Sierra's here as well."

Kate complied. "Okay . . . give it to me."

Lee Devlin and Sierra Dudicroft proceeded to tell Kate a horrific tale of a college weekend gone terribly wrong, of unchecked drug use, an accidental death, and a cover-up that had remained intact for thirty-four years and counting. As Kate listened, her mouth hung open in shock and disbelief.

"We wouldn't have known to look for this without that heads-up you gave us."

"What next?" Sierra asked.

"In your opinion, would what you found stand up in a court of law?" Kate asked.

"I don't know. One key link in the chain of evidence is a little iffy, but we have signed affidavits from the folks involved and I think they would testify if it came to trial. If nothing else, even if he beat the rap in a court, he'd be tried and convicted in the media."

Kate's mind worked at light speed. Then she stopped thinking and started praying. What would Jesus have her do with this? *"Render unto Caesar . . ."* It was her duty to let the people know the truth about the candidates they were voting for. Every voter had the right to understand what they were supporting when they cast their ballots—it was the only way democracy functioned effectively. What was the old computer acronym? GIGO—that was it. Garbage in, garbage out. Without truth in politics, the system would fall apart. Getting that truth out there to the voters was one of the reasons Kate was drawn to her career.

But she wasn't just a political operative. She was a Christian. And what were her duties as a Christian in this situation? With the evidence Kate now had in her hands, it was clear that, however horrible it was, the whole thing was just a youthful accident. He'd never meant for things to end in bloody tragedy and death.

Did Kate want to let this loose?

Her hands shook. She thought of all that had happened the last time she'd let a horrible secret become public. She couldn't bear to have another disaster like that one on her conscience.

She bowed her head and asked God for guidance.

Questions floated into her thoughts. *Did this terrible accident call into question the competence of the candidate? Would he govern badly now, or was his youthful stupidity behind him? He'd sworn to run a clean and honest campaign. Did he mean it?*

What was the right thing to do? As a Christian politician, not as a cutthroat political operative. She had a responsibility to her faith as well as to her candidate.

The answer came to her, along with that sense of peace she associated with letting her soul rule her actions and not just cold logic.

She could deep-six this information. The last thing she needed was to put a weapon of this caliber in Emily's hands. She'd done it once, and look how that had turned out. . . . How had Dozier put it? *"The only solution I see is for you to arm yourself but not necessarily her."*

Kate thought about what Wes had said—that her political actions from that point on should be governed by her faith, not by any simple calculation of political expediency. If she couldn't win this election on the merits of her candidate, then she didn't deserve to win the election at all.

It was the right answer for Kate.

She'd run this campaign on Emily's merits, not her rival's flaws.

Kate made up her mind. "Okay, here's the deal. Bury it."

There was a moment of silence on the other end of the phone. Finally Lee spoke. "You don't plan to use it?"

"No. Bury it—someplace safe and not connected to either of you or to me. Just make sure it's retrievable by remote if we absolutely have to deal with it later. I might need to destroy it in a hurry."

"But what about—?"

"And most important of all, *do not* mention this to Emily. Not a word of it. *Ever.* No written reports, no project names on the expense report. No voice mails, no e-mails. You don't mention this to anyone or bring it up unless I introduce the topic. Bill it to my personal account, not the campaign one. Okay?"

"You're the boss. Simple as that. I'll go make burial arrangements." Sierra dropped off the line, but Lee remained.

"Kate? I know your business is your business. But if I can add a personal note, I think you're making the right decision here."

"Thanks, Lee." She cast her eyes toward the heavens. *I know I am. . . .* She looked down. Her hands had stopped shaking. They were rock-steady.

The moment Kate hung up the phone, she knew she would have to push the disclosure and its appalling implications to the back of her mind. If she continued to think about it, it would color every word she spoke, every action she took, from here on in as she spoke about their rival.

She'd never be able to look the man in the eyes and keep her chin up. Or her lunch down.

But how easy would it be to forget a brutal death and a miserable cover-up?

★ ★ ★ ★ ★

There was no real "business as usual" in the world of politics, unless Kate considered "constant and uncontrolled chaos" the proper way to run a business.

January 3 was the start date for the early primaries in this election, but their preparation for it had started long ago. The day after Christmas, Emily had left for her thirty-ninth and longest trip to Iowa since starting her campaign eighteen months prior. From that point on, she had attended every banquet, every debate, accepted almost every invitation to speak as a presidential hopeful. She'd spend the better part of early December in Iowa and was returning to roost there for another week to comb through the state from top to bottom, west to east, conducting a whistle-stop campaign.

But instead of the more traditional train, she had chosen to ride in the biggest pickup truck available for her rounds of appearances. Occasionally, she'd make the Secret Service agent move over and drive herself into a small town simply for the perverse enjoyment of watching the expressions of the crowds as she climbed out of the driver's seat.

Instead of addressing a ballroom of thousands with her bigger-than-life image projected on two large screens flanking the stage, Emily would meet the people in their homes and workplaces. Walk and talk with them. Eat with them. Commiserate, find common ground, listen to their ideas, their complaints, and hopefully, their praise.

She would court them with her decisive politics, her easy wit, her hard-nosed stance on issues, and her sense of compassion. It was one of her strengths. Emily managed to play good ol' boy politics while still remaining a gracious lady. Kate admired that about her friend. It was a hard balance to maintain. As one media reporter put it, "Governor Benton does the political version of dancing backwards while wearing high heels with style. Better yet, she makes it all look so very easy."

Kate wondered if the public had any inkling how much effort Emily put into building her "everywoman" persona. For a girl who played horsey on the president's knee as a child, got married at the White House, and was raised every day in an atmosphere of privilege and power, keeping that veneer of everywoman in place was a real struggle.

Yet she did it. Well.

In Iowa, there was no earthly way for any candidate to reach every caucus location; there were well over two thousand of them, with meetings held in school gymnasiums, town halls, and living rooms across Iowa. But Janis Weems, the director of the state's field office, had extensive experience with the process and had helped steer Emily to a good mixture of large and medium-size voter areas, not to mention a few smaller ones for "Your opinion is valuable too" influence and media ops.

And while Emily wooed support from the good people of Iowa under the close watch of Janis and Kate's second-in-command and deputy, David Dickens, Kate led more Benton advance ground troops in New Hampshire in anticipation of the primary to be held there a little more than two weeks later. Tim Healy, an old friend from their Georgetown days, helmed their headquarters in Nevada and was instrumental in helping them define Nevada's new role in their campaign strategy. But because of the fact that one of Nevada's beloved sons, Senator Stephen Hyde, was also running, no other candidate was taking Nevada quite as seriously as the state might have wished prior to declaring its primary date change.

Nonetheless, Emily wasn't ignoring that state, or Michigan, either. Thanks to the wonders of modern air travel, she would be able to hit "Lunch with a Leader" in Whitehall, Michigan, then attend a dinner and rally in Greenville, New Hampshire, and be back in time for "Morning Coffee with the Candidate" in Blue Diamond, Nevada, the following morning.

No matter where she was, Emily tried to call Kate each night—whether from the back of the RV she used in the more rural areas, from a local bed-and-breakfast, or from the guest bedroom in someone's house. Emily didn't stay in hotels in Iowa. Even if there had been any five-star hotels there, she knew earnest candidates wouldn't stay in one. Not if they didn't want to be mocked on the local evening news and called an elitist.

Candidates in Iowa not only had to appreciate average citizens, but they had to be one themselves. At least they had to pretend they were average, everyday folks long enough to fool the Iowans if they planned to win, and they arranged their average lodgings accordingly.

Lacking an average, everyday background, Emily frequently called Kate to get advice on how to fake being normal. Kate, recognizing the caller ID, answered her cell on the first ring. "How's it going, M?"

"All I want is a stiff drink," Emily declared in a scratchy voice, worn thin from talking nearly continuously every waking moment for days. "If another yahoo complains to me about border control one more time, I think I'll scream."

"It's an important topic. The people in nonborder states need to know where you stand."

"I understand that. But I'd just sat there answering that same question for the idiot sitting next to him. I felt like saying, 'Open your stupid ears, Yokel. What have I been talking about for the last eight and half minutes?'"

"No, no, no . . . ," Kate teased. "You're using the Y words. I thought we agreed you wouldn't use any of the Y words—*yokel*, *yahoo*, *yo-yo*."

Emily snorted. "Farmer Fred is lucky I didn't use the F word."

It was a game they played. Emily would whine to Kate

about some harmless aspect of the campaign, never complaining about the big issues—spotty media coverage, poor crowd turnout, scheduling problems, or overwhelming exhaustion.

By venting over innocuous issues in a safe arena, Emily bled off enough of the building pressure so that she could deal with the more pressing issues and worries of the campaign in a much better humor.

After all, the Iowa caucus *was* a big deal. *As Iowa goes, so goes the nation* wasn't just an idle saying—it had history behind it. Come in first or second place in Iowa, and you were a lot more likely to become that party's presidential candidate in the end. And then there was the value of momentum.

America loved a winner.

If a candidate won Iowa, campaign contributions would pick up. After all, everybody wanted to back a winner. More often than not, they also wanted someone else to prove to them their choice was indeed a winner.

Iowa was great for that, even if it had meant campaigning hard there in the holiday season. At least they didn't have to interrupt their Thanksgiving holiday plans to go vote. For a while there, both Emily and Kate had feared that it might be a possibility. Their two years on the campaign trail would be grueling enough as it was. But each time the states jockeyed to be "First in the Nation," they inched their primaries earlier and earlier, adding weeks to the time frame, even threatening the holidays.

Having them in January was bad enough.

And Iowa's was to be held earlier this year by the standards of previous elections. It meant that Emily had pretty much campaigned continuously over the holidays. Her gift to Kate of an uninterrupted Christmas with her family had been a sacrifice of real hardship for Emily and the campaign that Kate would never forget.

But the media flurry accompanying a declared win in Iowa would result in national and international news coverage in which a candidate's name became associated with the word *winner*. The more times Americans heard this, the more likely they were to believe in the inevitability of the word. Even better, such media coverage cost them nothing.

Emily and Kate had blown vast quantities of their advertising expense budget on commercials for Iowa and New Hampshire—to the tune of $6.2 million dollars, a very large chunk of the remaining campaign contributions on hand. However, both of them viewed this spending as an investment in Emily's future.

Every presidential candidate—Republican, Democrat, or Independent—felt an unavoidable financial pinch in late December and early January. Donations were always down across the board, what with the holiday gift-giving season and increased competition from charitable organizations for donors' loose cash. Every campaign had increased its expenditures early in the race, thanks to political pressure laid on by all the early primaries. The whole race started in earnest nearly a year sooner than it had in earlier presidential elections. These days, many candidates—Emily included—started their campaigns as soon as they filed with the FEC. They hit the ground and started running hard with their campaign more than two full years before the actual election. Building a grassroots campaign in every state took time, money, and lots of manpower. Even when a candidate was independently wealthy like Emily, there were still limits to available funds.

But a win in Iowa, a strong showing or better in Mark Henderson's Michigan less than two weeks later, a very strong second-place finish against the hometown boy in Nevada four days later, and then a decisive win three days after that in New Hampshire—all that would turn the fundraising spigot on again and pour much-needed donations back into the campaign coffers. A new bumper crop of volunteers would also likely show up at the doors of their campaign offices throughout the country. So the way to achieve financial solvency, gain momentum, and generate media coverage was to travel the back roads of Iowa and do things the old-fashioned way.

It was traditional, just like admiring the butter sculptures at the Iowa State Fair. It was sometimes necessary to do things the old-fashioned way to grease the wheels of the new political machine. Besides, having Emily chow down on funnel cakes in front of the cameras in Iowa appeased the secret wishes of the American public to see their presidential candidates either cut down to size or humanized by the indulgent intake of untold amounts of fat and calories.

In their hearts, Americans still wanted to see their presidential candidates work the crowds, kiss the babies, and shake the hands of the common man, so the candidates complied. According to the field report from their deputy manager, Dave Dickens, Emily had found her stride on the road doing just that.

She charmed everyone, male and female, with her straightforward answers, good humor, and when the occasion called for it, sympathy. Kate had drilled that into Emily long ago.

"Sometimes you can't fix everyone's problems, but you can at least listen and offer your sincerest condolences."

Evidently, the lesson had taken.

At the moment, Kate was having a hard time following her own advice. Her meeting with Alexander Michaels, the New Hampshire state director, had been interrupted by a volunteer staffer with a minor medical emergency. As much sympathy as she felt for the young man and his physical discomfort, tempus fugit.

But her attention became even more split when she heard her cell phone *ching* once, the sign of an incoming text message. Since Alex was still dealing with the distracting problem, she discreetly pulled out the phone and read: `U at NH HQ? Can we meet? Nick`

Kate stared at the words, not quite comprehending them at first. The only Nick she knew was Nick Beaudry, and if the message was from him, then how had he gotten her private cell phone number?

In what universe did he think that campaign staff from opposing parties met routinely to chitchat, share trade secrets, or gossip?

Why in the world is he calling?

She thought for a moment. *Curiosity. That's why.* It was the same reason she was willing to text him back.

She typed: `Prove U R Nick.`

The answer came quickly. `12 at PO'B in NO`

It was definitely Nick Beaudry. The sudden heat of embarrassment filled Kate's face as she remembered when they'd all first met. It was in the crowd outside Pat O'Brien's in New Orleans during Mardi Gras. At Emily's insistence, they'd ended up sharing a minuscule bar table. Between the

four of them—Emily, Kate, Nick, and his friend Wendell—
they'd imbibed a dozen Hurricane drinks that night. At
least that's what Emily loved to tell. Truth be known, Kate
had had only one drink and didn't even finish it. Where
they went after that, no one quite remembered—what little
alcohol Kate had ingested had messed up her sense of direction. But the rest of them managed to keep their souvenir
Hurricane Glasses intact, which was no mean feat when
stumbling drunk through the streets of New Orleans in the
middle of Mardi Gras.

`Where?`, she typed.

`Hungry?`

`Always`

`Bagel Mike Close 2U Meet at 10?`

She consulted her daily planner. `OK`

It wouldn't hurt to listen to him. Even if it might be a
setup.

Meeting him in public had its complications, but doing
so in private would be far more damaging if news of it got
out. No matter how careful political people were, clandestine meetings always had a way of backfiring on them, their
campaigns, and their candidates. The whole Watergate mess
had left behind its share of object lessons, and that one had
been taken to heart by everyone on both sides of the aisle.

Kate had no qualms about her ability to keep campaign
secrets. But when it came to guarding the truth, it helped if a
political operative valued truth far more than the opponent
did. In this case, Kate knew that she held the truth sacred.
Nick, however, held it loosely, if he held it at all.

She wondered what he wanted. . . .

After Alex's staff crisis du moment was dealt with, he

and Kate went over the New Hampshire schedule in detail. Kate penciled in some suggested additional appearances for Emily based on what the field researchers had seen as holes in their demographics.

Alex hit a key, saving the changes they'd made in the centralized online calendar, then looked up. "Umm . . . can I ask a personal question?"

"Sure."

He pushed back from the desk. "What about you? Why don't you speak on Emily's behalf? I think you could make great political headway as her official spokeswoman."

Kate tried not to sigh. She'd answered this question more times than any other one that came up from the campaign's workers.

Now she offered her pat answer. "Emily's the headliner. I stay in the background. I always have; I always will. I can be more effective that way."

She gathered up the spread of papers she'd trailed across Alex's desk, then looked up at him. "You haven't met Emily's cousin Margaret yet, have you?"

"I haven't had the pleasure. But I'm supposed to meet her in an hour or so at the first of the appearances we've scheduled for today."

"Trust me. You'll find Margaret to be very engaging and incredibly persuasive."

And very well prepared, thanks to the intensive sessions the Virginia staff conducted, bringing Maggie up to speed on the party line, the current rhetoric, and the opposition. Even better, Maggie could be just a bit more open in her disdain for Mark Henderson's infidelities than Emily could. Maggie could mouth the words that Emily couldn't. Maggie and her husband, Pete Shaiyne, were living examples of how a couple suffering infertility problems could deal with the situation effectively. The Shaiynes' solutions covered the natal spectrum. They had one birth son, one adoptive daughter, and a set of fraternal twins, thanks to in vitro fertilization.

"Just be glad she's not bringing the kids. The last time the brood performed for the reporters, a food fight broke out. It made great copy, but a number of innocent bystanders took hits. Wet zweiback at twenty paces is not a pretty sight." Kate glanced at her watch. "I need to make a ten o'clock meeting at a place called Bagel Mike. Is it within walking distance?"

"Not particularly. But I have a volunteer with a car standing by to take you anywhere you need to go."

Said volunteer was Meredith, a bright-eyed coed from the University of New Hampshire who struggled against her better manners and obvious instructions to "not bug the higher-ups" and finally asked permission to ask just one question as they negotiated traffic.

Kate hid her smile. "Sure. Shoot."

It took the girl a few seconds to come up with the words for the question she was trying to formulate. Then she finally said, "What's in it for you?"

Kate had pegged the girl as just another dewy-eyed college volunteer helping the tides of democracy flow. Evidently she was wrong. This one was a thinker.

"Off the record . . . I could give you the usual song and dance about wanting what's best for America and knowing that former Governor Benton is the best candidate. Now, all that's true, but there's more. On some level, it's a power trip of sorts."

"That's a lot more honesty than I expected." The girl remained silent for a moment, then said, "If I could ask you a second question?"

Kate was curious to see where this would go. "Sure," she said.

"What kind of power trip?"

Kate made a mental note to learn more about this Meredith. "On a good day, I hope I'm actually shaping history for the better. On a bad day, I feel the same way. I help make Emily's success possible and history still gets shaped for the better. Anytime I can anticipate what's coming toward us better than the consultants we hire do, I win. Anytime I can accurately forecast the actions of an opponent and help Emily come into a situation prepared for their volley or their rebuttal, I win. And when I win, Emily wins. If Emily wins, in my opinion, we all win. And that's why I do it."

"So winning is the key."

"Absolutely. This is politics. Losers never even get in the door of the White House. I'm just as competitive as Governor Benton is, but I don't necessarily want the ultimate prize of the Oval Office for myself. I just want to see the right person behind that desk."

"But there *is* a prize for you, eventually, right? It's not like you're a hired gun or something like that. You've been with Ms. Benton for . . . like . . . forever. What sort of prize does that sort of loyalty win? I've studied you. You're smart. Maybe smarter than she is. You could run yourself. Why do you do all this for her instead of for yourself?"

"I know Emily—better than anyone else in the world knows her." Kate shrugged. "So I know she's the very best candidate out there, hands down. Far better than I could ever be. She's driven. I'm not. She's prepared all her life for this goal. I haven't. That's why I do it. She'll make the best possible president. As for my consolation prize, we'll see."

"White House chief of staff?"

Kate figured there'd been enough honesty in the car. "We'll see," she said. Although she'd uttered the necessary phrase *off the record*, she was pretty sure young Meredith was fishing for something to go on the record with. Smart kid—Kate promised herself she'd keep an eye on the girl. But they reached the bagel shop before the young woman could press harder and ask any further questions.

After stopping at the curb, Meredith held out a small business card to Kate. "When you're ready to leave, just call my cell. I'll stay in the general area."

"Thanks for taking care of me." Kate accepted the card with a smile. "But I'll probably catch a cab to go back to the hotel and work from there. So don't hang around on my account."

The young woman almost managed to hide her crest-fallen look. "All right. Nice to meet you."

"Thanks for the ride."

"You're welcome. And, Ms. Rosen? If you do become the chief of staff, I sure would like to apply for a position as a White House aide. I think I could be an asset to you. You have my contact info there."

Kate tucked the card into her day planner. "Thanks." After a brief hesitation, she added, "I'll keep this for the future. I promise."

A blast of icy wind hit her as she climbed out of the car, making her hurry to the restaurant door. Once inside, she didn't see Nick at first and wondered belatedly if the message had been nothing more than a setup. But she finally spotted him in a booth in the rear of the restaurant, where he was studiously reading a *USA Today*. He didn't look up until she got within feet of his table.

In any given situation—and that included the audience at the Oscars—Nick was usually the best-looking man in the room. Today was no exception. Although she hadn't seen him face-to-face in seven or so years, she'd seen the pictures. He'd changed very little. These days he had a slight amount of premature silver peppered through his dark hair at the temples. The combination of that and the light laugh lines now in evidence around his eyes served to add a hint of respectability to his traditional bad-boy good looks. Today he wore a dark turtleneck beneath a tweed jacket, looking like every coed's dream professor.

"K." He stood, ever the Southern gentleman when it came to manners. When it came to morals, Kate knew, he'd had a tougher time toeing the line. "Good to see you," he said. Leaning forward for an air kiss, he adapted quickly to her backward step, accepting the hand she stuck out instead.

Nick was the only person other than Emily to use her friend's pet nickname for her, and Kate found that uncomfortable. But she was curious about why he had contacted her. She wasn't going to call him on the bad habit until she found out why he wanted to see her.

Nick remained standing until she slid into the opposite side of the booth.

"I appreciate your coming. I wasn't sure if you would or not."

She shrugged. "Curiosity overrode my better instincts."

He shot her a boyish grin that she remembered all too well. "That's exactly how I felt when Chuck Talbot approached me. I'm sure you know all about that. You've got more listening posts than the DMZ in South Korea."

"Of course I do. That's one of my many skills. You're going to be named the new deputy campaign manager right after the primary. Congratulations."

He whistled. "News may travel fast, but rumor travels even faster. I'm pretty sure no one has figured that out other than you and Emily. The media certainly hasn't tumbled onto it yet. But nothing ever did escape your attention. I shouldn't be surprised."

She decided to take the remark as a compliment, whether he meant it that way or not. "Let's dispense with the small talk, shall we? Exactly why did you want to meet with me, Nick?"

He leaned forward and lowered his voice. "Because I wanted to draw up some ground rules for the upcoming months."

She studied his face, looking for the joke or the joker that had to be hiding there after a statement like that. Nick looked perfectly serious, which probably meant he'd taken up poker since she'd last seen him. "You know as well as I do that there are no ground rules in politics."

"There should be. You and I are a lot more alike than you know."

Utilizing a lesson she learned too late to do Emily any good, Kate made eye contact with Nick Beaudry and held it. His sincere facade wouldn't necessarily crack under unrelenting scrutiny, but it would crumble a bit. Kate had been able to make Nick twitch there at the end of his relationship with Emily. But this time, he held her gaze without turning away and without the slightest tic.

Hmm, she decided, *at least he thinks he's telling the truth.*

"I give." She leaned back into the booth's cushioning and crossed her arms. "How are we alike?"

The answer had to wait. A waitress interrupted them to take their order. Kate didn't even look at a menu but kept her gaze on Nick and her arms crossed. "Plain bagel, toasted; light cheese if you have it, regular if not; and black coffee."

Nick shot the waitress a thousand-watt smile. "I'll have the same but with cream and sugar."

Thus informed, the woman scurried away.

He tried that same high-powered smile on Kate. "Same as always. You know, I would have ordered for you, but I couldn't be sure your tastes were the same."

"Lots of things have changed," she said, keeping her poker face. "Maybe even me."

"Possibly."

"In any case, I don't think either of us has changed so much that we have anything in common."

"Other than Emily, you mean?" Nick leaned forward. "Cards on the table, K. We both know where the bodies are buried, but neither of us really wants to use that knowledge."

Kate felt the muscles in her back stiffen. She wondered if Nick really did know just how much she knew. But she put that thought away. Then she made her expression carefully nondescript. "Is that a threat?"

Nick pulled back. "Absolutely not. Not a threat or a veiled hint or even an innuendo. That's the point. I don't intend to use any insider knowledge I have of Emily to disrupt your campaign or cause her any personal grief." His face colored slightly. "I think I've done enough damage to her in the past. I have no desire to compound that error."

A kinder, gentler Nick Beaudry. Inconceivable. . . . In fact, Kate thought, *impossible.*

"You don't believe me." He ducked his head, then looked up with a blushing smile that took a decade off his face. "I can't say that I blame you. Not with my track record."

"Your track record speaks for itself. I have one or two good reasons not to believe you. Emily has dozens."

He nodded, then rested his arms against the table and laced his fingers together. "That's a conservative total. Between you and me, I gave her hundreds of reasons to never talk to me again, much less to ever trust me. But back then I was young, stupid, and full of myself. I listened to the wrong people and ignored the right ones." His expression softened. "Anything I could possibly do wrong, I did."

Kate stared at him, suddenly seeing the man Emily had fallen in love with, the person Kate had once called a friend. "I won't disagree with you. You had a great thing going and you screwed it up. Badly. But now you say you've changed? When? Why?"

He shrugged. "It'd be nice if I could point to a specific time and say on that particular day, at that specific hour, something radical happened to me and I made a miraculous change overnight. But both of us know that's much too convenient. Guilt takes a long time to eat away at you. What it leaves behind is overwhelming regret. The only way to get rid of regret is to confront the problem and ask for forgiveness."

The light dawned. Nick had been busy doing more than politicking. "AA?"

"Yeah." He nodded. "That and more."

"Like what?"

His blush returned, deeper than before. "Honestly? Religion."

"You found God? *You* found God?" Her words were edged with disbelief but not for the church. Only for him and the timing of his highly convenient conversion.

"Hard to believe, eh?" A distant look clouded Nick's eyes and his grin faded. "You should hear my older brothers start in on me. If I can't make them understand, I know I can't make Emily. But I was hoping that you would at least listen to me." He closed his eyes, then opened them, focusing on Kate. "That's why I texted you. And you came, K. I really appreciate it."

It was a lot to digest. Even harder to believe. "So let me get this straight. You're going to work as Talbot's deputy campaign manager, but you're not going to offer up any of Emily's deep, dark secrets against her at the strategy table. And you're doing all this because you found religion."

"Yeah. Don't get me wrong. I'll use what I know about her personality, her hot buttons, her fears, when her pride goeth, and when it doesn't. But I will not—and this is my solemn promise—will not in any way use my knowledge of any Benton family skeletons—"

The waitress popped up with the food just in time to hear the word *skeletons*. By her quizzical look, she had no idea who they were or what they were actually talking about, but they'd snagged her attention.

Nick shot the woman a heart-stopping grin and shook

his head. "Sorry about that, ma'am. Crime scene investigation over breakfast—we ought to know better." He turned to Kate. "So how's that autopsy going? Have you received the remains yet? They should have arrived in at least three boxes."

The waitress retreated fast, both fascinated and repulsed.

"One thing hasn't changed," Kate said once the woman was out of hearing range. "You're still incorrigible." She couldn't keep from returning his grin.

"Ah, but forgiven."

She studied his features. If Nick's claims were true, then he ought to look different, Kate decided. But other than the gentle signs of aging, he appeared just the same. He had the same tendency to a five-o'clock shadow at 10 a.m., the same quick wit, an obvious affinity to women, the same charm. . . .

But religion? Faith? A relationship with Jesus?

She examined his face harder, searching for an insincere light in his eyes, a crack in his earnest expression, anything that would support the idea that Nicholas Beaudry was pulling yet another fast one on her. Seeing nothing, and not sure what to think, she picked up their interrupted conversation.

"Back to what you were saying. Please define 'Benton family skeletons.'"

He looked around. "Here? Now? The walls have ears."

Inside, she cheered. She'd called his bluff. "For a man who won't give specifics, you talk a big game."

"But the point is—it won't matter what I know and what I don't know. As far as my participation in this campaign goes, it won't be a mudslinging competition. Chuck is pretty ironclad about that. That's one of the reasons why I respect him as a man as well as a candidate."

If you knew what I know . . .

Charles Talbot had been making a big deal in the press about his desire to run a clean, positive campaign. Then again, he did have his party's nomination all but sewn up. It'd been awfully easy for him to "play it clean" up to this point, since he had no real competition he needed to throw mud at. However, once Emily became his competition on the other side of the aisle, Kate was sure his tune would change.

Desperation did that to a person.

Kate suddenly realized the bigger implications of their little talk and she couldn't help but smile, which seemed to pique Nick's curiosity.

"What?" he prompted.

"Now I get it." She covered her mouth as if suppressing a giggle. "Talbot won't come right out and say it, but he knows Emily is going to win the party nomination and run against him. Please thank him for me . . . for his faith in her campaign."

Nick shrugged. "We *do* figure she has a better chance than everybody else. Henderson was her real competition. Now with him gone, all she has to do is not screw up, and she'll get enough delegates to win the nomination. He thinks she's got it in the bag."

"Of course Talbot thinks that; he's running unopposed. He's had it easy so far. But it's different for us. Even with Henderson out of the picture, there are five, maybe six real contenders still in the party backfield. Emily and I can't go into the end-zone victory dance anytime soon."

He sighed dramatically. "I love it when you talk football analogies." He pointed to her bagel. "Better eat that before it gets cold."

She closed her eyes, whispered a quick grace, and then took a bite, not to oblige him but to slake her hunger. How long, she wondered, had it been since she stopped to eat?

When she looked at him, his head was still bowed. A moment later, he opened his eyes, blushed slightly again, and grabbed a spoon to stir his coffee. "Okay. House rules: No politics while we eat, due to indigestion and all that. You look like you could stand to finish a few meals. We keep our opinions to ourselves while we eat. Agreed?"

What the heck? she thought. *But why not play along?* "Agreed."

"Want some of the newspaper?" He nudged the entertainment section of the *USA Today* across the table and picked up the sports section for himself. "If we decide to talk about it, no front page, no business section. Just the fun parts. Okay?"

Kate kept waiting for the other shoe to drop. But it never did. As they ate, they made innocuous comments on their individual sections—dissecting both the Saints' and the Redskins' seasons. Sports had always been a safe subject for them during the tumultuous years of his marriage to Emily. With Kate playing third wheel more often than she wanted, at least she and Nick found harmless common ground in their mutual interest in football. They'd even developed a friendly rivalry thanks to their divergent team choices.

In fact, the day after the Big Breakup, when he'd been arrested for DUI, Nick had actually called Kate. Whether it was for sympathy, for bail money, or what, she never knew. Out of loyalty to Emily, she'd hung up on him.

She drained her coffee.

"Want another cup? Our waitress is right over there."

"No thanks. I need to get back to work. New Hampshire isn't a done deal for us." She paused, then added, "Yet."

"Can I offer you a ride?"

Kate stared at him. He couldn't be serious. "Back to Benton campaign headquarters? You and me? Are you trying to destroy my career? smear my reputation? mess with my digestion?"

He laughed. "I guess that wouldn't look so good. What if I dropped you off a few blocks shy of the building. What Emily doesn't know won't hurt us."

"You mean, what Emily doesn't know won't hurt you. What happens to me if she has areas of ignorance is another story. I don't think it's wise for us to be seen together."

"You mean it's not safe?" He whistled. "That's news to me. Or maybe not. I bet Emily is still circulating copies of that 'Shoot to Kill' poster of my face."

Kate performed her best double take. "You weren't supposed to know about that," she said in a shocked whisper.

The look of surprise on his face was priceless. She waited a moment before bestowing on him her sweetest smile.

"Gotcha."

WHEN KATE GOT BACK to the office, she knew it was high time she sicced her favorite investigators on the newly reformed enigma named Nicholas St. Andrews Beaudry. She wanted to know where he'd been, what he'd done, *who* he'd been with since the divorce. Sure, she knew the basics of his public life after Emily—his term in the Louisiana State Senate and so on—but what about his private life? Something was going on here. There were rocks to be turned over, secrets to be uncovered. For once, that didn't give her insides the shakes the way it had since the Henderson catastrophe.

She might feel horrible about it, but it was her job.

Or at least it was another job for District Discreet.

And Nick needed looking at if a political opponent ever had. His past with Emily and his present with their biggest opponent made it imperative that Kate figure out what they were dealing with. She told the still, small voice of her conscience to shut up and started to place the call. Then she put the phone down.

Because of their almost-exclusively political clientele, the investigators had affiliated offices in practically every state capital in the nation. Kate knew that included Baton Rouge, Nick's home base.

It wouldn't take even a phone call. One e-mail and Lee Devlin would get Nick under her virtual microscope and report back on what and who made him tick. Lee wouldn't ask any questions as to why Kate was suddenly interested in information about Emily's ex-husband. Such requests didn't so much as raise an eyebrow when it came to the world of politicians and politics.

Kate sent the e-mail.

Four hours later, Lee called with some unusual news. "You're right; the governor's ex *has* changed," she said. "Turned over a whole new leaf, grown himself a conscience, or just plain turned his back on the devil. And all this seems to have taken place three years ago. That's when most of Beaudry's life went up in a puff of smoke."

"What happened?"

"Let's call it a string of unfortunate events. His mother died of cancer, his father had a stroke, and one of his brothers took his own life after a failed marriage."

Ouch, Kate thought. That'd be a heavy load for anyone, with or without a working conscience. Maybe Nick's sense of honor had been newly forged in the fire of disaster. Stranger things had happened.

"So that's what precipitated his sudden—what do we call it? Crisis of conscience? Enlightenment?"

"Maybe," the investigator said. "I've seen it happen before. When a man gets slapped in the face with proof of his own mortality, he'll do one of three things: stay down, sink lower, or try to climb back up. Beaudry appears to be a climber. And so far it appears as if his changes are permanent. He's been sober for two years. He didn't even backslide when his father finally passed away six months ago—or at least I haven't been able to dig up evidence of it, and that's good enough for me. More often than not, losing a parent is the real acid test for what a person's made of."

"So his religious conversion . . . ?"

"It's not something you can get a certificate of authenticity on, but it appears to me to be legit. When Nick's back in Louisiana, he goes to the Methodist church he grew up in. It's charming, but it's too small and too poor to do him any good politically. When he's in the capital, instead of attending some big, trendy nondenominational megachurch where he can get good press coverage and find lots of people to talk politics with—not that there's anything wrong with that, of course—he drives out to a nice little neighborhood church in the Virginia suburbs. If anybody would know how to use phony religion to build a political base, it's Nick Beaudry, but he's steering clear of that entirely. I think he might just mean it."

"So now he's the all new and improved Nick Beaudry." Kate harrumphed. "Am I supposed to believe he's taken vows of chastity and poverty as well?"

"Nope. Neither. He's not that different, though he does seem to be playing around less and shooting for permanence more. The arm ornaments are sticking around a lot longer. He likes women, and women like him. When I saw photos of him, I could see why. Yowza. So that part of his life hasn't changed. He appears to have a healthy dating life, and his finances don't seem to have suffered much."

"So I can't translate that to he still prefers loose women to debutantes and still worships the almighty buck?" she asked, almost sadly. It would be easier for her to believe that Nick hadn't really changed. Especially since he was on the other side of her political fight club.

"I said *dating* life, not *sex* life. Like I said, judging from the A-list of women he's dated in the last year or so, it appears as if he's looking more for a missus than a mistress. But he's not settled on any replacement for Emily yet. As to his funding, he's got a nice, conservative stock portfolio and he's scaled back his lifestyle considerably."

"Oh yeah? I bet he still drives a Porsche."

Lee laughed. "As a matter of fact, he does. But it looks to be the same one he bought while married to the governor." She paused. "And he hasn't so much as gotten a speeding ticket in it in the last ten years. I don't know what to tell you, Kate. We were both expecting to find dirt on the man. But from what I've unearthed, it looks as if he didn't sweep it under a rug but swept it out of his life. I don't want to go as far as to guarantee that he's a changed man, but it sure is looking that way to me. And trust me, I dug deep."

After she hung up, Kate pushed Nick's possible religious conversion out of her head and turned her attention back to the campaign's more immediate needs. Scheduling. Mail. Donations. Point papers. More mail.

Including a letter with no return address and with her name in big block letters eerily reminiscent of the "YOU WILL DIE" note.

Her breath caught in her throat.

Oh, no. . . . Not again. . . .

The postmark had been blurred or faked, but in either

case, she couldn't quite read details like an originating city or post office. The whole look of the letter screamed, *"Don't open me!"* Remembering the anthrax scares in Washington several years back, Kate didn't even want to touch the thing.

So she didn't.

Instead, she examined it carefully. Since it seemed thoroughly sealed, she used a tissue to pick up a corner of the envelope, slid it into a new manila envelope, and closed it. Then she put that in a plastic bag, sealed it with box tape, and left it on her desk beneath an overturned garbage can. Stepping out of the room, she motioned to the office manager, a sturdy woman named June who seemed to be the keystone to all the Manchester office operations.

"Excuse me, but who handles mail security here?"

The woman balanced her fists on her ample hips. "We've hired an outside agency to process all incoming mail." She nodded toward Alex Michaels's office. "The boss wants a daily breakdown—you know—amount of donations, letters of support, of complaints, weed out the crank mail, open suspicious packages, etc." She craned slightly to look into Kate's temporary office, spotting the upside-down can sitting in the middle of the desk. "Did something slip through?"

Don't panic the help, Kate told herself. *This could be nothing.* "I'm not sure. I just got something addressed to me, and quite frankly, I don't have a particularly good feeling about it. It's probably nothing, but I thought I'd better play it safe . . . you know?"

One quick call later and June had a security team member there to take care of the letter. Someone showed up with a biohazard box, sealed the letter, and whisked it away. Ten minutes later, the mail security guy returned and introduced himself as Ed Griggs.

"The contents weren't dangerous, at least as far as contamination of the paper went," he said. "But you were right about the sentiments, Ms. Rosen."

He handed Kate a xeroxed copy of the message found inside.

Repent Handmaiden of the Devil she who serves
The Devil will die by the hands of True Believers.

Kate stared at the crude letters with an odd sense of detachment. "Gee, it makes the 'YOU WILL DIE' note seem almost . . . pithy." Griggs gave her quizzical look and Kate shrugged. "It's not the first oddball threat I've gotten. The Secret Service dealt with the last one we received." She dropped the paper to the desk; even though it was a copy, the paper felt . . . tainted . . . by the words. "They should probably see this too. You'll need to give the original to the Secret Service, maintaining the chain of evidence from the moment it got into your hands. I'll keep this copy for myself. But we'll need a copy of the note and of the envelope, too, for internal security. I think we ought to attempt to discover where this came from ourselves."

"We've already contacted the Feds." The man puffed up slightly. "But I doubt they'll find anything we didn't. Chances are good the perp used gloves—thanks to those *CSI* shows, they all know to do that nowadays. There was nothing inside the envelope other than the one sheet of paper."

"No suspicious white powder or anything scary like

that?" She tried to find a disarming smile in her repertoire of tricks, but her humor was in short supply at the moment.

"No, ma'am. No threats, no fake threats, not even any cornstarch or baby powder. Just the message," Griggs declared. He tapped the sheet of paper. "And a weird one at that. It sounds like something some kind of zealot would spout. One who's been off the meds too long."

A chilling thought hit her. *And speaking of crazed zealots, exactly where is Daniel Gilroy these days? And his followers?*

"Uh . . . it does sound a little unhinged, doesn't it?" She drew herself up to her full height, but she was several inches shorter than the security head. "Thanks. Oh, one more thing . . . I really don't want news of this getting out. I'd like to keep the rumors around the campaign to a minimum."

Griggs shot her a snappy salute. "You call the shots, Ms. Rosen. Mum's the word."

After he left, Kate called Wes Kingsbury's cell phone and reached his voice mail. Rather than leave anything on record, she waited until she got back to her hotel room and called his home.

His wife answered.

"Anna? Hi, it's Kate Rosen. Is Wes there? I need to speak with him if he's not busy."

"Hey, Kate. Long time no see. Give him just a minute— he's up to his elbows in suds, giving Dani a bath."

"I bet that's quite a sight."

"Cuter than a calendar full of puppy pictures." There was a muffled noise as if she was covering the receiver. But Kate could just about make out the words.

"Honey? Phone's for you."

There were a few more muffled noises, including one that sounded like a baby's laughter and splashing water.

"Hang on for a second while we play tag team with her. He needs to dry off." She laughed. "Bathing Dani can be a real white-water adventure."

"I can imagine." Kate and Anna chatted idly about the baby's latest milestones. Normally, Kate was interested in babies—Dani, in particular—but today impatience distracted her from really enjoying the conversation.

Less than a minute later, Wes came on the phone. "Hey, Kate. What's going on?" Happy momma sounds joined the happy baby noises in the background.

"I'm not sure. I'm hoping you can help me. Are you still in contact with Daniel Gilroy? You remember? Crazed cult leader extraordinaire?"

"Not really. He stopped responding to my letters a couple of years ago. Why?"

"He's still in prison, isn't he?"

"You know? I'm not sure. Hang on. Let me step into my study. It'll be quieter." The sounds faded in the background. "Last I heard, he'd been turned down for parole. But that was some time ago."

Kate chose her words carefully. "If he does get out or is out now, would you consider him a potential threat?"

"To the public in general? No. I think that once we broke up the militia, he lost the one group of people he could easily influence. It'd take him some time—maybe years—to gather another crowd of followers who could be so easily controlled."

"Why?"

"The last group of followers was a gift to him from

his father. Gilroy inherited the group as a whole from his father's 'ministry' and hadn't actually collected or united them himself. I never figured he had the charisma to pull off something like that again."

"What about his attitude toward you? Do you consider him a threat to you or your family?"

Wes remained silent for a moment. "I never got that particular vibe from him. At least he never seemed to blame me for having any part in his incarceration. What few letters I got from him were pretty innocuous. Definitely not threatening." He paused for a moment. "Where are you going with this, Kate? Do I need to be worried? What's happened?"

"I don't know, Wes." The image of the note she'd gotten today floated through Kate's mind. "In the last few weeks, I've gotten two threatening notes. I thought the first one was for Emily and that I'd gotten it by mistake. But the second one came specifically addressed to me." She hesitated. "It seemed like something that Daniel might write. Or somebody like Daniel, at least. Does the phrase *Handmaiden of the Devil* have any significance to you?"

He sighed into the phone. "Oh, boy . . . that *does* sound familiar. Wait a second. I have my notes here." After a few moments of rustling papers, Wes spoke again, this time sounding much more serious. "Yeah, it's familiar. It was a term Gilroy used in reference to his wife, Connie."

Kate closed her eyes. Until this moment, the threat had been theoretical and the person behind it an anonymous, amorphous figure. But now Wes had offered some substantiation that the mystery man might indeed be Daniel Gilroy or at least somebody who knew him well enough to pick the same words to describe a woman. That was much scarier than an anonymous crazy writing her weird notes.

Kate squeezed the fear from her voice, unwilling to expose her weakness even to a good friend like Wes. "What a lovely nickname. Should I assume that he didn't get along with his wife?"

"They did at first, but it's a pretty sordid tale after the initial courtship. Connie was Daniel's father's assistant and instrumental in helping Gilroy Senior build his militia . . . er . . . flock. Then she married the elder Mr. Gilroy. But behind the old man's back, Connie helped Daniel engineer a takeover of the organization, pushing Gilroy Senior out. Then she divorced him and married Daniel."

"She sounds like a real charmer. And the family values for the group seem more than a little twisted."

"She was a real piece of work, all right. I think she was the one who made all the trouble go down in the end. It didn't take long for Daniel to realize he'd merely been her pawn. My theory is that she decided she needed to align with Daniel in order to get control from Gilroy Senior. But she must have figured it'd be easier to wrest control from Daniel than from Daniel's father. And it all would have worked except for the accident."

"What accident?"

"Connie and Gilroy Senior were killed in a car wreck two years before the infamous siege. The state troopers said it appeared as if they'd fought over control of the steering wheel, judging from scratches on Gilroy Senior's arms and the skin under Connie's fingernails. Pops lost control, drove off the road, and struck a tree head-on, killing them both. Daniel ended up with sole control of the militia without his father's help or Connie's organizational ability. In the two years he led the group, their numbers dwindled to about half the original size. They pretty much isolated themselves at the farmhouse to regroup."

"And now we don't even know if Gilroy is still in prison or not."

"Not right now, but it's easy enough to find out. I'm checking even as we speak. I just caught a friend of mine on instant messenger who works in Lorton at the correctional facility. He has access to the prison records from home and is looking for info on Gilroy right now."

"Thanks."

"And here comes the answer. . . . Let's see. . . ." There was a moment of eerie silence; then he spoke again. "Daniel Gilroy was released on parole right before Christmas."

"Oh, great." Her stomach flip-flopped. "So he *could* be the one sending the threats. But why me? Why am *I* suddenly getting these notes from him? I never even met the man. And you know how much I stay in the background. It seems like he'd be aiming at Emily, not me."

"Who knows? Maybe he's decided you're the Connie in the Emily equation—engineering the campaign from the sidelines but with an agenda of your own."

"But I don't have an agenda other than Emily's."

"I know, but we're talking about someone of questionable sanity who may be tempted to stretch an analogy beyond all recognition for the sake of justifying his delusions. Daniel was quite taken with Emily, even after his surrender to authorities. He thought, in his own words, that she was a 'mighty fine woman.' He failed to protect his father from the scheming Connie, so maybe he's planning to not make the same mistake again. Maybe he wants to protect Emily from the scheming you."

"But I'm not scheming."

"*I* know that. *You* know that. *Emily* knows that. But maybe *Daniel* doesn't know that. If this is Daniel at all. Look, have your security people contact John Ferguson at the Virginia Department of Corrections. I'll give him everything I have on Gilroy and explain the situation to him. If Gilroy contacts me, I'll tell the authorities everything he says."

"Thanks, Wes."

His voice softened. "Don't worry, Kate. Gilroy doesn't have a history of violence. If anyone is all bluster and no action, it's Daniel Gilroy."

"Are you sure?"

Wes lowered his voice. "Can I tell you a little secret? Remember at the cabin, years ago, when Emily pulled the clip from his gun?"

"Yes."

"Well, the clip was empty. The only bullet he had was in the chamber, and that was because he was too stupid to look there. The big militia man thought the gun he was waving around was unloaded. That's how nonthreatening he is."

Or how inept. Of course, that was several years ago. Hopefully, he'd not gotten any training on the darker arts in prison.

After thanking Wes once more, Kate hung up and immediately called Decker Bloom, the head of the security firm that handled all campaign security issues. After her explanation, Decker assured her that his people would investigate the Gilroy connection and beef up security around her, personally.

But to be doubly sure, Kate also called Agent McNally of the Secret Service and told him everything she knew. To her surprise, he already had information about Gilroy, since the man had been on their first-look list of "people of interest" after the first note had turned up.

"According to our intel, Gilroy is currently basking in the Florida sun, living with his older sister in her Sun City retirement apartment. We've had him under surveillance for some time now. I don't think he's any threat."

When Kate hung up, her heart rate dropped down from warp speed to merely insanely fast. With both sets of assurances, from Wes and from McNally, she realized she could afford to feel marginally better. Maybe, just maybe, she could concentrate on the dozen or so campaign reports that needed to be reviewed.

Instead of thinking about a lunatic coming to kill her.

She called room service, ordered a cheeseburger and fries, and after a second and third thought, plus a trip to the bathroom scale so thoughtfully provided by the hotel, she called back and added a chocolate sundae to her order.

Sometimes, a person just had to ignore the calories and splurge.

That night, Kate was almost asleep when Emily called with the day's update, giving a rundown of the good and less-than-good moments. But this time, she sounded different— she sounded . . . happy.

"M, you didn't drink a lot tonight, did you?" Kate tried to not sound suspicious.

"Not a drop, K. It's just that we had a really great day. Good venues. Great responses. I really felt like I reached the people today. I think . . . nope—I *know*." A note of awe crept into her voice. "I really believe we can pull this off."

If Kate had entertained any notion of mentioning Gilroy and the second threatening note to Emily, she decided against it then. The last thing she wanted to do was douse Emily's infectious enthusiasm and good mood.

Kate closed her eyes, sent up a quick, fervent prayer requesting guidance, and reached deep to tap what her mother always called the "Rosen Reservoir." She even found a bit of good humor stashed there as well as a sufficient amount of inner strength.

"Don't sound so surprised," she chided. "It's not like that wasn't our plan from the beginning. As that great Greek philosopher Homer said, 'D'oh!' You know you're going to win."

"Theoretically, sure. But now it's all coming together right in front of me. The people are responding. We're getting more enthusiastic crowds and bigger crowds—a lot bigger on this leg of the campaign."

"I'd say that's a pretty good return for the six million we invested in advertisement."

"Now, wait. Only half of that was Iowa. How's our other half of the investment going? How's New Hampshire?"

"Full of interesting people, one in particular." She almost said "two" but decided again not to burden Emily with the suspected antics of Poison-pen Gilroy—or whoever was writing the threatening letters.

"Who?" Emily demanded.

Kate drew a deep breath. "Nick."

There was silence on the other end.

"He asked for a meeting."

"Over my dead body," Emily said in an equally dead voice. "Better yet, over his dead body."

"He didn't want to talk to you. He wanted to meet with me."

More chilled silence.

Kate continued. "He called to arrange a meeting with me, and I agreed."

"Kathryn Marie Rosen," Emily began in warning, "you know how charming and slimy he is. You can't trust him. For heaven's sakes, don't meet with him."

Kate drew in a fortifying breath. "Too late. I already did."

Emily split the air with a single icy expletive.

"Don't worry. We met in a public place and all I did was listen to him. And his message was simple. He said, and I quote, 'I don't intend to use any insider knowledge I have of Emily to disrupt your campaign or cause her any personal grief.'"

"I'd like to cause him some personal grief," Emily grumbled. "Tell me you didn't believe that load of bull. Please?"

For some reason, Kate decided to not enlighten Emily concerning the news of Nick's newfound faith. It would only serve to rile her friend up even more.

"He's changed," Kate said. "He says he's been to AA."

"Considering that he was drinking his way straight to cirrhosis of the liver, good for him." Emily's ice-queen act began to melt under the heat of her sarcasm. "So he's, what? somewhere in step eight? making amends to all those folks he done wrong?" She affected a Southern accent. "Why,

Momma, Dah-dy, I so-o-o sorry I'm such a disappointment. Will y'all ever foh-give me?"

"Don't be crass," Kate scolded.

"If he's asking for apologies, why hasn't he called me? I figure I rank above you—probably even above Momma and Daddy—in the 'need to forgive' list."

Telling Emily that Nick's parents were both gone wouldn't help at all now. Emily had appeared to like them, even after she'd assigned Nick to the innermost ring of Dante's Inferno.

"Maybe he hasn't gotten that high in the to-do list yet," Kate said. "Or maybe he knows you're in no mood to listen. Not that I think it would be a good idea for you to talk with him. In any case, it appears Talbot has realized you're going to come out of Iowa as the winner and he's trying to get us to agree to a clean, positive campaign. After the primaries are over."

Emily chuckled. "This is really priceless. You know what this means, don't you?"

"Yeah. That he's already pegged you as the party's nominee."

"Well, there is that . . . but more importantly, he must know we found dirt on Talbot and now he's running scared." Emily began to speak faster as her sarcasm gave way to anger. "The only thing Talbot can think to do to stop us is to hire Nick as his not-so-secret weapon and then send him to you with his fake 'Let's keep it clean' message. This is just priceless."

Red-hot glee filled Emily's voice. "I am *so* going to love blowing that sanctimonious Talbot right out of the water. And if Nick is a not-so-innocent bystander in that explosion, all the better. Collateral damage."

"But—"

"But nothing. Talbot's plan to use Nick to throw me off my game is going to backfire in his face. Trust me, Chuck Talbot is going to rue the day he invited that snake into his camp." Emily released a belly laugh.

"But—," Kate started, but Emily interrupted her efforts again.

"Hush. This is rich. We don't even have to do anything, say anything, or use whatever it is that you found on him that you won't tell me about. All we have to do is simply sit back and watch it crumble from the inside."

"Whatever you say, M." But Kate wasn't sure she meant it.

KATE WISHED SHE COULD BE IN IOWA, if only to distract Emily from her fixation on her ex-husband and Charles Talbot. Emily may have needed Kate to help keep her impatience and her temper in check, but Kate needed to run New Hampshire while Emily concentrated on Iowa. It was hard to wait, even harder to stay in the Manchester headquarters on the actual day of the Iowa caucus.

Emily's campaign had everything riding on the results, and Kate felt almost as if she was shirking her duty by not being at Emily's side, even though she was pulling round-the-clock duty in New Hampshire.

This particular night, everyone in the New Hampshire office was staying late, wanting to be together to celebrate what they were sure was the upcoming victory in Iowa. Kate manned a direct connection via computer to the Iowa and Nevada headquarters as well as to the Virginia base camp so all four groups of the hot spots in Emily's campaign could stay in constant contact. So far, news from Iowa had been mixed but tending in Emily's favor.

Emily's top opponent had been Henderson. In his absence, a retired four-star air force general named Wright was expected to be her strongest contender in the state, according to media reports. In the credit column, the general had the bearing of a male authority figure, which appealed to the older party members, both male and female, plus he had a strong oratorical voice. When he said something, his ringing baritone made him sound as if he really meant it and so should you. On the negative side of the ledger, he came across to many younger voters as an autocrat, expecting everyone to jump whenever he issued an order. That impression might just be fact. Running his campaign like an extremely strict military organization, he'd limited his ability to adjust his plans to the rapidly changing political climate of the campaign.

In particular, he hadn't been able to turn and go after Emily full-time once Henderson had bowed out. And the lost opportunity might have done irreparable damage to his campaign efforts.

Media reports already suggested that Wright's ramrod, standoffish demeanor had played against him on the grassroots caucus trail, even to an Iowan public predisposed to liking the military.

Like his slogan said, "Wright is might" and don't you forget it. . . .

However, Iowa did.

The caucus entrance polls were substantiating the early media reports. The good people of Iowa had not been impressed with Wright's paternal but strict "I know what's best for America" pose. Emily's "We have a plan for America" concept had fared much better.

But not enough to be securely, clearly in first place.

At least not yet.

Early returns with only about a quarter of the precincts reporting put Emily in second place, trailing slightly behind Senator Burl Bochner but well ahead of General Michael Wright. Whether Emily would hold that position through the rest of the night or not, especially as the bigger urban precinct results rolled in, remained to be seen.

Emily had all but forecast Bochner's potential as the front-runner the day before. Bochner had been flexible and had come on fast once Henderson was out of the way. "The trouble is, he's a man advocating virtually the same things I am," she'd said. "He'll appeal to the same voters I do, but he'll score points off of their familiarity and comfort with male representation. Just like Henderson before him. I don't like this at all."

Kate knew her role in Emily's world was to point out the obvious. "But he's still a first-term senator. He has virtually no experience in Washington. You, on the other hand, know the Washington culture, the political clime, the names, the faces. You're a known quantity within and beyond the Beltway. You've seen what government's about nearly from the day you were born."

"Trust me—the folks in Iowa don't really care about the Beltway. To them it's just a highway with more traffic than they've ever seen before."

Ten minutes later, with 50 percent of the precincts reporting in, Emily had pulled into the lead.

An hour later, with 75 percent of the precincts' results,

Emily was ahead by a comfortable margin but not enough for her win to be considered a clear victory that would catapult her to the front-runner for the party at the convention. Theoretically it was still possible for her to fall behind, even in Iowa, but if the current trend held, she'd win.

But Emily wasn't ready to rest on her laurels for more than a few minutes. She called Kate back immediately. "I'd hoped to get a strong enough win here to blow out the rest of the competition, but Bochner has made a solid showing. We can't count him out or, for that matter, Wright either," Emily cautioned. "That's why I want you to look harder into both of—"

"Stop," Kate commanded. "Don't say it. This is not the time. We need to count our positives. The volunteers, not to mention the field office staff, have been working awfully hard for you. You need to let them celebrate *their* victory, as much as yours. And to do that, you need to celebrate with them. Janis and I had a long talk about timing. She'll give you the cue when your win is made official and when it's time to go into the ballroom for the hoopla. Are you comfortable with the speech?"

There was a burst of noise in the background. Kate looked at the television screen and saw that the network news had cut into regular programming. She turned up the volume slightly. "This is an NBC News special report."

The camera cut to the national news desk in New York. "This is George Lacken reporting. With 85 percent of the precincts reporting in, it appears as if Emily Benton, the former governor of Virginia, has won her party's Iowa caucus in what our experts are calling a guarded victory."

"Guarded?" Emily growled in her ear.

"Iowa is a critical first step to Ms. Benton's winning the party's presidential nomination, and she's expected to hold her own in Michigan, now that Senator Mark Henderson has pulled out of the race," the newsreader intoned. "Former Governor Benton comes from a family with a long history in American politics. Her father was the late House Representative Henry Benton, perhaps best known as the man who intercepted would-be presidential assassin Edward David Sharbles and took a bullet meant for President Haynes. Her uncle is former President William R. Benton and—"

The echoing voice from Emily's phone died down as she evidently muted the sound on the television. Kate did as well.

Emily sighed. "One of these days, they're going to talk about me without trotting out my family's bloody laundry. Sure, I'm proud of what the Bentons have done, but I'd rather not have Dad's death mentioned every time somebody runs a clip of me on television."

"I don't blame you, but you know the media." Kate changed the subject as quickly as she could, not wanting to feed into Emily's foul mood. "Even though they're supposed to be all about 'news,' they love to tell a story they've told a thousand times before. Forget them, M. Go out there and be a gracious winner for the people who supported you."

"Yeah, yeah. For the little people. Yada yada."

Kate ignored Emily's complaint. "Hey, I haven't congratulated you yet. It's a big first step, but you did it. Congratulations."

Emily was silent for a moment; then she spoke softly, no longer talking to her campaign manager but to her oldest and best friend. "Big Henry would be proud of me, wouldn't he?"

Kate knew the politically correct answer. But it happened to be the truth as well. "Your dad was always proud of you, Emily, win or lose; you know that. Tonight you won. Go make nice with the cameras."

"Thanks, K," Emily whispered. She sniffed and then her voice grew stronger. "After today, the Benton legacy won't be all about bloody laundry."

"It sure won't. Now go smile at the cameras." Kate hung up.

Bloody laundry, indeed.

Like most of America, Kate would never forget the day of Big Henry's death. But unlike most of America, Kate was supposed to have been there, standing in the crowd next to the man, taking advantage of having a college roommate who was a member of the best known political family in the United States. It'd been Kate's bad luck to get a stomach virus the day before. So instead of a front-row seat, hopefully witnessing history in the making, Kate had stayed home, trying to keep saltines down, and watched the event on C-SPAN.

Later that night, when Emily finally got home, she gave Kate a highly detailed, up close version of the day's events. She seemed to have a cathartic need to purge herself of the memories. A burden shared . . .

Between Emily's personal account and what Kate saw in live coverage and endless replays, she had a good idea of what had happened. . . .

✯ ✯ ✯ ✯ ✯

It was April.

Emily and Kate had both been looking forward to their

upcoming summer jobs on the Hill, interning as legal researchers for the Honorable Matthew R. Benton, member of the U.S. House of Representatives, aka Emily's cousin Mattie.

However, it wasn't their new positions that was providing them a chance to stand on the steps of the Capitol and witness what was being touted as an historical appearance by the president. It had been an invitation from Emily's father, Big Henry, one of the most powerful lobbyists in the District. Kate was at home, kicking herself for missing the opportunity of a lifetime to be in such august company and see the president in person as he signed a major bill. Emily had promised to tell her everything.

She eventually did.

The weather had cooperated with clear skies, a strong sun, and pleasant temperatures in the low seventies. A good-size crowd of dignitaries framed the tableau, the front left open for the media and spectators, held at bay by a defensive line of Secret Service agents.

Sitting in bed, Kate watched as the camera panned across the throng. She easily spotted Big Henry. His nickname had more to do with the amount of power he wielded than his towering height, but he still stood well over six feet tall. Emily stood to his side, sedately dressed for the event in a conservative burgundy suit. She'd wanted to wear a bright red dress, but Kate had talked her out of it. Emily's youth, her attractiveness, and her blonde hair were enough to make her stand out in that sea of older, dark-suited men. After the Great Clothing Debate, she and Emily had settled on something "Not black, not navy, not gray. . . . And absolutely no pinstripes."

Years later, when Emily's internal censors had shut down for the night thanks to a very large quantity of tequila shooters, she'd bemoaned the fact that she hadn't worn a pastel pink outfit instead.

"It would have shown the blood better," Emily had declared in a slightly slurred whisper. The next morning, she either didn't remember having said it or chose to forget that she had. Emily never mentioned it again and neither did Kate.

Standing at a podium, the president had made his remarks concerning the bill he was about to sign, which mandated a cut in farm subsidies. He cited the inordinate number of large corporations that had replaced the family farms—the original intended recipients of subsidies. Plus, he alluded to the vast amount of crops the U.S. exported overseas. Yet there were food shortages within America's borders. His points were valid but so had been the points of those opposing the bill. The vocal opposition protesting the loss in their subsidies had been forced to stand behind barricades a safe distance away. The separation had kept their complaints at this photo op down to a minor roar and their faces out of the frame.

The right time to protest, Kate knew, had been long before the bill was being signed.

But some people never learned. . . .

Kate figured that a public signing, although rare, was this administration's way of thumbing its nose in public at its detractors. This was a Benton accomplishment too, not just the president's alone. It had been Big Henry's lobbying efforts that had pushed the bill through both sides of Congress, and his influence and power had brought the bill to the steps of the Capitol for the president to sign. Big

Henry had sat down months ago and, in confidence, explained to Emily and Kate exactly what steps he would take to assure the bill would pass. Typical of Big Henry, it had been the sort of eye-opening lesson in practical politics that was rarely taught in classrooms. Kate knew just how many lessons like that Emily had witnessed, simply as a result of being her father's child.

Emily's political education had begun in the cradle, in Kate's opinion. And Kate couldn't think of a tougher school.

On that day, as the president moved from the podium to the signing table, there was a commotion in the crowd. Someone shouted several expletives. Heads turned, attracting the attention of the Secret Service. One man pushed the president down. Most of the agents moved in the direction of the disturbance. That was when a second man emerged from the other side of the crowd, his gun raised. The sound of his threats was lost in the larger noise of the first disturbance.

Only Emily's father seemed to have seen the man in time to react. Big Henry lunged forward, intercepting the would-be assassin by wrapping big beefy arms around the man and letting his weight and momentum pull the man down to the hard granite steps. Big Henry's actions evidently spoiled the shooter's aim.

The first bullet struck the podium.

When other people, including Secret Service agents, were moving away from the struggle, Emily moved toward her father, but her cousin Matthew, who stood just behind her, grabbed her arm and kept her from entering the fray.

Big Henry and the assassin struggled for the gun.

There was a second muffled pop.

That bullet struck Big Henry point-blank in the chest.

By then, Secret Service agents were running straight for the shooter, but they were too late.

Although fatally injured, Big Henry still kept his arms around the assassin, refusing to release him until the Secret Service agents disarmed and cuffed him.

Once relieved of his duty, Big Henry collapsed.

He was dead before the shooter hit the ground beside him.

Kate could never forget the image, frozen in her mind forever, immortalized in wire report photos, in the evening news, and in every newspaper across America and the world.

Big Henry.

Lying on his back, staring blankly into the noonday sun.

The most famous footage of the tragedy showed his still body, the only movement being that of his blood, which had pooled beneath him and was cascading like a scarlet river down the white granite steps. It was a visual that Kate and most Americans would never forget.

Emily tore herself free of her cousin's grasp and ran to begin CPR on her father.

Two of the congressmen in attendance were medical doctors and they immediately rushed to Big Henry's side to help.

It was already too late.

Later, the autopsy would show that the bullet had hit Henry dead center in the heart, obliterating the organ. And yet, he'd held on to the assassin, not because death had frozen his arms in place, but because even though his heart had stopped, his brain had insisted on continuing its mission: don't let the man kill the president.

Emily remained beside her father, crying but not hysterical to the point of uselessness. Instead of being a distraught and overwrought daughter who had to be prevented from interfering with lifesaving measures, Emily spelled the doctors as they all continued to attempt resuscitation. When she was pushed down by the Secret Service, who were worried that other assassins might still lurk in the crowd, she relented but stayed close to her father, whispering soft encouragements in his ear as if her outpouring of love would help him hang on to life.

America had watched as one doctor reached over and grasped the arm of the other, then shook his head. *It's no use*. It had been eerily easy to read his lips. *He's gone*.

One astute news photographer won a Pulitzer for his shot of Emily at that moment, next to her dead father, her young and beautiful face twisted by devastation, fear, and anguish.

And her hands, still coated with his blood, reaching for her father.

From that moment on, America knew the name and face of Emily Benton. They'd witnessed and shared her pain. They considered her a heroine and branded her father an American hero. His full and fascinating life as a political power broker was eclipsed in the public eye by his last selfless act, a split-second move that saved the president's life.

America also knew the name Edward David Sharbles, the man who tried to kill President Haynes. Instead, Sharbles murdered prominent Virginian citizen and Washington power broker Henry W. Benton.

A high school dropout, Eddie Sharbles was the son of an East Texas farmer who was barely making a living raising feed crops. By Eddie's narrow interpretation of the bill, the reduction of farm subsidies would put his father out of business, and they would lose the land that had been in their family for four generations. Eddie's overly simplistic solution was to use a gun to prevent the president from signing the bill. His plan had been to force him to tear it up instead.

In his off-kilter logic, the destruction of the actual paperwork of the bill would have ended his family's problems.

When interrogated, he'd reportedly been shocked that anyone had thought he had gone there with the idea of killing the president. He'd simply needed the gun as leverage. Only, he didn't understand the word *leverage*. His defense attorney had supplied that word and then had to explain its meaning to his client. Unable to understand the concept, Sharbles clarified his motives by saying he knew he needed to bully President Haynes and he had simply chosen the same weapon to bully the president as had been used against him by other bullies. His family, aware of his intellectual shortcomings—reportedly due to medical difficulties during his birth—had never anticipated Eddie would go to such illogical and unexpected extremes to try to help them with their problems. Neighbors were quoted as saying, "He was always such a good boy," the hallmark of Heisman Trophy winners and serial killers alike.

But none of the posttrauma revelations and deconstructions of motive and opportunity would bring Big Henry Benton back from the dead.

In Kate's studied opinion, Emily changed that day. Sure, before her father's death she'd always voiced dreams of holding political office someday. But after the shooting, her aspirations solidified, and her ambition went into overdrive.

Her hazy dreams, as well as her political acumen, grew sharper and more focused.

Kate decided Emily's renewed dedication was an understandable reaction to her father's death. To Emily's credit, she didn't allow ambition to completely replace her sorrow but instead used the power of her grief to fuel her refocused ambition. As a result, she became a real shark in law school, not necessarily ruthless but unwilling to put up with unnecessary obstacles or people who tried to stand in her way. Luckily, Kate could keep up with her, and she managed to remain in Emily's good graces through school and well beyond, becoming Emily's silent partner in law school, then in politics, and always in the bonds of friendship.

Until tonight, they'd celebrated every victory together as a team. State senator. Lieutenant governor. Governor. Kate felt a little lost, having to remotely join in the excitement of Emily's first presidential primary win on what had been and still remained a very long road to the White House.

As Kate watched the bedside clock in her New Hampshire hotel room change from 11:59 to 12:00, she told herself there would be more victories ahead to share. If everything went as planned, exactly one year and sixteen days from now, Emily would be sworn into office as president of the United States.

Kate rolled over in bed, hugged her pillow, and smiled herself to sleep.

By noon the next day, the two last-place finishers in Iowa's primary had announced their withdrawal from the presidential race. Neither had been serious contenders for president, so it was no surprise to Kate, who had written them off days ago after seeing how little time and money they'd spent wooing the good people of Iowa and Nevada, Michigan and New Hampshire, Florida and South Carolina. The early primaries were important, and each one had to receive Emily's full attention, which is exactly what she and her staff had given them, even if two of the states had favored sons.

Now only six candidates remained for the party's nomination, including Emily.

And Tsunami Tuesday, February 5, was looming large.

What bothered Kate most was Burl Bochner's campaign. As Emily had mentioned, the major difference between Burl and Emily wasn't agenda, per se, but gender. But in addition to his political platform and all-American clean-cut looks, Bochner also had a photogenic wife and three adorable moppets. Or maybe they were Muppets. They certainly weren't human, not with their cherubic expressions, freshly pressed clothes, and ability to deliver sound bites that would make the most hardened member of the press corps grin.

Kate had actually witnessed the children, little more than toddlers, sit still for hours in the hot sun at political rallies without throwing a single tantrum. In fact, they hadn't even fidgeted or broken a sweat.

She'd concluded at the time that they must have been Robo-Kids.

Kate had only just learned that the oldest Bochner offspring had been left home with his grandparents for this leg of the campaign, ostensibly because, as a high schooler, he couldn't be as easily schooled on the campaign trail as his younger, elementary-age siblings. Kate, suspecting that there was more behind that reason, had done some digging. She'd discovered that the eldest Bochner boy had been in some minor trouble with the law; he'd been cited for street racing on two occasions and had been questioned three times concerning the appearance of graffiti on a nearby municipal water tower.

At least his alleged graffiti artwork had been in support of his father's political ambitions. It was nice to see he had done his bit for the good of the campaign.

With no evidence of drug use or underage drinking, such minor transgressions weren't the sort of information the press could or would use against his father. As far as Kate was concerned, every candidate's minor children were sacrosanct. If she needed dirt on the candidate, she'd go after the grown-ups.

After much soul-searching, Kate had come to terms with the use of research into Emily's political opponents in the course of the election. In light of what had happened to Henderson and his wife, Kate had decided that she needed to look just as thoroughly at the spouses as she did the candidates. Had she done so, then maybe all of them would have realized that Henderson's wife had been far more fragile than they'd ever imagined.

Thanks to the Internet, background facts and details could be more easily checked, and lies and sins of omission caught faster.

Following her ironclad policy, Kate vowed to acquire the information honestly and to use it ethically and truthfully. After that, all bets were off.

And may God have mercy on her soul.

So, as the campaign heated up, Bochner's wife, Dr. Melissa

Bonner-Bochner, was fair game. However, she appeared to be everything she was cracked up to be—a devoted wife as well as a college professor of engineering on sabbatical in order to support her husband's presidential bid. Her family loved her; her fellow academicians loved her; her students loved her; the charities for which she tirelessly worked loved her. . . .

She'd make a great First Lady, Robo-Kids aside.

Unfortunately, Emily had no potential First Gentleman in tow, great or otherwise. But to her surprise, Bochner had been frankly and publicly supportive of Emily's single status. Kate had a sneaking suspicion that the highly independent Dr. Bonner-Bochner might have influenced her husband's opinion.

Kate closed her laptop. Evidently the battle with Bochner would be played aboveground in the bright New Hampshire sun.

If they ever saw the sun. . . .

It'd been snowing off and on all morning as bands of bad weather passed through the New England area. Emily was due to land in an hour if the next threatening storm held off.

Her upcoming speaking schedule was an ambitious one, but that would be true for every schedule for the next ten months. Emily was slated to spend two days in New Hampshire covering fourteen different events and speaking engagements. Then she'd fly overnight to Nevada, where she'd spend two cram-packed days in Reno, Carson City, Laughlin, and Las Vegas, ending in a candidates' debate. Once she returned to New Hampshire, she'd do another whirlwind tour of the state, hitting every possible hamlet, and then cap off the campaign by participating in yet another candidates' debate the night before the primary.

Senator Bochner, like Emily, had worked two days into his schedule to stump in Nevada. The other four candidates evidently belonged to the school of tradition and were concentrating solely on the New Hampshire primary, which, in Kate's opinion, was a strategic mistake. Even if Senator Hyde of Nevada was a shoo-in to win his own state, the candidate who took second place would be extremely important in terms of maintaining momentum.

☆　☆　☆　☆　☆

Sure enough, when Emily emerged from the Nevada caucus in second place with a one point lead over Burl Bochner, the network news pundits ignored Hometown Hyde's expected win and concentrated on what they called the more important second-place race.

Emily left Nevada an hour after the totals were announced and arrived in New Hampshire six hours later, just in time to start the day. Kate gave her a short debrief, then bundled her off to start the grind all over again.

Despite the lack of a full night's sleep, Emily arrived at her morning meetings looking fresh, alert, and every inch a presidential potential. It wasn't until she reached the third afternoon meeting that she hit the wall.

"I don't think I can take another step." Emily took another chug from her bottle of water, stifled a yawn, and slumped in her seat toward the limo door. "If I could just get a twenty-minute nap . . ."

Kate noted the tremor in her friend's hand and the circles under her eyes and made a command decision. With one phone call, Kate arranged for Emily to cut short her next engagement—a coffee shop appearance—and to delay her arrival at the next location, thus creating a thirty-minute gap in an otherwise impenetrable schedule. She even made sure Emily was served decaf at the coffee shop.

During that break, Emily stretched out across the backseat of the limo and took a fast nap, from which she emerged looking remarkably revived. A quick refresh of her makeup and she was off to meet a group of high school teachers to discuss her "Value Education, Value Educators" program.

Kate, on the other hand, didn't have time for a rest. By eight o'clock that night, she was feeling a sense of malaise that she feared was evidence of something a simple nap wouldn't fix.

In the wee hours of the next morning, Kate's worst fears came true. Even as she curled up on the bathroom floor, fighting yet another wave of nausea, she ran through a mental checklist, planning a work-around for her absence from the morning events. Neither the flu nor food poisoning could completely stop her, not as important as her duties were.

Once she was able to drag herself back to the bed and the hotel room stopped spinning, she spent the next fifteen minutes figuring out a contingency plan that spread her day's duties across the entire staff. Then she sent text messages to various campaign personnel, giving them the temporary assignments. Her last message was to Emily, informing her of the problem and the alternative plans that were now in place.

Finally Kate fell asleep.

When she awoke at noon, she marveled that the room was no longer revolving in swooping circles and her stomach wasn't lurching.

She got up, found her footing, and went into the bathroom to splash water on her face before tackling the fifteen messages waiting for her on her cell phone. Most were from the people she'd texted, acknowledging that they would cover for her and offering wishes of a speedy recovery.

The voice messages from Emily went from understanding to progressively panicked.

Message two: "Hey, this is Emily. I got your message. Don't worry. David is supposed to be here shortly, and until he lands, Alex will cover for you."

Message seven: "David's plane was delayed in Philadelphia. Alex is still covering."

Message nine: "Whatever you do, call me before you turn on the news."

Kate's stomach immediately clenched again.

KATE TURNED THE TELEVISION ON just in time to watch the view switch from a well-known news anchor in his shirtsleeves to an on-site reporter from a local Manchester affiliate.

"—outside of the New Hampshire headquarters for presidential candidate Charles Talbot, where approximately thirty minutes ago, an unidentified gunman entered the building and began firing. One campaign worker was killed and two others injured. Governor Talbot was not present at the time. He was speaking at the morning service at Antioch Baptist Church. Officials say that the gunman escaped in the resulting melee and is still at large. The names of the deceased and injured have not yet been released. But we do know that the victims were transported to Catholic Medical for treatment."

They switched to a split screen with the network studio, the field reporter relegated to the right-hand side.

"Carl, have they released any information about the gunman?" the anchor asked.

"All we've been told is that he's a white male between the ages of forty-five and fifty-five, wearing jeans, a white T-shirt, a navy blue jacket, and a red ball cap with a black insignia. Probably the most bizarre aspect of the case is that witnesses say the shooter's shirt read *V4M*, which as you know is the text slogan meaning 'Vote for M' in reference to current front-runner in this race, Emily Benton. Ms. Benton's camp has not released a statement as of yet, but officials believe that the gunman was acting on his own volition and isn't directly connected with former Governor Benton's campaign."

Kate turned off the television, walked into the bathroom, turned on the shower, and stepped—pajamas and all—into the icy cold stream of water.

For once, she was relatively certain this disaster wasn't her fault. But that didn't make it any less a disaster, so she prayed for those injured and for the family of the dead campaign worker.

Then she got to work.

Twenty minutes and four terse calls with Emily later, Kate sat in the New Hampshire campaign headquarters, hair still damp, sipping a mug of weak tea and fighting a rising nausea that wasn't food related. While riding over in the cab, she had dictated a first draft media response over the phone to the main headquarters in Virginia. Once she arrived at the office in Manchester, it'd been nearly impossible to get through the gauntlet of media that waited outside the front entrance. The last thing she'd wanted them to think was that her ragged looks were due to fear rather than food poisoning. An off-duty Manchester cop and campaign volunteer had given her safe passage through a back door, unseen by the hungry press corps.

Once inside, she isolated herself in the conference room and hammered out a second draft of the statement, then e-mailed it to the Benton inner circle of legal, political, and media advisers who were already on e-mail alert. They vetted it, made changes particular to their own expertise, and sent their recommendations back to her in record time.

Now she sat at the conference table, staring bleakly at the finished product as the words on the page swam in and out of her vision. The statement covered the salient points without sounding overly defensive. Another key to not looking or sounding defensive would be to have someone other than Emily make the statement. If folks at the various campaign stops asked her specifically about the attack, Emily would make the appropriately sympathetic remarks and say a statement was forthcoming.

Even during the best of times, Kate didn't want to face the press, but in her current condition? No way. But Dave Dickens would be there shortly. He would be the one to deal with the cameras and deliver the press release.

Kate and Emily had courted Dave for their staff not only because of his rock solid experience running the campaign for the Democratic candidate in the 2004 race but also because Dave had the polished delivery and trustworthy looks of a network news anchor. Most people believed he was working for Emily solely so he could become the next White House press secretary. But Kate knew Dave's real goal was to make the jump from his current position to a network news desk. She thought his chances of doing that were pretty good. His odds would get even better once Emily became president.

Plus, it wouldn't hurt them to have a familiar face who admired their politics riding a network anchor desk once Emily got into office.

Dave dashed in moments later, changed into a crisp white shirt, and reviewed the copy for all of five minutes. Then he stood in front of the cameras and delivered the statement flawlessly—almost without consulting his notes—to the platoon of reporters who had been camped out by the main entrance, awaiting an official response from the Benton camp. After presenting the statement, he deftly sidestepped the persistent souls who clamored for more information by pleading ignorance of the actual details of the crime and referring any subsequent inquiries to the Talbot camp, the hospital, or the local police.

"Let me close this press conference by saying that Ms. Benton, along with her staff, extends her deepest sympathies to the family of the deceased, to those injured in this terrible tragedy, and to their families. We'll keep all of them in our hearts and our prayers. Thank you."

The last bit was an ad lib but a suitable one in context, even if anyone who really knew Emily wouldn't use her name and the word *prayer* in the same sentence.

Bentons didn't pray for things to happen. They made them happen.

Once the press had their ration of attention, the glory hogs drifted away, allowing the headquarters staff to get back to the business of conducting the campaign, watched from a distance only by the serious political reporters. Even the seasoned pros understood when Kate issued the order to bar them for the day.

Still feeling under the weather, she retreated to Alex's

corner office, where she commandeered his couch as her recovery center.

After a while, Dave came in to check on her. "You look terrible," he said from the doorway. "Can I get you anything? Hair of the dog?"

"I'm not hungover," she said, pushing herself to a semi-upright position. "I got food poisoning or something last night."

"Or something," he echoed, his grin more teasing than doubtful. "Like out-and-out exhaustion. Seriously, can I get you some tea or a Coke?"

"Thanks, but no thanks. Have they released the names of the victims?"

"Not yet. And no one in the Talbot camp is talking. Of course, they don't talk to us during the best of times. But they're not talking to my buddies in the press, either. They've battened down the hatches over there, I think."

"Let me know if you hear anything."

"Will do." As he turned to leave, he paused to shoot her a sympathetic look over his shoulder. "All kidding aside, if there's anything I can do for you, please let me know. We can't afford to have our fearless leader working at less than 100 percent." He lowered his voice to a conspiratorial stage whisper. "Emily may think she's in charge, but we know who the real power is. . . ."

Ugh.

What a thought.

And what a burden. . . .

Was she really that central to the campaign?

And if she was, what did it mean for this moment?

Alone again, Kate debated whether she should contact

Nick. After the shooting, he was probably knee-deep in cops, hysterical volunteers, and who knew what. And did she really want to make a habit of talking to the opposition at the drop of a hat?

Then again, having a madman with a gun shoot the place up wasn't exactly a drop of the hat.

Given the circumstances, though, she felt like she should contact Nick. She wanted him to know that Emily's campaign really didn't send idiots with guns to take out their opponents.

Kate compromised between her urge to touch base and her cautious side by sending Nick a text message. `Hope U R OK. Call if we` . . . She changed it to `I can help.`

Five minutes later, her cell phone rang.

"K?" It was Nick and he didn't sound good at all.

Poor guy.

What could she say?

In the end, she went with "How's it going over there?"

There was a sudden flare-up of voices in the background. "Hang on and let me go someplace quieter." A few moments later, the noise abated. "That's better. Sorry. I've had better days."

"What happened?"

"Pretty much what you've heard on TV. Some idiot with a semiautomatic came in and started shooting, strafing the place. He hit three people and one of them died—one of our local staffers."

"I'm so sorry."

"Me too. It was mass bedlam. People screaming, the gun firing, glass breaking." His raspy voice grew softer. "It's like I'll never get the sounds out of my head. The only good thing to come out of the horror is that I know I'm Christian now. I prayed like I've never prayed before, for everybody, even the shooter. And when that campaign worker was dying in front of me . . . and I couldn't do anything to help . . ."

Her stomach tightened. "How bad is it? Should you even be on the phone right now?"

"Probably not." He paused, then added in almost a conspiratorial tone, "I'm one of the ones that got hit."

The phone nearly slipped out of her grasp. "Nick! Are you okay?"

"I'm fine; I'm fine. I caught one in the arm, but it only grazed me." He released a short bark of tense laughter, then a grunt of pain. "Funny word—*grazed*. Like that makes it hurt any less. But I suppose it could be lots worse. I lived."

"Where are you now?"

"In the lobby outside the ER. They've just discharged me and I'm waiting for the car to come around to pick me up. I can't wait to get back to the hotel and take one of the horse pills the doc gave me. According to him, I'll be out the rest of the day."

"What about the other person who was hit? Who was it?"

There was a brief period of silence. Then he spoke. "I . . . I can't say. The police don't want us to mention any names. They haven't been able to reach his family yet. You understand, right? And you can't mention me either. We're keeping my injury under wraps."

"Of course." It was her turn to hesitate. The question had to be asked, and although this was probably not the best time or the best situation, at least it wasn't the worst. She closed her eyes and plunged ahead. "Nick, they mentioned the shirt the man was wearing. You don't . . . you don't think that we—that Emily has anything to do with this, do you?"

His lack of response was deafening as well as frightening.

"Oh, c'mon. You can't believe . . ." She started again. "We've handed out thousands of those shirts across the nation and sold tens of thousands of them on our Web site. Just because the gunman was wearing one of them . . ."

More silence.

Rising frustration made her stomach clench in protest. "Nick, if nothing else, you can't possibly believe that *I'd* have anything to do with this, do you?"

He finally responded. "You? Of course not, Kate. But Emily? I can't be sure. After all, the last time our paths crossed, she threatened to shoot me if she saw me again."

"Now you're just being ridiculous. You know she didn't mean it literally."

"Do I? Look at what she did to me after our big blowout. And more recently, what she did to Mark Henderson. The woman doesn't make idle threats. If she wants someone out of the way, she'll find a way to remove them from the equation."

Kate's stomach did a somersault and she clutched the phone harder for fear of dropping it. What did he know about their involvement with Henderson's withdrawal?

A new flare of pain sliced through her. She hated playing games with the facts.

"Emily didn't *do* anything to Mark Henderson," she said. That was a technical truth, at least.

"Okay, we'll play it that way. In any case, I'm not going to argue with you. All I know is that when the gunman came into the office, the staff had already pegged him as either a

troublemaker or a kook. One of the staffers had been outside and watched him zip his jacket to cover up the Benton
T-shirt, so they figured he'd shown up to be simply a pain in
the neck—you know, disrupt the office.

"We let the guy come in, figuring we could film it and use
it against you guys, maybe post it on YouTube. We expected a
stupid stunt but not a harmful one. He didn't say anything—
just stood there looking a little crazy and lost. So the staff
decided to boot him out of there. But when they asked him to
leave, he pulled out the gun and started taking potshots."

Kate heard a noticeable tremor in his voice.

"But here's the scary part. When he walked in there, he
asked to speak to me. He didn't ask for Chuck Talbot. He
asked for me—used my full name. The receptionist even told
him she didn't think they had anyone named Beaudry working there. Nobody among the campaign's volunteer staff
knows who I really am. As far as they're concerned, I'm just
some guy named Nick and they have no idea why I'm here.
The press hasn't even stumbled onto my connection with
Talbot's campaign yet. Only you and Emily know that I'm
working for Chuck."

"You can't believe—"

"Sure I can," he said, not letting her finish. "I know exactly how much M hated me, how much she still hates me.
She's a Benton. Bentons don't forget, and they definitely
don't forgive. If you were me, wouldn't you be more than a
bit suspicious today?"

Indignation swelled inside her, filling the places that guilt
had hollowed out. "Nick, I promise you, before God, that
Emily had absolutely nothing to do with this. And you know
I wouldn't lie to you."

"Can you be sure?" He didn't sound convinced. "Listen, Kate, I know you well enough to be sure you had nothing to do with any plans she had to hang Mark Henderson out for public humiliation. You wouldn't have stood for it. Everybody knows he could have been nailed on the bribery charges alone. And that's probably what you advised, right? But no, M had to go for the kill, didn't she? If I know her—and trust me, I do—then I'm sure she orchestrated the whole ugly thing behind your back. Got those tapes into Henderson's wife's hands, didn't she? In the worst possible way? Right?"

Kate clamped her mouth shut. What could she say that wouldn't make this worse?

"Look, Kate, I trust you. You've always played straight with me even when I didn't deserve it. You play fair in politics, too. So I know you'd never have gone along with a media attack on Henderson's private life, much less arrange a physical attack on me. But what makes you so sure Emily didn't plan, coordinate, and execute something like this without your knowledge?"

"She couldn't have," Kate said.

"Are you sure? Like I said, she's done it before."

He's just fishing, her conscience cried. Despite his bravado, Nick couldn't possibly have any proof concerning Emily's involvement in Henderson's scandals. If Nick had a shred of proof, he would have brought it to Talbot's attention or, better yet, to the media's attention. And somebody surely would have used it against Emily by now.

Unless Nick's plans are to create maximum exposure and the greatest damage after the primaries, when it'll be a head-to-head race between the two candidates from the major parties . . .

Nick interrupted her thoughts. "Just think about it, okay, K? You tend to wear blinders when it comes to Emily." There was a noise in the background. "It's part of your charm. I gotta go. Ride's here," he grunted. "Talk to you later."

"I'm glad you're okay," Kate said. She hesitated. "I'll pray for you and the others."

Nick released a ragged sigh. "Thanks. So will I."

Kate closed her phone and grasped it in a white-knuckled fist. There was no way on God's green earth that Emily had done anything like hiring or otherwise coercing a mono-grammed gunman into attacking Talbot headquarters. It was crass, risky, and downright stupid. Emily might be crafty; she might have taken a calculated risk or two . . . dozen in her lifetime; but no one could ever call her stupid.

And having the gunman wear a Vote for Emily shirt while carrying out the attack was much too stupid for anything her friend might pull.

Kate's conscience swiftly added, *Not that Emily'd ever send a gunman . . . even if it wasn't stupid.*

But Kate's thoughts drifted back to Nick's cryptic com-ment: *"Look what she did to me after our big blowup."*

Exactly what *had* Emily done to him?

Kate rose from the couch, moved somewhat unsteadily to the door, and locked it. Once she reached the relative safety of the couch again, she speed-dialed Lee Devlin's home number. The phone rang several times before a young child answered, "Devlin residence."

"May I speak to your mother, please?"

Although the voice was that of a six- or seven-year-old, the child had obviously been taught phone manners. "Who is calling, please?"

"Tell her it's Kate Rosen. Thanks."

"Hang on." A second later, a small hand failed to cover the receiver well enough. Kate heard a bellowing "Mom! It's for you. . . ."

After a few moments, Lee picked up. "I got it in my office. Thanks, Sarah," she said with obvious affection to the messenger. After a click, signaling that the child had hung up, the tone of Lee's voice changed completely. "Now remind me again why I gave you my home number?" she complained. "This had better be good."

"You're not watching television."

"No. I was in the middle of making my daughter a snack. What now?"

"About two hours ago, a gunman opened fire in Charles Talbot's New Hampshire headquarters. One killed, two injured. Luckily Talbot wasn't there."

Lee murmured something under her breath.

Kate continued. "This next part doesn't go beyond you and me, okay?"

"Agree."

"Nick Beaudry was one of the injured. According to him, the gunman asked for him by name."

"Beaudry was there? Since when did he start hanging around Charles Talbot? I thought we were looking at him simply because he was one of Emily's loose ends."

Kate ignored her question. Even if Lee had already drawn a line between fact A and person B, their standing confidentiality agreement would keep her from spreading the news. But that wasn't Kate's concern now. "Lee, when you were investigating Nick, how far back did you go?"

"Hmmm . . . let me log in to the office's database. Hang

on." She was on the phone again in less than a minute. "For your most recent request, I only went back four or so years. But our files actually go back to the original request you made when he started dating Emily. You know, the typical background stuff—nothing too checkered beyond the usual cockeyed Louisiana politics. Sure, we knew he drank a bit more than could be considered merely recreational, but that wasn't the sort of glaring flaw we were looking for. I did scan the older files this last time around, but I spent most of my time on his postdivorce life, with a heavy concentration concerning his private life in the past four years."

"Do you have any data on the time period immediately around the big breakup with Emily?"

"You mean the brouhaha at the party or his arrest the next day?"

"Give me everything you've got, including what led up to the arrest. ASAP."

"Sure. Listen, if I remember right, Sierra has some sealed documents not included in this file. As soon as I get ahold of her, I should be able to have her unlock them and I can report those back to you as well. But while I'm waiting, I'll dig in and see what I can reconstruct."

"Thanks."

Kate spent the rest of the day conducting damage control. There were two basic ways to do that—either patch the holes and hope the resulting fix would hold or distract the media with something more interesting. In most cases, a carefully calculated leak or two would redirect the media into "straying" in more controlled territory. But there were precious few things to reveal about a woman who had practically grown up in the public eye.

At least, few things that the Benton campaign really wanted to bring to light.

For instance, Kate absolutely didn't want to bring up the "what Daddy did to me in Mexico" story. It would only play well as a last-stand defense against speculations—make that *accusations*—about the real reasons behind Nick and Emily's childless state.

And no one needed to know about the DUI that Emily had sidestepped in New Orleans. At the time, even Kate hadn't known her friend had the forethought to carry a second wallet that contained a series of bogus IDs supporting a completely faked identity. It was awfully easy to sidestep criminal liability when all the paperwork was filled out in a fictitious name. It only took a small bribe a day later by a friend of the family to facilitate removing the fingerprints of "Olivia Davis" from the system.

As far as Emily was concerned, the DUI had never happened. And the lack of evidence completely supported her. As far as Kate was concerned, that little dodge had given her sleepless nights, but she had justified it because she knew Emily only drank for effect. She never indulged privately and never to excess. For Emily to have overdone it, she had to have been dealing with some major issues. The problems with Nick had pushed her into behaviors she had never exhibited before or since that awful time.

Then there was the plagiarism scandal. In that particular situation, Emily really hadn't done anything wrong . . . at least initially. Emily had simply been the individual who'd recognized the striking similarities between two papers, the one she was reviewing for a fellow student and the original that she had read only a week or so earlier. All she'd done was give their law professor both papers and let him draw his own conclusions. At first, she was thankful he'd kept her name out of the resulting student court hearing. Then she became more than a bit resentful that the professor took full credit for having discovered the literary property theft. To make things worse, he turned the whole experience into a CNN news story and ended up writing a book exposing the pressures placed on students in graduate school.

However, he failed to take into account the tendency of the Bentons to exact revenge when they believed they were maligned or mistreated. Emily got her retribution when she combed through the good professor's book and substantiated a dozen or more instances where the man failed to credit the original source of the material he had used without attribution.

Word for word.

The press had a field day with *her* findings of *his* plagiarism.

What goes around, comes around. . . .

Even that wasn't illegal or immoral. But it sure was vindictive.

In Kate's experience, political candidates usually fell into one of two groups—those who shunned bad PR and those who embraced it, believing that bad PR merely created an opportunity for a public rebuttal, not to mention the chance to get in the last word.

Emily fell into the second camp, so Kate took full advantage of the unfortunate attack on the Talbot headquarters to stump Emily's platform in front of the voters—in a positive way.

In her next few speeches, Kate had Emily refocus the public spotlight on gun control and increased funding for mental health programs, both key planks in her platform. What better example could they cite than the recent unfortunate attack on the Talbot campaign to demonstrate the need for stricter control of guns and better care for the mentally ill? The press ate it up. They stopped asking if the shooter's T-shirt had any significance and whether the Benton campaign was in some way connected to the attack.

And Kate pushed any thought that it might be possible down to the farthest reaches of her mind. She repeatedly reminded herself that she'd never once seen a whisper of such an intention in Emily. No matter what the provocation, she simply couldn't imagine Emily using violence like that.

Especially since she refused to think about it.

Meanwhile, whether it helped or hurt, the news hoopla that surrounded them kept Emily firmly in the thoughts and minds of her constituents.

As Emily always said, "People won't vote for someone they don't remember."

Emily was many things but never forgettable. Kate grinned. She couldn't forget Emily for even a minute.

But the media circus didn't stop Kate from worrying. Maybe Nick was playing her from the start, deliberately planting that seed of doubt in Kate's mind in hopes of causing friction or, better yet, fracture between her and Emily. If so, the only person she could blame would be herself if she allowed that seed of doubt to germinate. There was no way

Emily would ever orchestrate anything this horrendous, devastating, or overt.

Emily never used a sledgehammer when the flick of a finger would do.

Nick wasn't even on Emily's radar anymore, right?

Once again, Kate told herself she wasn't going to think about that whole mess. Instead, she decided to continue fighting the good fight for the rest of the day—for God, country, and Emily, in that order. When it ultimately came time to tally the votes, she found her reward in the results: Emily pulled out a victory in New Hampshire with 37 percent of the vote. Burl Bochner had a respectable second-place win with 18 percent and retained his position as a potential threat to Emily's campaign.

It wasn't until a couple of hours after the New Hampshire victory party that Kate and Emily finally got back to the relative quiet of Kate's hotel suite.

Emily propped her feet up on the coffee table and nodded toward the bar fridge. "Get me a beer while you're up."

Kate, having already collapsed into an upholstered chair near the window, groaned. But she rose from her seat to retrieve a can of beer for Emily and a diet soda for herself.

Emily made a face at Kate's choice of beverage. "That thing is nothing but water contaminated with artificial coloring, artificial flavoring, and artificial sweeteners—nothing but chemicals, you know." She admired her beer can, then rolled its smooth cold surface across her forehead. "And this is 100 percent all natural ingredients. Barley, hops, yeast, water, and time. Nothing harmful to man can grow in the ferment of a good beer."

She raised the can in salute and then opened it. "That's

about the only good thing that came out of my marriage to Nick. He did teach me how to appreciate beer."

Kate took a tentative sip of her soda. So far, the Talbot campaign had been able to keep Nick's name out of the news. His name hadn't even showed up as a victim of the shooter.

But she knew she couldn't keep the news from Emily any longer. "Uh . . . M? Speaking of Nick . . ."

"Do we have to?"

"Seriously. There's something I need to tell you."

"Hang on." Emily took a deep gulp of beer and settled back into the soft couch. "I need a lot more fortification before we start talking about him." After another long draw from the can, she gestured for Kate to continue. "I'm ready. Shoot."

Kate cringed over the unfortunate choice of words. "It's about the shooting yesterday. Uh . . . Nick was one of the people who was injured."

"You're kidding me! Really?" Emily took another sip. She looked interested but not worried. "How bad was it?"

"A bullet grazed his arm."

Emily made a face. "That's all?"

"It could have been much worse. One of the volunteers died."

Emily released a harsh bark of laughter. "How does that old chestnut go? 'I really missed my man. But my aim is getting better'? Better luck next time, eh?"

"Give it a rest, Emily." Kate knew there was no real use in scolding her for such irreverence. Nick was and always would be a sore spot for her. But she couldn't joke about something so serious. Her conscience, still sore from the strain she'd been under for so long, couldn't take it.

Emily's sigh dripped with overly dramatic exasperation. "Don't look so aghast, K. I'm not saying these things in public. I know better. I'm only saying them to you. In private. Since no one has leaked this in the press, I guess he called you to tell you his little sob story. Probably wanted to build up a little sympathy for himself."

"No, I called him."

Emily's smirk faded away to a concerned stare. "I'm really getting worried about you. I can't just sit here and let Nick get his hooks into you. He's still the same vindictive, untrustworthy, unreliable, smarmy—did I say untrustworthy?—person he was before I ditched him. Nothing has changed. Think about it; his best revenge would be to stop me by compromising you."

"He's not getting any 'hooks' into me. And he's not going to use me against you. I won't let him. You know me better than that."

"Well . . . you're right. I guess I do." Mollified, Emily drained her beer. Rather than ask Kate to get her another one, she rose and fetched one for herself. "But God help you if you're keeping anything else from me."

It took a moment or two for Emily to realize how threatening her harsh words sounded, and she scrambled to correct herself. "Oh, man, K. You know I didn't mean to sound so grumpy. Let me try again. I appreciate that you've shouldered a lot of things on your own, not bothering me while I was on the road. So is there anything else I need to know?"

Kate hesitated. Should she tell Emily about the second threatening note now or later?

Emily put down the second beer, unopened. "What is it?" She studied Kate's face. "I can read you like a book, my friend. If something's bothering you, then it's bothering me, too. You know. Sisters. Compadres. Arm in arm. Hand in hand." She waited expectantly, and when Kate said nothing, Emily cocked her head, real concern filling her eyes. "What is it, Kate?"

Yep, they were closer than sisters in some ways. Emily knew things about Kate even her mother didn't know. It had been that way since they were roommates in college. Kate realized there was no way to gloss over what had happened. *Time to rip the bandage off the wound.* She reached down, found her briefcase, and thumbed through the files until she found the one with the copy of the message. She held the sheet of paper out for Emily's inspection. "I got another threatening note. This time addressed to me and delivered to the office here."

Emily gawked at her, then at the note. "When?"

"Three days ago." One look at Emily's distressed face and she quickly added, "But I reported it. Both the Secret Service and our own security team know all about it. They're on top of things."

Emily stared at the note and dropped to the couch. "I can't believe you kept this from me, K. That stuff about Nick—in the long run, it's just not that important. But this is about you and your safety. That's critical to me! I love you like family. Never mind what you mean to my campaign."

"What was I supposed to do? You needed all the support you could get out there on the road. I didn't need to distract you with my problems."

Emily shot her a perplexed look. "But your problems are *my* problems." She stared at the note, recognition dawning in her eyes. "I bet I know who sent this. It had to be Daniel

Gilroy. I remember him using that same phrase when he was talking about his ex-wife."

"I thought that too. I called Wes right after I got it and picked his brain. He thinks Gilroy isn't really a violent man— and he isn't likely to act on any threats he might make."

"Especially if he's in jail," Emily said.

Kate swallowed hard. Emily wasn't going to like her answer at all. "The problem is—Gilroy's not in jail. He's been paroled."

EMILY'S RESPONSE SHOULD HAVE BLISTERED the paint from the walls. She slammed her palm against the coffee table, the sound ricocheting through the room. "I can't believe the Feds let him free without even warning us. Those idiots!"

"He did his time."

"Still . . ." She rose from the couch and stalked to the minibar. "He had a thing for me. I should have been notified." When Emily got upset, sometimes a six-dollar package of chocolate-covered macadamia nuts or a three-dollar Snickers bar could take the edge off. Kate hoped today was one of those times.

Emily rummaged around the small fridge until she found something suitably sweet and expensive. "In any case, I agree with Wes—I never got a sense from him that Gilroy was actually dangerous." She held out a yellow bag of M&M's, but Kate refused. Emily tossed some into her mouth and continued. "Gilroy's confused—yes. Crazier than a bedbug—

sure. But violent? I don't think so. We're not talking Waco or Ruby Ridge here. That whole cabin siege scene was pretty much a complete farce. He gave in without even a whimper. His followers ran away behind his back and left him to take the rap for everything himself. But that didn't matter. He was already crumbling. I think he knew what was at stake." She tipped the bag up and poured a few more candies into her mouth. "But that language. It sure sounds like him. I wonder . . . Is everyone basing their accusations on the fact that he always used that 'Handmaiden of the Devil' line when talking about his wife?"

"Not really. The Secret Service isn't sure it's him. They've had him under surveillance and he's not made any suspicious moves. You don't think it's simply a coincidence, do you? That someone else just used that same phrase?"

"Not by accident, at least. There are no coincidences in politics, and I suspect that applies to crazed cult leaders too." Emily stood and began to pace the room, the chocolate and sugar evidently having hit her system with carb-fueled energy that needed to be bled off. "This guy is targeting you. It goes without saying that you'll have to stay in Virginia rather than head to Florida with me."

"Now, wait—"

Emily cut her off fast. "We've been working for over eighteen months to build up the key state headquarters so they could function at peak efficiency for the primaries and beyond. I'm not saying that the hard work is over. . . . Far from it. But you need to have faith in all the hard work you've done so far, that we've done together."

She spoke rapidly without even pausing to catch her breath. "We can manage South Carolina and Florida just fine with you working your mojo from Virginia. We'd discussed this possibility even before the note writer became a royal pain in our rumps. The week after Florida is going to be a logistical nightmare anyway. I think I'd rather have you manning your regular desk in preparation for it. You'll have better control from there."

"Emily, I appreciate your flexibility, but—"

"But nothing. Once I get out of Gilroy's backyard, then it's back to work as usual for you—some on the road, some back home."

Emily finally paused to draw in a deep breath, which calmed her somewhat. "And while you're home, you put in your time at the office. No lollygagging around with that mutt of yours," she teased. Then her face softened. "How *is* my Buster boy, anyway?"

Kate knew this was Emily's way of temporarily closing the subject from further discussion. She played along. "Buster's doing fine. Every time I come back, Kaleesa has taught him a new trick. Soon his vocabulary will exceed mine."

A rare look of nostalgia filled Emily's eyes. "I really miss hanging around my favorite pooch. I still think we should have made him the official campaign mascot." She used one hand to trace an invisible banner in the air. "Buster for Benton."

"Buster Barks for Benton," Kate countered.

"Buster Bets Benton Buries Bochner!"

The word games made Kate smile and remember why she felt so close to Emily.

But as amusing as this was, it didn't change the fact that somewhere, somebody had Kate in their sights.

They were dancing around the real topic and they both

knew it. But it was a game they played—pretending for a few minutes that the big, hairy complication didn't exist by burying it under a pile of off-subject pleasantries.

Emily was the one who broke protocol first. "Listen, K, I know you're worried about all this. About Gilroy. But trust me, he's all bully, no bite."

"That's pretty much what Wes said. And the Secret Service."

"Which means it's true. After all, you heard it from unimpeachable sources like the good Reverend Kingsbury and now from me, the next president of the United States. . . ." A small smile of satisfaction creased her face. "I do like the sound of that."

"What? 'The next president of the United States'?"

A twinkle glittered in Emily's eyes. "That and *unimpeachable*."

"Don't get too big for your britches, girl. Remember Clinton and Monica Lewinsky."

"None of my dates have blue dresses," Emily shot back.

Kate had to admit that Emily had her there.

The next few days were intense.

Insane.

Exhilarating.

And that was merely back at M Central. On the road, Kate knew Emily was experiencing twice as much exhilarating insanity, judging by her frequent phone calls and text messages.

The calls were mostly updates on the events and requests

for advice, but buried in the news were Emily's assurances that although Gilroy had not surfaced at any event, that didn't mean he was elsewhere.

Like Virginia.

Kate had tried to tell Emily that she didn't need a private security firm assigned to watch her at all times. But Emily insisted. And when Emily insisted, people listened.

Kate ended up with a detail of watchdogs assigned solely to guard her, which was as awkward as it was embarrassing. Finally, after one and a half uneasy, uncomfortable days of constant scrutiny, with two security men running unnecessary interference between Kate and practically every person in her path, known or unknown, she called the agency.

"I thought your people were supposed to protect me from stalkers, not *become* my stalkers," she complained.

The head of the agency laughed. "Ms. Benton said you wouldn't last two days."

"She was right. I can't stand this. You're interfering with my job." Kate tried not to glare at the man standing next to her office door. She knew his counterpart was sitting in their car just beyond her window.

"You do realize, ma'am—this is for your own safety." Their boss sounded amused rather than apologetic.

Her grip tightened on the telephone. "Trust me—I'm not safe if I'm walking around in a constant state of irritation. It's bad enough having your people stomp around my yard every couple of hours, but inside too? My dog, Buster, is going crazy."

"Yes, ma'am. . . . I understand the dog is all howl and no bite."

"So far, but I don't know how long he can hold out. If

they keep bribing him with Milk-Bones, I'll have to put him on a diet."

After much discussion, they came to the agreement that one member of the security detail would accompany Kate in her car from her home to her office and remain within a discreet distance during any intermediate stops or appointments. The other man would trail them in his car. But she made it plain that her home and her office would be considered sacrosanct. Once they performed a single but thorough internal sweep of each location, all other surveillance would be conducted from the outside of the building.

But despite all arrangements, the one thing the security company couldn't protect her from was the person who leaked to the press the existence of the two threatening notes.

It wasn't just a leak. It was a well-orchestrated and obviously deliberate disclosure, released to several key news markets simultaneously. Had she wanted to alert the media, Kate couldn't have selected a better way to do so if she'd arranged it personally. That, of course, meant that most everyone believed she *had* leaked the news herself. Instead of spending her time admitting that yes, she had received those threats, she had to defend herself, saying no, she hadn't leaked the news.

To complicate matters further, the Talbot headquarters chose the same time to announce that Nicholas Beaudry had been hired as deputy campaign manager, and yes, he was the same Nick Beaudry who had been briefly married to Emily Benton.

Gee. What a coincidence. Dueling press releases at thirty paces.

Kate tried to ignore all the questions that flooded her office, whether in person, on the phone, or in her e-mail in-box. Instead, she spent her time, energy, and the better part of the day shutting the questions out and tracking the leak back to its source.

After a couple hours of tracing and retracing, she reached the stunning conclusion that the leak came from within. In fact, every clue she unearthed pointed to a single volunteer, Cassidy Gates, who by all appearances was a sweet, unassuming high school senior getting work-study credit for helping with general office duties—filing, answering phones, stuffing envelopes. After speaking with her, Kate realized that either the girl was a world-class actress, or maybe someone much smarter than her was taking advantage of her naiveté.

But who?

Rather than grill the girl, Kate sent in her assistant, Caroline, whose gray-haired granny looks and Southern drawl hid political acumen of the steel-trap variety. Kate trusted Caroline. Better yet, so did all the other staffers. The mother-confessor of the office, Caroline would be the one to entice out, ream out, squeeze out, or otherwise determine who had used Cassidy's access to interoffice-only information to knock a chink from Kate's walls of privacy.

Thanks to that violation, reporters who had spent untold days badgering her about Emily now turned their unwanted attention on Kate's personal life. When the press realized her neighbors didn't know her and her campaign staff wouldn't talk, attention turned to the members of her church. But the staff and congregation there understood how much Kate cherished her privacy and everyone closed ranks.

Buoyed by her church family's unconditional support, Kate couldn't help but develop a renewed sympathy for anyone on the lens side of relentless media scrutiny who didn't belong to such a community of trust.

She also thanked God for the security team who made it possible for her to slip safely past the camera gauntlet outside of the headquarters when she needed to. Unfortunately those same security grunts were of limited use when it came to wading through the increased quantity and variety of mail she was getting on a daily basis.

Some of the letters she received fell in the hate mail category, but most of them smacked of being copycats. Kate had finally become desensitized to the contents after the first dozen or so. She no longer got the shakes. In fact, she didn't even get worried.

But her new public profile meant she received a larger number of letters from people sent directly to her—a third of them blaming Emily for having sent the shooter, a third praising Emily for having sent the shooter to the Talbot campaign, and another third wanting to defend Emily by helping identify the shooter. The last category contained by far the most interesting letters she received. Kate got variations on the theme from every flavor of nutcase—from a legion of tinfoil hat–wearing conspiracy theorists to a bunch of psychics and everything in between. The writers either claimed to be the shooter themselves or declared they'd seen him in their dreams or in their space-time machines or foretold by an ominous thunderhead in the western sky.

She prayed for the writers. They needed grounding that Kate figured only a healthy relationship with God could give.

But despite all this "help," no one had identified, much

less caught, the New Hampshire shooter or the writer of the Handmaiden note—now thought to be one of Gilroy's erstwhile disciples—or the other dozen or so missives of doom that her security team and the Secret Service thought might be remotely related to the initial notes.

However, one good thing about politics—both the candidates and the press had short memories and would eventually move on to other issues if they continued to hit a brick wall of silence.

Eventually.

So after a hundred or so repetitions of "No comment," the press finally accepted the fact that neither Kate nor anyone connected with the Benton campaign would say anything further to keep the story alive. They drifted away to the next scandal, someplace else.

As relieved as Kate was to not be photographed every time she stepped out of the building, she still had her security watchdogs trailing her, complicating her life. At least when she dragged her detail along with her to church, she felt a bit better, as if some good might come of their exposure.

Yet complaints to Emily fell on deaf ears; her friend was adamant about taking the threats seriously until proven untrue.

In order to maintain some semblance of normalcy, Kate tried to never stay late at the office; it simply made her security detail that much more prominent when she was the last to leave. The last thing she needed were pictures of her walking out of headquarters in the obvious company of one burly man and being tailed by another. Publicity like that simply wasn't good for the campaign. So she always made sure that when she left, it was as part of a crowd of office workers. That way, things felt and looked much more normal in her life even if she could never forget she was someone's target.

She prayed a lot these days, for strength, for mercy, and for somebody to find the shooter before he could do any more harm.

Driving home, Kate tried to make very small talk with her current closemouthed protector, a large and pathologically fit man named Lew. Buster didn't like the man at all. Her dog sat in the backseat, emitting an occasional growl at the guard when not distracted by the passing cars. Once they reached her house, the three of them waited in the car while Lew's eminently more personable partner, Sidney, checked the house. As usual, today he proclaimed it safe and she and Buster ditched their guards at her front door. Once inside, she breathed a sigh of relief. Buster flopped down in the middle of the floor and promptly fell asleep.

After nuking a frozen dinner, Kate tried to watch television only to realize—drat her luck—that the few shows she'd managed to see in the last six months were all being rerun that night. She turned to a stack of unopened DVDs sitting on the coffee table, ones that should have been sent back in the mail months ago. She flipped through them. Nothing sounded very interesting to her.

She pulled out her Bible. She hadn't had nearly enough time to read it lately. She'd settled on a favorite selection from Psalms when her cell phone rang. It was Lee Devlin.

"Sorry to call after business hours," Lee began.

"Don't worry about it. I did that to you last time, so I guess it's your turn. Got something new?"

"On Nick. Yes. A couple of things. First, it turns out

that those sealed files Sierra had were nothing more than his juvie records. They were supposedly sealed by the courts, but she'd gotten ahold of them somehow. She won't let me open them, but she assures me there's nothing really useful there that applies to his life today. A single charge of grand theft auto made by one of his uncles whose car Nick 'borrowed.' A couple of underage drinking raps."

"Nothing earth-shattering, then."

"Not there. But I did find something interesting about his DUI after the Big Breakup."

"What?"

"When he was pulled over, he failed the field sobriety test but blamed it on an inner ear problem. So he requested a Breathalyzer test—it wasn't mandatory in those days in Maryland. When he took it, he blew a 0.09, which was just under the cutoff at the time of 0.10. He should have gotten off right there. However, there was a scuffle that ended up with him being arrested for driving under the influence and striking an officer."

"Ouch."

"Exactly. But it doesn't add up. I've seen the pictures. Trust me—if Beaudry hit the cop, he didn't leave a mark on the man. The cop, on the other hand, must have had quite a time waling on Nick. He looked as if he'd done a demolition derby without the benefit of a car and was the last man standing. He had no serious injuries, but he had to have been hurting. When Nick finally arrived at the jail, forty-five minutes later, they did a second Breathalyzer test and he blew a 0.18."

"The results doubled? While he was handcuffed in the back of a police car? How's that possible?"

"Best way I can figure is Nick might have had a couple

more shots of undiluted whiskey poured down his throat while being forcibly held down in the back of the cruiser. It'd account for the injuries and the delay in reaching the station. Nobody ever seemed to question the fact that it took forty-five minutes for them to reach the booking facility that was only five minutes away under the worst conditions from the arrest site. Maybe the officer needed time to let the alcohol metabolize into Nick's bloodstream. Or maybe he took that long so the news media could get situated in the perfect place to get those front-page pictures. They were stunning."

Kate recalled several "beauty" shots of a bedraggled, bleary-eyed, and bruised Nick, handcuffed and being marched into the building. Considering how badly he'd humiliated Emily the night before, Kate hadn't felt any sympathy for him at the time. Nor had she asked any questions about his injuries. She'd only figured he'd resisted arrest after a night of hard drinking.

But now she began to see there might be a different side to Nick's story. Had he been deliberately set up for maximum humiliation after the breakup?

If so, then by whom?

Other than Emily, Kate was the only other person who could have pulled something like this off with so little prep time.

Besides Emily. . . .

Hmmm. . . .

✫ ✫ ✫ ✫ ✫

Kate didn't have time to ponder the past, even if such thoughts were justified because of the new facts in evidence.

The present and Emily's campaign were much too pressing, the future far more compelling.

Florida and its 210 delegate votes were up for grabs. Emily's schedule had started with speeches in Miami; then she headed northward. When she called from Orlando, she seemed to be in an unusually nostalgic mood.

"I wish you were here, K. I know how much you'd love it. I can see the big castle in the distance."

"You mean Cinderella's castle."

"You know, it looks a lot bigger than the version at Disneyland."

"That's because it *is* bigger. It's Sleeping Beauty's castle in Disneyland. Different princesses, different castles, different sizes."

"That was still the best vacation I ever took," Emily said, sounding almost wistful.

"Same here, thanks to you."

"Not me. It was all thanks to Dad. He's the one who arranged everything."

"True."

Kate had been around Big Henry only a few times before he died, but she'd found him a surprisingly congenial man—outside of the political arena. Inside politics, he frightened her to death. She'd never seen a man with so much power at his fingertips. He was like Zeus flinging thunderbolts at his enemies with pinpoint accuracy. To Big Henry's credit, he seemed to use his power wisely. Then again, he seemed awfully careful about what he allowed outsiders to see. Despite her friendship with Emily, Kate had always been an outsider among the Bentons. That is, until Big Henry's death.

The very first time Kate had met Henry Benton face-to-face was on the tarmac as she, Emily, and two more friends climbed down the stairs of the Benton family private jet. They'd all left Dulles thinking they were headed for Florida, but the plane's pilot had filed a different flight plan at Big Henry's orders. Unbeknownst to the girls, they were headed for sunny California instead.

"What do you have up your sleeve, old man?" Emily asked her dad, shading her eyes from the bright sunlight. She pointed at the unmistakable arches of the LAX control tower. "Unless I'm crazy—and trust me, I'm not—this is *not* Florida." She glared at her father. "Why did you divert us to Los Angeles, Dad?"

He hugged his daughter and bestowed the famous Benton grin on the rest of them. "I just wanted to give you and your friends the vacation of a lifetime. It's not every day that your daughter not only gets into law school at Georgetown but does so well in the first semester. I thought you and your friends might enjoy a little pampering."

A few hours later, all four girls were stretched out on massage tables at The Beverly Hills Hotel, being pummeled by four of the best-looking men Kate had seen in some time.

That afternoon, at Big Henry's request, they shopped in the boutiques of Beverly Hills to find new cocktail dresses. What they cost was of no consequence, thanks to Big Henry, who paid for the dresses with his platinum card. The gift also included matching shoes, purses, and jewelry from famous stores Kate had only heard of in Hollywood gossip columns and certainly had never shopped in before. The cost of college and law school had placed a serious crimp in her finances. She had scholarships and student loans, but it was still hard on her and her parents. These days, her ideal place to go fashion shopping was more budget barn basement than Beverly Hills boutique.

But Big Henry wouldn't listen to her protests as he insisted the girls each buy the perfect ensemble as his gift.

Then that night, with the girls all dressed in their new finery, they stepped into a white stretch limo that pulled up outside their private bungalow at the famous hotel.

As the limo glided up the ramp onto the interstate, Kate and the other two girls speculated which of LA's legendary hot spots they might be going to. Emily listened to their theories but refused to tell them anything other than a guarantee that it'd be a night to remember. At least, that's what her father promised. Even she didn't know where they were going until they got there.

To their amazement, instead of pulling up in front of Spago or Chasen's, the limo pulled into the parking lot of Disneyland.

Kate glanced down at her new six-hundred-dollar heels. "Are you serious? An amusement park? In these shoes?"

Emily grinned. "Don't worry. I know what's going on now. You'll be fine."

The driver opened the door and helped them out onto the sidewalk. There, they watched tired families carrying exhausted children in mouse-ear hats toward the parking lot, back to their minivans, back to Suburbia, USA.

Back to the ordinary world that they'd left behind early that morning.

"Wait here," the driver directed. Then he walked over to a small building sporting a Guest Services sign. While the driver negotiated, Emily listened to her friends' whispers as they huddled together on the sidewalk, talking about how they felt totally out of place in comparison to the shorts and T-shirt set entering and exiting the park.

The driver returned with four bits of paper in his hand that he gave Emily.

"I'm not complaining. Don't get me wrong—I've always wanted to come here—but aren't we a bit overdressed for the 'Happiest Place on Earth'?" Kate asked.

Emily could hardly keep the smug look off her face. "Not the part of the park where we're going. We're wearing the right clothes, and trust me, you'll be happy."

They entered through the turnstiles and followed Emily as she marched through the park with purpose, passing groups of kids and parents, walking by shops selling everything Mickey and past pushcarts hawking various food items. Emily obviously knew where she was going and wasn't tempted by the sights along the way. The rest of them couldn't help but be distracted by the attractions.

Theresa Charles, the youngest of the group at twenty-one, lagged for a moment at the entrance to the Pirates of the Caribbean ride. "Hey, this looks fun. Do you think we could—?"

"Later." Emily didn't even break her stride, causing Theresa to rush on her somewhat precarious new heels to catch up. "We have a reservation."

"For what?"

"Dinner." Emily came to a halt outside an innocuous-looking door, lifted a brass plate exposing a speaker grill, and pushed a button. Someone answered and asked her name. When Emily gave it, a buzzer sounded and the door clicked open.

"This is like . . . out of a spy movie or something," Theresa said in awe.

Kate stared at the brass plaque beside the door, remembering an offhand remark Emily had made a couple of months ago. "This is Club 33, isn't it?"

Emily smiled broadly. "Right. The best-kept secret in Disneyland."

That previous November as they had celebrated Emily's birthday with candles stuck in doughnuts, she'd recounted her past parties, including the sixteenth birthday bash her family had thrown for her at the überprivate Club 33, hidden smack in the middle of Disneyland's New Orleans Square. That particular night the park had stayed open late solely for the extensive Benton family—all the aunts, uncles, and cousins many times removed, not to mention the families of some of Big Henry's political cronies.

Had the story come from anyone else, Kate would have discounted most of it as either a lie or overt bragging. But considering the lifestyle Emily had always known as normal, a private party at Disneyland was nothing more than a typical Benton family celebration that she remembered with fondness. Emily had recounted the occasion with the same sense of nostalgia and affection as Kate did her sixteenth birthday party at Kings Dominion amusement park with a handful of buddies. The only difference was that Kate and her friends waited in line for rides like everyone else, dined on corn dogs and lemonade, spent too much money trying to win stuffed animals, and were picked up at closing time by her dad in the minivan.

Somehow Kate didn't think corn dogs would be on the menu this time.

After they entered the building, they stepped onto an elevator Emily called the French lift and ascended to what was perhaps the most elegant restaurant Kate had ever seen, much less dined in.

That evening, Emily introduced Kate and her friends to "the other life"—attentive, eager waiters, excellent food, an unbelievably expensive wine, decadent desserts, and then carefree after-dinner drinks on the balcony overlooking a faux New Orleans, where they watched the evening fireworks from a spectacular vantage point, unattainable by all but the most elite.

Emily pointed at a group of sunburned college girls in the midst of the milling crowd below them. "Any ordinary slob can roast themselves on a beach for spring break and then get drunk on cheap booze and wake up in some guy's bed with a hangover," Emily declared. "I have higher standards."

Then she lifted her glass of five-hundred-dollar-a-bottle wine. "Ladies, let me propose a toast. May we always have the wisdom and find the funding to choose the Better Life."

"To the Better Life," they all echoed.

Theresa pointed in the general direction of Sleeping Beauty's castle. "You think I could just, like . . . sublet that place for my 'better life'?"

Emily laughed. "Next thing you'll be telling me is that you think it should come with its own handsome prince."

"Well . . ."

"Hey, if you want the best, then go for it. But as nice as that piece of real estate may be, I have my eye on another."

Jocelyn Kirby, their fourth partner in crime, snagged

a piece of chocolate from the plate that sat by her elbow. "What's wrong with the castle? Not big enough for you?"

"No, the house I'm thinking of is white."

Jocelyn hiccuped with laughter. "Surely you don't mean one in the burbs with a white picket fence, 2.5 children, and a dog?"

Emily shot her a mock glare. "Wash your mouth out."

"She means *the* White House," Kate said, reading her friend's face.

"Don't be funny," Theresa said.

"Get serious." Jocelyn hiccuped again and reached for another piece of chocolate.

Kate studied Emily's expression. "She *is* being serious," Kate declared. She addressed her friend. "If anyone could do it, Emily, I think you could."

Emily turned and stared at Kate as if seeing her for the first time. "I'm glad to find someone who not only understands me but agrees with me, too." The air crackled between them, as if a new connection was being forged between two casual friends, strengthening it into a political partnership. "I'll need help along the way—people I can trust who are willing to work beside me as well as behind the scenes."

"But who don't particularly want the limelight themselves, right?"

"Exactly."

Giggling, Theresa lifted her glass and tried valiantly not to slosh its contents onto her new dress. "Then, to the White House!"

Jocelyn matched the gesture and the words.

Kate glanced at the other two, then solemnly picked up her own wine glass, still mostly full. She decided to change the toast to something much more appropriate. "No, not to the position. To the person. Here's to Emily, who someday *will* become the first female president of the United States."

Emily had met Kate's gaze with a look of unmistakable determination, ignoring their other two companions. "And you, my friend, are going to help make it happen."

FLORIDA—ORANGES, PALMETTO BUGS, AND VOTERS. The Benton campaign goal? Admire the first, avoid the second, and charm the third.

But even from a thousand miles away, Kate knew it was a monumental task. There were seventeen varieties of oranges, forty-one species of palmetto bugs, and almost an infinite assortment of Florida voters. Young, old, male, female, white, black, Cuban-Americans, Mexican-Americans, native Floridians, snowbirds, U.S.-born, naturalized citizens, Christian, Jewish, farmers, nonfarmers, rural, urban, military, civilians, and many more classifications, perhaps more than any other state in the Union outside of California and New York.

Long considered an elector-rich swing state much sought after by presidential candidates in the late stages of the election, Florida had made itself even more pivotal in the political process by pushing up its primary date, which meant it was now one of the must-win-for-momentum states in the early primary season calendar.

That change in date, along with several others in other states, had caused earthshaking complications in this presidential campaign. In previous campaigns, the first Tuesday in March had been nicknamed Super Tuesday because of the large number of states that held their primaries on that date. But an even larger number of states had overhauled their election calendars and now the first Tuesday in February 2008 would be the big day when more than twenty states would hold their primaries or caucuses. The press had several names for the day—Super Duper Tuesday, Giga Tuesday, or Kate's personal favorite, Tsunami Tuesday.

But no matter what you called it, the first Tuesday in February would try the campaign staff's patience, challenge their logistics, and otherwise turn their world upside down.

After all, not even a candidate with a private jet at her beck and call could easily visit twenty different states in seven days. Not even Wonder Woman . . .

So taking the early states had become essential. And Florida was the biggest of the early states.

With over 1,800 delegate votes at stake, the Tsunami Tuesday night tally would identify and validate the two strongest party front-runners, and it would be a head-to-head match from that point on. The other candidates might hold out and continue to campaign after that, but it'd be futile. They'd simply be throwing good money after bad, trying to save face or prove some heartfelt political point. More likely, everyone but the two front-runners would throw in the towel and slink back home to be mostly forgotten by the nation.

Kate had already put her money on Burl Bochner as Emily's chief competition. He was running a smart campaign, calling attention to but not harping on his traditional family structure, something that Emily lacked as a divorcée with no children.

So the Benton strategy was to concentrate on issues rather than personalities and to spend more time and effort in the states with the heavier populations and, therefore, larger number of delegates to win over: first Florida, then New York, New Jersey, Illinois, and California.

And Emily jumped the first hurdle, receiving a resounding 66 percent of the Florida votes, resulting in 138 delegates from that state. That brought her total delegates won to almost 200. However, that wasn't even 10 percent of what she needed to win the nomination.

Even if she made decisive victories across every Tsunami Tuesday state, Kate already knew Emily wouldn't have enough delegate votes to win. Not yet, at least. But the momentum would be critical to sway the undecided, who—more often than not—waited to see who was winning so that they could vote with the prevalent majority.

Once Emily left Florida, Kate had planned to reconnect with her on the road. She felt confident that the protective measures instituted by Decker Bloom and Bloom Security would give her all the peace of mind she needed to get back to the task at hand: how to make sure Emily won in most—if not all—of the Tsunami states.

If she did win, their work wasn't over by a long shot, not even when Emily reached the magic number: 2,181 delegates at the convention in the corner pocket. Her focus would simply change. Instead of battling on a double playing field—

campaigning against her fellow party members while still paying close attention to the other party—she'd be able to focus solely on her campaign against Charles Talbot.

Kate had some ideas about how to make that contest interesting. But first she and Emily had to concentrate on the members of her own party.

Unfortunately, Tsunami Tuesday still squatted at the end of a large, dark tunnel, full of logistical nightmares and a schedule for Emily that would reduce the heartiest athlete to a quivering mass of Jell-O. Successful politicians often said that the most important trait a good politician had to possess was stamina. Emily counted stamina among her greatest assets.

She was definitely going to need it.

Her schedule had been vetted by the best in the business, Miriam Smart, who knew precisely how to coordinate the split-second timing necessary to maximize Emily's appearances and minimize her downtime. No item was added or removed from the schedule, nor were any changes distributed to the troops, until they'd been initialed *MS*. The letters stood for either Miriam Smart or perhaps Master Scheduler. No one was exactly sure.

Thanks to Miriam's careful stewardship of Emily's time, whenever the candidate wasn't courting fellow party members in person, she would be shooting supplementary footage for a new set of television commercials, cutting more than two dozen "Quick Bites" sound clips a day to be used as morale boosters, tailored to each of the individual state headquarters, thanking key volunteers by name.

Miriam had every moment of Emily's day booked solid, including breaks for snacks and naps. With years of experience under her belt, Miriam not only knew how long it took to get from any airport to a downtown hotel in five-o'clock rush hour, but she had three different preferred routes programmed into Emily's GPS, each ready to take depending on traffic.

Beyond that, Miriam knew which entrances to a venue had the most flattering light for photo ops and which ones would allow a bedraggled candidate to bypass the awaiting press unobserved. She knew how long it would take Emily and her entourage to walk from one city venue to another and what bakeries might be handy along the way for informal meet and greets.

Curious Americans, thanks to the equally curious American press, appeared to enjoy hearing about Emily's "obsession" with finding the perfect chocolate chip cookie recipe. It had started as a casual comment about needing a little something to tide her over one long day on the campaign trail. Comedy pundits joked that Emily's vice president choice should be Mrs. Fields. The media magnified her search for a simple cookie into a fixation. It all made for fabulous press, and Kate gladly ran with the concept since it added a warm homebody element to Emily, who really wasn't much of a warm homebody.

But the most important thing that both Miriam and Kate knew as they made their plans was that all schedules existed mainly to be changed. They had to remain flexible so as to take advantage of last-minute opportunities, unavoidable delays, and unfortunate cancellations. That's what made Miriam the campaign's best asset—her skill in projecting the cascading changes necessary to resuscitate a mortally wounded schedule, accomplishing the retrofit literally in minutes. Then there was her lightning fast ability to get the changes to all parties instantaneously, thanks to e-mail, cell phones, and network file sharing. Perhaps Kate's greatest talent was that she knew when to step back and allow Miriam to work unhampered and uninterrupted.

They were in the middle of a surprisingly unhectic schedule review meeting at M Central when one of the staffers burst into the room.

"Lost another one!" the young woman exclaimed proudly. "Raintree just stepped out of the ring."

"One more down, three to go," Kate responded, not even looking up from her notes. The news meant one less bottom-feeder to worry about, which was good because she had bigger catfish to fry if Emily was going to win this thing.

Kate pressed on with the meeting. "Okay, in the area of communications, do you have the plane outfitted with everything you need to record and transmit the sound bites?"

She waited for a response, and when she heard only silence, she looked up, startled by the expressions of the people sitting at the table. "What?"

Her assistant, Caroline, glared at her.

"What's wrong?" Kate repeated.

Caroline pointed to the crestfallen staffer still standing at the door. "We just got some encouraging news. How about letting us celebrate for a minute or two?"

Kate glanced around the table and saw the same look of failed expectation mirrored on all of the faces. Then she realized her faux pas, a violation of her most important rule: people first.

She'd learned that one in Bible school before she'd gotten

her permanent teeth. It wasn't like her to forget it. *Stay with me, Jesus, for I'm a goof-up without you. . . .*

She used her pen as a bookmark as she closed her day planner and stood up. "You're right. I apologize." She turned to the staffer waiting in the doorway. "I'm sorry. I didn't mean to brush you off. So when did this happen?"

The young woman looked somewhat mollified. "It just came across the wires that he's holding a press conference. CNN is about to cover it."

"Then crank up the tube so we can all watch." Kate could feel the tension caused by her gaffe draining away as they all focused on the coverage of the speech.

They crowded around the television set, watching the candidate bow out of the running as gracefully as he could. He'd been a long shot at best, with an awkward, uneven delivery that had failed him miserably during the few debates he'd participated in. His discomfort with the format was palpable, and he'd been woefully unprepared for some of the questions the moderators and participants asked him. Even his best answers had made him look uninformed. Probably the death knell to his success was his consistent and unfortunate mispronunciation of *Des Moines*, which didn't exactly endear him to the people of Iowa. He regularly mangled the word *America* too, managing to get a few more vowels into it than the Founding Fathers had ever intended. He'd finished the Iowa caucus with slightly less than two percent of the primary vote.

After James Raintree finished his speech, the whole group of Benton staffers cheered in unison. Caroline turned off the set. Kate stepped back and allowed the staffers to discuss what they'd just witnessed without her input.

"You know, if he'd been half as eloquent when campaigning as he was just then, he might have been able to hang on a bit longer." As always, Mario Medina, their deputy communications director, found something encouraging, no matter how backhanded, to say about the guy. Behind his back, the staffers called Mario "Little Mario Sunshine." Backhanded compliments weren't Mario's usual style, but in the case of James Raintree, it was the kindest thing anyone could say about the erstwhile candidate.

"You call that eloquent?" Miriam opened her laptop and began typing, no doubt coming up with a contingency plan to parallel the slight changes they were making to the California part of the schedule. "I've never been able to associate *that* word with him. Ever."

"Not actually eloquent *per se*," Mario admitted. "But his 'I'm takin' my marbles and goin' home' speech was far better delivered than any other one he's made so far."

"I kinda liked his incoherence," Caroline said. "It had a certain naive charm. Remember when he said that in his travels to foreign countries, he'd liked New Mexico best?"

"Yeah, then he said he was worried about the border security there. Nobody asked for his passport when he left Arizona." Miriam grinned at the thought. "I was standing backstage when he said that. I was sure his campaign manager was going to faint. You gotta love a man who says what he thinks. Especially when what he thinks is good for Emily."

The staffers all laughed.

Kate realized this was the sort of banter and camaraderie that fused talented individuals into a cohesive team, giving them a sense of unity and purpose. Political ideals and Emily's charismatic personality were enough to draw the staff initially to the Benton camp, but it was the bonds of respect and friendship they formed that helped keep them focused and dedicated to the task of electing Emily as the next president. That was the part of politics Kate liked. The camaraderie in a common cause.

For a few of them, trashing the other candidates as the common "enemies" helped foster their closeness too.

That was the part of politics Kate wasn't so fond of. But it worked. It forged them into a team, and as Emily's team, they were succeeding on a national level.

In fact, at all the various headquarters for Emily's campaign across the nation, it was getting hard to tell the paid staffers from the volunteers when it came to spirit and dedication.

The results of that solid fusion of talent and the drive of thousands of people united behind one cause were reflected in Emily's poll numbers.

Kate usually thrived on the energy and synergy of such group dynamics. But thoughts of her hate-mail writers' motives kept derailing her, interrupting her concentration. As a result, she knew she was overcompensating and trying to zero in too tightly on a single subject. Her preoccupation was limiting her effectiveness. To be truly effective as campaign manager, Kate needed to get back to her usual duty of juggling a dozen big, hairy tasks simultaneously.

But first . . .

She caught Caroline's attention and winked. Caroline understood the silent message and walked over to the iPod that was hooked up to the office's intercom and sound system. Normally the unit played a mixture of quiet jazz and

Emily's official campaign song, "Together We Rock." Of course, after nine months of constant repetition, the tune had lost some of its sheen for the regular staffers, but they pretended to still love it, even after the 3,463rd time they heard it.

But Kate had a weapon hiding in the iPod, one that she activated on select occasions as much to bolster her own flagging energies or attention level as that of the staffers working in M Central. It was the best and most beloved team exercise they had, *exercise* being the operative word.

"Everybody!" Caroline bellowed, her voice surprisingly robust despite her gray-haired, grandmotherly looks. "Dance. Now."

She hit the button and the opening vocals echoed her words. Then the music kicked in with a driving beat that few people, if any, could ignore. Those on the phone politely asked their callers if they could be placed on hold. Those carrying armloads of material dropped their burdens to the nearest flat surface. Everyone stood and began to dance. Some were fine dancers; some merely swayed to the music. Others used the tempo and the time to stretch and do a few simple exercises. Participation was never mandatory, but almost everyone seemed to enjoy joining in; those who didn't tolerated it with good grace. One of a group of younger staffers would take center stage and do an energetic if not impressive mini dance routine, ending in a round of applause. Caroline had told Kate that despite the impromptu appearance of the dance, the competition was fierce for those sixty or so seconds in the limelight. Wannabe lead dancers had actually set up a secret schedule as to who would perform next as the featured "spotlight dancer."

Of course, the real purpose of the short but enthusiastic dance break was to help clear mental cobwebs, to get the blood flowing, to continue building a sense of unity, and the most important goal, to give everyone a chance to not only smile but share a smile with each other.

As the applause ended for the day's featured performer, everyone returned to their current tasks with lingering smiles, Kate included.

Maybe I should get on the list of performers.

She recalled one young man's split at the end of his routine and she shifted uncomfortably in her chair.

Or maybe not.

However, the dance break was just the kick in the pants she needed to get back into the swing of things in a better mood. After the scheduling meeting, she headed to her office, where Buster had just roused from his nap and was attacking a rawhide bone.

"You and me, kid," she said, scratching his ears. "All the way to the top. Emily might not want you to poop in the Rose Garden, but we'll find you a piece of the White House lawn you can call your own. Executive dogs pooping on the White House lawn have a long and glorious tradition. You'll fit right in."

She settled at her desk. She was trying to concentrate on a field report from the Florida office when, rather than using the intercom, Caroline thundered in unannounced and flipped on the television set. She then stood back, crossed her arms, and waited. Kate joined her, mimicking her stand.

"*General Hospital?*" Kate asked.

"Not quite. Even more important. Watch."

A CNN newsreader filled the screen. "This just in. After

reports of suspicious noises and signs of an illegal campfire, military police at Fort A.P. Hill have found and detained a man identified as Daniel Gilroy. Gilroy is wanted for questioning in connection to threatening mail sent to the staff of former Virginia governor and presidential hopeful Emily Benton."

A picture of Gilroy flashed on the screen.

"He's also listed as a person of interest in the attack on the Manchester, New Hampshire, office of presidential front-runner Charles Talbot. That shooting attack resulted in the death of staffer Terry Pinchot. Two other campaign staffers were injured as well. Law enforcement officials were observed moving boxes of evidence from the campsite."

Kate sagged against her desk. *Thank you, God. Thank you, God. Thank you, God.*

"They got him." Caroline reached over and gave Kate a quick hug. "He's in custody, so you don't have to worry about him anymore."

Kate's mind filled with a sense of relief as well as a sudden exhaustion. It'd been hard to keep her spirits and her energy levels up when fear and concern sat firmly like an enormous boulder across her shoulders. She'd been starting to have real sympathy for Atlas and his whole world-juggling act.

Although she knew she ought to forget all this Gilroy business and get back to work, her curiosity kicked in. That's why she was glad when, an hour or so later, Agent McNally of the Secret Service called her with an update. As she had guessed, even though the Talbot HQ shootings had occurred on New Hampshire soil, the federal government had claimed jurisdiction over the case since that situation

involved a candidate under their protection and events occurred in multiple states.

It seemed that Daniel Gilroy had ended up in the hands
of the FBI for questioning.

The lawyer in her wanted to be there in the room, watching and interrogating, when they questioned him. The potential victim in her wanted to observe from behind the
safety of a bulletproof window. In either case, she wanted to
see his eyes when the Feebs grilled him, judge his reactions
for herself. It wasn't as much morbid curiosity as that she
wanted to know his motives. She wanted to know if he did
it for sure, and she wanted to know why he did it. Plus, if
she could beard the dragon in his den, so to speak, then she
could feel completely in control of her life again.

But the Feebs politely asked her to butt out when she
asked if she could watch them question Gilroy. They put up
a solid stone wall around their suspect. The only information she received was from McNally, who assured her that
the evidence against Gilroy was very strong. She pulled every
string she had to talk to the accused but to no avail. The only
solace she could find was in the fact that at least Gilroy was
in federal custody and no longer a direct threat to her.

If nothing else, Kate could get back to work secure in the
knowledge that even if the Feds couldn't prove Gilroy sent
the notes, he would have his parole revoked because he'd
left the state without permission. No matter what additional
charges he faced, he would go back behind bars.

The threat level surrounding her could finally drop to
where it usually was during a campaign and Kate could call
off her dogs—of the security kind.

No more escorts. No more chase cars. No more tough

men looking over her shoulder and gauging possible angles of attack.

Kate couldn't help but grin.

Thank you, God, for freedom from that worry at last.

Her silent prayer winged its way to heaven.

✯ ✯ ✯ ✯ ✯

After the Florida primary, Emily made her way out of the South on a private plane with a brief swing through the capitals of those Southern states participating in Tsunami Tuesday—Montgomery, Alabama; Atlanta, Georgia; Nashville, Tennessee; and Little Rock, Arkansas. Kate took a commercial flight and caught up with her candidate in Atlanta.

Together they toured the four heavyweight states of Tsunami Tuesday, beginning with Albany and Buffalo in one day, then spending a full twenty-four hours in New York City, with neither of them sleeping in the city that never sleeps.

New York was a double whammy because of the whopping number of delegates up for grabs and also by being the news media capital of the nation. Luckily Emily was popular with both groups.

Besides providing the usual sound bites to the local press, Emily appeared on both *The Daily Show* with Jon Stewart and *Late Night with Conan O'Brien*. The Letterman camp wasn't pleased at all with her refusal to appear on the *Late Show*, but they didn't protest as loudly as they might have. It all had to do with the bad blood between Emily and Dave. Kate had never heard the entire story of the incident that sparked it—ancient history, Emily always said—but she followed Emily's orders to always turn down any and all of their offers, even refusing to accept the canned hams and baskets of muffins sent by Letterman's booking staff.

The next day they spent in New Jersey, visiting Trenton and Atlantic City. Then after an overnight flight, Emily stumped in Springfield, Illinois, before heading to Chicago, where she attended two afternoon speaking engagements and ended the night at a women's empowerment dinner sponsored by Oprah Winfrey.

From Chicago, they flew to California, stopping on the way in Denver and Salt Lake City.

After a day and a half of stumping in California, Emily was to spend the night before Tsunami Tuesday in Los Angeles, yukking things up with Jay Leno on *The Tonight Show* as his first guest. Leno's staff had wanted to line up three well-known Hollywood bachelors to be part of a public matchmaking attempt in a parody of *The Dating Game*. But Kate had quashed that concept fast, believing that it weakened the message Emily needed to deliver. Leno good-naturedly agreed to let go of the comedy piece, saying that the American public didn't need any assurances of Emily's sense of humor and such fun and games could wait until after she was elected. The guest slot would be sedate in comparison to Leno's original plans but just as effective.

Emily always made his day just by being on his set, he said.

Jay could afford to be nice since Emily had already made a considerable contribution to his ratings during the February sweeps the previous winter. When she'd declared her candidacy on *The Tonight Show*, they'd performed a good comedy bit about campaign slogans that really had people talking around the office watercoolers the next morning. The clip had reigned supreme on YouTube for at least a week.

After reading through some of the best fake slogans Emily could use, Jay had told a joke about how Emily's campaign could save money by taking all the old "W" banners and bumper stickers created for George W. Bush and turning them upside down to read "M" for Emily. It was just a throwaway line, but that bit of silliness had inspired Kate.

She'd worked with Emily's advertising firm, and together they came up with the text-messaging slogan *V4M*, which worked well not only on cell phones but on bumper stickers, lapel pins, billboards, Internet banner ads, and even in hand signals.

Kate had papered the country with it, thanks to Leno's offhand bit of humor.

But Emily agreed—this Leno appearance wasn't the right time for dating jokes or over-the-top comedy bits. She didn't have the time to waste on silliness in her ambitious and detailed schedule, even if George Clooney was mentioned as one of the three possible dating-game bachelors. Both Emily and Kate had had a moment when they wavered in their sense of purpose after they'd heard that. But they'd stuck to their plans—and it was just Jay and Emily out there tonight in one of his more serious tête-à-têtes.

Kate was watching the show from the greenroom when her cell phone vibrated. She glanced at the readout. *Unknown Caller.* So far, her cell number had remained private, so she took a chance and answered. "Hello?"

"K? It's Nick."

"Hey. How are you doing?"

"The campaign's going great. As for me personally, I

heal fast. Still a little gun-shy though." He managed a mild laugh.

"I can imagine." She fumbled for the next thing to say. Somehow it didn't seem right to inquire about his interpretation of the latest polls—the ones that showed Emily and Talbot heading for the election after the primaries.

"Awkward silence," Nick said. "I can understand that. Let me get to the point. I have a friend who would like to meet you and me somewhere."

"You and me . . . ," Kate echoed.

"I know; I know. No cross-pollination of campaign staffs and all that. But what he has to say is important. We both need to hear it. Where are you?"

"Burbank."

"Oh, that's right. She's taping *The Tonight Show*. I think I'll watch Letterman tonight. When will you get back to Virginia?"

"Wednesday afternoon."

"Can we meet Wednesday night?"

"The campaign numbers are getting tight." Kate hesitated. "I'm not sure that's really a good idea."

"Trust me. It is. I'll call you with the location."

"Nick, really—"

"I'll make sure it's someplace safe, somewhere we can't been seen or overheard. See ya tomorrow."

Kate knew she'd be there.

But what would she hear?

TSUNAMI TUESDAY ENDED with Emily and Kate in Los Angeles. Emily had partied more than she probably should have, but the California primary had brought out a slew of high-profile supporters in the entertainment industry and beyond. Because they were spending time in elite, well-known company, the Benton campaign's usual media coverage had tripled, meaning Emily worked it for all it was worth, and she and Kate didn't "close shop" until the wee hours.

Even then they were too wired to sleep.

And Emily wasn't on her best behavior.

She stalked around the hotel suite, ramped up on the caffeine she'd used to stay awake for almost twenty-four hours straight. Kate knew getting Emily to bed soon would be like trying to calm a six-year-old hopped up on Pixy Stix.

"Where's my hairbrush?" Emily yelled. "Has anyone seen my stupid hairbrush? How hard is it for you people to lose it in a postage-stamp room like this?"

Their travel assistant, Loretta Keene, who handled Emily's clothes, hair, and makeup, looked as frazzled as Kate felt as she scanned the spacious room for the missing brush. Kate watched the woman clamp her mouth shut rather than respond in kind to Emily's ravings. To help alleviate the stress, Kate joined the search, getting on her hands and knees and checking under the furniture. Loretta and Kate both knew that once Emily released a little steam, she'd realize how unpleasant she'd been, apologize, and perhaps everybody could actually get some sleep.

But first they had to find the dratted hairbrush.

Kate spotted it on the bedside table partially hidden behind the clock radio. "Here it is." *Right where you left it,* she added silently.

Kate picked up the brush and made momentary eye contact with Loretta while she spoke to Emily. "Why don't you let *me* brush out the hair gel?"

Emily hesitated for a moment, then nodded.

Kate glanced at Loretta again and tilted her head toward the door. *I'll handle it from here. You run.*

Loretta gave her a tight smile in response. *Message received.* The woman slipped out of the room, trying not to appear too eager to escape.

Kate envied her a little. She began to slide the brush gently through Emily's blonde bob, praying that a technique that had always worked so well in her own life would be equally as effective now. The ritual of brushing hair had been one of the ways Kate and her mom had often ended a long day. Sometimes it was easier to clear the air or share the day's events when two people, no matter how close they were, weren't facing each other.

After a few moments of silence, Emily finally spoke. "You know, my mom used to brush my hair like this."

"Mine too."

"It was a battlefield of sorts."

Kate faltered for a moment, startled by Emily's unexpected description.

"Battlefield?"

"She'd make me kneel in front of her chair, face the wall, and tell her everything I did that day. If she didn't like what I had said or done—" Emily rubbed her temple—"I knew it. Boy, did I know it. I used to gauge the success or failure of a day by how much hair had been left in the brush."

Kate remained quiet, and another silence stretched.

"I guess it wasn't that way with your mom," Emily said.

"Nah, it wasn't. More like a bonding ritual. We used the time to share. Talk about the day, our plans. That sort of stuff. I always found it relaxing. And sometimes, even now when I go home to visit, we still do it. We end up sitting in the bedroom and talking with her brushing my hair, just like the old days."

"I hated it when my mom made me do it. That's why I cut my hair off when I turned sixteen."

While growing up, Kate, like most Americans, had seen her fair share of photographs of the Bentons in the media, mostly formal shots released to magazines and newspapers. Their life as paparazzi fodder tended to go in cycles that matched the political climate.

As Emily's closest friend, she'd seen the casual family snapshots too, chronicling Emily's earlier years. She remembered seeing shots of a cherubic young Emily with waist-length blonde hair and then photos of a slightly older Emily, her long hair gone and replaced with a dramatically short haircut.

"It must have been a shock for you both."

"It shouldn't have been," Emily retorted. She took a deep breath and continued. "She simply didn't expect me to rebel in quite that manner. But she knew I was both a Benton and a Rousseau. Bentons take charge and Rousseaus manipulate. I simply used the strength of one side to remove the control of the other." Her shoulders sagged a little. "Things were never the same between me and my mother after that."

There was nothing Kate could say to respond to this, so she simply continued brushing in calm, even strokes. But she thought of the love she and her mother shared unconditionally, and she thanked God their relationship had been so close and so simple. And she prayed that Emily would find the peace she needed. Soon Kate could almost feel the tension flow out of Emily in palpable waves.

"I miss her sometimes," Emily finally said in a quiet voice.

Kate realized she could take the statement two ways and she chose the least innocuous. "Your mom?"

"Yeah."

"If you feel like you need to visit her, we could probably clear some time in mid-May for a quick trip to Paris."

"That's not what I mean."

"Oh." What else could she say? Kate couldn't imagine the circumstances that would cause such emotional distance between her and her own mother. Sure, it'd been hard for her mother to let go, but then again, Kate's mother believed in influence, not manipulation. Her security in Christ gave her the freedom to love all those around her unconditionally. It was a gift that Kate hoped she'd inherit one day. She still struggled with showing the fruit of the Spirit as effortlessly as her mom did. That influence stayed with a person, wherever they went in life. Unlike Emily's mom, who clearly bartered love and manipulated the young Emily. Maybe that was why Emily was so tough. That manipulation stopped the moment she jerked herself out of her mother's grasp. It was a tough lesson and she'd apparently learned it well.

And it was still ruling her life, if Kate's observations were right.

"Thanks." Emily suddenly stood up, shaking off the momentary reverie, and held out her hand for the brush. "I needed that breather. I have to admit everything's happening faster than I expected. But don't get me wrong; I like what's happening." A gleam of determination danced in her eyes. "I like it very much."

It was just like Emily to turn off one emotion and go right back into business mode. She'd learned it young, maybe as a defense mechanism in the meat grinder of her famous family. Kate had learned out of necessity not to question such changes but to simply roll with them. In this case, it gave her an opening she'd been looking for. "So, what about Bochner? What are you going to do about him?"

Emily didn't hesitate in her answer. "If he announces that he's pulling out of the race tomorrow, then it means he really *is* a party man. I'll admire him for that."

"Enough to offer him VP?"

Emily picked up the hairbrush and began to brush her own hair. "I have to admit I've thought about it. He's a smart man, his military experience will definitely be an asset to us, and I think we could get along. At least he's remained civil during our debates."

She dropped the brush and reached instead for the telephone on the bedside stand. "I'm going to head to bed now. See you in the morning at—" she consulted her planner sitting on the bed, running her finger down the agenda— "seven sharp. G'night."

Summarily dismissed, Kate paused at the door to glance at Emily, already dialing. If she was using the hotel phone, that meant she was calling someone within the hotel. It didn't take a PhD to guess it was Chip McWilliamson.

As Kate headed to her room, she tried to turn her thoughts far away from Emily with Chip. There was something about the young man that Kate didn't like, but she was still unable to put her finger on the exact problem. *Young* might be the operative word, but *opportunistic* wasn't far behind. However, his references were impeccable; she knew that because she'd checked them out personally. Twice. Kate tried to tell herself it was simply a form of jealousy on her part—that she was sharing a close friend with someone else now, and any reservations she had were understandable in that context.

After all, Emily had the right to enjoy some personal time, even if she chose someone inappropriately young, somewhat inexperienced, and just a bit smarmy.

As Kate fumbled with her key card to enter her own suite, her mind jumped to the right description.

Someone convenient.

And since when did Emily do anything simply because it was the convenient thing to do?

★ ★ ★ ★ ★

After she got home, Kate didn't call Nick, despite the reminder message he left on her answering machine. She
wasn't sure why she hesitated, but in the long run, it didn't
matter. Nick called her again in the late afternoon.

"Can you meet me at eight?"

Her instincts said, *No. No way.... Absolutely not!*
"Nick, I don't think it's a good idea for us—"

"It's about Gilroy."

"Can't you just tell me over the phone?"

"There's someone you need to meet."

She closed her eyes and sent up a prayer. *God, please
tell me what to do. Am I seeking revenge or just wanting
closure? I can't tell.*

The answer didn't come attached to a lightning bolt. She
found it within her own heart. She didn't want retribution
or revenge. Just to understand why and then close the door
on the fear and get on with her life. Maybe Nick had his
hands on a key that could help her do that. "Where do you
want to meet?"

He gave her directions to a house near Chantilly, several
miles beyond the Beltway on U.S. 29. Kate knew the area
well enough to not need a map. "That's a little ways out in
the burbs, isn't it?"

"We're less likely to be seen or recognized. Neither of us
wants to be seen consorting with the enemy. I figured a little
precaution seemed in order."

By seven thirty, the worst of the rush-hour traffic from
D.C. radiating out to the suburbs was over. Kate made good
time and reached the neighborhood a few minutes early.

New to the world of clandestine meetings with the enemy, she wasn't sure whether she should wait in the car until the scheduled time or simply walk up to the door early. Stay in the car and someone might drive by and recognize her. Then again, the house had a For Sale sign; no one would think it odd if she were seen looking around the property.

A light rain had begun to fall, and when she stepped out of the car, she felt somewhat shielded from curious onlookers by her plain black umbrella. Thank heavens, her unique pink plaid one had suffered irreparable damage during their last storm.

Before she could knock, the door opened. A pleasant-looking man greeted her. "Ms. Rosen? You're early." He moved back and opened the door farther, gesturing for her to enter.

"I hope that's not a problem."

"Not at all. Please come in."

When she stepped inside, her footsteps echoed in the empty foyer. Through the archway to her right, she saw a cavernous living room with a fireplace at its end. To the left, an ornate but unlit chandelier hung low in the middle of the space, suggesting it was meant as a dining room. Neither room had furniture.

The man reached out a hand. "My name is Kevin Cho, and you called me because you wanted to view this property." He opened his pad folio and pulled out a home flyer with a business card stapled to its corner. "Most people make notes on the flyer when they tour a place. So afterward you might want to take a quick peek at the house and jot down a couple of remarks to substantiate that you were actually here."

"S-substantiate . . . ?"

Nick's voice reverberated from the rear of the house. "We're back here."

Kevin, the real estate agent, gave her a salesman's smile. "They're in the kitchen. Through that hallway." He paused. "And if you do become interested in the house, please let me know. I'll be upstairs so the three of you can have some privacy."

After the man headed up the curved staircase that presumably led to the bedrooms, Kate walked tentatively down the hallway. It blossomed into a large gourmet kitchen with gleaming steel appliances and sleek black cabinets. Nick and another man sat on stools at the counter, playing cards.

At the sight of her, Nick hopped down and took several steps toward her. "Thanks for coming." It was an awkward moment—as if he was unsure whether to shake her hand or offer her a hug. Kate solved his problem by doing neither. She still had her doubts and she didn't exactly hide that.

"Why am I here, Nick?"

"Because my friend has some information that you need to hear."

The other man stood up, crossed over to her, and instead of holding out his hand, reached into his jacket and pulled out his wallet.

"Jim Trainor. FBI."

She glanced at the identification long enough to recognize the seal and his name. Her heart quickened.

He continued. "I was one of the people who questioned Daniel Gilroy. And I wanted to talk to you about what he said."

Kate remained perfectly still, her instincts whispering for her to be suspicious. "What's wrong with this picture? If the

FBI wants to talk to me, all you guys have to do is respond to the dozen or so calls I've made to you. Or even crook your little finger and I'd make a beeline to the Hoover Building to talk." She pinned him with a glare. "Why go through Nick to talk to me? Why all this?" She glanced over her shoulder, indicating the empty house beyond.

Trainor shrugged artfully. "I'm sorry for all the pseudo-spy stuff, Ms. Rosen. My superiors don't know I'm here, but Nick thinks you need to know. I agree. I could lose my job if anyone learns why we're here. So we have three reputations to protect." He paused and added a cryptic "If not more."

Trainor turned back to his stool and plopped down, gesturing to the empty seat beside him. "Please?"

She looked at Nick, who nodded toward the counter with a silent *sit and listen* request.

Kate hesitated. What real harm would there be in listening to what the man had to say? At best, he might have some real information. At worst, she'd have wasted two hours and inadvertently rekindled the ember of desire she'd buried for a beautiful house like this in the burbs.

She took a seat at the counter and crossed her arms, then uncrossed them, realizing how petulant she must look.

Once Nick was settled next to her, Trainor began. "I was one of three people who questioned Daniel Gilroy once he was brought into federal custody. We started with the threatening notes. He denied any knowledge of the first note you received. We did find fingerprints on it, but they weren't his. They've yet to be identified. We don't believe he sent it."

"But the second note?" she prompted.

Trainor pulled a copy of it from the file folder sitting in front of him. "Gilroy admitted he'd written that second note. He then launched into a rather long-winded explanation of his philosophy of government, but it was mostly incomprehensible. Once he got to a stopping place, we asked him why he wanted to harm you. That's when . . . that's when his weird answers got even weirder."

"How so?"

"At first he talked about seeing you and Nick conspiring against Emily and how upset that made him."

Kate turned to Nick. "Gilroy must have seen us together at the bagel shop in New Hampshire." She returned her attention to Trainor. "But we weren't conspiring. We were just talking. In public, no less."

"In any case, then he started telling us about how his stepmother, Connie, tempted him into betraying his own father, and he compared that to you, Nick, and Emily."

Kate and Nick looked at each other. "Huh?"

"Gilroy blamed his stepmother/wife for . . . How did he say it?" Trainor thumbed through his folder, pulled out a report, and read, "'. . . for blinding me with my own greed, enticing me to deceive my own father and to steal that which was rightly his.' It seems that after she married Senior, she talked Junior into ousting the old man from his own power base."

Kate supplied the next part. "Then she divorced Senior, married Junior, doing so because she thought she could get control of the group from Junior. But she and Senior died in a car accident, leaving Junior with complete control."

Trainor and Nick stared at her, both somewhat surprised.

"That's old news." She shrugged. "I did my homework. But what does any of that have to do with Emily?"

"It took a while, but we finally figured out that he was trying to draw an analogy between the betrayal he'd experienced with the betrayal that he thought was about to be sprung on Emily."

"By Kate and me," Nick supplied. "But why would he even care about what happens to Emily? I can't imagine she's his favorite person. She brought him to justice, literally."

"We asked him about that, and it turns out that while incarcerated, he spent most of his time conjuring up a . . . for the lack of a better word, a fantasy love life centered around the woman who 'saved' him from himself—Governor Emily Benton."

"O-o-okay," Nick said, obviously fighting some sense of incredulity. "So he thought Emily loved him. . . . Then his note to you must have been a warning that he knew you were being enticed by the devil and that *he*, the devil—meaning me—would die. Not you."

The revelation sat in Kate's stomach like a stone. "He was warning *me* in advance about his plans to attack Talbot headquarters?" She turned to Nick. "I had no idea. . . ."

He raised his hands in mock surrender. "I don't blame you. It went over my head just like it did everyone else's."

Trainor pulled out a copy of the "Handmaiden of the Devil" note. "Yeah, a little punctuation would have helped." He took out a pencil. "This is how we all read the note." He added the missing bits so that it read: *Repent, Handmaiden of the Devil! She who serves The Devil will die by the hands of True Believers.*

"This, as it turns out, is how he said he meant for it to be read." Trainor erased the first changes and added different punctuation. Now it read: *Repent, Handmaiden of the Devil, she who serves. The Devil will die by the hands of True Believers.*

LAURA HAYDEN

Kate stared at the words. "Gilroy thought he was helping Emily? By killing Nick?"

Trainor nodded. "He said he knew that if the temptation was removed—i.e., Nick—you might redeem yourself and faithfully serve Emily again."

"But we . . . ," she faltered. "But Nick and I . . . we're not . . ." She looked helplessly at Nick, but instead of agreeing, he flushed slightly and turned away.

Trainor stepped in to end the awkward silence. "I know. But Gilroy sees what he wants to see. In his own situation, had Connie been removed from the equation, he believes he and his father would have patched up their differences."

"Oh." Kate sat for a while, trying to digest the revelation. Both revelations. She never should have agreed to meet with Nick in the first place. Pure and simple. Nothing had been said at the bagel shop that couldn't have been said over the phone. She didn't need to meet him again, learn how much he'd changed, see how he'd worked hard to regain his respectability. . . .

Dear Lord, deliver me from temptation. . . .

Luckily Nick couldn't read her thoughts. He reached over and patted her hand. "The man is a certified nut job. A wacko. A flake. A raving lunatic." His attempt to laugh bore more than a hint of hollowness, then died off to silence.

"I'm sorry you were injured, Nick," she said at last, finding the words. "And I'm even sorrier that I didn't listen to my first instinct."

"Which was?"

"Not to meet with you. I told myself there was nothing wrong with hearing you out. Well, I guess now we know I was wrong." She sat at the counter lost in her thoughts—not ones of accusation but of regret, of should-have-knowns. Then something hit her. She turned to Trainor.

"Why hasn't the FBI released its findings? Why is this considered some big, deep, dark secret?"

Jim Trainor looked her dead in the eye. "Because we think Daniel Gilroy is lying or that someone is using him."

Both she and Nick gaped at him.

The man tapped the note sitting on the counter. "We do believe Daniel Gilroy wrote this note. But we believe it was delivered seven years ago. To his wife, Connie."

At their stunned silence, he continued. "The original note was used at his trial as proof of his mental state. I think you'd agree that it makes him sound pretty unhinged. When we pulled the case file on him, we discovered that someone had replaced the original note with a xeroxed copy." His face darkened. "The last time the evidence file for that case was pulled prior to our request was at the hands of District Attorney Peter Shaiyne."

Kate heard the words but discounted them immediately.

But judging by the look in Nick's eyes, he'd also made the Benton family connection and he obviously thought it was possible. "So you're suggesting that Emily got her cousin's husband to pull the complete files—evidence included—steal the original note, replace it with a replica, and then . . . ," he hesitated as if wondering if he should say his thoughts aloud. "Then Emily sent the original to Kate in order to implicate Gilroy. But why?"

"Public sympathy, perhaps? Or free publicity. Or perhaps the relationship between you and Ms. Benton isn't as finalized as you both thought."

"That's ridiculous." Kate and Nick spoke the words simultaneously.

Nick crossed his arms and stared at the agent, his body language a true reflection of his disbelief. "Okay, let's assume for the sake of argument that Emily did this for reasons we haven't yet determined. Then why is Gilroy lying and helping her cover this up?"

Trainor tapped the copy of the note with the pencil. "A man will do a great deal to win the favor of a woman he loves . . . or at least lusts after."

"And a betrayed woman never forgets . . . ," Nick added darkly. "If Emily is manipulating Gilroy for any reason, it's because she still hates me and has no qualms against using him. He was a tool in Connie's hands. How hard would it be to lead him astray again?" A mixture of emotions reflected in his face—regret, confusion, and anger. "You know . . . Emily never forgave me for our marital problems. I guess 'going over to the enemy' and joining Talbot was the last straw for her."

Trainor picked up on Nick's train of thought. "So you think it's possible she used the man's infatuation against him and sent him to New Hampshire to kill you?"

Nick nodded and Kate shook her head.

"No way," she said with a building sense of resolution. "This is all crazy talk. Even if I could possibly accept that my best friend might have—in a moment of weakness—sent me that note in hopes of stirring up some controversy, I can tell you categorically that she did not conspire with Gilroy. She didn't meet with him, play on his affections or whatever, and send him off with orders to shoot Nick."

"Why? Why can't you believe she hates me enough to do something like that?"

"Three reasons." Kate held up her forefinger. "One, because the man was completely inept with guns. Wes will corroborate that. If Emily were to send in a shooter, I guarantee he would have been an expert marksman and would have gotten his target. If Emily sent somebody after you, Nick, you'd be dead. And no one else would have known it was a setup and no one else would have been hurt. And two, Pete Shaiyne is smart enough to figure out how to get the evidence without leaving any trail leading back to him."

"And three?"

She fought to control her rising anger. *Help me, dear Lord. Make me an instrument of your peace here. I don't want to lose it now.* She spoke in a low voice. "Nick, I realize what you're doing. Trying to use rumor, conjecture, and maybe even some pure lies to put a wedge between me and Emily."

Kate stood up, her arms crossed. "Sorry, boys, it didn't work." She shot Trainor her coldest, most contemptuous glare. "If I see or hear from you again, I'll be talking to your superiors about this little meeting. And you . . ." She turned to Nick, fighting to keep her indignation from turning into a righteous fury.

"If you really have found God, then you need to ask his forgiveness for this stunt. God knows, my faith says I should forgive you, but I can't find it in me right now. For both of our sakes, don't you ever call me again."

✫ ✫ ✫ ✫ ✫

Kate was lucky she hadn't been pulled over for speeding on the way home. Twice, she looked down at the speedometer to discover she was pushing ninety. It wasn't like her to let her emotions overrule her common sense.

No, that was something Emily was more apt to do.

Kate's stomach flared and she almost pulled off to the shoulder of the road to throw up. Once she reached home, emotionally and physically drained, she dragged herself inside, crawled into bed, and gave herself permission to have a good cry.

But she had no tears.

All she had were a thousand questions running through her mind, threatening to keep her awake all night.

Could Emily have gotten so mad at Nick, so upset by his involvement with Talbot's campaign, that she'd take such a drastic action to have him killed? It was a complicated question that had to be broken down into its component parts.

Did Emily hate Nick?

Yes.

Did Emily hate Nick enough to want to kill him?

Maybe.

Did Emily hate Nick enough to arrange to kill him?

No. Emily's vindictive streak was such that she'd much prefer watching him live in fear of death than watch him actually die.

Kate grabbed that small thread of logic spun from her faith in her friend and held on for dear life. Then she reached out to find other threads of logic and braided them together to give her a stronger lifeline.

Emily wouldn't have made Nick a martyr.

She wouldn't have cut a sensitive deal with an unstable person.

She wouldn't have sent a threatening note to scare her best friend.

Divide and conquer were tools of desperation. And since Emily wasn't desperate, the person behind this just might be Talbot via his henchmen Nick Beaudry and Jim Trainor.

And the flicker of something for Nick that hid in her heart? It was no more than Christian concern for another human being. Nothing more than that.

Kate allowed herself a small smile as she decided that this had been nothing more than a test of her faith in Emily.

And she passed.

EARLY MOMENTUM in the primary race had been the first critical goal of their campaign plans. The overwhelming success of Tsunami Tuesday took that early momentum and turned Emily into a force to be reckoned with. In fact, their early success caused the remaining primaries to become Benton landslides. True to Emily's prediction, Bochner had stepped out of the race the morning after his distant second-place finish on Tsunami Tuesday and only two mostly inconsequential candidates remained, neither of them holding more than a couple dozen delegate votes each.

Working under the radar, Kate started the machinery to initiate private talks with Bochner by first contacting his campaign manager, Sheila McIntosh, feeling her out about the vice presidential slot. They'd met several years ago and had a basically congenial professional-to-professional relationship. Kate was encouraged by her honesty and the answers she relayed to some very tough questions asked of her about her boss.

In Kate's opinion, Bochner and McIntosh had played it smart by playing it clean. There would be no unfortunate insinuations to be swept under the rug and no private retractions necessary in order to bring Emily and Bochner into the same room. The same could be said about Emily and Kate—they had found no need to use what little dirt they'd turned up against the man. Life was always easier if you started with a clean playing field.

And Kate's resolve to conduct her political life in accordance with her personal values hadn't been tested again as it had early in the primary cycle, for which she was profoundly grateful.

Best of all, Bochner would give the ticket a grounding of Midwest sensibilities. It was the only region in which Emily lacked a personal or familial presence. Her Virginia upbringing gave her a theoretical foothold in the South, even if she didn't personify a true Southerner. Then there was the fame or, in some cases, infamy associated with the Benton family name both in the Northeastern states and on the West Coast. All she lacked was a strong relationship with mid-America.

But a decidedly male vice president born and raised in the Heartland, his Chicago-born academician wife, and his family of three picture-perfect male moppets (and one less photogenic and somewhat rebellious teenage son) would help sway the holdouts who still found gender a big roadblock to stumble over or around. Add to all that Bochner's four-year stint in the army and he looked like the perfect running mate on paper and, in Kate's estimation, in person as well.

After several calls, first from one manager to the other,

then one candidate to the other, they set a date for a face-to-face meeting.

When they finally met, Emily held out her hand first and Bochner accepted and shook it warmly. "It's so nice to have a chance to talk without microphones being shoved in our faces," she said.

"What's the old joke?" Bochner flipped up the collar of his sports jacket. "Please step closer and talk into my lapel?"

His bit of humor helped break the ice, and Kate watched as Emily relaxed a bit. At one time, Bochner had been known as the boy wonder of the House, thanks to his youthful face and eagerness in facing his duty to his country in the political arena as well as earlier in a uniformed capacity. In the intervening years, he'd matured in looks and tempered his enthusiasm without losing it completely. His constituents, as well as the press, described him as a dedicated Everyman.

Kate excused herself to allow the two to talk alone, something Emily had insisted on and with which Kate had readily agreed. The day's discussions would be more philosophical and theoretical ones. No immediate offer would be made as a result of their confab. No promises made. Bochner also knew he wasn't the only person under consideration as the running mate. Emily had meetings arranged with three other potential vice presidential candidates.

But Kate had her money on Bochner. There was just something about the man she respected—his style, his grace, his deeply felt faith. She thought he brought qualities to a Benton/Bochner ticket that would make it even more viable against a Talbot/Whomever one.

Three hours later, Emily emerged, shook hands with Bochner once more, and they went their separate ways.

Kate waited for Emily to report, but she said nothing. Finally Kate stuck her head in Emily's office and prompted with a "Well?"

"I'm not sure." Emily wore her inscrutable look, which meant getting details from her would be like getting state secrets from a closemouthed spy.

"Politics, personality, or what?"

"I can't put my finger on it. Let me think for a while—digest everything that was said."

"Is he at least a possibility?"

"Yes, he's still in the running."

Kate didn't pry any further. Instead she pulled out the master calendar to brief Emily on her updated travel schedule.

Kate had set up an ambitious pattern of travel for the next few months until the convention was held in Denver in August. Emily's rotation included two weeks on the road, talking, visiting, and otherwise speaking directly to the people, then back to Virginia for a couple of days to recharge her batteries and reassess their plans; and then she'd strike out again. Kate spent part of the time on the road with Emily but just as much time, if not more, holding down the fort at the main headquarters and making plans for the next volley of speaking engagements.

The tone of their campaigning had changed once Emily's candidacy was all but official. Now she had new responsibilities to her party and its leadership and, because of that, spent a lot of time behind closed doors talking international and domestic policies with higher-up party officials. Many of the cities they chose to visit were because Emily needed to have a closed-door meeting with an organization or group headquartered there. In addition, funds still needed to be raised, and that meant organizing and attending various "Benton for President" galas in major metropolitan areas.

By the end of April, they'd raised another $34 million. By the end of May, they'd reduced the number of days in the air or on the road between locations, spending more concentrated time in a specific area—staying for days rather than hours in one general part of a state. During this time, they had more meetings with Burl Bochner as well as one other potential vice president. Two earlier contenders had removed themselves from consideration for reasons they didn't disclose.

Their loss.

July was a patriotic blur, tinged in red, white, and blue. It wasn't until the end of the month that Emily finally made her decision of a running mate. She'd used Kate as a sounding board initially, discussing each candidate's attributes, their shortcomings, their influence, their political agendas, what philosophies meshed with hers and what didn't, which personalities she respected and which qualities she could tolerate.

Which ones she couldn't stand . . .

When the discussions petered out, Kate knew Emily had made her decision. Kate's money was still on Burl Bochner, but Emily was keeping her decision close to the vest.

August was more of the same. Kate couldn't allow herself to call it the "grind" because the intensity was ramping up, but in some ways, it *was* just more of the same—harder, faster, more concentrated—travel, speaking engagements, and fund-raising.

All work and very little play.

Plus the party convention loomed ahead like some giant

behemoth. Their initial campaign tactic had been to keep the gender issue on the back burner, not ignoring it by any means but presenting it as simply one of the qualities this worthy candidate happened to possess. There had been female candidates for president before and there would be again.

But now they were treading in—for the lack of a better word—virgin territory with Emily about to be named the first female, party-nominated presidential candidate. Gender would jump to the front burner, especially with the unprecedented selection of a female convention chair and female cochairs.

It didn't help that one of the more irreverent online news sites came up with a lead story headlined, "Political Chastity Belt at the Convention—All Women, Locked Up Tight. No Men Need Apply." Their tabloid-style story insisted that Emily was considering only fellow females as her running mate. More serious news agencies had jumped on the story and it had started a fair amount of debate as to whom she would choose—a man or a woman.

The media was betting female.

Kate figured the smart money should know better.

In reality, Kate knew Emily hadn't interviewed or otherwise talked with any women for the job. When asked, Emily had said, "I'm gearing up to win the election, not make a statement on any amendment, equal rights or otherwise."

Emily had intended to wait until the morning after being crowned as the party candidate to name her choice for vice president, but the pressure and burden of travel reached such a point that she and Kate decided that an official running mate could take up some of the slack for them, allowing the Benton campaign to literally be in two places at once.

So, on August 5, Emily climbed the steps of the beautifully recreated Governor's Palace in Colonial Williamsburg, Virginia, and spoke to the crowd and the cameras assembled.

"Thank you for coming. I appreciate having you with me as we take a new step on this journey together."

She indicated the large historical building looming behind her. "Colonial Williamsburg. More than two hundred years ago, the pursuit of freedom, independence, and equality fueled a movement that continues to influence the world today. People like Thomas Jefferson, Patrick Henry, and George Washington played major roles in defining the true meaning of freedom and liberty; and many others have helped build this great nation by going about their everyday lives. It's important to have our history come alive in a place like this."

Her smile bore just the right amount of nostalgia. "I loved coming here as a child. One day when I was eight years old, I told my father that I wanted to live in the Governor's Palace someday. He had to break it to me that this wasn't where the governor of Virginia actually lived."

There was polite laughter in response.

"As you know, I did end up spending four years in the executive mansion as the governor of Virginia, so I guess I did fulfill that childhood dream in a way. But—" she thumbed over her shoulder at the house behind her—"it would have been cool to have lived here, don't you think?"

The laughter increased in intensity.

"But we aren't here to talk about the goals I've set and fulfilled. I'm here to discuss the aspirations I'm still striving to reach. This morning I've had the privilege to speak with several courageous, talented patriots who, at my request, have discussed at length the qualities and desires they possess to become my running mate and candidate for vice president of the United States of America."

The camera flashes increased as the press realized this was *the* speech they'd been waiting on for at least three weeks since rumors started running rampant about her possible running mate.

"Each of the individuals with whom I've spoken could effectively fulfill this role, and all of them have the qualities to lead our country in their own right. However, I can choose but one person to be my running mate."

The murmurs in the crowd included whispered speculations, ranging from the ridiculous to the sublime.

"The person I've chosen understands American values and has defended those values here and abroad in service to his country."

Kate watched as the crowd's speculations narrowed to two politicians whose military service had been an important part of their biographies.

"He returned from a military career to become a champion for the very people whose freedom he fought to protect. He's a family man whose character, experiences, and talents have prepared him well for leadership.

"I'm pleased to announce that, with your approval, my candidate for vice president of the United States of America will be Senator Burl Bochner from Missouri."

The crowd erupted in applause, indicating their enthusiastic approval of her selection.

Kate watched from the sidelines as Emily continued praising Bochner in public, something she hadn't really done much in private. Behind closed doors, he simply was a means to an end. If she wanted the presidency, she needed a second who possessed the elements that America thought she needed and didn't have. And that included a nuclear family and testosterone. Bochner appeared ready to throw his lot in with Emily's, to take the right stances, make the right remarks, shake the right hands, but to never, ever steal the spotlight from the candidate herself.

As long as Senator Bochner remembered he was second in command, second in importance, played second fiddle in all other areas to Emily, he'd do just fine indeed.

Welcome to my world, Kate thought. *Hold on, because it can be a bumpy ride.*

Burl Bochner came to their campaign with a complete staff of his own, people who had worked with the same sort of tireless dedication as the Benton staff to make their candidate outshine the competition. But now their mission was different; Bochner was no longer the star quarterback but a tight end who might be asked to run or catch, depending on how Emily called the plays.

How *Emily* called the plays. . . .

The mission of his core staff was no longer how to spotlight Burl as a single person but how to present what strength he brought as part of the Benton team. However, no matter how much of a valued player Burl Bochner might become, it would remain the Benton team who shaped the campaign. One of Burl's first duties was to learn that it was the party line he needed to espouse—Emily's interpretation of it and not necessarily his own.

After several days of intense review of Benton platform programs, Kate sent a couple of her staffers along with Bochner and his traveling crew while he made his maiden voyage representing the team of Benton/Bochner in '08. The encouraging reports that came back included words like *brilliant* and *team player*. He entranced the press as well, and their news footage of his appearances showed him to be enthusiastic, well-spoken, and best of all, well-versed.

Everyone—from the most critical pundits to the average woman on the street—felt that Emily had made the right choice of running mates.

And Kate couldn't help but agree.

She prayed that Emily thought so, or things could get ugly fast.

AUGUST IN DENVER.

Instead of being covered in several feet of winter snow, the mountains off in the distance were brown and bare with only small patches of dirty snow hiding in the shadows. In the city itself, summer temperatures had soared to record highs, and Kate felt every degree of heat and every foot of altitude. Fifteen minutes in the sun walking from the hotel to the convention center and she was searching for water. Fifteen steps up to the next floor and she was panting for breath.

It hadn't been that hot in Virginia only a few days earlier at the Benton farm. Or maybe it was the vast number of trees that shaded the mansion and outer buildings that made the summer heat more bearable. Emily had retired to her family estate near Charlottesville to work on what amounted to the most important speech in her life. That didn't necessarily mean writing every word herself but working with Hugo

Bills, quite possibly the best and, more importantly, the hottest political speechwriter around.

In Kate's opinion, Hugo was quite an enigma. She'd never met anyone who could write with such heart and compose such moving words and who, in real life, could be such a complete waste of carbon. He was the biggest jerk she'd ever met. He was loud and demanding; he drank too much and made raunchy and inappropriate jokes at the worst possible times.

He tested her patience and her ability to turn the other cheek on a regular basis.

Yet he and Emily worked well as a team. That wasn't to say that they got along well. Kate conducted her business while staying in the main house, and Emily and Hugo worked in one of the guest bungalows, ostensibly for the privacy but in reality so no one could hear their screaming arguments. But despite the rancor, together they were able to craft a speech that absolutely awed Kate when she read it, with its stirring eloquence and precision in defining Emily's goals for the country and its people.

As thrilling as the written words were, when Kate listened to Emily practice it aloud, her recitation sent actual chills up Kate's spine. At that moment, she knew that when Emily delivered her acceptance speech at the party convention, the speaker of those words would go down in history, not for being the first woman to reach this lofty stage of American politics but for being a brilliant politician and astounding orator.

Then, that day came. . . .

The Benton staff had a temporary office on the club level of the Pepsi Center, where the party's national convention was in full swing. Between the tight security, the crush of delegates filling the arena below them, and the astonishing number of media people each vying for a chance to see, photograph, or better yet, speak with Emily, Kate had been going nonstop for over twenty-four hours straight without any sleep and barely any food.

All she had to do was hang on a little while longer. . . .

But an hour before Emily was about to be introduced and make her grand entrance into the convention hall, Kate had the closest thing she'd ever had to a panic attack. Her pulse shot up, it became hard to catch her breath, and suddenly her most important task was to get out of the incredibly shrinking room by any means necessary.

And yet she knew she shouldn't, couldn't, leave.

The only person who noticed her mini-meltdown in the making was Wes Kingsbury, who had risen from unofficial religious adviser to a more official position. He'd come on board to head the Religious Initiatives office under Kate's supervision. The Office of Religious Initiatives might have started as Kate's idea, but she soon realized she needed someone else who shared her vision to chart this course into previously shark-ridden governmental waters. A similar office had been tried under President George W. Bush and had been too quickly politicized, underfunded, and undermined. Kate wanted it to be a true reflection of Christ's mercy, open to all and a beacon of light in the political and governmental darkness. Wes had been her one and only choice to head up the mission, and he'd quickly accepted the tentative position.

If Emily benefited from having Kate's conscience help her make decisions, then she'd be doubly blessed when Wes also had an official position within Emily's White House.

But right now, all Kate could think of was figuring out how to survive the next fifteen minutes in the crowded room. Wes saw her distress and maneuvered through the throng until he was next to her. He leaned over and whispered in her ear, "You okay?"

"Sure," she lied. In her mind, she was plotting the path of least resistance to the nearest exit. Once she got outside, she was going to either keel over or scream; she hadn't decided which.

"You don't look okay. You look like you're about to pass out."

"I'm just a little tired," she offered as an explanation.

"It's more than that. C'mon." He grabbed her arm and began to follow the very same path Kate had plotted in her mental escape. But what she'd thought might be an exit turned out to lead to an outside balcony. Wes held open the door and she stepped out into the dry heat of a sweltering Colorado summer.

"Take a few deep breaths," he suggested as he led her to the railing, closing off the noise behind them by shutting the door. "Take a few minutes. Admire the view."

She stared bleakly at the jagged horizon of the Rocky Mountains that managed to be majestic and imposing yet brown and bare at the same time.

"God's playground," he said quietly.

Kate pointed to a large amusement park much closer in the foreground. "Much more beautiful and serene than man's playground."

"It's an interesting juxtaposition, don't you think?"

"True."

They could both hear some faint screams, presumably

coming from the roller coaster that peeked out over the tops of trees and buildings at the end of the park.

"Political conventions are a lot like roller coasters," Wes said in his best "I'm a preachin' man" voice. "Lots of ups and downs, unexpected turns to the left and right. Some of them even turn you upside down, swing you around, make you go backwards. There's some laughter, some screaming—"

"—and some puking," Kate added.

"That too. But in the end, you complete your journey and that's when you realize you were never in trouble at all."

Kate knew exactly what he was doing and appreciated the distraction. But she spotted what she considered a flaw in his sermon. "But the problem is, you end up in the exact same place you started."

"Hmm . . ." He rested his elbows on the balcony railing. "You have a point." He tilted his head for a moment, then began again in a slightly comedic voice. "Political conventions are a lot like amusement parks. There are many rides to choose from—ones that go up and down, sideways, around in circles. Some are slow and some are lightning fast. Sometimes, you have to wait in line a long time, longer than the time the actual ride takes, but the moment you step off, you're ready to get back in that line again."

Not to be outdone, Kate took his analogy a step further. "Then again, after a long, full day of riding every ride, eating all the great junk food, getting a bit too much sun, drinking expensive fruity drinks that turn your tongue blue, buying one too many expensive souvenirs, you get back to the car and you slump over the wheel and say, 'Now that was a great time. I'll never forget it.'"

Belatedly Kate realized that her heart wasn't hammering as hard and her breath was easier to catch. His insidious little plan to help her gain control of herself had worked. "Then you try to stay awake during the drive home and eventually collapse onto your bed, exhausted."

"Exhausted but happy," he added. "Kinda like you're feeling right now?"

"I've got the exhausted part down pat."

He studied her face. "But you're not happy?"

She managed to paste on a tired smile. "Sure I am. Phase one is all but accomplished. We're here." She gestured to the melee behind the glass doors. "We've made the convention and in less than an hour, Emily's going to make history by walking out of here as the first female presidential candidate to win either major party."

"And then the fright ride starts up all over again?"

"Yeah." Kate nodded. "I think that's what just hit me. We do exactly what we've been doing for over a year and a half—hit the road, campaigning all over again. Same places, new faces. We have to continue to work aggressively, to be on the offense to get our message and our team to the people. But we also have to be on the defense and repel incoming barbs, innuendos, and insinuations."

"But isn't that what you're doing to Talbot and Mason? Trying to distract them from delivering their message by lobbing similar accusations so they spend more time cleaning up than reaching out?"

She spread out her hands. "Welcome to the wonderful world of politics. We spend more of our time twisting the knife or rotating the roasting spit than we do turning the other cheek."

"You've been with Emily for a long time. You knew this when you signed up for the big race. I think you've done a remarkable job of handling your responsibility to Emily but holding yourself accountable to a higher authority."

Kate sighed. "I hope so. I knew that politics can be an intense and sometimes dirty business. But even if I had a pretty good idea of the work involved before I got into it, no one goes out of their way to point out all the details of the seamy underbelly."

"Why would they? It's not what you'd call a great recruitment tool."

"You're right." She reached over and patted his arm. "Don't pay much attention to me. It's the exhaustion talking. That's all. Yeah, I'm tired but I'm not disillusioned. I'm still in this for the long run. But boy, will I be glad when November 4 finally rolls around. Maybe I'll get some sleep then."

"Plus, you'll get a great corner office on Pennsylvania Avenue with an amazing view."

"And Emily will get an even cooler oval-shaped one. And we'll be able to make the world a better place. That's the goal." Kate turned from the view and leaned against the balcony railing, facing the glass door and watching the throng of people milling about inside the room. "And I, for one, can't wait until that happens."

"I know what you mean. It's been a long time coming. But remember, even with God's help, you may find that the Rose Garden isn't always a bed of roses."

She grinned at his analogy. "Don't I know it. The job comes with a completely new set of thorns. I might not know exactly what those thorns are, but at least I know in advance that I have to watch out for them. I suppose that little panic attack was just a demonstration of good sense."

Wes rested his elbows on the railing and looked toward the mountains. Kate turned and mimicked his position. After a moment of contemplative silence, he spoke. "The chief of staff position won't be an easy one."

"No job is. Especially that one. But it's going to be a bit easier with you working with us in an official capacity."

"I'll do what I can. But the real trick will be to keep the new responsibilities from isolating you from the things you hold dear—your relationship with your family, your friends, and more importantly, your God. The White House can be an ivory tower sometimes and—"

They both heard a noise behind them. Emily had slid open the glass door and was shading her eyes from the sun. "What are you two slackers doing out here?"

"Praying," Wes deadpanned.

"Dear Lord, give them whatever they asked for. They're that good." Emily stepped out onto the balcony and shut the door behind her. "Now how about praying for a break in this heat? I thought Denver was supposed to have cool, comfortable summers." She fanned her face as if suggesting that eighty-five degrees of dry Colorado heat was far more uncomfortable than ninety-five degrees and 95 percent humidity in D.C. "Better yet, pray that this insane circus comes off as planned and we can get back to our real business of whuppin' the competition."

"Emily!" Kate instinctively looked around, hoping that no one had overheard her statement from a nearby balcony. She didn't put it past certain less savory members of the media to have parabolic microphones pointed in their direction at all times. It had happened before. Even some politicians weren't above it. Nixon had routinely bugged his opponents. The Watergate break-ins had been just another string in the president's bow, another tool to keep his eyes and ears on what he referred to as his "enemies list." Kate didn't want any listeners mistaking Emily's nervous face-tiousness for her real sentiments.

"I'm just kidding; you know that." Evidently Emily re-membered the parabolic mics too, if only a moment too late. She quirked one eyebrow as if telling Kate, *Okay, I screwed up. I'll get out of this.* "The convention is a critical step in our journey. I don't mean to diminish its importance or its sense of tradition. It's just that I find the hoopla some-times . . . straining."

Good recovery, Kate thought to herself.

Wes turned away from the majestic view and faced Emily. "I think a prayer wouldn't be out of place at the moment."

Emily, obviously mindful of unwanted ears, nodded. "Good idea."

Wes reached over, grasped Emily's hand, and then placed his other hand on Kate's shoulder. He closed his eyes. "Dear Lord, please watch over our Emily here as she steps into a new arena. Give her the insight to see into the true hearts of her constituents, give her the wisdom to know what they need and what they want, and give her the strength to do what must be done in accordance with your will. Please keep her strong in mind and body to serve you as she serves your people.

"Help her use that same wisdom and grace when she reaches the White House, to lead a great nation into even more greatness."

Kate peeked.

It'd been a habit she'd tried to break since childhood. Sitting in a hard pew and listening to a thoughtful, albeit long, prayer, she would sometimes take quick glimpses of the faces around her. She'd watch her father concentrate on the preacher's words as if trying to memorize them. Her mother would wear a look of bliss and contentment that always filled Kate with a similar sense of satisfaction.

In Wes's face, she saw strength and commitment. He might be primarily an academician, but in his heart and in her eyes, he was still a man of the cloth. If her own pipeline to God was often clogged with the flotsam and jetsam of a complicated everyday life, it was good to know that she could turn to Wes and be assured that his line of communication was clear and his advice sound.

Kate listened more closely to his words as she scanned the imposing mountains in the distance. She'd needed this moment and Wes had instinctively known it. That thought alone brought her a sense of comfort, making the pressures of the day ease somewhat to a more manageable level. She glanced over at Emily, expecting to see her friend reflect some of the same inner peace, but instead, she saw boredom in Emily's expression, her mouth tight with impatience, her other hand tapping an irritated cadence on the railing.

For a moment, Kate allowed Emily's discontent to override her own feelings. Almost everyone connected with the campaign had learned early to heed the adage, "If Emily ain't happy, nobody's happy."

Kate, more than anyone, kept a constant watch on Emily's emotional status and had a host of tricks and diversions to lighten her dark moods and narrow her focus or, when called for, a list of excuses to explain her actions or reactions. Often that'd been the most exhausting part of Kate's job.

But Kate knew that right now Emily's apparent sense of annoyance was merely to mask her very real emotions of anxiety and fear. Even though those were reasonable reactions considering the profound burden she was about to accept, Emily's upbringing didn't allow her to display such sentiments. She went with undiluted bile instead.

As if reading Kate's mind, Wes added, "And, Lord, please help guide Kate as she works with Emily. Help them both to stay on the path, temper their decisions with your wisdom, use their energies and power to serve you."

A sense of renewed joy filled Kate and an uncontrollable smile made her lips quirk. The spirit of the Lord . . . what a remarkable medicine.

Straightening, she reached up and covered Wes's hand with her own, hoping to draw the strength she needed to better grasp this newly regained sense of emotional balance. Somehow, she knew he had strength to spare, thanks to the strength of his own faith. He squeezed her fingers lightly and completed his prayer, ending with a quiet, "In God's name we pray, amen."

Both Kate and Emily echoed, "Amen."

He turned to Kate, noting her smile. "Better?" he asked.

"Absolutely," Emily answered quickly for them both, already pivoting toward the door leading back inside. "Thanks, Wes. Let's get inside. I'd better get ready. I go on stage in less than twenty minutes." She paused and gave them her brightest and most intense smile.

"Time to get this party started."

✫ ✫ ✫ ✫ ✫

Any lingering doubts in the crowd of delegates concerning Emily Benton's potential presidency faded away the moment Dozier Marsh began the carefully crafted speech they'd written for him. It was designed to prove that, although he was eightysomething, he still understood and was a master of the theatrics of politics. His speech ended with a resounding introduction of Emily as the *next* President Benton, which was her cue to step out on stage.

When she did step into the spotlight, the noise generated by the crowd must have outshone that of any other individual who ever graced a stage at the Pepsi Center—be it pop star, athlete, or any other type of performer.

After the thunder of applause finally abated, Emily mesmerized the audience with a speech that both clarified her positions and reflected a unified party line. The enormous crowd erupted once again when "Benton/Bochner '08" campaign signs unfurled behind her.

Kate watched from a discreet place in the wings as the last vestiges of her earlier panic faded into excitement tinged with well-deserved relief. Sandwiched between Dozier and Emily's uncle Bill, she watched Emily expose a side of herself that she usually kept in check. It reminded Kate of her friend's younger, more idealistic self, before she'd developed some of her sharper edges.

This was the Emily Benton that Kate wanted to—expected to—see sitting behind the big desk in the Oval Office. This was the person who would keep a great nation great. Maybe even make it greater. . . .

"You look almost like a proud momma right after her

first child's been born," Dozier Marsh whispered to Kate, slipping a grandfatherly arm around Kate's shoulders.

"I feel like that."

He reached in the breast pocket of his coat and pulled out a cigar with a pink "It's a girl" band on its cellophane wrapper. "Congratulations, Mom," he said, offering her the cigar. "It's a president."

☆ ☆ ☆ ☆ ☆

It was a whole new ball game.

Because the other party's convention started four days after theirs ended, Charles Talbot was home in Cincinnati, busy preparing for his part of the tradition. Even shoo-in candidates had to craft the perfect speech and then deal with the pomp and circumstance of the proceedings. That meant he wouldn't be on the road for at least a week, leaving everything wide open for Emily to chip away at his support in those areas that were teetering either way. *Swing states,* Kate thought. *Gotta love them swing states.*

"Every time the press mentions the other convention, I want them to mention me as well," Emily demanded. "Put me in the most visible places you can find where I can generate the most news coverage and take the best advantage of the other party while they're distracted."

And that's exactly what Kate did.

The "V4M: Coast-to-Coast" bus tour started in Washington, D.C., and over the course of two weeks took Emily and Burl to thirty-seven cities across the United States from the East Coast to the West. Emily excelled in the larger metropolitan areas, whereas Burl's down-home qualities played well in the more rural areas.

At the end of the tour, Emily and Burl had developed a good rapport but not necessarily a great friendship. Then again, a president and vice president didn't necessarily have to be best buddies. It was almost traditional for that relationship to be strained. John Nance Garner, FDR's veep for eight years, had framed the dilemma of the vice president's job perfectly when he'd famously stated, "The vice presidency ain't worth a pitcher of warm spit." Not surprisingly, considering his choice of language, Garner hailed from Texas. Like Truman, another of FDR's veeps and the one who assumed the presidency after FDR's death, Garner was never particularly close to the president. He was just added on to the ticket to beef up the chance of pulling in the Southern vote after being FDR's strongest competition in the primary.

Given that running mates were traditionally picked out of political expediency rather than true friendship—more to round out a ticket with strengths the main candidate didn't have than to forge a political partnership—the process almost guaranteed that the president and his VP were polar opposites in temperament, upbringing, and political constituency. Close relationships, like the one shared by George W. Bush and Dick Cheney, were the exception in presidential politics, not the rule. Rumor had it that JFK couldn't stand LBJ and that Al Gore wasn't on the Clinton invite list for intimate gatherings.

But Burl was proving to be an asset.

Kate flew out several times during the two weeks, catching up with them in some of the larger cities. She watched the change in dynamics between the two of them. Emily finally started to relax around Burl when he revealed that beneath his choirboy good looks, he had a wicked sense of humor and an occasional weakness for Belgian beers.

After the tour, Emily took a few days to recuperate from two solid weeks on the road. Unlike Kate, Emily's childhood had not included spending a lot of time riding the American interstate system. Even in those days, the Bentons flew on their private jet; the Rosens drove in their Chevy station wagon.

"I feel like everything is moving—the floor, the chair, the bed," Emily complained the first night back on terra firma.

"You'll get over it. Trust me."

Although Emily had two days off to recharge, Kate couldn't afford to shirk her duties for two hours, much less two days. Their goal now was to garner organizational support—to court various groups to get their official endorsements or at least platforms from which to speak to their particular needs.

In some cases, invitations were automatically extended to Emily. In other cases, Kate had to play the "We would like to be invited" game. In either situation, the end result was the same—whether it was presenting her immigration program before the Congressional Hispanic Caucus or affirming her ironclad support of women's rights to a national gathering of Girl Scouts or speaking about her support of affirmative action to the Congressional Black Caucus Foundation.

Emily spoke, people listened, and then they applauded.

Simple as that.

At least that's how it appeared from the outside looking in. In reality, Emily had become more demanding about her schedule, requesting changes that had Kate, Miriam, and the staff scrambling to accommodate. Kate figured M's uncharacteristic insistence on second-guessing the schedule was a product of her anxiety over the upcoming debates with Charles Talbot.

"We need to cram, like in college. I need a few days of peace and quiet," Emily said, "in a place where I can really concentrate." They all understood that a poor performance against Talbot would mean losing all the ground Emily had made up in the last two weeks. However, this was the first instance that Kate could ever recall where Emily suffered from pangs of doubt that lasted for more than ten minutes. No matter what, at the end of the day, Emily had complete and total faith in her own abilities to succeed.

But now that faith seemed to be wavering, and Emily's way of coping these days was to find small faults in those around her. Kate hated it, but she knew that Emily was struggling with fears that she'd fail. That brittle insecurity made life at M Central resemble a walk through a land-mine field, as they all coped with her short temper. Loretta, Emily's traveling assistant, was the first victim of her grow-ing discontent.

"We need to replace her," Emily told Kate. "She actually tried to get me to wear an off-the-rack number she'd picked up in some back road bargain barn. And did you see the footage of me at the veterans' meeting? My makeup made me look like I'd gotten stuck in the tanning bed for an hour too long. I was Bob Barker orange."

"Have you said anything to her?"

"That's not my job. It's yours. Find me someone else. Preferably someone with better taste."

Kate bit her tongue and figured she'd try to dissuade Emily from following through later.

She didn't have to. By the next morning, the storm clouds had passed and Emily swore she couldn't imagine life on the road without Loretta. *Her* faithful Loretta who unpacked every bag so that Emily walked into an air of familiarity no matter where in the world her hotel room was. Loretta who knew not to speak to Emily in the mornings until after handing her boss a cup of scalding black coffee and a *New York Times* with key articles flagged with color-coded adhesive markers: red for Republican items, blue for Democratic, pink for women's issues, yellow for medical news, and green for those articles that could provide humorous fodder for the upcoming day's conversations and speeches.

It'd been a tradition since Emily's first day on the road. Of course, what Emily didn't know was that Kate told Loretta which articles to flag.

Now Emily was in a good mood. But that didn't mean she wasn't still demanding.

"Okay, here's the deal," Emily said. "I know we planned to spend my debate prep time at the house, but I don't think that's wise."

Kate knew asking "How come?" would be an exercise in futility. Besides, she'd planned for this. She had lined up three potential locations to offer—any of which could provide Emily the privacy she craved, the structure to accommodate her staff, and the security to keep her safe.

Maybe a last-minute change in locale wasn't a bad idea. The number of anonymous and not-so-anonymous threats Emily received had increased since the convention. Kate didn't like to think about it, but assassination was a constant threat, even for a potential presidential candidate. Four presidents had been killed while in office—Lincoln, Garfield, McKinley, and JFK, and eleven more had faced serious attempts on their lives. Every president since Richard Nixon had had to deal with an attack.

It made the whack-job threats and notes she and Emily were getting all more unsettling to Kate.

Neither Kate nor Emily was taking any chances on reducing security, no matter how much Emily wanted a quiet break from the road.

Kate figured that a sudden location change, if they picked the right location, might throw off attackers, so she went to work determined to pull off the move seamlessly for Emily.

As usual, Emily was more concerned with seeing results from her request, not with the workload required to make it happen. Kate reminded her of the chaos she was causing. "I want you to appreciate how hard it is to find suitable places that are available on such short notice. There are a lot of folks in the office who will have to stop what they're doing to restructure this for you."

"Yeah, yeah, I appreciate your hard work and all that." Emily grinned. "And I'm such a pain in the rump. But you're brilliant. You know you've had this covered for weeks. Now quit stalling and tell me my choices."

"What makes you think I've come up with more than one possibility?"

"Because you're an overachiever. C'mon. Spill the beans."

Kate did just that. First was an exclusive private ski club in Winter Park, Colorado—off-season, of course. Second was a four-bedroom cottage on the grounds of the Grand

Hotel on Mackinac Island. The third choice was a full floor containing two of the most elegant suites in the Marriott Wardman Park in the District, thanks to pure luck in timing and a campaign volunteer who knew a friend who knew a friend who knew the hotel's manager.

The Michigan site was in Mark Henderson territory, and it wouldn't hurt to spend a little extra time in his backyard to charm the constituency that he hadn't felt compelled to push in Emily's direction.

So as Kate had expected, Emily chose the Grand Hotel. But Emily surprised her. She told Kate she'd picked it as much as a treat to the advisers who would be flown out to grill and rehearse Emily as for herself.

"After all, don't you folks deserve a few perks?" she asked. "I'm going to be too busy to enjoy it, but you guys should have fun."

With Emily in a better mood, the campaign efforts ran smoother despite the sudden chaos. Kate personally contacted the special advisers for the session with Emily. All agreed to the location and date change except one.

Marjorie Redding refused.

"Look, Kate," she'd said, "it's not that I don't want to help, but my only granddaughter is getting married that weekend. I simply can't make it. But I can send you the next best thing."

Kate couldn't wait to see what Marjorie had up her sleeve this time.

MARJORIE'S NEXT BEST THING turned out to be her assistant and protégé, a woman named Maia Bari, a woman so exotically beautiful that she literally stopped all conversations when she walked into a room. Kate figured that if Maia came with Marjorie's highest recommendation, it didn't matter what she looked like. It simply meant she was the best.

When time came for Emily to go into IDP—Isolated Debate Prep—mode, Kate arrived a day early at the hotel to oversee the advance troops. The island offered several complications in logistics beyond the well-known "no motorized traffic" rule, which seemed to impact the Secret Service more than anyone else. But Agent Perkins assured Kate that they would be able to maintain security despite that challenge.

Emily arrived in a fine mood, mentioning at least four times that she much preferred flying to driving around in "some decommissioned rock-star bus."

Once she was settled in on the second floor of the cottage,

she began meeting one by one with her advisers, there to grill her, instruct her, inform her, support her, and in the case of Maia Bari, dress her.

Francesca Reardon, Emily's policy adviser, had the first session, and when the woman finally came downstairs, Kate couldn't read anything from Francesca's usual expression. No matter the situation, no one did "quiet dignity" quite as well as Francesca Reardon.

"So, how's it going up there?"

Fran tilted her head and spoke in the measured tones of an elocution teacher. "If she keeps focused, she'll be splendid in the debate." She lowered herself to the chair next to Kate.

"She's not focused?"

"Not as much as I'd like. Then again, she has to prepare herself to cover a wide variety of areas. Every four years, the number of topics a candidate has to master expands almost geometrically. Twenty years ago, no one asked questions about stem cell research. Now every candidate has to have enough understanding to write a doctorate. Plus there's end-of-life care, geopolitical history, global warming, environmental science, alternate energy sources, social issues, education, and a thousand other subjects. I feel as if I'm prepping some kid for an Ivy League grad school exam. In the old days, they stuck to politics. Must've been nice."

"We have a medical/technology adviser coming in tomorrow morning."

Fran sighed. "I know we do. I just think I'm getting a little . . ." She glanced through the window to the porch beyond, where Dozier was enjoying a cigar and holding court with Chip McWilliamson. "I was going to say a little long in the tooth, but standing there is proof that there is *no* age limit in our particular field."

Kate smiled. "Sharp as a tack, our Dozier is."

Fran's face creased with a smile. "Yes, he'll be wheeling and dealing beyond the grave."

Kate studied the two men. Dozier was making wide swooping gestures with his lit cigar. Chip stood perfectly still, wearing a respectful but slightly forced smile.

Fran rose. "I'll go rescue the young man. Dozier is probably lecturing him about people the boy's never even heard of." She headed for the porch.

Moments later, Chip stepped into the living room, waving away the cloud of cigar smoke that still clung to him.

"I wanted to talk to you about . . ." Kate watched his attention go elsewhere and his face grow slack. That could mean only one thing.

Maia Bari had walked in.

Sure enough, when Kate turned around, she saw Maia gliding into the room. Kate was sure the woman had left thousands of gaping men in her wake.

"Miss Rosen?" she said. "I don't know if you remember me, but I'm Maia Bari."

"Please, call me Kate. I'm so glad you could come help with the campaign on such short notice."

"It's my pleasure. I've been hoping for a chance to meet Miss Benton for some time now. To work with her is quite a coup."

Her English was flawless, with a touch of an upper-crust British accent. "I took the liberty of bringing some clothes and accessories for the candidate with me. You also have outfits that Miss Benton is contemplating for the debate?"

"We don't stand on formality here. It's Emily. And yes, she brought four suits with her—three new and one she's worn before and particularly likes. You can go on upstairs, if you like. She's free right now. First room on the right at the top."

"Excellent. Thank you."

After that, she walked gracefully up the stairs.

Had Kate not elbowed him in the ribs, Chip probably would have stood at the bottom of the stairs, staring after the woman for another hour.

"Get a grip, Chip!" she whispered.

He shook himself and had the decency to blush. "Sorry, Kate. It's just that she's . . ." Words failed him, and he glanced toward the stairs.

"Stunning? Gorgeous?" Kate supplied. "A goddess stepped down from Mount Olympus?"

"Something like that."

"Just remember: Our Hera? She doesn't share."

He looked at her perplexed. Evidently his undergraduate education hadn't included the classics, nor reruns of *Hercules* or *Xena*. Kate sighed. Time to make the landscape crystal clear.

"Roll your tongue back into your head. You're here to work for Emily. Maia's here to work for Emily. That's the only thing you two should have in common—Emily. Not each other."

His blush deepened, which Kate took as a signal that he'd understood her meaning. Good thing too. If he did anything to upset the status quo—to turn any amount of affection away from Emily and toward Maia—heads would roll.

Starting with his.

✫　✫　✫　✫　✫

The rest of the scheduled review times went well. Emily came out of the tête-à-tête with Maia raving about the girl's insight and how her skills might actually exceed that of her mentor, Marjorie.

Kate found that hard to believe but appreciated the young woman's hard work and dedication. Her efforts really shone on the third day of debate prep, when Kate, Dave Dickens, Dozier, the rest of the advisers, and a handful of staffers created their own rehearsal debate.

After a few rough moments at the start, Emily got into the swing of things, letting her natural eloquence shine through. Had this been the real thing, she would have wiped the floor with Charles Talbot.

But this wasn't the real thing, and the real Charles Talbot had most likely been approaching the problem in the same manner—having his staff prep and grill him as well.

So what would happen in real life was anybody's guess.

Two days later, the debate became reality.

All of the preparation, the rehearsals, the efforts by Emily and the staff resulted in what political pundits hailed as a classic showdown. Emily fared well against Talbot. She managed to smoothly work in all the essential points of her campaign, as well as some of her successes in the past, including her pet highway project. Talbot had been on his A game too and managed to turn the topic around several times to his extensive experience in foreign policy.

Kate knew that the key now was to keep Emily from diving into her own "woulda-coulda-shoulda" deconstruction of the debate. Rather than allow Emily to start a self-recriminating analysis of her performance, Kate forced her to attend a post-debate rally where, after some coaxing, Emily took the stage with the guest performer, one of her favorite singers. Kate knew Emily could sing—now she had it on tape so America knew it too.

While the party raged, the advisers and staff pored over the debate footage, and the next day, they offered Emily their recommendations for changes in the second and third debates. To Kate's relief, those suggestions were mostly minor ones; everyone agreed Emily had done a solid job of presenting herself and her platform.

Kate's sense of accomplishment lasted until Nick called two days later.

He started the conversation with "Please don't hang up."

Curiosity overruled her instinct to hit disconnect. "What do you want now?"

"We have to meet."

"No."

"Things are happening. It's going to hit you two hard and fast and there's nothing I can do about it other than warn you."

"Do they pay you to be this cryptic, or is double-talk just second nature with you?"

"I'm serious, Kate." Nick's voice lowered as if he was afraid of being overheard. "I don't particularly feel any loyalty to Emily—you know that." A note of panic crept into his voice. "But I do . . . to you. You've always been there for me, even when I messed up totally. Now it's my turn to return the favor. I had no idea that answering a simple question could possibly result in something like this. I can't believe I'm doing this."

Kate's heart began to race. "What are you talking about?"

"Not here. Not now. We have to meet. I'm in town. You?"

Kate closed her eyes. She had six hours before she was supposed to leave for Seattle, where she was joining Emily at a series of town hall meetings in Washington and Oregon. Could she take the risk of having another meeting with Nick? Could she risk avoiding it?

Lord, what should I do? Is he leading me down the paths of temptation? Politically or personally?

"Kate . . ." He was pleading now. She'd never heard him do that. Ever. Not even with Emily when times were good.

She gripped the phone tighter. "I'm headed out of town this afternoon, but my plane doesn't leave until six. I can meet you at Dulles at three." She added, "And this better be good."

"It's not good, Kate. It's not good at all. But it's important. . . ."

Three hours later, the limousine service dropped Kate off at the curb. She went inside, checked her single bag, then called Nick's cell. "I'm here. Now what?"

"What concourse are you flying out of? I'll meet you there."

"But how can you get past security?"

"Don't worry about that. Just tell me your gate number."

She gave him the information and headed for the security checkpoint. Once safely past that, she took the shuttle to the concourse where they were to meet. She found him dutifully waiting for her. He looked haggard, his five o'clock shadow darkening his strained features. Before she could speak, he gestured for her to say nothing but to follow him.

Great. Another person worried about surveillance. . . .

Feeling like a reject from a bad spy movie, Kate trailed Nick through the crowd of travelers. Finally he stopped at an unmarked door cut into what appeared to be a temporary wall. He turned the knob. It was unlocked. He entered. Kate followed and found herself in a construction area, empty of anybody but Nick.

"We won't be disturbed here," he explained. "Or overheard."

She glanced around at the wires and ductwork hanging down from the exposed ceiling. A thin coat of dust covered the counter, suggesting that no one had worked in the space in a while.

"Very Spy versus Spy. Should I watch out for an anvil falling on my head?"

His expression was grim. "Not yours. Emily's."

Kate scowled at him. "So what happened to your promise to keep the Benton family skeletons in the closet? Or is this about something else?"

"I didn't break my word. At least—not intentionally. When we were gearing up for the debate, Chuck and Wayne kept quizzing me hard about Emily. What did I consider to be M's hot-button issues? What sort of rhetoric gets under her collar? What subject might cause her to have a knee-jerk reaction? What she was immensely proud of in her personal life? Since they weren't looking for the specifics, just general concepts, I saw no problem in answering them."

"But then they asked . . . ," she said, leading.

He shifted uncomfortably. "Which of her accomplishments as governor did she consider her greatest? To me, that was a no-brainer. If a reporter asked you that, what would you have answered?"

"Simple. The highway project."

"That's what I said too. It's not like it's a deep, dark secret. She was quoted saying it in the *Washington Post*. Anyway, they started asking me other questions. Did the phrase 'the Loompaliki River' mean anything special to her? or the name Gablonski?"

Kate recognized the second reference; Gablonski had been Emily's first horse. But since it seemed important to Nick, and especially to Talbot, she volunteered no information.

Nick correctly read her silence. "Don't worry. I'm not fishing for the answer. I found out after the fact that it was her favorite horse's name. And the Loompaliki River was the made-up name she gave the creek behind the stables."

Kate recalled the few times she'd visited the stables at the Bentons' horse farm. "That can't be right. There's no creek back there."

"Not anymore. There used to be. It was diverted years ago to form the lake in the west pasture. M told me about it because the neighboring farms raised a stink about the water rights issues."

"So what's the problem? The name of a horse and a long-gone creek. They don't add up to certain doom in a presidential election."

"I didn't think so either." Nick looked around, spotted a shrouded row of chairs, and pulled the plastic sheeting away. A fine cloud of dust sifted through the air. "You better sit."

"I'll stand, thank you. Just tell me what all this has to do with the highway project and why I should be worried."

He sat down, facing the window. Sunlight valiantly tried to shine through the dirt-streaked glass, but only a few muddy rays penetrated the panes.

"How much do you know about it?" he asked. "The highway project, I mean."

She thought back. "A fair amount. I'd gone back to my law practice once she got into the governor's office, but we stayed very close." Kate narrowed her gaze. "Don't stall, Nick. Just come out with it."

He rubbed the back of his neck. "Four days ago, a barge broke loose in the Potomac and struck one of the main northbound lane bridge supports near Morgantown. No one was hurt, but the bridge was closed down so the inspectors could make sure there was no structural damage. After what happened in Minneapolis in '07, nobody wanted to take any chances. But there's been no announcement yet about why the bridge hasn't opened again."

"Why hasn't it?"

"The inspectors took a core sample of the concrete. Tomorrow morning, a report will be released that shows that the wrong grade of sand was used in the concrete bridge supports. Someone used a cheaper grade of sand which, in turn, has caused the concrete to not be as strong or as long lasting as it should have been. Now they have to replace all the bridge supports."

"Some contractor shortchanged the state. Sure, that's bad. But why is it Emily's problem?"

"A company named Two States Bridgeworks got the bridge contract. They subcontracted out the construction of the concrete foundations for the pylons. Two States provided the preliminary specs as well as the construction plans and materials list. The subcontractor turned in invoices showing that they bought and paid for the proper grade of sand."

Kate had participated in enough construction lawsuits

to understand the implications. "Seems to me either the materials supplier or the subcontractor was to blame. I don't think it's a problem for Emily."

"Wrong. Chuck had his investigators look into the subcontractor, who's since gone bankrupt due to a host of lawsuits. The investigators also looked into Two States' financial records and discovered the business is owned by a holding company called Loompaliki River Ltd."

"Coincidence. Maybe she didn't make the word up and it's real—some obscure river in Africa or somewhere. Like the Limpopo. That's a real place."

"It turns out that Loompaliki River Ltd. is owned by an offshore holding company called Gablonski International."

The sounds of the busy airport faded from Kate's hearing. She had to clear her throat before she could speak. "Nick, stop beating around the bush. What does Talbot have on us that's got you in such a panic?"

"Chuck paid an obscene amount of bribe money to a banking official in the Bahamas. He has a list of the board of directors of Gablonski International."

Nick looked Kate straight in the eye. "Every last one of them is a Benton."

KATE WANTED TO SINK into the seat next to Nick and cry. She wanted to scream, kick, and throw an Emily-type fit. She wanted to do anything and everything other than what she knew she had to do. Gathering every ounce of control she possessed, she said, "So?"

Nick jerked his head up, a mixture of shock and disappointment filling his face as well as coloring his words. "You knew?"

She couldn't bear to see the crushed look in his eyes, as though he believed she'd let something like that happen. "No. But there's no reason to believe Emily knows anything about it either."

"Oh, c'mon, Kate. We're talking the Bentons here. They live in each others' pockets. If they could reproduce without going outside of the family, they would just to keep the bloodline pure. We're not talking a case of simple nepotism—like getting your nephew or cousin a job with the state. We're talking kickbacks and illegal payments on a grand scale. The preliminary findings show that the Bentons had a finger in practically every aspect of the highway construction—from the surveying crew to the heavy equipment to the paving company. They even owned a piece of the company that built the tollbooths."

"I know Emily. She wouldn't think twice about letting her family businesses bid on the highway deal—but she'd blow her top if she thought a subcontractor was shortchanging the project. She wouldn't stand for it. It wouldn't just be bad for the project—it would be bad for her reputation. That project was part of her legacy. She didn't know about the problems. I'd stake my reputation on that."

"You will be, and it's already too late to save it." Nick shook his head. "You may be right, but it won't matter. Chuck's going to take your girl out of the running."

Kate let the words settle in for a few moments before she spoke again. "How bad is it going to be?"

"Chuck's people have proof of financial irregularities to the tune of millions in illegal payments. It's probably going to go even higher. She won't be able to duck this one or talk her way out of it. Her campaign is toast. Emily is going down tomorrow. Hard."

"Tomorrow?"

"Chuck's planning a press conference at noon. During the speech, the staff will be blanketing the media with e-mails containing enough proof to trigger a massive investigation. The damning evidence will be e-mailed to every major news outlet in the U.S. and abroad. They'll get the absolute unvarnished proof in their hot little hands by the time he finishes his statement. By nightfall, Emily will be lucky if she could win president of her book club. Her political career will be in shreds."

Numb, Kate sat down before she fell.

"I'm sorry, Kate." Nick reached forward to touch her, but she jerked away. "I just wanted to warn you and to assure you that I had no part in this. This whole thing has been as much of a shock to me as it has been to you. I only found out yesterday. I never thought Talbot would stoop that low. This was supposed to be a campaign on the issues, not a mudslinging spectacular."

"It's politics, Nick," Kate said.

"It's not the politics I signed on for," he said. "I've worked hard to get my life back on track. I've asked for forgiveness, made amends however I could. I'm living a better life now. The one I hope God wants me to live. I'm not as mature in my faith as you. And I don't have the strength to stay with these people, hoping to change them without worrying they'll change me back to who and what I was."

"I wish I was as strong as you think I am," she said.

"But you are. You've been Emily's best friend for years and yet she hasn't . . . infected you. If anything, your influence is turning her into a better person. Will she ever completely submit herself to Christ? I don't know. But it won't be because you haven't shown her the better way. You lead by example, and we can all feel his presence in your life. Even Emily. I think it's why she listens to you when she won't listen to anyone else. I envy you that. I wish I could have a little of that kind of influence with Chuck, but I've failed. I sat in on that meeting with his dirty tricks department, and my stomach turned. I think that somehow *he* turned that shooter loose on the headquarters the day I got shot."

Nick sighed. "To think I thought Emily might have done it. Emily's takedown is just the beginning. Talbot's got plans I won't tell you about. For his campaign. And for his presidency. I can't imagine he's serious about them, but he says nothing's going to stop him. I will tell you that his plans terrify me. And I don't think that I, or anybody else, can make him change them. I'm getting out. Now."

Kate thought back to the evidence on the man she'd hidden deep, out of Emily's reach. "After what I've learned, I'm not surprised. I don't know that you *can* redeem him. He's done . . . some pretty bad stuff."

"You talk like it's all in the past. Trust me. He's been *doing* a lot of bad stuff. He'll *keep* doing a lot of bad stuff. He's just really good at hiding it." Nick reached over and grabbed her hand. "Kate, if he wins, America is going to suffer. Badly. As much as I hate to say it, Emily needs to become president. She's the better choice. Especially with you at her side."

Kate's mind churned ahead at warp speed, considering and discarding dozens of scenarios and actions. It was definitely a shock. But what was more shocking to her was the obvious solution she came up with, the command decision she made without hesitation but with the courage and conviction she found inside herself to start the process.

She'd promised God and herself that she was going to run this campaign on the merits of her candidate because she believed Emily was good enough to sweep the country on those merits.

But this turn of events made that vow moot.

She had to follow Christ's teachings. She had to learn

from his words and deeds. And now she knew what the lesson she should apply to this situation was.

She thought of Jesus at the temple in Jerusalem overturning the tables of the moneylenders.

They had defiled the temple.

Now Emily's opponent, a man with blood on his hands, thought he was going to defile this election.

He was wrong.

God, give me the strength to do what I must. It's not just Emily's future at stake here but the fate of a nation. . . .

"Nick, did you mean what you just said? You're out?"

"Yeah. My resignation's already written and sitting on his desk. I can't be a party to what he's about to do. I can't continue to support him now that I know what kind of person he is. This was just the last straw. Why?"

"Then call Talbot and let me talk to him."

Nick looked confused. "Why? There's nothing you can say that can stop him. I spent all day yesterday trying to do that."

"Just get him. Now." *Do it before I lose my courage and collapse. Dear God, be with me. . . .*

Nick sighed but reached in his jacket pocket, pulled out his cell phone, and punched a few numbers. After a moment, he spoke.

"Chuck? Nick. Look, I don't know how to tell you, but . . ." He stalled as if unsure how to explain to his boss that he'd just spilled the beans early, and to the enemy camp, no less. "Aw, never mind. Hang on. Someone wants to speak to you." He held out the phone to Kate and hung his head. "In some ways, it was a nice job while it lasted. I got to talk to you again. . . ."

Kate's hand trembled as she accepted the phone. She prayed her voice wouldn't quiver as well. "Governor Talbot? This is Kathryn Rosen, Emily Benton's campaign manager."

Talbot's voice boomed in her ear. "Well, Miss Rosen! I must say that this is a surprise. Why do I have the pleasure of speaking with you today?"

She'd always thought his deep voice sounded distinguished and authoritative. But now it sounded smarmy and cheap. "It's come to my attention that you have arranged a press conference tomorrow to release some information about Emily."

There was a moment of silence; then the man had the unmitigated gall to laugh out loud. "You know, I never did quite trust Nick. Not really. I always wondered if he still had the hots for his ex. I suppose this proves it. Looks like I shouldn't have been so upset when that little surprise I arranged in New Hampshire almost took him out of the picture. We sure got a lot of good press out of it, didn't we? I thought at the time it might not be worth nearly losing my secret weapon campaign adviser. Guess I was wrong."

What? Kate thought. Had Talbot just admitted to setting Gilroy loose? Didn't he care that Gilroy had killed a member of his staff? What kind of man was she dealing with?

But Talbot was still talking.

"I bet Nick's hoping to get back in the ex's good graces and back in her bed by divulging details about tomorrow's press conference to her."

"Actually I'm the only person he's told about your plans. I haven't informed Emily yet."

Talbot took a moment to digest what she said. "I suppose *yet* is the operative word."

"Correct." She fought her natural tendency to add a per-functory "sir" when addressing him. He deserved no such respect. "You will call off that press conference."

"Now why in the world would I do that?"

"Because this presidential campaign is going to be about issues. We're going to let the voters decide based on the platforms the candidates present to them, not underhanded political mudslinging. You said so yourself."

"Well, I didn't realize I had a gold mine's worth of mud to sling when I said that."

"Your gold mine is actually a field of clay. Here's the deal. We won't—"

"Pardon me, Miss Rosen," Talbot sneered, "but you're in no position to call any shots at all. The way I see it, I'm holding all the cards and I'm not in the mood to bluff. It's simple. She's going down tomorrow. If you have any sense whatsoever, you'll walk away from her today. You're a smart woman. Save yourself."

Kate squeezed her eyes shut, glad that he couldn't see her. It was far easier to play this sort of no-bluff, one-hand-takes-all poker over the phone. But she knew what she had to do.

"You don't have all the cards. And my hand beats yours. October 7, 1973," she said.

He acted as if he hadn't heard her correctly. "Pardon?"

She stood and began pacing the dusty room as she pulled from her memory the details that Lee Devlin and Sierra Dudicroft had ferreted out at her request. Emily had wanted ammunition against Talbot, and Kate had gotten it. She'd swallowed her revulsion and done the task and discovered truths she'd decided were too terrible to use against an honorable man. Carmen del Rio had pointed her in the right direction and District Discreet had flushed out the facts.

In spades.

Kate had buried the evidence. But that was before she found out what kind of person Talbot was. She'd given him the benefit of the doubt, and he'd faltered. He'd dug up dirt—but that was just politics. Setting a madman on his own people for publicity's sake? And laughing about it? Talbot was someone who could take a great country and corrupt it beyond belief. She never wanted to be president herself, but she wasn't about to let this snake sully the process. God had put her in this place, with the information in her hands, for a reason. She was sure of it.

Lord, put the right words in my mouth. If I fail now, millions will pay the price for my failure.

"Don't tell me you've forgotten the day, Chuck. Let me repeat it. October 7, 1973. That's the day your girlfriend almost died. Well, it was nighttime, actually. Angela Kaye Kasdan, a poli-sci major at Ohio State, just like you. You and Angie had been staying at the lake cabin your parents owned and the both of you had been doing coke all weekend. But high or not, when Sunday night rolled around, it was time to head back to campus."

Kate fell into a pattern she'd learned in school; any good trial lawyer knew that you had to keep referring to the victim by her name.

"You drove Angie's car because she was too wasted. But you really weren't in much better shape, were you? The two of you were only a couple of miles from campus when you missed a curve in the road and plowed into a tree. You thought Angie was dead, so—smart boy that you were—you had the presence of mind to drag her out of the passenger's seat and shove her body behind the steering wheel, making it appear as if she'd been driving. Once you'd set the scene, you removed all evidence that you'd been in the car. Then you walked back to campus and somehow managed to get into your dorm room without being seen."

There were no sounds coming from his end of the phone, but Kate assumed he hadn't hung up.

She continued. "You had no idea she survived the crash. Pity you didn't keep your head and show some courage and try to save her. I guess it was good luck for you, bad luck for her, that she came out of the experience in a persistent vegetative state. It cost you ten thousand dollars, but you bribed two of your suitemates into swearing you'd been in the dorm all weekend, sick with the flu. They also swore that they'd overheard you break up with your girlfriend over the phone that previous Friday. With her unable to contradict you, you covered your tracks well."

When Kate looked over at Nick, he was gaping at her.

"At least you thought you got away with it. I have a signed affidavit from one of those roommates who will admit to having taken the hush money from you. I've got pictures of the bills you gave him. And—talk about a sharp guy—your buddy had had a feeling that you might be destined for greater things, so he was even smart enough to preserve the bloody shirt you were wearing that night. I guess he figured it might be worth more someday than that initial five grand you paid him. I've been assured that, despite its age, any half-decent forensics lab will be able to determine that the shirt has bloodstains from two individuals—you and another person.

"You could never prove . . ." Talbot's voice trailed off as if he realized he'd already said too much.

"Because Angie finally passed away six years ago? Sorry, wrong. Don't you remember? Angie had an identical twin sister, Diane, who is still very much alive. A forensic lab should easily be able to prove what happened using DNA testing, to prove that the second blood sample came from Angie by testing it against Diane." Kate was on a roll now, with all her earlier fear transformed into the excitement of doing the task the Lord had given her. This moment, this mission, was why he had led her into politics. "We're talking a 100 percent certainty, Chuck, because identical twins have identical DNA."

There was an uncomfortable silence on the other end. Then Talbot finally spoke. "I have no idea what shirt you could be talking about."

If this was the best he could do . . .

"Your varsity football jersey, Chuck. The one with T-A-L-B-O-T printed on the back. Remember? Number twenty-three? It's still an important number for you, isn't it? You even have *NMBR23* as your personalized license plate. Every year on the anniversary of the accident, you sent her twenty-three roses. In fact, you just placed that order at the florist's four days ago for the roses to be placed on her grave. I've got a copy of the receipt."

Talbot released a barrage of expletives that made Kate's hands shake. But it didn't make her back down. Nothing could at this point, short of a bullet to her brain.

"I'm sure you know the statute of limitations didn't start counting down until the day she died, six years ago. That's why you could still be charged with leaving the scene of an accident, failure to provide aid, failure to report a crime, tampering with a crime scene, and I'm sure a number of other felonies. Even if the case doesn't put you in jail, the press will convict you of all those things and more in the court of public appeal. Like Ted Kennedy and Chappaquiddick. Every time he even thought of running for president, somebody mentioned Mary Jo Kopechne, and his presidential ambitions sank as fast as his car did. It would be worse for you. I've got everything I need to make sure Angie gets her posthumous revenge."

"You little—" He sputtered some of the worst obscenities Kate had ever heard, spewing his rage-filled hatred for almost a minute straight. She held the phone away from her ear, not willing to subject herself to such filth. Kate's own heart began racing to the point where she wondered how long she could last before it wore out and stopped completely. It occurred to her that Talbot had to be in worse shape, and he was much older than she was.

In her mind's eye, she pictured the man, keeled over, suffering from a heart attack.

For a horrible second, the picture looked good to her.

What have I become? How can I live with myself after this? But it has to be done. . . .

Finally Charles Talbot spoke again, his voice gruff and uneven. "Put Beaudry on the phone. Now."

"Sure. But before I do, I just want to point out that Emily Benton is an honorable woman. She'd never stoop to mudslinging until the first stone was cast. You brought this on yourself when you cast that first stone, Talbot. I think an aggravated vehicular homicide rap trumps any claims of financial irregularities by Emily, don't you?" She waited for her words to sink in and then added in her best, breezy tone, "Here's Nick."

She handed the phone back to Nick with a remarkably steady hand. A moment after that, the adrenaline rushed out of her body as quickly as it had flowed in. She sagged to the seat, a boneless, quivering mess. If Nick said anything further to his boss, Kate didn't hear it. The blood thrummed in her ears, blotting out all other sound.

After a while, she realized Nick was no longer talking on the phone and instead, sitting next to her, watching her intently. She drew a deep, shaky breath. "Did Talbot say anything else I should know about?"

He nodded. "The press conference is on hold. You've scared the stuffing right out of him." Nick stared at her. "Is all that true? You have statements? and his bloody shirt? real proof?"

"Yes. I've got it. Even if I promised myself I'd never use it. Enough evidence to possibly bring in a guilty verdict in a criminal trial. We should probably tell him there's no use breaking into my place. The evidence isn't there or at my office. It's in a safe-deposit box at a bank I don't regularly frequent, and I'm not the only person with access or a key. I know it's a cliché, but I've left the usual letters that will get that box opened by the authorities if something happens to me."

Nick tilted his head and studied her face so intently that she felt self-conscious.

Finally she turned away from the heat of his stare. "What?"

"I never dreamed you could do something like that. Emily? Sure. In a split second. But you? It's like you were channeling her. I've never seen you so . . . so . . ."

"Devious? Manipulative?" Her stomach soured. "Vindictive? It surprised me, too. But I think I had more than my own strength to draw on—it felt to me like that moment was meant."

"To me, too." He stood and walked over to the dirty window, where a plane was pulling up to a nearby Jetway. "It was almost like you were . . . on a different plane of existence. I expect that sort of behavior out of Emily." He turned around and gave Kate a long, hard look. "Why didn't you just call Emily? let her be her own hatchet man?"

Kate leaned forward, holding her stomach and fighting her building nausea. *Adrenaline overload.* "Like I told Talbot, Emily knows nothing about this. The evidence rested in my hands and my hands only, and I never planned on using it. Or on telling Emily."

"Honestly?" He dropped into the seat next to her. "Why not?"

"I couldn't tell her. You know Emily. You don't put weapons of mass destruction in Emily's hands if you don't have to. She just might use them. You saw what she did to Mark Henderson. She tends to be a little . . . trigger-happy."

"A little?" He leaned forward, matching her position as if these new revelations were causing him a similar pain. "What are you going to do when she becomes president? She'll have access to all sorts of secret weapons. Real ones. Nuclear and otherwise."

"I know. That's why I plan to be there at her side. That's why I've enlisted Wes's help. She listens to us. Between the two of us and her own native talent, she'll be the best president this country has had in decades. I've known her since she was eighteen. She's the best leader I've ever seen. People listen to her. She gets things done. She just has moments where she loses her way. That's when she looks to me. And I have my own agenda. Wes and I hope to revive the faith-based initiative office and really make a go of it. Emily has promised to back us to the hilt. She keeps her promises to me. I hope to find the right place for religion in the White House. Not running the government—that's Emily's job. But reaching out to help others and providing a framework in which people of faith can do good in this country and all over the world. Emily's giving me the platform, but I've dreamed of this mission since I was a kid. We discussed a thousand times in college what we could do together if Emily made it to the White House, then more seriously when her political career began. By the time she was elected governor, we were dead serious about it. We've got fabulous ideas. Think of it: Emily, me, and Wes. . . . Don't you think we can accomplish miracles?"

"So you're her voice of reason? the angel on her shoulder?"

"Reason, yes. Angel, no." Kate grasped for any amount of humor, even macabre, that she could find. "And somehow I don't think your boss would use either of those descriptions when it comes to me."

"True." A moment later, he added, "Ex-boss. That's for sure."

An uneasy silence fell around them, one she broke as her sense of guilt swelled beyond control.

"Nick?"

"Yeah?"

"Did I make the right decision?"

"Second thoughts?"

"Right now, I don't particularly like myself. I swore I

wouldn't use that file. I promised myself I hadn't sunk that low. Then he came at me like that. And it felt like he wouldn't stop at anything. It seemed to me that God wanted me to use that file." Kate paused, searching for an answer within herself and finding none. She'd been so sure just moments ago. "Did I do the right thing?" she whispered.

Nick remained silent for a long moment. He moved next to her and put his warm arm around her shaking shoulders. Then he finally spoke. "Yeah. Maybe." He drew a deep breath. "I don't know."

She rested her head on his shoulder. "That covers a lot of ground."

They both sat back in the slightly dusty chairs, and Kate reached over to take Nick's hand. Beyond the temporary wall, the airport bustled with life, the people having no idea what sort of political and criminal machinations had taken place only feet away from them.

Permanent decisions made behind a temporary wall.

Kate could scarcely believe it herself.

"What now?" Nick asked.

"I don't know," Kate said. "I need to take some time. I need to think. To pray."

"Me too."

"I have a plane to catch." Reluctantly she stood up, untangling her fingers from his. "You?"

"I have to go back and see if I can still salvage my reputation." He tried to smile. "You'd think I'd be used to this by now. It's almost operatic, the way my life comes crashing down on me at regular intervals."

"True." She paused to meet his pained gaze. "I'm sorry you got caught in the middle of all this, this time."

"Me too. But—" he stood—"I'm glad you were able to stop it. Maybe God did put you here, with that information in your head, just so you'd be able to stop it."

"Do you think so?"

He nodded. "I suspect so. If I find out anything else, I'll let you know immediately."

"Thanks."

Kate brushed herself off, took several steps toward the door, then turned around. Somehow words just weren't enough. "I really mean it. Thanks, Nick. For everything. Emily didn't deserve your help. But I'm so glad you trusted me to take on Talbot."

He shot her a tight-lipped smile that almost made it to his eyes. "Yeah, that you did. I can't think of anyone else I've ever trusted as much." He sighed. "You know, Emily could learn a thing or two from you about being a politician."

18

KATE TRIED TO MELT into the flow of travelers hurrying to their next destinations. She was shaking again. She felt almost as if she had a neon sign above her head flashing "Blackmailer! Evil woman!"

She found an empty waiting area near her gate and leaned up against a corner where she could see anyone approaching her and couldn't readily be overheard. Relief poured through her when she dialed District Discreet and was put through immediately to Lee.

"I hope you remember where the burial plot is." Being cryptic on the phone now seemed simply a way of life.

"The Kasdan death? Indeed I do." Lee didn't have to be as cryptic since there was no danger of her being overheard.

"Well, I had to resurrect the body today. But I told only two people."

"Your boss and who?"

"No, not Emily. The opposition. Talbot himself."

Lee whistled. "You *did* count your fingers after you handed him that information, didn't you? He plays for keeps, that one."

"I know. He meant to crush us. He sure came after me like he wanted me gone forever. I used the only weapon I had that I thought would stop him. I think I did the right thing. But I'm a basket case."

There was silence that Kate could only assume fell under the category of *stunned*.

But Lee had worked in D.C. long enough to draw a crooked line between two points. "Defensive retaliation? A case of tit for tat?"

"In a manner of speaking. More than that, though. What I need from you is more on the tat."

"What'd she do now?" They both knew the *she* was a reference to Emily.

"It's not what she's done now but what she may have done fourteen or so years ago. I'll text you the basics in a moment. I'm in a public place. But please mark this as highly sensitive, my eyes only. Send nothing to my office and bill this directly to my personal account."

"This is getting to be a habit. It's really that bad?"

"I don't know." Kate looked at her watch. "I think she might be innocent, but the situation surely isn't. Not if what Talbot was threatening is true. I'm about to fly out, so I'll be out of pocket for a while. Let me know as soon as you have something."

"Gotcha. Awaiting your text. Have a safe trip."

Kate disconnected and relayed in text a very brief version of the information Nick had given her. After she finished, she walked over to the counter at her gate and bought an upgrade to first class.

If she was going to spend the next several hours alone with her conscience, she at least wanted to have a comfortable seat while she wrestled with it.

It was a very long trip.

Six hours later, Kate landed at Sea-Tac lamentably sober despite the liquid refreshments the flight attendant had tried to serve her. She'd had a single glass of wine with her dinner and failed to lose herself in the not-so-funny comedy movie that played on her personal video console. When she got to the baggage claim area, she found an eager young campaign volunteer waiting for her.

She never quite got his name—Chad or Tad or Vlad—but by the time she arrived at the hotel, she knew all about Chad/Tad/Vlad's sloppy roommate, adorable cat, ungrateful brother, scatterbrained sister, and clueless parents. In some ways, his constant chatter was a relief, dulling the persistent ache of her overwhelming disillusionment.

Was this what politics was? A clash of titans over privilege and decadence? Backroom threats and underhanded manipulation of your opponent? What about all her dreams of politics as a catalyst for change for the better?

The trip wasn't over a moment too soon.

When Kate reached the hotel, she checked in, left an "I'll talk to you in the morning" message for Emily, and hung the Do Not Disturb sign on her door. Settling back into a fortress of pillows she built against the headboard, Kate opened her laptop and checked her e-mail. When she saw no report from Lee, she debated calling, but her body screamed that it was after midnight on the East Coast and it was high time she got some sleep.

Although exhausted in mind, body, and spirit, Kate slept

only for fitful half hours at a time. She kept waking up, her body shaking almost uncontrollably as her mind insisted on rehashing the phone conversation with Charles Talbot over and over again. It was as if she needed to experience all the delayed emotions she'd sidestepped earlier—fear, panic, shock, disgust, anxiety, and an almost perfect sense of being in the presence of destiny, of finding a moment where she was an instrument of God's will. Had she imagined that? used it to justify bringing Talbot down?

What did it all mean?

She was a frail mortal. It was likely she'd never get the answers to those questions.

Dear Jesus, be with me and be my strength. I need you now.

Finally she slept, but she woke long before dawn. Rather than deal with more constantly interrupted sleep, she got up, made a pot of coffee, and waited for 5 a.m. to roll around. At 5:01, she called District Discreet.

Lee sounded almost breathless. "G'morning. I got your message. I'm still tracing back the ownership of the various companies involved in the highway construction. Right now, about a third of the contractors involved seem to have at least one Benton hiding in the woodwork. Another third probably paid a kickback to a Benton-owned firm. Who knows about the remaining third? It's going to take time to unravel the sub-subcontractors from the subcontractors. I'm having to wait for many of those records."

"My source said it required a rather large bribe to a Bahamian official for one offshore account."

Lee laughed. "That's because someone must have been in too much of a hurry to go through government channels. Or maybe they read too many spy thrillers. The rules changed in 2002. If you ask the right questions with the right appearance of authority, you can get Bahamian banking records. It just takes a little time.

"I didn't know that. Evidently Talbot didn't either. He reportedly dropped a bundle to get them."

"Good—he's got less money to spend on political attack ads. Guy's a piece of work. Anyway, I've managed to get a large number of construction inspection reports from both the Virginia and Maryland departments of transportation. Lucky for you I have a cousin who's retired from the West Virginia highway department. He's going to help review them with me, and yeah, he'll keep his mouth shut."

"Good."

"But so far in just scanning them, I've found no overt complaints of slipshod work, inferior materials, or anything like that. In fact, the whole project seems to have come in early, under budget, and according to my cousin, it's considered a model highway construction project."

Kate padded over and poured a second cup from the miniature coffeemaker. "It doesn't matter if they lined the roads with gold. Taking any kickback is a violation of the Virginia Public Procurement Act. Then add to that the ethics of the governor's family owning a piece of most of the companies used on the project."

"Yeah, I don't think you could write that one off to coincidence. It'd turn voters to Talbot in droves. But it's not like leaving your girlfriend to die. I'll get back to work unless there's anything else."

"Thanks, Lee."

The woman hesitated before she spoke again. "I have to

admit—working for you is always interesting. You know it's our policy not to ask questions, but this is one time I really wish I could ask you a thing or two."

"And I wish I could answer them. Maybe later."

"Gotcha."

After she hung up, Kate sat on the bed. She was too caffeinated to go back to sleep and too tired to be of much use to anyone. Her only recourse was to sweat some of the caffeine from her system. She dressed in shorts and a T-shirt and consulted the hotel directory for the gym location as she pulled on her running shoes.

No one was there, which was how Kate preferred it. With her iPod blasting something loud and fast, she got down to the serious business of exercise. She'd run almost two miles when she heard a raised voice.

"Well, look what the cat dragged in." Emily stood in the doorway next to a Secret Service agent Kate didn't recognize.

"Hey."

Emily stepped up on the machine next to her and turned it on. "You don't call. You don't write," she said in mock complaint.

"Did too. I got in late last night, so I left you a message."

"Late night, early morning. It's a grind, isn't it? Don't worry. Just twenty-nine more days of this and then we can relax."

Kate kept her pace steady, wishing she could do the same with her quickening heartbeat. "I don't think we should consider the presidency a more relaxing position. It's more like a four-year final to the campaign season's midterm."

"Sheesh. You're in a mood today." Emily turned up the speed of her machine, effectively ending their conversation. Rather than get caught in the "I'm running faster than you" contest, Kate kept plodding along at the same rate. Even when Emily inched her speed up twice as if to bait her, Kate kept her pace.

At six miles, Kate started a slowdown, cool-off process. In response, Emily kicked her machine into overdrive and did a scaldingly fast final mile before ending her exercise.

"You ought to cool down," Kate advised.

Emily mopped the sweat from her face. "Aha! She speaks! So what bee got in your bonnet, oh great campaign manager?"

"I'm just tired. That's all." She didn't want to talk for fear of blurting out something she shouldn't. But silence would only exacerbate the situation. "It's been a long eighteen months. We hit the road in an hour. I'll meet you in the lobby." Kate picked up her towel, shook it out good in hopes of dislodging any errant notes of doom or danger, then slung it around her neck.

"Wait up." Emily rushed forward to fall into step with Kate. "I've seen *tired* and I've seen *angry* and this looks a lot more like *angry*."

"Later, Emily. This isn't about you. At least, not exactly."

"But I want—"

"*Not now.*"

It was probably the first time Kate had raised her voice to Emily since their campaign efforts started three years ago. Or maybe longer than that.

But in any case, it felt almost . . . good. What had happened to her in that airport construction area? Had it really changed her so deeply? *Lord, what are you doing to me?* But whatever had happened to her, Kate's words stopped Emily and her friend backed down.

"Uh . . . well . . . okay. I'll see you downstairs in an hour."

"Fine." After she spoke, Kate wondered if she was enjoying Emily's discomfort a bit too much. Rather than make amends, Kate simply left the room, trying not to notice the slightest hint of a smile on the face of the Secret Service agent who stood just inside the door and had overheard the entire interchange.

Once upstairs in her hotel room, she showered and got ready for the first of four meetings for the day. With any luck, she could minimize her contact with Emily and pay more attention to managing the appearances.

She needed time alone to internalize what had happened to her. Whatever it was, it felt like she'd turned into a new and different person. Was this what it felt like when the Lord worked through a person? Or was the strain of campaigning for so long finally driving her mad?

Lord, do you want to weigh in on this for me?

Something deep inside her was changed. It was like she'd found a new level of meaning in her life, and it left her off-balance until she could adjust to it.

Emily had felt it too.

And it had shocked the breath right out of her.

Kate couldn't help but smile.

The morning started with another "Donuts to Democracy: Breakfast with the Candidate" meeting at a large tech firm in downtown Seattle. Kate remained in the background there and left early to coordinate the next stop.

Open-air locations required high-level security coordina-
tion, and you couldn't get more open-air than a downtown
farmers market. It was photo op rather than a speech. There,
as with most other produce-related stops, Emily would be
expected to pay respect to the local crops. Every locale
meant another homegrown specialty, and Emily had to
admire, taste, and enjoy them all in public, whether she actually liked beets, butternut squash, or homemade scupper-
nong preserves. In this case, Emily lucked out and munched
happily on an apple as she toured the produce stands.

While Emily noshed and networked, Kate managed to
get away long enough to call Nick.

"'Lo?" he slurred.

"Nick? That you?"

He made a vaguely positive grunt, sounding as if he was
either still drunk or nursing a grand mal hangover. She supposed these might be the times that tried a man's sobriety.

"Have you been drinking?" she said softly.

"No." It was a quick but decisive denial.

"You really need to call your sponsor."

"You should trust me." His voice grew clearer. "Really
trust me after last night." Nick groaned. "I haven't been
drinking. I was mugged."

Alarm spread through Kate like wildfire. "Oh no! Are
you okay? What happened?"

"Nothing much, actually. Two guys jumped me in the
parking garage at my apartment. The folks who live next
door pulled in right behind me and scared the guys off. But
not before I managed to smash their beer bottle with my
head and their bat with my knee."

"Did you call the police?"

He laughed, then groaned. "Of course not. The reason they used a beer bottle was so I'd be stinking of booze when I tried to make a report. It would have played right into Chuck's hands."

"You think he's behind it?"

"You bet I do. I don't have any proof, but the timing sure stinks. When he gets mad, he gets vindictive. It's one of the reasons I quit. Been there, done that. Remind you of someone you know?"

She ignored his gibe. "You need to leave D.C."

"I'm ahead of you there. My bags are packed and I'm booked on a flight to Baton Rouge tonight. But I'm actually going by train instead and taking the Crescent to New Orleans. When the going gets tough, the tough get the heck out of Dodge City. Chuck may think he has connections everywhere, but I know more cops and crooks in Louisiana than he ever will. I figure I'll be able to use both groups to protect me."

"The good ol' boy network?"

"The Cajun equivalent." Nick paused. "But nothing's changed. Thanks to you, Emily's political career is safe. You've short-circuited his plans. I don't know what he'll try next, but you have a pretty powerful trump card to stop him."

"So I don't have to worry about a press conference?"

"Nope. And he's none too happy about that. Ergo, the attack. Take his unhappiness out on my hide."

"Good. I mean . . . bad." Kate faltered for the right words. "I mean . . . I'm so sorry all this has happened." Although she wanted to thank Nick for sticking his neck out, she was still a bit wobbly after the emotional train wreck of their last meeting. At least she'd managed to salvage the basic tenet that she'd kept sacred for twenty years in politics. No manufactured scandals or clever tricks. Only the truth used honorably. A smart offense didn't need dirty tricks, and an effective defense was not afraid to dig hard and dig deep and use what they found in retaliation only.

She'd lived that core belief last night.

Nick hadn't asked her to violate her principles. As far as that went, Emily hadn't asked her to either.

Whatever Kate had done, she'd done entirely on her own.

She started again. "Nick, I really want to thank you for—"

"Whatever you do, don't thank me," he said, interrupting her. "Forgive me instead."

"For what?"

"For going to work for him in the first place. We both know I did it just to get at Emily. For that, I am truly sorry. If anything, I should thank you."

"Whatever for? Getting you beat up?"

"Nah. That was Chuck's doing. And the more I think about it, the more I think it was Chuck's doing that I got shot."

"I think so too. That's part of the reason I took him on last night. . . . That FBI guy—how did you meet him?"

"Chuck introduced me."

"After that, how well did you get to know Agent Trainor?"

"Not well enough. I did think it was odd that none of what he told us ever came out in the press." Nick's accent deepened as realization evidently dawned. "Son of a gun . . . it *must* have all been a setup. All that hush-hush stuff was to keep either of us from pursuing more information. As long as we both thought the FBI was investigating, we didn't need to do anything more. What if Chuck set me up from the beginning as the victim and Emily as the fall guy? He knew I'd be the first one to believe Emily sent Gilroy. I'm so stupid."

"If you were stupid, then I was too," Kate offered.

"No, you weren't. You said to his face that you thought it was a load of bull. I'm just not cut out for this, am I? Good thing I'm headed back to Loo'siana," he said, his natural accent thickening like the Mississippi mud. "It's better to dance wid' the devil you know. . . ." He sounded totally deflated. "Well, thanks anyway for believing me—believing *in* me. Trust me, I'll remember that. I gotta go. As they say, *Laissez les bon temps roulez*." Nick paused. "Uh, Kate? Is it okay if I keep in touch?"

Her heartbeat quickened for a moment. Was it? "Sure, Nick. I'd like that."

"Thanks. Bye."

She pocketed her phone. His new revelations should have left her with a bigger, better sense of resolution on two fronts. But she'd already made a mistake by accepting the obvious explanation.

Kate looked up to see Emily reach the end of the row of produce stands, signifying the end of the appearance. After signaling the transportation captain, Kate inserted herself into Emily's conversation with a serious man who appeared to be grilling her about farm subsidies.

"I remember when your father said—"

Kate physically stepped into the conversation, bestowing her best smile on the man. "I'm so terribly sorry to interrupt, but I'm afraid Ms. Benton has another engagement. It's a school, and we don't want to hold up the students' schedule because we're late. I'm sure you understand."

The man did. Emily wrenched free from what was probably an uncomfortable conversation about her father, moved toward the exit, and climbed into the limo. They headed off to the next activity, a town hall meeting held in a suburban high school.

With Emily having no children of her own, it meant they'd had to promote the relationship she had with her large extended family of cousins. Emily's cousin Steve Tremont lived in the area and had readily agreed to trot out the next generation of Tremonts for a photo op. Even better, his eldest daughter, Brittany, age fourteen, looked more like a Benton than the rest of his children. She bore a strong familial resemblance to Emily.

At the girl's school, the two of them laughed like old friends as they posed, mirroring each other's stance and expression, looking more like mother and daughter than the real pair. Kate couldn't help but believe it would sway those voters who remained on the fence, wondering if a female presidential candidate who was single and had no offspring could possibly understand the needs of the family structure and their values.

They'd probably be amazed to learn this was only the second time Emily had ever met the girl. The child was another Benton politician in the making, judging by her willingness to play along as if she'd known Emily for years. Of course, it'd taken the incentive of a new laptop to charm her into compliance so that Brittany became Emily's new closest young cousin—charming, personable, and cooperative.

The last event of the day was with an independent filmmaker who was finishing his pro-Benton documentary. At least it was purported to be pro-Benton. Kate held a healthy amount of skepticism because she knew that filmmakers wanting this kind of access to a presidential candidate often presented themselves as sympathetic, when underneath it all, they were like sharks, showing only their fins above the water while they trolled for scandal and corruption.

Everybody wanted to be the next Michael Moore.

Kate made sure to limit the access the young man received. It was far easier to control a situation than to clean up the aftermath.

With that in mind, she thought back to Daniel Gilroy's attack on Nick. If Talbot had indeed masterminded the incident, he certainly hadn't managed it well. You don't throw a loaded grenade into a crowded room when you only want to injure one person. The man didn't strike Kate as being so callous as to consider the death of one of his campaign workers as an unavoidable but necessary casualty of friendly fire.

Did it even matter whether Gilroy had acted on his own or in concert with someone else?

The important thing was that he was locked up and no longer a threat to anyone. And Talbot was neatly hog-tied too. Kate only hoped all the ropes would hold until after the election.

She pushed that thought firmly from her mind and pulled out the next spreadsheet she needed to review.

Oh, how she wanted to look forward to a nice, clean campaign.

KATE MANUFACTURED a reasonable excuse to not be on-site for the second presidential debate, but the third and final debate was harder to duck.

"I need you," Emily whined. "This jerk Talbot is really getting under my skin and I need you to keep me centered. To keep me focused." She added in a dark voice, "To keep me from tackling him at the podium and plucking his well-groomed head bald."

But that meant Kate would have to see Charles Talbot face-to-face. She wasn't sure she could stomach that, not after their invective-laced phone conversation. If Emily thought *she* was having a hard time keeping her cool around the man, she had no idea what Talbot did to Kate's blood pressure. . . .

But when it came time for the show—Kate couldn't think of it as anything else but a show—she gathered her courage and watched the procedure from the wings of the stage. They'd chosen a college auditorium for the last clash.

But *clash* turned out to be the wrong word. Football

teams clashed. What Emily and Charles Talbot did was play an elaborate game of chess, one strategy masking another, each of them thinking two or three . . . dozen moves in advance. They started with a classic opening and it was as if they'd studied the same "How to Play Chess" book.

Avoid moving a piece twice. Or mentioning a topic twice. Make your point well the first time and move on.

Make sure to develop the pieces on both sides. Both candidates fought to present themselves and their agendas as being planted firmly in the middle of an issue, rather than wildly to either extreme. The conservative Talbot tried to lean more to the liberal side of issues and the more liberal Emily tried to anchor herself closer to a conservative center.

Don't play a piece beyond your own side of the board during the opening stage. There was nothing to be gained by coming out of the corner swinging. The debate would degenerate into modified name-calling soon enough.

Search for weak spots in the opponent's position. That was the end goal for both prior debates and the third one as well. Robbed of his ability to bring up Emily's questionable involvement with the highway project, Talbot pounded away at every other possible soft spot. He even glanced once or twice in Kate's direction during one such attempted drubbing as if to dare her to say something in retaliation.

She prayed for strength.

Apparently something in Kate's gaze had the power to shake him. He lost his train of thought, and Emily scored points.

However, their unspoken agreement held. There was only one verboten topic; any other subject matter, any new discoveries, were fair game.

After all was said, done, and rebutted, the conservative political experts declared that Talbot had won the debate by a slim margin and liberal pundits stated Emily had tipped the scales in her direction by an equally narrow amount.

In other words, it was anybody's game.

Emily and Kate returned to the hotel in an unusual silence that Emily broke when they stepped into the elevator along with the Secret Service detail.

Emily crossed her arms. "Is it me, or were you and Talbot having a telepathic conversation back there? He'd glare at you, you'd glare back, and it was almost like you could see words floating in the air between the two of you."

"Nonsense."

"Don't give me that. You've been acting weird since Seattle. And don't tell me it's just stress. Trust me. I know stress. This is something . . . more. I can almost feel power and pain rolling off you in waves."

Kate glanced at the back of the Secret Service agent who stood between them and the elevator door, filling the gap with broad shoulders. "I don't like the man. I don't trust him. And I don't want to talk about it anymore." She tilted her head toward the bodyguard. "Not here. Not now."

As they reached their floor, Kate pushed past the agent and positioned herself to exit first. If that broke protocol, she didn't care. She had to get out of the elevator before she dissolved into a bundle of nerves.

Emily called after Kate as she made her escape to her room. "Wait up."

"No. I said later." Kate's tone brooked no argument, not even from Emily, used to having her way at all times.

When Kate reached her room, she didn't turn around

to see the expression on Emily's face. She already knew it was a combination of concern, consternation, and confusion. Once safely inside, Kate leaned against the closed door. Things couldn't stay like this—her dodging Emily, refusing to explain. Either Kate figured out how to deal with this or she was going to go stark raving nuts.

Lord, what do I do?

Wes.

He was the only person who could help absolve her.

＊　＊　＊　＊　＊

The next night, Kate sat in Wes Kingsbury's living room, laughing at the antics of his cherubic daughter, Dani. She was amazed at how motherhood had tamed but not extinguished the fiery Anna.

"You look fantastic," she said as Anna scooped up the baby to blow kisses on her round little belly.

"Thanks. I don't need a gym membership when I have to run around tending to the kiddo here for sixteen hours a day. It's like pumping iron with a weight set that keeps getting heavier every day."

"I never thought my sister-in-law would give up the Stair-Master for actual stairs, but she did now that she has kids and a three-level town house."

"Having kids changes your perspective, if not your architecture," Anna said with a grin. "You'll have to excuse me. It's Dani's bedtime, so I'm going to head upstairs and give you two some peace and quiet."

After saying their good nights, Wes stood and gestured for Kate to follow him into his book-lined study. Once she was comfortably seated there, he closed the doors, giving them an added measure of privacy.

He propped against the corner of the desk. "You've been very congenial tonight, but I can tell something is bothering you."

Kate nodded. "I need advice. I need answers. I need . . ." She felt something crumble inside of her, and a new flood of emotions threatened to turn her into a soggy mess. "I need help," she said, hanging on to her control as tightly as she could.

Wes abandoned the desk and sat next to her on the couch. When he rested his hand on her shoulder, everything bottled up inside of her broke loose.

She told him the entire sordid story, every fact, every conjecture, and every suspicion she had. Kate didn't hold back anything about Emily, telling him about the irregularities surrounding the highway project. She talked about her doubts but also her belief that Emily was capable of taking kickbacks but not of letting that bridge be built wrong. What Kate didn't mention was her own conversation with Talbot, the one that had spiked his guns. It was only after she finished that she realized how badly she might be compromising, or at least complicating, Wes's friendship with Emily. Kate immediately began to apologize, but Wes shut her up quickly.

"You're not telling me anything new. I've known Emily a long, long time." He paused to correct himself. "Okay, so you *are* telling me a lot of things I didn't know, but you're not destroying my illusions about Emily. I've always known she's had the capacity to do something under the table. I think deep down inside, you knew that too. We know we need to make up for that particular shortfall in her qualities. But like you, I think the bridge thing wasn't her style. The money and the family firm finagling control of the job—that's another matter. . . ."

Kate nodded. "It's quite a disappointment to learn that your idol is almost entirely made of clay. So what do I do? This . . . animosity and resentment I have is affecting our relationship. How can I support her for president when right now I can barely hold a conversation with her?"

"Why can't you talk to her? Why can't you simply tell her what you learned and let her respond? You might find that she regrets having done it."

"Are we talking about the same person? I don't think the word *regret* is in her vocabulary."

Wes said nothing and instead leaned back, giving Kate a critical once-over that she felt all the way to her shoes. "What?"

"There's something else going on. What is it?"

"Nothing."

He crossed his arms. "We can't begin to untangle this mess unless you're honest with yourself."

She sank into the comfortable leather couch, wishing it could swallow her whole. "I did something I'm not proud of and . . ." She closed her eyes and tried to find the right words. "And I'm mad at Emily for putting me in the position where I felt I had to do it."

"What'd you do?"

"I . . . I blackmailed Charles Talbot." Kate's voice broke along with her control. Tears fell as she named her offense, her sin, for the first time. "I think I might have been called to do it. But I still feel like my soul is shattering. I'm not the same. What have I become?"

Wes's expression didn't even flicker. He didn't look disappointed or disgusted. If anything his lack of response was
more frightening than anything she could imagine. Had he
held no high expectations for her either? She'd expected
shock, even censure for her sin, but Wes remained quiet.

Like any good psych patient, she felt compelled to fill the
silence. "I'm mad. At myself. I'm supposed to be better than
that. But I folded. I'd been sitting on this information for
months. I didn't even tell Emily because I was scared she'd
pull another Mark Henderson on me and use what I found
without provocation."

"You worried that she'd take this information and use it
to fire the first volley at Talbot?"

"Yeah." Kate nodded. "Here I thought I was taking the
moral high ground. That I was so much better equipped to
safeguard the information than she was. But the moment
I learned Talbot was going to hold a press conference and
reveal all this wretched stuff about Emily and the highway
project kickbacks, I reached right into my bag of tricks. I
didn't hesitate for a moment. Not one second thought. I just
pulled that loaded weapon out and I fired it point-blank at
Talbot."

"And you stopped him."

Kate buried her face in her hands, trying to stop the tears.
"Yeah, I stopped him."

"What had he done?"

"Does it matter?"

"I know you. It had to have been bad. Really bad. Maybe
bad enough to violate more than your own moral values.
Maybe bad enough to be considered a capital crime?"

"Y-es."

"Are you sorry you used this knowledge?"

"Yes. Maybe. No. Maybe all of the above. I'm sorry that I sank to fighting scandal with scandal. But I'm not sorry that Talbot knows he didn't get away with what he did back then. He essentially killed a girl he loved with his carelessness, and he ran away from the responsibility of his actions by bribing the witnesses." Kate hadn't meant to confide that. Or had she? Should the severity of Talbot's crime be a consideration? Or was she just trying harder to assuage her own guilt for sinking to his level?

"Someone died?" Wes emitted a soft whistle. "I take it you haven't told Emily about this."

"No, of course not. About none of it—not even what Talbot uncovered about the highway project, not that he planned to release it, and definitely not what I found out about him."

"And you resent her for this. Being unable to confide in her because you fear her reaction."

"Yes, Dr. Freud."

"So let me ask. What happens if you tell her?"

Kate's imagination went into overtime. "She'd want to expose him to the world, even at the risk of revealing her own guilt. But he already knows his secret has been compromised. If he's smart, he's trying to clean it up. He's probably looking even harder into Emily's background, trying to find something else to hang over her head."

"What will he find?"

That was the real problem; Kate had no idea what ghosts still haunted Emily's past that could be used against her. The highway thing had taken her by surprise. What other messes were out there festering? "I don't know," she whispered. "I had no idea about the highway project. Who knows what else is lurking in the shadows? I guess this proves I don't know Emily as well as I thought I did."

A sense of despair dried her tears. "What do I do, Wes? How can I forgive myself for what I've done?" She looked at him, instantly mesmerized by the expression of serenity on his face. "Did I do the right thing?"

"Ask God first. Did you live up to his plan for you? Or did you fall short? If you're truly sorry, ask for his forgiveness and then ask for his guidance to help you make the right decision next time."

"There's always going to be a next time, isn't there?"

"Of course." Wes shrugged. "Politics is a difficult business. Honestly, it could use a little more religion."

"A little more?"

He smiled. "Okay, a *lot* more." Wes rose from his chair and offered Kate a hand. After she stood, he reached for her other hand. "You're a good person, Kate Rosen. You may call it your conscience speaking, but I call it your heart and soul. Listen to both and you won't be led astray." He paused, then squeezed her hands. "Would you mind if I said a little prayer on your behalf?"

She nodded. "I need it."

Wes closed his eyes. "Well, Lord, as you can see, it's been a tough week for Kate. It's been a stressful time and she needs your help. She's in a unique position to influence the woman who just may be the next president, and this is a serious responsibility that Kate wants to do well and in your name. Please help guide her. Help her weigh all decisions and make the wise ones. Protect her from those who want to manipulate her in the wrong direction. Bless her, Lord, and forgive her if she veers off your path. Show her that the way back takes only one step at a time. Watch over her and keep her and Emily in your loving care. In his holy name, amen."

It wasn't that Kate suddenly felt all her cares and worries lifted from her shoulders. But she felt better equipped to handle the myriad of problems that still hung around her neck and loomed in the distance.

The main one being Emily Benton.

✫ ✫ ✫ ✫ ✫

The next morning, Kate flew to Kansas City, where Emily was starting a series of postdebate rallies in the Midwest. She knew what she had to tell her friend wasn't going to be the sort of discussion one should have over the phone.

Instead of going backstage, Kate chose to sit in the audience, joining the other Benton supporters, their enthusiasm infectious and familiar. She'd forgotten how exciting a rally could be, how the speeches, the music, and the ceremony could whip up a crowd.

The woman standing next to Kate was particularly caught up. "Isn't she wonderful?" she shouted to Kate as she clapped in rhythm to the music.

Kate nodded.

"She's going to make such a wonderful president."

Kate stared at this Everywoman, representing an important part of Emily's constituency. "Why?"

The woman stopped clapping.

"Why are you going to vote for her?" Kate repeated.

The woman took very little time to formulate an answer. "Because I like how she thinks, what she says, what she's willing to fight for. And even better, she has real experience. She practically grew up in politics." Her eyes began to shine. "The male politicians in Washington, D.C., really respect and listen to her." She pointed to the stage, where Emily and Burl Bochner stood, drinking in the palpable love and support. "It's time for a change and she's going to do it."

"You really think so?"

The woman smiled. "Honey, I know so."

After the rally, Kate worked her way backstage and ran into Maia Bari, whom she hadn't expected to see but who seemed genuinely pleased to see her. The young woman gave her an awkward hug. "You don't know how much I appreciate being allowed to work with Emily. I never knew politics could be so . . . thrilling."

Kate almost asked, *And when did I supposedly hire you?* But instead she played along. "She seemed in fine form tonight."

"She feeds off the fervor of each crowd." Maia was slightly breathless. "I am simply amazed at her stamina."

Kate turned her attention to Emily, deep in an animated discussion with the people clustered around her. "She's amazing, all right." She turned back to Maia. "I'm headed to the hotel to check in. Can you tell Emily I'm in town? She wasn't expecting me. I need to talk to her tonight when she gets back to her suite."

"I'd be delighted to give her the message. I know she misses your counsel while traveling."

Kate faded into the throng, deliberately staying out of Emily's line of sight. Once outside, she took a quick cab ride to the Hyatt Regency Crown Center, moved her things into one of the bedrooms in Emily's private suite, and tried to distract herself with e-mail until Emily arrived.

Two hours lapsed before there was a sharp rap on Kate's door. When Kate opened it, Emily stood there with an opened bottle of champagne.

"Hey, K."

"Hey, M." Kate pointed to the champagne. "What's the occasion?"

"You tell me. You're the one who showed up unexpectedly. I thought you were doing the nose-to-the-grindstone stuff back at M Central."

Emily stepped back and Kate followed her into the living room area. Kate gestured to the couch. "There's been a . . . complication."

"Hang on." Emily kicked off her shoes, unbuttoned her jacket, and dropped onto the couch, propping her feet on the coffee table. She uncorked the half-filled bottle and took a healthy swig.

"That's better. Dom Pérignon . . . take me away!" She giggled. At least Kate assumed it was a giggle; Emily so seldom did that. Then she shushed herself. "No, no, seriously . . . it's high time you told me what's wrong. The next three weeks will pretty much be me, Loretta, and Maia in the rock-star bus, going from pillar to post, and I need to know what's wrong now."

"Oh yeah . . . Maia." Kate tried not to sound defensive. "When did she become part of all this?"

Emily made a dismissive gesture. "Since I met her and realized how much she can help me. You're changing the subject. Maia's not the problem. What is?" A sharp look in Emily's eyes suggested that the earlier air of frivolity had been more theatrics than real inebriation.

No matter, Emily did have a right to know that her family's involvement in the highway project was no longer a secret from everyone. She needed to know that the news had essentially fallen into the hands of the enemy. But that didn't mean Kate had to tell Emily exactly what information she'd used to stop Charles Talbot.

"C'mon, K. Spill it."

Kate sat down in the chair facing Emily and laced her fingers together in her lap to keep her hands from shaking. "You heard about the barge that hit the toll road bridge near Morgantown, right?"

"Sure."

"You know that raised some questions about the bridge's construction."

"Yeah. So?"

"It appears that the company who built it used inferior quality materials."

Emily clucked sympathetically, but Kate put up her hand. "Spare me."

Her friend's eyes opened in rare surprise at her retort.

Kate continued. "Your unworthy opponent started looking into the firms involved, and after a lot of digging and more than a couple bribes, he uncovered enough information to strongly suggest, if not outright prove, that members of your family have a majority ownership in more than just a few of the companies involved."

"That's ridiculous. You can't believe—"

"He knows too much, Emily. Then again, you really didn't cover your tracks very well if someone knows what to look for. Gablonski International?" Kate sighed and shook her head. "You named the company after your horse?"

Emily didn't respond for nearly a minute as if weighing

another lie over admitting the truth. Finally she shrugged. "It seemed like a good idea at the time."

"Then you don't deny it?"

"I don't deny that I am on the board of directors of a company called Gablonski International, but you can't believe anything Upchuck Talbot says about the company."

Kate's anger flared. "Do you think I'm a complete moron? I didn't take anything on face value, not from the likes of him. I had my investigators—"

"Our investigators," Emily corrected.

"They're *my* investigators when they're doing work for me. They've substantiated most of what Talbot claimed. You or someone in your family had a piece of almost every company that won a construction bid for that project."

Emily took another swig from the champagne bottle. "Is it any wonder? I come from an extraordinarily large family, and those who aren't politicians are extremely shrewd business owners. Sure we own construction firms. And we also own banks, hotel conglomerates, and a host of other companies. You can't shake a stick in Virginia without hitting a Benton and their works."

"You violated the law."

"Just a little. But I wanted that job done right. We built an incredible highway."

"Really? What about the problems with the bridge?"

Emily sighed. "See what happens when you hire a subcontractor outside of the family? We subbed out to a smaller firm and they're the ones who substituted cheaper materials and pocketed the difference. It was them, not us, because had we known, we would have taken it over ourselves. We would have gladly lost money rather than build an unsafe bridge, especially on Virginia soil."

Alarm grew in Emily's eyes as if she was finally seeing past the gauzy curtain caused by the champagne. "If Talbot knows about our involvement, we've got to act fast before he releases anything."

Emily stood, the empty bottle hitting the carpet with a loud thud. Swaying slightly, she made a failed attempt to pick it up, then waved away the effort. "Forget it. That's why we have maids." She shoved the bottle under the couch with her foot.

Belatedly Kate realized that this wasn't Emily's first bottle of champagne that evening.

"You've been awfully closemouthed about what you actually found on Talbot, and I respected that. But I think it's high time we uncrated whatever secret weapon you found and use it. I sure hope it'll be enough to shut him up."

"About that, I—"

Emily kept talking as if she hadn't even heard Kate. "You brought all the gory details with you, right? And you're ready to stay up all night strategizing? If we plan to stop him, we have to hit him hard and hit him fast."

"Emily . . ."

She ignored Kate and began to slam her fist into her opposite palm in a classic pugilistic gesture. "We need to keep pounding him hard so that he doesn't have time to breathe. We need to—"

"Emily, stop!"

She rolled her eyes. "Don't start that sanctimonious stuff with me, Rosen. This is serious. If you don't want to be a part of it, fine." She pointed at herself. "If *I* don't strike first, then *I*—"

"If you'd just shut up you'd learn that I did it already," Kate shouted.

Emily's mouth gaped open. "Huh?"

Kate turned away, no longer able to look her friend in the eye. "I struck first. I stopped him."

"Really?" Emily's shock disintegrated into something much too close to utter delight. "You really did it? On your own?" Emily reached over and tried to hug Kate, but Kate inched away, not wanting to be touched.

"C'mon, don't be like that, K. Admit it. You loved telling off that smarmy meat puppet for the special interest groups, didn't you?"

God help her, but Kate *had* entertained the briefest moments of . . . destiny. Not when telling him but when realizing her gambit had worked. She'd told herself it was relief. But she worried that it had been pride. And everybody knew what pride preceded. . . .

"See?" Emily wagged a finger precariously close to Kate's nose. "I'm right. I can read it in your face. It felt wonderful telling off that self-righteous sanctimonious scumbag. Don't ever tell me you didn't like it. You've been trying to play Little Miss Perfect Priss lately, but admit it. You're no better than I . . ."

Emily's voice trailed off and a look of surprise creased her face. "Oh, well. I think I must be drunk." She dropped carefully onto the couch and even reached down to retrieve the empty bottle and place it on the table.

"Here I am, screaming like a banshee. And why? Am I mad that you did what you did? No way. I appreciate it.

More than that, I'm honestly grateful. Proud, even. You had my back when the bad guys came." She plowed her hand through her carefully arranged hairdo. "I'm a real piece of work, aren't I?"

The Emily Benton who looked up at Kate was the old friend she remembered, the old friend she hadn't seen in quite some time. "It was the Henderson thing," Emily said with a sense of finality and a hint of dejection. "That's where I went wrong. And that's when you decided not to trust me."

Kate said nothing.

Emily stood and walked with very carefully controlled steps over to the window, pushing the curtain back to reveal the city lights below. "I can't say that I blame you. If it's any consolation, I realized soon after it happened that I really should have listened to you." She stared outside as if she couldn't look Kate in the eye while making her confession. "You were right about Henderson. I suspect you've been right about Talbot too."

"That's the problem. I'm still not sure I made the correct decision," Kate admitted.

"Nonsense. You stopped him, right?"

"For now."

"For pete's sake, don't start doubting yourself. If he gets wind of your hesitation, he may decide to call your bluff."

"But I wasn't bluffing."

"There's only one way to make sure." Emily pivoted sharply. "Tell me what you have on him."

Kate had expected this, and she stuck to her guns. "No."

"Now hear me out." Emily returned to the couch and sat primly on the edge of the cushion, her hands folded in her lap. "Charles Talbot is the type to act first and then second-guess himself. I've seen him do it in the debates. So when you played your hand, he backed down. Fast. But now he's had time to think about the situation. He's thinking, 'Maybe I acted too rashly. Maybe she wouldn't follow through.'"

She lowered her voice as if afraid of being overheard. "You have to admit that you don't have a reputation as a real cutthroat. He might decide to take the chance that you're all talk and no action. But the one thing that will stop him is if he thinks *I* know everything. He knows that I won't hesitate to use what we know."

A sudden chill enveloped Kate and she wrapped her arms around herself. Emily was making sense in a perverse sort of way. In essence, Kate would merely be handing her friend and colleague an empty gun, its ammunition already spent. What would be the harm in that? She'd even brought the file, which was stowed in her briefcase.

Emily read her indecision as easily as a billboard. "This isn't like with Henderson, K. The damage has already been done."

Damage.

That one word cinched her decision.

"No."

Resolution began to build inside Kate like the rosy glow of sunrise on a darkened horizon. "We're going to take our chances. He played his hand. I played ours. Now we just sit back."

"By *we* you mean me."

"No, I mean *we*. We're in this together, remember?"

Emily stooped to pick up her discarded shoes, disappointment rolling off her in waves. "I don't like this," she admitted. "I want to do something . . . proactive."

"I know you do, M. But you also know that will quite possibly blow up in your face. This time, you have to trust me. The only way any good can come out of this is if you and Talbot both believe you've reached a stalemate."

"With no one caught in the cross fire." Emily's eyes clouded slightly and she held her shoes close to her chest. "Like my family."

Kate grabbed the subject thread and pulled as hard as she could. "Exactly. Talbot didn't just threaten you. He threatened everyone in your family who's involved in any aspect of the construction project. We don't want collateral damage."

Emily stood unmoving, lost in thought. After a few moments, her unfocused stare sharpened. "Okay. We play it your way. But there's one thing I need to know."

"What?"

"How bad was it? You don't have to tell me any specifics, but this thing Talbot did. Was it bad?"

Kate nodded.

"How bad?"

"Someone died."

For one infinitesimal moment, Kate thought she saw a smile of triumph play on Emily's lips. But it was gone as quickly as it started.

"Too bad." Emily nodded toward her bedroom. "Well, I gotta hit the sack. Tomorrow morning I get to cram myself in that sardine can we call a tour bus so I can meet and greet Ma and Pa Kettle and show them that I'm just a good ol' girl. G'night."

BY NOVEMBER 4, Kate calculated that they'd raised and spent almost a half billion dollars on Emily's presidential bid. The candidate herself had traveled nearly that many miles in planes, trains, and automobiles and on foot through crowds of constituents, thrilling the faithful and winning over the undecided. All told, Emily had spent less than forty nights in her own home in the two years since announcing her bid for office.

Excited and exhausted, Kate accompanied Emily in the media procession as she went to her home precinct and cast her vote. Kate had done so earlier by absentee ballot so she wouldn't have to work in a trip to her own polling place along the rest of her responsibilities.

The press hounded them all day, in the car, at the campaign headquarters, by phone, by e-mail, and by ambush. Reporters acted more like paparazzi than respectable mainstream media representatives as the press trailed them that afternoon. Even when they were on the road, reporters followed them as they drove to the Marriott Wardman Park, where the election night party would be held. Emily had a suite on the top floor, where she could wait in relative privacy for the results to come in. *Relative* was the key word because besides the inner circle from the campaign, a steady stream of Benton kinfolk came and went during the day, paying homage, delivering good wishes, and showing the type of solidarity that Kate had learned to appreciate during the course of the campaign.

Emily's uncle Bill held court on one side of the room, telling anecdotes about his own presidential election day. To Kate's amazement, Emily didn't seem perturbed by his usurping of the limelight, and instead, she listened with rapt attention along with everyone else as if she hadn't already heard all those stories a thousand times.

Once five o'clock rolled around, they began to get more information—exit poll reports, updates from CNN, or some other bits of news. The whole group would chew over the numbers, analyze the trends, and somehow manage to find a positive meaning in the resulting calculations or speculations.

Kate sat back and watched, not necessarily amazed but still impressed at the collected political knowledge represented in the room. The Bentons were truly America's political family, and they supported and protected their own without hesitation. Kate had seen that on the road and now she saw it here again.

But the tenor of the room changed when the first polls started closing. The family realized that being supportive meant giving Emily room to wait for the results in private.

They excused themselves to the ballroom downstairs, where people were awaiting state election results.

During a lull in the reporting, Kate went downstairs to take a peek at the arrangements. A balcony overlooking the stage had been sectioned off for their use and she stood in the modified press box, surveying an enthusiastic crowd who cheered and booed depending on the state election return being shown on the huge television screens at the front of the large room.

As Kate turned to leave, she felt her cell phone vibrate. She answered with a "Just a minute" and headed for the door, waiting until it closed behind her, choking off the worst of the noise, before she spoke again.

"Hello?"

"Kate? It's Nick."

"Hi. How are things going? You still in Louisiana?"

"Yeah. I'm fine. No assassins on my tail. So how's the wait?"

"Killing us."

"I can imagine. Emily's never been what I'd call a patient person. I just wanted to call and wish you good luck."

"Me? Don't you mean Emily?"

"No. Emily can take care of herself. If she wins, I wish you good luck with your new position as chief of staff. If she loses, I wish you good luck dealing with her."

"Funny."

"Honest." There was an awkward pause; then he spoke again. "Well . . . I don't want to keep you on the phone, Kate. You might have to explain who you're talking to and even I don't want to antagonize Emily today of all days. So in any case, good luck. To you both."

"Thanks. Bye."

Odd call, Kate thought. But it was kind of him and not necessarily out of character for the "new" him, she decided. She took the elevator upstairs and, once she entered the suite, noticed that the crowd had thinned out to only a handful of people. Dozier Marsh and Dave Dickens sat in the corner, drinks in hand. Chip McWilliamson sat at the desk, huddled over his laptop, typing furiously, with Burl Bochner hanging over his shoulder. But Emily was nowhere to be seen.

"Where's Her Majesty?"

Dozier thumbed over his shoulder toward the bedroom door. "Playing clotheshorse. Maia brought her some things to try on."

"Today?" Kate crossed the room and knocked on the bedroom door. "It's me. Can I come in?"

She heard several rustling sounds, and then someone said, "Come in."

When Kate entered, she saw several dress bags laid across the bed and a couple of shopping bags on the floor. Melissa Bonner-Bochner sat in the chair.

"Emily," she called out. "Kate's here. Come out here and show her the outfit before you take it off." Melissa turned to Kate. "You're going to love it. Maia is a genius."

Emily stepped out of the bathroom, decked out in a stunning teal suit—tailored enough to look professional but with enough draping in the skirt to be feminine. "So? What do you think?" She preened, turning in a circle for Kate's inspection.

"Beautiful," Kate said, meaning it. "So is this suit going to replace the one we picked out earlier as *the* acceptance outfit?"

"From your mouth to God's ear," Maia responded automatically. She colored slightly. "I mean about the acceptance, not the clothing choice." She busied herself by zipping the next dress bag. "Mrs. Redding simply asked me to pick up a few things for Emily's consideration."

Emily laughed. "Marjorie is trying to distract me."

"Oh no," Maia added quickly, "she merely wants you to look as perfect as possible on stage. This will be your big moment and you should be mindful of your appearance."

It was hard to believe that someone so exotically beautiful and worldly looking could possess an outlook quite that innocent and simplistic. Marjorie had a deal with a couple of designers who could probably build their careers based on this exposure alone.

Maia turned her attention to the scattered bags. "If you are satisfied with this outfit, then I must go now. I shouldn't disturb you any longer. You have many important things to do today." She looked up and smiled. "I am pleased to have been a small part of it."

Emily picked up the dress bag and hung it in the closet. "You don't know how much I appreciate this, Maia."

"My pleasure, Miss Benton."

"How many times do I have to tell you? Call me Emily."

The young woman's smile magnified. "I hope to be calling you President Benton—"

A roar from the living room interrupted her.

Dozier knocked on the door. "If you're decent, get out here. The returns are starting to come in."

* * * * *

East Coast, South, Midwest . . . As the results came in, the tension mounted in the suite. By 7 p.m., Talbot had won the first four states called and put himself in a thirty-three vote lead right at the start.

To everyone's surprise, Emily remained almost circumspect, her calmness masking what Kate suspected was a fear of failure, a word not usually found in the Benton family lexicon. "Well, this is not the rout I was hoping for," she said.

Dozier drained his highball glass. "Don't fret, honey. Things'll pick up soon enough."

An hour later, the tides had indeed changed and Emily picked up ten of the next twelve states, garnering a fifty vote lead. Wes Kingsbury popped in to say hello but immediately headed downstairs since he'd been asked to speak and lead the invocation.

By 9 p.m., Emily's lead had been cut to twenty-seven votes, but she still was in first place with over 145 votes. In typical fashion, Emily spent more time complaining about the states she hadn't won than celebrating the ones she had.

Dozier was the only person brave enough to take her on. "You only lost Texas by a hair, and you had solid numbers in New York."

"I wanted both."

Dozier contemplated his empty glass, twirling the ice cubes with his forefinger. "You're going to win, sweetheart. Mark my words. Just be patient."

By 10 p.m., her lead widened to a little over forty votes, but Emily's anxiety began to infect everyone else in the room. Kate found herself pacing in front of the large window and had to force herself to stop and admire the view of Washington National Cathedral, its lit towers reaching for the heavens.

Between ten and eleven, the reports began to come in

faster. Until then, the staff had kept Emily mostly away from the television so she wouldn't blow out her voice yelling at the political pundits who had spent all night analyzing every single aspect of her campaign from her platform planks to her platform shoes.

"Pennsylvania!" Chip called out, the Internet reports beating the network news coverage by scant seconds.

Ten minutes later, he caught Kate's eye and mouthed, *California*. After a quick calculation, Kate realized that Emily lacked only twenty-six votes. Florida, yet to be called, held twenty-seven votes.

Kate made a command decision; it was time to move to the private box off the ballroom. Victory was within their grasp. She wanted everything to go smoothly. Emily had barely gotten settled in the private balcony when more reports flooded in, showing the rest of the states falling like dominoes in her favor.

At 11:27 p.m., November 4, 2008, all four networks plus CNN declared Emily Benton as the next president of the United States.

At 11:35, Charles Talbot made a frigidly polite and extremely brief call to Emily, conceding the election.

At 11:50, Burl Bochner introduced Emily. When she took the stage, the throng of her supporters screamed and cheered.

Energized by the excitement, Kate climbed the stairs two at a time to the private box to watch. Dozier, Dave, and several of the senior staffers were there. Dozier gave her a boozy kiss on the cheek. Dave, at the far end of the row of spectators, shot her a thumbs-up.

From her lofty vantage point, she could see the entire

ballroom, from the bunting-draped stage to the crowd who had paused in their celebration to listen to their candidate speak.

Their president.

Kate wanted to capture the feeling, drink in the moment, memorize every sight. She never wanted to forget this feeling, this place, this time.

Emily had won. They had won. Although it had been the goal from the beginning, it seemed unreal. Surreal.

Maia joined Kate at the balcony rail. "Emily looks beautiful, doesn't she?" she said, close to Kate's ear. "Every inch a president."

Kate nodded.

"I do not understand why anyone would not vote for her. Charles Talbot would *not* have made a good president. He is not a nice man."

"I agree." *Please stop talking so I can enjoy this.*

"I read the papers that Emily had about him. About the terrible thing he did when he was young. That poor girl . . ."

All sounds blurred together in the background—Emily's voice, the applause, everything. The last vestiges of trust she had in Emily shattered into a thousand pieces. Disillusionment replaced excitement. Fear uprooted faith.

All Kate had left now in her broken moment of glory was a burning desire to know why, when, and where Emily had chosen to betray their friendship.

Kate wrapped her hand around the young woman's fashionably thin arm and pulled her from the rail until they stood at the back of the balcony box. "Where did you see those papers?"

"She had them on the touring bus. When I asked her

about them, she told me she got them from you. That you had found information that Charles Talbot would not like the American public to know about."

Kate stared at Maia's perfect, guileless face, the light of absolute innocence in her eyes. Then she turned and caught sight of Emily in the television monitor—shrewd, calculating, and triumphant. She pushed Maia toward the door at the back of the balcony and into the room behind it, where they had all waited earlier. A bartender was policing the area, picking up dirty glasses, and two security personnel stood at the far door.

"Why?" Kate said in a terse whisper.

"Pardon?"

"Why are you telling me this?"

"I do not understand." Maia had perfected the look of wide-eyed innocence.

"Drop the act. You don't think I didn't investigate your background, do you? You've been in this country since you were four. You grew up and went to school in Hoboken. That stilted ESL dialogue and this 'I don't understand your foreign ways' act is growing really thin."

Maia's eyes widened; then she shot Kate a not-so-innocent smile that completely changed her flawless face from a naive beauty to a calculating one. "You're more like Emily than I expected," she said, the tinge of foreign accent gone. "She saw through me pretty fast. I thought it'd take you a while. But it's a wicked good gimmick, don't you think?"

Kate ignored the question. "Tell me about the papers."

"What about them? You had them; Emily wanted to read them." Maia leaned closer with a conspiratorial whisper. "You really should have locked the door to your bedroom.

She simply waited until you were asleep and then she sent me to retrieve them. It's not like they were hard to find or anything. I got the file, made a copy of it in the business center, and sneaked the originals back in place without you ever knowing. I didn't even read them while I was copying them," she said proudly, as if expecting praise for the expediency of her crime.

The logistics were certainly possible and Emily's motives were crystal clear. But not Maia's.

"Why are you telling me this? And why here and now? Don't tell me that guilt is weighing heavy on your conscience. I'd find that a bit hard to accept at the moment."

"Nah. It's because I want to be honest with you. After spending three weeks on the road with Emily, I realize that I desperately want to work with her. And if you're going to be her chief of staff, that means working for you. You have the reputation as a real straight shooter. What'd happen if you hired me and then learned what I did? You'd have me thrown out on my rear end before I could take another step. I don't want to start my career in politics trying to hide a lie like this. I respect you too much for that."

Maia was saying all the right words, but the sentiment behind them seemed more than a bit forced, not to mention the logic was somewhat strained.

She was telling Kate she'd be trustworthy because she'd just confessed to her breach of trust.

"Look, I didn't have to tell you anything," Maia continued, almost pleading. "You never would have found out. And it's not like Emily used the papers to expose Talbot to the world. All Emily did was make sure Talbot received a reminder of his upcoming college alumni meeting two nights ago. You'd already inserted the knife; all she did was point out the scar to him."

"Sure she did," Kate said. "All she did was drop a veiled hint that she knew what happened and where. She didn't care if she made a liar out of me. She didn't care that I'd promised to bury that stuff forever. And she'd promised to respect my decision!"

Maia grew defensive. "I didn't say I agreed with her actions. I'm just telling you *what* she did." An honest light lit her dark eyes for the first time. "I really do want to work for you. I want to help you help Emily. I have an advantage because she sees me as someone she can mold in her own image. I can tell you things. About what she's planning. She likes confiding in me," she said, her sense of pride obviously outweighing her common sense.

Such idealism. Here Maia thought she had hidden her worldliness behind a naive facade, but the girl wasn't nearly as experienced as she thought.

Kate almost didn't have the heart to burst her illusions. But some things had to be done. Otherwise it wasn't fair to the innocent bystanders.

"No," she said. "Emily sees you as someone she can use to her own advantage. If the Talbot thing had blown up in her face, who would have been the fall guy? Not me. And certainly not her. No, you were the one who stole the files from me. Your fingerprints will be on the originals, not Emily's. I bet the e-mail to Talbot even came from an account only you have access to. If Talbot raised a fuss, Emily would have made you the sacrificial lamb."

Kate had to give the girl credit. It took only a second for realization to dawn.

"She . . . she used me?"

"Of course she did. That's what she does best. Give her an opportunity and she'll do it again. Both of you are beautiful, smart, ambitious women. The difference is that she's mastered the art of being ruthless without people realizing it. And she'll stop at nothing. You might think about that before you take her as a role model, much less a boss."

Maia glanced at the door to the ballroom balcony and the door on the opposite side of the room that led to the hallway. "I . . . I've got to think this over." She inched her way toward the hallway.

"You do that. Think long and hard."

As Kate watched the young woman make a hasty exit, she thought back to her earlier conversation with Wes. The stakes were higher now that Emily had won the election. Soon she would be at the center of the most powerful government on earth, controlling the visible reins of the country as well as its invisible strings of power. As White House chief of staff, Kate would be in the best possible position to influence, guide, and if necessary, temper Emily's actions.

But Kate asked herself the same question she asked Maia.

Do I really want to work for someone I can't trust?

Can I withstand a constant bombardment of my values, my faith, my morals?

Do I go or do I stay?

Kate stared at the television monitor that showed Emily and Burl standing with clasped hands raised high in the classic victor's stance. The camera panned the stage, showing various party higher-ups—Melissa Bonner-Bochner, Dozier, Dave Dickens, Wes Kingsbury. . . .

Kate turned away from the television set.

Two doors led from the room. Two paths.
Which one should she take?
Right now, only God knew what would happen next.
Kate prayed she would make the right decision.
And took the first step.

A NOTE FROM THE AUTHOR

Allow me to let you in on a secret. I've never really liked politics. I'm not likely to jump into a heated political discussion. I've never felt compelled to sway people into supporting my candidate, whoever that might be. Maybe that's a funny thing to admit after what you just read, but it's true.

So this is less a novel about politics than it is about the trials, tribulations, and heavy burdens of people who work in politics. As the famous philosopher Stan Lee said, "With great power comes great responsibility." To me, that's one of the key issues of this series. Emily will be facing some pretty stiff challenges that come with the office of president. Will it be enough for Emily that Kate is her conscience? Or will Emily realize that she must forge her own relationship with God to responsibly wield the power of the presidency? With Emily's soul and the fate of the country in the balance, I know what I'm hoping will happen.

Emily is a stubborn woman. Then again, Kate is a patient one.

I just hope that Kate's patience lasts longer than Emily's stubbornness. . . .

ABOUT THE AUTHOR

Born and raised in Birmingham, Alabama, Laura Hayden began her reading career at the age of four. By the time she was ten, she'd exhausted the children's section in the local library and switched to adult mysteries. Although she always loved to write, she became sidetracked in college, where the lure of differential equations outweighed the draw of dangling participles.

But one engineering degree, one wedding, two kids, and three military assignments later, she ended up in Colorado Springs, Colorado, where she met people who shared her passion for writing. With their support, instruction, and camaraderie, she set and met her goal of selling her first book. She now has published ten novels, including the First Daughter mystery series, as well as several short stories.

The wife of a career military officer, Laura has moved with surprising frequency and has now returned to her native Alabama. Besides writing, she owns Author, Author! Bookstore and is the head of the graphics department for NovelTalk. com. When not at the keyboard of her computer, Laura can be found at the keyboard of her piano.

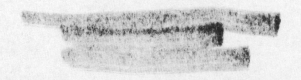

WATCH FOR THE NEXT BOOK
IN THIS GRIPPING POLITICAL SERIES

✴ ✴ ✴ ✴ ✴

RED, WHITE, AND BLUE

✴ ✴ ✴ ✴ ✴

Releasing fall 2008!

CP0240